WORTHY OF TRUST AND CONFIDENCE

By the Author

Actual Stop

Worthy of Trust and Confidence

Visit us at www.boldstrokesbooks.com

WORTHY OF TRUST AND CONFIDENCE

by

Kara A. McLeod

2017

This Trade Paperback Original Is Published By
Bold Strokes Books, Inc.
P.O. Box 249
Valley Falls, NY 12185

First Edition: March 2017

Credits
Editor: Shelley Thrasher
Production Design: Stacia Seaman
Cover Design by Melody Pond

For Riley. Just because.

CHAPTER ONE

E arth to Ryan!"
     At the sound of Meaghan Bates's vaguely irritated voice, my eyes snapped up to meet hers. I blinked, startled and confused. "What?"

"Hello?" Her tone held rich notes of anticipation as she cut a sideways glance toward the television that played soundlessly in the corner of our shared office. Clearly, she thought I should have some clue what she was asking of me. I hated to disappoint her, but…

"What?" I asked again.

Meaghan raised her eyebrows at me expectantly, and when I continued to goggle at her, she waved the hand not resting on her mouse toward the television and mimed pressing a button on a remote. She looked dangerously close to irritated.

"Oh." I searched the disaster that was the top of my desk somewhat ineffectively with my left hand and finally managed to locate it underneath a pile of paperwork at least four months old. How had it even gotten there? I frowned at the gadget for a second before I tossed it to her awkwardly.

Meaghan caught it with a huff and turned the TV off to fix me with a dark glare. "Okay, what is going on with you?"

"Huh?"

"You just made me watch *Jersey Shore* reruns for like fifteen minutes!" Her voice became shrill. She tossed the remote onto the top of her own desk, folded her arms across her chest, and leaned back in her chair.

"What? I did not!"

"Yes, you did, too. At first I thought you put it on to be a smart-ass, but even you wouldn't let the joke go on for that long."

I wrinkled my nose in distaste and fussed with the strap of the sling that held my right arm against my chest, trying for easily the millionth time to get it to sit on my shirt rather than rub against my neck. She was right. I did hate that show, more than words could ever adequately express. That I hadn't even noticed it was on said a lot about my state of mind. "I'm so sorry. I didn't realize. You should've said something sooner."

"No kidding. So, what's got you all tied up in knots?"

I tensed, and the fingers of my good hand curled reflexively around the strap, giving me away. When I realized what I'd done, I shoved my hand into my lap and forced myself to relax, but Meaghan's knowing look told me she'd caught the gesture.

A lot of different topics were clamoring for top billing in the theater of my mind, and I didn't care to talk about any of them. I chewed my bottom lip as I considered how to dodge the question. "I'm just really tired, Meaghan."

She narrowed her eyes at me and studied me suspiciously. "Haven't you been sleeping?"

"No," I told her truthfully. "Not very well." I sure as hell wasn't about to tell her why.

"Didn't they give you drugs to help with the pain?"

"Yeah. They did." And if I thought taking them would help, I might've considered it. Perhaps. But as they seemed to only make it harder for me to fight my way out of my nightmares, they were no longer an option.

"But you're not taking them."

"No."

She sighed noisily. "Why not?"

"I can't go back to full duty if I'm on the kind of medication they're giving me."

"Ryan, you can't go back to full duty until you can actually use your right arm. You shouldn't even be here now. You were released from the hospital, what? Twenty-four hours ago?"

It'd actually been less, but I wasn't going to tell her that. "I was bored at home." That wasn't a lie, but it wasn't the entire truth either.

Meaghan smirked at me and raised her eyebrows. "Allison

couldn't think of any way to keep you entertained?"

My insides suddenly felt ice-cold, and that chill spread throughout my veins at an alarming rate. In retrospect, I didn't think I could've been more unprepared for any question. No, that wasn't strictly true. I'd have been equally taken aback if she'd asked me whether I thought a lion would beat a tiger in a fight to the death. That might even have surprised me more. But not much.

Now that I thought about it, I'd have rather she'd asked me the lion question. I'd have stressed a lot less over the answer. I wasn't certain how to respond to what'd actually come out of her mouth. I didn't know where things stood between Allison and me—not after yesterday, not after she'd left so abruptly and in such a horrendous mood, though she'd assured me it had nothing to do with me—and I was participating in whatever it was we were doing. I definitely wasn't equipped to explain the situation to anyone else.

I tried to calm my racing heart and come up with a suitable response quickly. A long pause would've made Meaghan even more suspicious than she obviously was and therefore more likely to press.

"What?" My voice broke on the word, and I tried not to wince. So much for not arousing suspicion.

"What? She's your girlfriend, isn't she?"

I froze, and all my normal bodily functions—breathing, heartbeat, thought—shuddered and ground to a halt. "Wh—what makes you say that?"

"Please, Ryan. I'm not an idiot. And she should really be here. Where is she, anyway?" Meaghan spat out the words like they'd tasted terrible and she couldn't wait to get them out of her mouth.

"You don't like her." I hadn't realized it until I'd said it, but as soon as I'd voiced the thought, I recognized it was true. Meaghan's reactions to mentions of Allison's name as well as memories of her expression during their last few interactions skittered through my mind, and I wanted to smack myself for not noticing it before.

"What?"

"Allison. You don't like her. Why?"

"I like her fine," Meaghan insisted, but her gaze darted away from mine to study an uninteresting spot on the wall, belying the statement.

"Now who's keeping secrets?"

Meaghan exhaled noisily and stood up, keeping her back to me as she stalked around the edges of the room. Her posture was rigid and wire-tight as she prowled. I watched her warily.

"Okay," she said finally. "You're right. I hate her."

"*What?*"

Meaghan shot me a quick glance out of the corner of her eye and waved one hand airily. "I mean, I don't really *hate* her, hate her. But you're my friend, and she hurt you. I can't forgive her for that."

"Hurt me? What are you talking about?" Allison had been nothing short of amazing the entire time she'd been here. In my drugged-up state, I'd seriously considered trying to have her canonized. I'd demanded someone get me the number for the pope and everything.

She scoffed. "Really, Ryan? That's how you're gonna play this?"

"What?"

"You're gonna make me say it, aren't you?"

"Say what?" Had something happened at the hospital I couldn't remember? I'd been out of it for a lot of the past couple of days, but Allison would've said something. Right? I mean, before she'd taken off like someone had set her chair on fire.

"Okay, fine. Just remember, I tried to avoid this. So this is your own fault."

"Oh, for crying out loud. Spit it out already."

"We all knew."

"Who all knew what?"

Meaghan's lips quirked in a small, indulgent smile. "When you and Allison were together before? Back when she was still in NYFO? We all knew."

My ribs crackled and snapped as a vise-like pressure gripped me hard and radiated up and down my chest. It didn't even occur to me to deny it. That's how utterly shocked I was. "You all knew? What do you mean you all knew? Who's all? How?"

"Please. The chemistry between you two was off the charts. Frankly, a few times I thought the walls might catch fire with the heat you guys were throwing off just being in the same room and making it a point not to look at each other. Not even the most oblivious of the guys could miss that." Meaghan's smile grew wider as she teased me.

"Shit." I doubted Allison would be particularly pleased with that revelation. However, she'd mentioned some of the guys on the detail hadn't seemed at all surprised when she'd said she needed to come back to New York after she heard I'd been shot. And she'd seemed more amused by that than anything else, so maybe she wouldn't be as upset as I feared.

"Were you guys trying to hide it?"

Well, I hadn't been, necessarily, but Allison had certainly had concerns. And it had nothing to do with her not wanting people to know she was dating a woman, which is what most people would assume. She would've had the same attitude toward the situation if she'd been seeing a male agent. It'd been more a matter of keeping her professional life as separate from her personal life as possible.

I, on the other hand, was slightly less concerned about those sorts of things, but that was mostly because I was a master at pretending things weren't happening. If I didn't hear about the gossip, I assumed it wasn't going on. Allison, however, had taken a much more cynical view of the situation and attempted to avoid that pitfall.

I wasn't about to get into any of that with Meaghan, though. I was afraid she'd take it the wrong way, possibly deliberately, and dislike Allison even more. Instead, I said, "Allison's a very private person. So, we didn't exactly want to advertise it."

"Yeah, that's kind of what we all figured."

"Wait! You all actually *talked* about this? Are you kidding me? Please tell me you're kidding me." I don't know why I was so flabbergasted. That right there had been the whole reason Allison hadn't wanted anyone to know. It was jarring to hear someone admit to gossiping about us.

"If it makes you feel any better, the guys didn't talk about you two being together as much as you'd think they would. And what they did say was probably not what you'd expect."

"How lovely." My tone was petulant and bitter.

"It was, actually. I expected them to focus on the usual things guys focus on. You know, how hot you two were and how they'd kill to watch, which one of you was the top, did you use a strap-on, that sort of thing."

"Oh, I'm sure they did talk about that. Just not when you were around."

Meaghan chuckled lightly. "No. Definitely not when I was around. Even our guys aren't that crass."

"If you say so." There was an extended lull in the conversation.

Eventually, my curiosity got the better of me, and I hated myself a little bit for it. "So, what did they say, then?"

"They thought you guys were good together and that you complemented one another nicely. It was pretty cute. Everybody seemed really happy you were so happy. And the way they figured it, no one else had the stones to handle Allison half as well as you."

"Pptthh. I didn't handle Allison." Not then and certainly not now. I couldn't imagine anyone handling her ever.

"You know what I mean. She's super focused and intense. And occasionally standoffish and guarded. She's just…Much sometimes. Intimidating. Larger than life. But you softened her, made her more relaxed, more approachable. Less the uber-perfect big, bad federal agent on a fast track to promotion and more human. And she balanced you perfectly because, let's face it, you're almost never serious about anything."

"That's completely not true. I'll have you know I'm deathly serious about my all-consuming hatred of Peeps."

Meaghan rolled her eyes, but she was smiling. "See? I rest my case."

"I think your case needs some serious work, Counselor. Or at least a pie chart. Juries love pie charts."

"Anyway, my point is, we all thought you two were pretty perfect together."

"I'm thrilled to hear that."

"No, you're not."

I agreed. "Not even a little bit."

"So…" Meaghan pursed her lips as though she were unsure how to phrase her next statement. "She's the one, isn't she?"

"The one what?"

"A couple weeks ago, when you and I were on the way to that interview for your friend in WFO, I asked you who made you swear off love. It was her, wasn't it?"

Heat blazed across the surface of my skin, and I averted my eyes as I made a show of scratching the hollow of my cheek in an effort to hide my expression. I wasn't sure what to say. Maybe there really wasn't anything to say.

Meaghan nodded, as though my silence was all the confirmation she needed. "And that, right there? That's why I hate her."

"Oh." That was actually rather sweet. I sniffed and coughed awkwardly. "So, it's like the time I told Benton if he made one wrong move I'd hide his body so well they'd find Jimmy Hoffa before they found him?" I clarified with a tight smile, referring to one of her ex-boyfriends from years ago.

Meaghan matched my smile with a smirk of her own. "Yeah. Just like that."

"When's the last time you heard from him, anyway?"

Meaghan scoffed. "It's been a while."

"Damn, I'm good!"

"You're also trying to change the subject."

"Can you blame me?"

"I guess not. But you should know by now I never fall for that. So, where's your girlfriend? Why isn't she here taking care of you?"

"Entertaining me, you mean?"

"Whatever."

"She had to go back to DC."

"Why?"

I almost shrugged but caught myself at the last moment. Thank God. My shoulder hurt like a son of a bitch when I was sitting completely still. Moving it at all was akin to setting it on fire. With a blowtorch. After dousing it with lighter fluid. "Dunno. Her boss called her back."

Meaghan rolled her eyes. "You'd think they could cut her a little slack. She was here for what? Two days?"

"Three," I murmured, even though I was pretty sure the question was rhetorical. "And she never once left the hospital."

"Well, it's not like the detail would fall apart without her. She should've stayed."

The call from her boss demanding her return had seemed odd, but it wasn't the request itself as much as her reaction to it. She'd become immediately furious and had been really short with him on the phone, though she'd refused to tell me why, instead attempting to placate me with lies along the lines of she was just upset to be leaving me in my time of need. I hadn't believed her, but I hadn't called her on it, either. I knew better than to force her to talk before she was ready. I also hadn't wanted to risk her turning her ire on me.

"She never would've done that," I said, forcing myself back to the conversation. "And I don't blame her for leaving. It's not a big deal."

"It's a huge deal. You wouldn't have left her."

"Probably not. But she and I are very different people. I don't hold her loyalty and dedication to her job against her." It was actually one of the many things I liked about her.

"Well, I do."

I chuckled. "Thanks. I appreciate that. I think. But could you maybe try to…" I wasn't sure exactly how to ask for what I wanted.

Meaghan rolled her eyes and threw up her hands. "Fine. I'll try to be nice to your girlfriend. Happy?"

"Very. And she's not my girlfriend. Not technically." At least I didn't think she was. We hadn't really clarified what we were to one another. Not officially. I mean, we'd said "I love you," so maybe it was implied, but I wasn't about to make assumptions. Not without talking to her first. And seeing as how I hadn't heard from her since she'd left for DC the day before, I'd say she didn't appear to be in a talking mood at the moment. I ducked my head self-consciously and examined all the paper circles dotting the floor around my desk, casualties of my three-hole punch. I suddenly realized I really needed to vacuum and wondered if Meaghan would see that for the distraction technique it was.

"Why not? If she's playing games with you again, I swear to God I'll kill her."

I ignored the idle threat and considered my response. The question bubbling up behind my lips had been gnawing away at my insides for days now, and as much as I detested voicing my concern, maybe it was time to solicit a second opinion on the subject. And I sure as hell couldn't talk about it with Allison. I took a deep breath.

"It's not too soon, right?" I asked, my voice a barely audible whisper. I didn't lift my head, but I did peek at her from underneath my eyelashes so I could study her reaction. "You know, after…"

Meaghan's expression softened, and I could see sympathy in her golden-brown eyes. "Oh, Ryan. Is that what's been bothering you?"

I nodded and went back to studying my carpet, running my fingers through my hair and scratching my scalp. That wasn't exactly a lie, either. That was one of the things that'd been bothering me. It just wasn't the one that'd been bothering me the most. But my problems didn't necessarily need to be tackled as a group. They could be managed singularly, so I didn't utter the rest of my woes for the time being.

"You're afraid of what people will think if you're with Allison so soon after Lucia's death."

I flinched. It wasn't so much what other people thought as much as my own feelings on the subject, and my own feelings were telling me I might be being disrespectful to Lucia in some way. "It just seems... discourteous somehow."

"You seeing someone else?"

"Yeah. I mean, it's only been a week."

"Well, didn't Lucia break up with you?"

"Yeah." Despite the fact that Lucia and I hadn't exactly been exclusive and that what I'd felt for her hadn't held even a tenth of the intensity of what I felt for Allison, her sleeping with someone else and then dumping me had still stung. The blunt reminder landed like a sucker punch and made my breath hitch.

"And it was about a week or so before...everything, wasn't it?"

"Uh-huh."

"And you and Allison had started things back up again a few days before—" Meaghan seemed uncertain how to phrase it nicely.

I smirked at her bitterly. "The incident?"

"Is that what we're calling it?"

"It's what headquarters is calling it, apparently." My father had let that slip on his last visit to me in the hospital. The moniker had left me less than pleased.

"Why am I not surprised?" She waved her hand dismissively and went on. "The point is, you and Allison started before that day."

I sighed. "Yeah, I know that, and you know that. But nobody else does." And though it was irrelevant what anybody else thought or knew or when, it still felt borderline inappropriate. To me.

Meaghan laughed. "Ryan, everybody else knows that."

"What?!"

"Honey, you guys left the bar together after the wheels-up party—a party she shouldn't even have still been in district for, might I add—and you showed up at work the next day with a hickey on your neck. It wasn't too hard to figure it out. And you know how fast word travels."

I groaned and buried my head in my hand as my cheeks heated up. "Oh, God."

"Since when do you care what everybody else thinks? Screw 'em."

"Meaghan, you know as well as I do how this all works." I was becoming extremely frustrated with her for being deliberately obtuse. "I refuse to throw the gossip sharks even the tiniest bit of chum." Well, even more than I evidently already had. And I really hated that, by default, Allison had become rumor bait right along with me. I knew how much that bothered her. I would've shielded her from that if I could have.

"Sorry, sweetie. I think that might be a little out of your control."

"Fantastic."

Meaghan laughed at my distress. "Come on. You should be used to it by now."

"I am. Doesn't mean I have to like it."

"No. You don't." She hesitated for a bit, and I could see she was working herself up to something. "You wouldn't…I mean, this isn't going to…Uh, you're not going to break up with her because of what people might or might not say about it, are you?"

"What? No! Of course not. I love her. It's just…been eating at me. That's all. I'll get over it eventually."

"Good. Because you deserve to be happy. And if Allison is the one who makes you happy, then…Just…Good."

I smiled at her and shook my head. "You need to work on your enthusiasm."

"And you need to go home and get some sleep."

"Ugh, Meaghan—"

"Nope. I don't want to hear it. Get out of here before I call Mark in for something."

I shot her my darkest look, unable to believe she'd threatened to sic the boss on me. "Low blow."

"Hey, I play to win." She picked up the receiver to her landline. "Are you really going to make me do this?"

I rolled my eyes and stood up with a huff. "No. But only because I'd hate for you to have to try to explain to him exactly why you summoned him. I'm a fantastic friend like that."

Meaghan grinned and set the receiver back into its cradle. "Yes, you are. Now get the hell out of here."

"You're the reason why female agents have a reputation for being bitches, you know that?"

"I do. And I revel in it. Now go. Take your drugs and get some rest."

"Okay." I headed toward the hall but paused in the doorway. "Thanks for the talk."

"Stop stalling."

I shook my head and stepped into the hall.

"Ryan?" Meaghan called.

I stopped but didn't turn around. "Yeah?"

"Anytime."

I grinned and made for the elevators as fast as my aching body would carry me, praying to any deity who might be listening that I wouldn't run into my boss on the way.

CHAPTER TWO

The second my feet hit the pavement in front of the building, I concluded there was no way in hell I was going home. Not yet. I had no idea what direction my thoughts would stray if I sat in my apartment with nothing to distract myself, and I had absolutely no desire to find out. I could only take so much wallowing, and after three days in the hospital, I'd already had my fill. Sure, I knew intellectually I was smack dab in the middle of slogging through the five stages of grief and some wallowing was to be expected, but what I really wanted more than anything at the moment was a break from feeling anything.

I slipped my ear-buds into my ears and chose the playlist on my iPod I was most likely to sing along to had I been at home alone or in my car and not out roaming the streets. The music did as much to soothe my angst-ridden soul as the warmth of the sunshine on my shoulders, and the dim protest of muscles too long underused was welcome.

My first stop was the Verizon store down the block to replace the cell phone Lucia had shattered when she'd hurled it to the ground during her last precious minutes of life. I'd begged Rory several times during my convalescence to pick me up a new one, but she'd never gotten around to it. I couldn't be upset with her for that, though. She'd split her time between her shifts at the hospital where she worked and visiting me, and even sleep—a normally precious commodity for her—had gotten pushed to the back burner. I couldn't very well tell her I'd rather she run errands than spend time with me. Not when she'd gone so far out of her way to see me as it was.

I tried not to get mired down in memories of the spiteful sort of triumph that'd glittered hard in Lucia's eyes as she quoted from memory an innuendo-laden text message from Allison right before she'd thrown my phone to the sidewalk. It wasn't easy. The mean smile that'd twisted her lips was permanently seared into my brain. As was the look in her eyes as the life drained out of her body. Would there ever come a time when something didn't remind me of the moments leading up to her death? It probably wouldn't be any time soon.

I chose a new smartphone as quickly as possible and held it in my hand as I ambled slowly back out to the street. My mind snagged on the idea of calling Allison and held there, making it impossible to think about anything else. I still hadn't heard from her, but that wasn't necessarily a surprise as much as it was a disappointment.

My hands shook a little, and my heart galloped wildly as I typed in the number I'd never forgotten even after I'd deleted it from my phone to ensure I'd never be tempted to drunk-dial her after we'd broken up. I paused before hitting the call button. It'd probably be a good idea to think of something to say before I took the plunge.

I started moseying down the street with no particular destination in mind, staring at the phone in my hand as I went. I could just call to say hi, right? Just because she'd gotten all upset the night before for reasons that were still a mystery didn't mean I couldn't act as if everything was normal, did it? Except it wasn't, and I knew it, and my acting skills were nowhere near good enough for me to be able to pull it off. I let out a forceful breath and frowned.

I supposed I could wait for her to reach out to me. But waiting for things to happen wasn't really my style. I was much more proactive. And letting her set the pace and make the first move felt way too much like the way our last relationship had played out. I didn't want to force her into anything, but I wasn't about to take a completely passive role this time around, either.

Guess who finally got a new phone?

I texted her after several long moments of agonizing over what to say. It was a cowardly move, choosing not to call, but I managed to convince myself it was for the best, that she was probably working and couldn't talk anyway. The notion made me feel marginally better about myself.

The seconds dragged by with the same lack of urgency you'd find in growing grass, and my grip on my phone was tight enough to cramp my hand. I wrinkled my nose and huffed as I shoved my phone into my pocket. I wasn't the girl who waited by the phone for her girlfriend to respond to her overtures. No freaking way. I was the kind of girl who—

My phone buzzed, and my heart immediately soared. So much for not being that girl. Part of me was disgusted with myself but clearly not disgusted enough not to fumble for my phone immediately. I yanked it free and swiped hastily at the lock screen.

Who is this?

Was she freaking kidding me? What the hell?

Joking. Congrats.

I rolled my eyes and shook my head. Jesus, the woman was an epic pain in my ass.

Very funny.

Working. Sorry. Talk later.

While I was glad my theory about her working had been correct, and that my choice to text rather than call was validated, I couldn't ignore the emptiness that seized me. Feeling like the last unwanted deviled egg at a picnic, I resumed my wandering. My leg felt like it was being repeatedly prodded with a hot iron, and my back ached along the entire right side, but I was determined not to go home yet. I had less than no interest in returning to my quiet apartment to flounder in despair and self-loathing, and there was a greater-than-average chance of that happening if I went back there. Especially after that non-conversation with Allison. Shit. How the hell was I going to occupy myself?

A brilliant idea struck me, and I stepped to the curb, holding my left hand aloft to hail a cab. I gave the driver the cross streets of my destination and sat back in the seat to idly watch the world go by.

Not long before "the incident," I'd been looking into a counterfeit case for my friend Sarah in DC. Initially, it hadn't seemed like much. A man, later identified as Amin Akbari, had used a phony one-hundred-dollar bill to purchase a few small-dollar items in a grocery store in Maryland. We got leads like that all the time, and more often than not they turned out to be dead ends. Half the time, the people with the bills had no idea they were even counterfeit. And the other half of the time, the folks couldn't tell us who'd sold them the bills because they had no other information for the contact who'd given them the fake notes other than a street nickname or a number that turned out to belong to a burner phone. Sarah and I had honestly both thought nothing would come of the Akbari interview and that'd be it. Case closed.

We were partially right. Nothing had come of the interview itself. Akbari had more or less clammed up and denied everything. However, when I'd run routine database checks on some of the personally identifying information I'd gleaned on him through the Joint Terrorism Task Force computer systems, I'd made a startling discovery: Akbari appeared to have connections to subjects who were targets of terrorism-related investigations. I'd been sure I must've run the wrong phone number because no way could I have fallen headfirst into a case like that off a one-note pass in a grocery store. I'd had to ask Sarah to verify the number for me, to make sure I hadn't written it down wrong.

The day I was shot, I'd asked Sarah to send me copies of whatever documents she'd pulled the subject's telephone number from so I could verify that I'd been running down the right information. I hadn't received the records until a few days later, and the hospital stay had put a damper on any follow-up investigation I'd planned to conduct. Since I was out now, I figured I might as well go into my JTTF office—I was one of several USSS reps assigned over there—where the rest of the paperwork related to this case was stored and start unraveling the mystery. I didn't need two good arms to follow paper trails.

I managed to sneak into the office and make it to my desk without being waylaid too much. Most of my squad mates were already gone for the day, so I didn't have to answer very many questions about how I was doing. That was a huge relief, as I wasn't in the mood to talk about what'd happened. Truth be told, I wasn't sure if I ever would be, although a small part of me was disappointed I wouldn't be able to pump anyone for information about the investigation into who'd killed Lucia. Whatever. They wouldn't have told me anyway.

I accessed the FBI email account I'd been given when I joined the task force and quickly printed out the documents I'd forwarded to myself after Sarah had sent them to my Secret Service email account. Included in the email was a scanned copy of a frequent-shopper card application for the grocery store Akbari had passed the counterfeit bill in. That Sarah had thought to inquire if he'd filled out an application at all had been a fluke stroke of luck on our part and a grave act of stupidity on his because he'd slipped up and used a burner phone number for that application we probably would never have connected to him without that document.

I frowned as I studied the printouts of the papers Sarah had sent me, and I highlighted the pertinent pieces of information I wanted to run for easy reference. Then I began the painstaking task of looking up telephone number after telephone number, following the trails of associations down the rabbit hole into Wonderland.

The research process was slow and awkward, to say the least. I'd never thought about how proficient—or not—I might be with my non-dominant hand when trying to perform everyday tasks such as taking notes or using a computer mouse. If I had, I sincerely doubt I'd have imagined the situation to be even half as bad as reality was turning out. If I'd known this morning what I knew now, I might've reconsidered even showing up to work today. Maybe. Okay, probably not.

Fortunately—or unfortunately, depending on your point of view—the telephone number I'd investigated before I was shot had been the correct one. I hadn't copied it down wrong, which meant we'd inadvertently stumbled onto something a lot bigger than we'd originally thought.

Akbari's burner phone—the one from the grocery store frequent-shopper application—had made several calls to another number the FBI database had associated with someone named Vafa Fallahi, including one about eight hours before the counterfeit bill was passed.

Fallahi was intimately associated with Naser Golzar, who was currently under investigation for the material support of terrorism, meaning the FBI suspected he was funding an extremist group somehow.

And Golzar was already confirmed to be a close associate of Mahmood Rostami, who we'd actually just arrested on that same charge a couple of months ago. I hadn't participated in the interview following his arrest—though I'd been part of the arrest team, and, if I remembered correctly, Rostami's apartment wasn't too far from

Akbari's—but I obviously knew the guys who had. I emailed them quickly to ask them to hit me up when they had time to chat. I wanted to ask them a few questions.

After several long minutes, I also obtained identifying information for the three people that Fallahi, Golzar, and Rostami had each contacted the most often, as well as the dates, times, and durations of all the telephone calls I was referencing to make my case. I added a note to my paper to make a pictorial chart to spell out the associations as soon as my right arm was out of its sling. I preferred visual aids whenever and wherever possible because they made it easier for others to follow along as I explained the case to them. And if I wasn't mistaken, I'd need to enlighten a lot of other people soon.

I also wanted to find information regarding who Akbari was calling now. He'd gotten a new burner phone when he'd relocated to New York several weeks ago—a number I'd basically strong-armed him into giving me at the conclusion of our interview—and, as far as I could tell, that number wasn't on the FBI's radar. It wasn't included in their databases yet, at any rate. I doubted any of the Feebs were even looking at him. I'd only gotten a hit on his old number because of the open case on Fallahi. If a confidential informant hadn't identified that burner phone as Fallahi's and if someone hadn't subpoenaed Fallahi's phone records and uploaded the results to the network server, I wouldn't have even gotten that far.

And whether it had any ties to an FBI case or not, I needed to know who Akbari was talking to on that new burner phone. I was particularly fascinated with the very first call Akbari had made once Meaghan and I left his apartment the night we'd interviewed him. I was fairly certain he would've called someone. We'd made him nervous with our inquiries, and he'd have wanted to be reassured he wasn't about to be thrown into a federal prison. I was dying to know who he'd reached out to for that reassurance.

I picked up the hardline telephone at my desk and awkwardly dialed a number from memory. Listening to it ring, I continued to scratch notes onto my notepad.

"Counterterrorism. Popovic." Assistant United States Attorney Gregor Popovic sounded distracted as he answered.

"Hey, Greg. It's Ryan O'Connor. How are you?" I hoped whatever

I was interrupting wasn't too important. I also prayed that whatever had his attention wouldn't so overshadow my request that he completely forgot to do what I asked.

"Hey, Ryan. What's up…Wait!" I could practically hear the wheels turning in his head, and I cringed, knowing where this was going. "Didn't you get…I mean, I thought I heard…Are you okay?"

"Yeah, Greg. I'm fine." *Please don't ask me anything else. Please, please, ple—*

"So, is it true?"

"Is what true?" Why hadn't it occurred to me he was going to have a million and one questions? Why hadn't I just sent him an email? He was going to ask for one with all the details anyway. I should've just jumped straight to that.

He cleared his throat, and a brief, awkward pause on his end followed. "Did you really get shot?"

"It's true. I really did get shot."

"And you're back to work already?" He sounded surprised.

"I'm on light duty," I told him, though that wasn't strictly true. I was probably still listed as being on sick leave, but that didn't have any bearing on this situation. "I can't carry a weapon or participate in… Well, anything, really. But I can do paperwork."

"Wow. Well, I'm really glad you're okay."

"Thanks."

"So, what can I do for you?"

"I need you to cut subpoenas for a couple of phone numbers for me. The quicker we can get these results, the better."

"No problem. Just email me a quick synopsis of the case and the info you're looking for, and I'll have them to you before I leave for the day."

"Thanks, Greg. I really appreciate it."

"Any time, Ryan. Take it easy, okay? I want to lock up Jhalawan soon," he told me, referring to one of my other cases. "And I don't want to do it until you're ready. I want you to be the one to put the cuffs on him."

I laughed. "You and me both. I'll hit you up the second I'm cleared for full duty."

"I'll hold you to that. Talk to you later."

"Bye, Greg."

I hung up and went to work drafting the email he'd requested. With any luck, I'd have the results by the end of the week, and then the picture of this scheme would come into sharper focus. And in the meantime, while I waited, I'd just have to come up with a way to occupy myself so I didn't drive myself crazy feeling guilty about Lucia and confused about whatever the hell was going on with Allison.

Somehow, I suspected that'd be easier said than done.

CHAPTER THREE

Now that I'd gotten the ball rolling again on this investigation, I didn't want to waste any more time. Sure, I probably should've gone home to get some sleep, but that concept had largely been eluding me for days anyway. I couldn't think of a good reason not to put it off for just a little while longer. Not when I had questions I needed answered. So instead of going home, I headed back to NYFO.

The Secret Service is different from almost every other law-enforcement agency I've ever worked with in that we're all a lot closer to one another than agents from other entities. Not just the New Yorkers, either. The entire outfit is that way. Our protective mission necessitates that we spend a great deal of time with each other outside the normal confines of our jobs. We travel together, we eat together, and occasionally we have to sleep together. Actual sleeping, not sex, although that does happen on occasion, too, as Allison and I can attest. We also tend to hang out with one another a lot more on our off time than agents from other organizations do. It really is like a family.

And in the spirit of family, I decided it was time I sought out the man I saw as my big brother to help me piece all of this together. I had a few questions about that counterfeit note Sarah had sent me a picture of that I needed his opinion on. If anybody could help me understand this whole case, it'd be him.

I rapped my knuckles lightly on his doorjamb to get his attention, secretly relieved he was actually in. Time had gotten away from me, and I hadn't realized how late it was until I noticed the lack of bodies and noise as I made my way to his office. I was lucky to catch him.

"Rico?"

Rico looked up from his desk, surprise etched on his handsome face. He blinked at me once, and then a broad smile broke across his features. Immediately, he was on his feet and coming out from behind his desk to enfold me in a gigantic hug.

I tensed, trying not to hiss too loudly from the pain his embrace sparked in me. I didn't want him to know he'd hurt me, and the emotional benefits of the clinch far outweighed the physical detriments.

When Rico finally pulled back, he kept his hands on my biceps and held me at arm's length. His gaze was critical as he studied me. He narrowed his eyes slightly and pursed his lips.

"Not that I'm not glad to see you, but what the hell are you doing here?"

I rolled my eyes and deftly stepped out of his grasp so I could settle myself into the chair on the opposite side of his desk. "I missed you, Rico. And I simply couldn't stand to be apart from you for even another minute. What can I say? The heart wants what the heart wants."

Rico smirked. "Very funny."

"Okay, you got me. I'm not actually here for you. I came to ask permission to date your wife."

"Now that I wish was the truth." Rico cocked his head to the side and scrutinized me intently, his dark eyes searching. "She's been asking about you. She wanted to visit you when you were in the hospital, but I managed to stop her. I knew you wouldn't want her to see you like that."

I grinned at the thought of Rico's fiery spouse. "Yeah, she told me. In language way too colorful for an innocent girl like that to know. I'd yell at you for corrupting her, but I kinda think you deserved all the things she was saying about you."

"Funny you should mention that. Because several of the phrases she used to lambast me sounded exactly like things you've said to me on occasion. So, if anyone could be accused of corruption here, I think it's you."

"You'll have to prove it. And Paige will never give me up."

"Sisters before misters?"

I laughed, unable to believe those words had actually come out of his mouth. "Something like that."

"So, now that you've been unleashed on the world at large, please tell me you'll let my wife come over to cook for you and generally dote on you and shower you with affection. I'm fairly certain I'll never have sex again if you say no."

I pretended to consider it, rubbing my bottom lip with my thumb as I attempted to hide my grin. I was enjoying watching him squirm. I probably would've let it go on a little longer, too, if he hadn't used the wounded-puppy-dog eyes. I laughed again.

"Oh, my God. You're pathetic. I can't believe you need my help to get laid. Step up your game, man! Okay, okay. Fine. She can come over. But not tonight."

"You got a hot date or something?"

I ignored the dull ache that blossomed inside me. He had no idea how much I wished that were true, and I refused to tell him. "If you can call arguing with my sister—which is probably what I'll be doing—a date, sure."

Rico's expression turned mischievous, and he shot me a sly grin. "Your twin sister?"

I wrinkled my nose at him. "Yes, my twin sister. And for the hundredth time, no, you can't meet her."

"Oh, come on."

"Absolutely not."

"But why?"

"Because I don't trust you with her, that's why. God only knows what you'll tell her. And I don't need her getting any ideas. The woman has enough dirt on me as it is."

"Ryan. Come on. I'll be good. I promise."

"Now I know you're lying. Since when you have ever been good? Does that whining work on Paige?"

Rico feigned hurt. "Hey! I do not now, nor have I ever whined. I sweet-talk."

"Well, then, you had to know that wasn't going to work on me because I'm immune to your charms."

"I just persuaded you to let Paige and me come over," Rico reminded me, looking way too smug for my tastes.

"I said Paige could come over. I never said anything about you."

"We're a package deal. She'd be lost without me."

"Yeah, because she wouldn't know what to do with all her newly acquired free time. She's used to spending most of her waking hours cleaning up after you."

"True. But she knew what she was getting into when she married me."

"I'm still not convinced she wasn't coerced somehow. I've launched a formal investigation into the matter."

"Because you aren't busy enough. Seriously, though, what the hell are you doing here so late? Most of the office went home hours ago."

"I could ask you the same thing." Not that I wasn't thrilled he'd been here because I seriously doubted I'd have been able to force myself to wait until the next day to have this chat with him, but it was pretty late for him to still be at his desk.

Rico's lips twisted into a mirthless smile. "I'm the midnight response guy. Well, one of them. I just came in to grab a quick workout before my shift started."

"They still make a big shot like you take response shifts?" I'd just spied the assignment board hanging adjacent to his desk and glimpsed who his partner was for the evening.

"Yeah, well, someone has to show the rookies how it's done."

"Good thing they paired you up with Eric Banks then, huh? What's with all the midnight shifts, anyway? Is he being punished again?"

Rico snorted and rolled his eyes. "When isn't he being punished?"

Eric Banks was only a couple months out of the academy and still as green as the Emerald Isle but not smart enough to recognize or accept it. In short, he was an absolute pain in the ass. And everybody in the office knew it. "What'd he do to piss you off now?"

"Not *just* me. The SAIC of Hurricane's detail."

I grimaced and sucked in a hissing breath between my teeth. It's never a good idea to land on any SAIC's radar for screwing up. It's even worse when you piss off the SAIC of another office or division. That's the fastest way to end up with numerous bosses looking to end you. "Ooh. That's not good."

"You know what else isn't good? Driving the president's daughter with one hand while drinking coffee with the other."

"He didn't!"

"He did. He also turned down the wrong street, and the motorcade ended up having to square the block."

"Shit! Didn't he check the route before they left?"

"Nope. And apparently he had plenty of time to do it, too. Which is part of why SAIC Quinn is so pissed."

"Understandable. Why was he driving Hurricane anyway? Shouldn't one of the detail guys have been doing it?"

"Normally, yes. But one of them had a family emergency come up while Hurricane was at an event, so they snagged Banks off post to have him drive the limo back to the res." He shook his head. "All he had to do was make it one mile without fucking up, and he couldn't even manage that."

I hummed in the back of my throat. "So why's he working response with you instead of manning the duty desk?"

Rico scowled. "Because apparently he's managed to make a mess of that, too, so they don't want him up there."

"How do you mess up midnight duty desk? Nothing's going on."

"You fail to answer the phone when the alarm company calls to report that the alarm's going off at the warehouse where we store the hard cars. Which means you fail to send the response guys to check that everything's okay. And the AT of Special Operations ends up getting a call at home in the middle of the night."

"Jesus."

"Yeah, it's been a real treat around here lately," Rico quipped. "But I doubt you're here to check up on Banks. So what's up?"

I slid the printout of the counterfeit hundred Akbari had passed in the grocery store in Maryland a few weeks prior out of the envelope in my hand and handed both to him. I'd already examined it myself and had formulated a theory regarding its origins, but I wanted Rico's take on it. "What can you tell me about this?"

Rico took the offered document without comment and studied it, his brows pulled down in concentration as he scoured the page. Some of the details he no doubt wanted to verify were indistinguishable on the photocopy, and he was touching key places on the images with the tips of his fingers. Sarah had thoughtfully made notes on the page with a pen, pointing out all the flaws in the bill that made it easily identifiable as a fake, but I knew Rico well enough to know he still longed to see them with his own eyes.

I watched him in silence as he studied the image, smiling at his contemplative expression. I hadn't realized how much I'd missed working with him. I'd always had such a blast storyboarding cases with him. We worked well together, and I'd always felt we could get to the bottom of any case if only we could put our bickering on hold long enough to give it proper attention.

Rico interrupted my reflection. "Did you look this up in the system yet?"

"Nope. I wanted to get your opinion first. I wish I had the original, but Sarah couldn't send it up to us without involving proper channels. Chain of custody and all that."

Rico was studying the printout again and appeared to be only half listening. He shook his head absently. "Nah. It's fine. She made really good notes. I think I can get what I need from them."

I leaned back in his chair, struggling to find a semi-comfortable sitting position. Wincing, I pulled at the strap of my sling with my left hand so I could move my right arm a little, simultaneously grimacing at and reveling in the pull of muscles. Then I rubbed the sore spot on my neck where the nylon kept chafing. Finally, I crossed my right knee over my left and bobbed my foot as I waited.

"Is it something you've seen before?" I wanted to know.

Rico took a deep breath and let it out slowly. "It is, yes. This is an updated version of the old Iranian note."

The room suddenly seemed unreasonably warm, which contrasted sharply with the icy consistency of the surface of my skin, and I heard a distant sort of buzzing in my ears. I uncrossed my legs gracelessly, and my foot hit the floor with a dull thud. My left arm fell at the same time, and my hand curled around the arms of the chair so hard my palm ached.

Rico merely went on, clearly oblivious to my distress. I wasn't sure if he'd even picked up on the implications of what he'd just said. "You can see the changes they made here and here to make it more passable." He gestured to the spots in question with the tip of his pen. "But they haven't managed to correct this flaw here"—another indication—"that has always been the signature on this type of note. I'm beginning to think they haven't noticed it. Or they don't think we have. Anyway, we've been seeing it up here a lot in the past few months, but I didn't realize WFO was seeing this new version in DC already."

"What did you just say?" My voice was a harsh whisper I could barely hear over the rapid-fire staccato of my heart. The pounding underscored the buzzing in my ears quite nicely.

"Hmm?" Rico finally looked up from the paper, his expression vaguely puzzled.

"What did you just say? About the Iranian note?"

"Oh. Yeah, that's what this is. The latest version of the Iranian note."

I'd thought as much when I'd first seen it, but I'd been out of the counterfeit game for a while now. Those changes he'd just remarked on had given me pause, had made me doubt my initial gut instincts, and I'd needed him to confirm my suspicions. Fuck. Sometimes I really hated being right.

If I believed in coincidences, I'd have remarked that this sure was one hell of one. Unfortunately I didn't. No freaking way was I buying that the counterfeit bill I'd been looking into that just happened to be linked to Iranians had absolutely nothing to do with the recent assassination attempt on the president of Iran. Not even with a leprechaun, a four-leaf clover, and a whole box of Lucky Charms did stars align like that if they weren't somehow related.

But how were the two incidents connected, exactly? I needed some trails to follow here, some new puzzle pieces that'd bring the whole picture into sharper focus, because with these gaping holes, I still couldn't quite wrap my mind around it. I was hoping my pending subpoena results would provide me with something to go on because if they didn't, I was going to be shit out of luck.

Rico blinked once, and then his eyes grew wide as realization flooded his features. "Holy shit."

"No kidding," I said dryly, pleased he'd finally caught up.

"What the actual fuck?"

"You tell me, dude. Because I'm absolutely clueless."

Rico frowned in thought and tapped the tip of his pen on the top of his desk in a familiar rhythm. I could see his rapid-fire thought processes playing out in his eyes as he pondered this new information. Something else must've occurred to him suddenly because he favored me with an odd look and then abruptly stood. I watched as he hurriedly shut the door to his office and then sat back down.

Rico leaned forward a little so his weight was resting on his forearms as he fixed me with an intense stare. "What are the odds that this bill and you getting shot while working Iran are related?"

"Fairly high, by my reckoning."

Rico shifted his attention to an innocuous spot on the rug to the left of my chair. A shadow passed over his features, and his lips twitched. I knew him well enough to know he was debating whether to voice the notion that'd just popped into his head. "Do you think maybe you were the intended target?"

A thought crossed my mind, cloaked in the form of the pervasive nagging feeling that'd been plaguing me lately. I frowned as I reached for the ever-elusive answer to the as-yet-unidentified question. As always, it scampered easily from my grasp, forcing me to chase it. Usually, it managed to evade me effortlessly. Now, however, called into stark relief by Rico's words, the idea suddenly solidified and turned on me, crashing down to nearly crush me in an oppressive wave. The effect simultaneously rendered me physically ill and made me see some of the odd specifics of my recent dreams in a completely new light.

What kind of an assassin missed their target by such a wide margin? I mulled over the finer points of his theory to test their merit. I could feel my face crumpling as I considered the question and weighed it against what I already knew to be true. Things like my proximity to the protectee at the time the shots were fired, for example. It seemed to me only an amateur would be that sloppy. And hiring someone untested for such an important mission as the assassination of the president of a foreign country felt like an obvious faux pas. So, either something had gone horribly wrong, or the would-be assassin's aim hadn't been as off the mark as I'd originally thought.

"I think it's very possible I could've been," I said slowly, rolling each syllable around in my mouth before releasing it to hang close in the sudden silence Rico's question had left in its wake.

"You think the guys who're manufacturing this note wanted to make sure you never connected it to them?"

I heard him, sort of, but I didn't even bother trying to respond. My insides abruptly twisted into angry knots, and bile rose in the back of my throat, threatening to choke me. I swallowed, attempting to banish the sour notes from my tongue. I felt nauseated and too small within my body, the shell of which had broken into a cold sweat. While you could expect such a violent physical reaction to the news that someone wanted to kill you and even deem it appropriate, the unexpected sensation still took me aback.

"You okay?" Rico's voice drifted lazily to me as though from a great distance, sounding muffled and slightly distorted.

I forced myself to refocus on his face, setting my mouth into a grim line in response to the concern playing there. Something inside me broke, washing away the sickness beneath a sluicing torrent of anger, the heat of which instantly banished the cold that had enveloped my body.

"I'm fine," I replied curtly. What a bald-faced lie. I wasn't fine. I was furious. And beneath that, more than a little terrified.

"Bullshit." Rico stared at me defiantly, practically begging me to fight with him. I probably would've, too, if for no other reason than to let off some steam, but my BlackBerry went off just then, distracting me.

Pushing the fury inside me out of the way enough so I could breathe, I opened the email I'd just received. The subpoenas were in. Gregor had just forwarded them to me so I could submit them to the appropriate telephone company. He'd marked them urgent, too, and had given the recipient only a few days to respond. Perfect. I grinned widely, my mouth no doubt stretched in such a way that the gesture seemed vaguely maniacal, and stood up, snagging the envelope and the copy of the counterfeit bill off his desk.

"Where are you going?" Rico wanted to know.

I wanted to tell him everything. About Akbari's connections to Fallahi, Golzar, and Rostami. About the implications behind those connections and what I'd suspected they hinted at. I wanted to lay it all out for him so I could get his opinion so badly I was about to burst. But I couldn't. I couldn't talk to anyone about it. Not yet. Partly because I still had numerous unanswered questions, but mostly because I simply wasn't allowed to discuss any terrorism-related cases with anyone outside of the JTTF. That was why Meaghan was no longer involved and hadn't been since I'd first realized what kind of a case we'd stumbled upon. I had to do this alone.

Instead of giving in to the urge to spill everything, I wiggled my phone at him before slipping it back into its holster on my belt. "I'm going to track down the assholes who thought they could get away with trying to kill me."

CHAPTER FOUR

By the time I'd finally made it home—which had been an adventure in itself since I was now perpetually tensed waiting for the sound of gunfire and searching for snipers in every window—I was that strange combination of exhausted yet wired. Sleep wouldn't come either quickly or easily. I groaned as I tossed my keys on the kitchen counter and wandered over to the couch to settle into its cozy depths, squirming in an effort to get comfortable.

The cut on the outside of my thigh had been healing nicely, or so I'd been told. It didn't hurt nearly as much to move my leg as it had a few days ago. The spots on my back where my vest had caught two of the bullets, as well as the one where the doctors had cut me open so they could stop the internal bleeding, still ached. So did the back of my right hip where my handcuffs had stopped a round, and I was glad I didn't sleep on my back because that would've been downright impossible. Even sleeping on my left side—the only option available to me at the moment—had been quite a feat, requiring a precise configuration of pillow placement to keep pressure off the cut marring my forehead.

The unexpected ringing of my phone interrupted that line of thinking, and my heart jumped. A near-blinding sort of hope burst inside me but was spectacularly dashed when I read the caller ID. I swallowed against the disappointment that threatened to choke me as I answered the call.

"Hey, Rory." I tried not to sound as dejected as I felt but failed.

"Hey. Am I interrupting anything?"

"Not really. I was just thinking about going to bed."

"How are you feeling?"

"I'm okay."

"How'd you sleep last night?"

"Terrible. Which reminds me, can I take Excedrin PM?"

"Not with your Vicodin!" Rory sounded aghast that I'd even suggest such a thing.

"And if I'm not taking my Vicodin?"

"Why wouldn't you be?"

"I don't want to. Look, can I take the Excedrin or not?" I was really hoping it'd help me get a good night's sleep, but somehow I doubted it. It was just a feeble attempt to get some solid rest. I'd concluded I'd be much less of an emotional basket case if I weren't so utterly exhausted.

"Sure. Knock yourself out. Pun intended. But please, for the love of God, don't drink alcohol with it."

"Why the hell would I do that?"

"I don't know. Just don't."

"Okay." I bit my lip for a moment as I mulled over my next words. "I'm sorry I snapped at you at the hospital yesterday."

"I'm sorry, too. This whole situation has me a bit off balance, but I shouldn't have taken it out on you."

"It's my fault. I was a pain in the ass."

Rory laughed. "So what else is new?"

"New York. New Jersey. New Hampshire."

I could practically hear my sister rolling her eyes. "That joke hasn't aged well."

"New Brunswick? New Kids on the Block."

"Don't quit your day job. You wanna know a secret? You lasted a helluva lot longer than I would've if I'd been in your position. A lot longer than I thought you were going to. I honestly thought you'd have made a break for it the second your intubation tube was out."

"Believe me, the thought crossed my mind. If I'd been able to keep my eyes open for longer than eight seconds in a four-minute period, I probably would've had a better chance of formulating a solid escape plan."

"So, the secret to keeping you in one place is drugs?"

"Actually, I think it's technically unconsciousness by way of drugs."

"I'll have to remember that. Speaking of your recently acquired freedom, what are you doing tomorrow?"

"I thought I'd stop into the office at some point. That's about all. Why?"

"I was going to drop by."

I teased her. "Checking up on me?"

Rory snorted. "Hardly. I was going to offer to take your stitches out, but if you don't want me to…"

"Really? I thought they couldn't come out for several more days at least."

"For the ones on your head and your leg, that was a conservative estimate. There's no reason they need to be in that long. The ones on your back need to stay in a little longer."

"Hmm." I thought about how to fit that into the plan I'd already mapped out, mentally juggling my schedule around to make room. No way was I going to turn that offer down.

"Oh, my God!" Rory exclaimed, sounding horrified. "You took them out already, didn't you?"

"What? No." Sure, I'd been tempted, but the reality had been way too gross. I'd opted to leave that to the professionals.

"Okay, good. We can meet up after my shift. We can have a late lunch, and I'll take care of them for you."

"Thanks, Rory."

There was a pause on my sister's end of the line. "I do have an ulterior motive."

"Ooh. Scandalous! What's up?"

She hesitated again. "I was hoping you'd go to the cemetery with me first."

Oh. I hadn't seen that request coming. I was stunned into silence. Normally, it required blackmail, bribery, or both to get Rory to visit the graves of our biological father and our older sister, Reagan. I chewed on my lower lip, trying to recall if she'd ever suggested going to the cemetery and couldn't think of a single time.

"I know it's not when we usually visit," Rory went on, her voice soft, her tone borderline embarrassed. She exhaled noisily. "But I… this whole thing with you has made me think about them. A lot. I don't know. I just feel like it's something I have to do."

I smiled spontaneously at the admission. "Sure, Rory. I'll go to the cemetery with you tomorrow. I'd like that."

Rory let out a sigh of what I could only assume was relief.

"Thanks." A comfortable silence settled between us before Rory shattered the moment by asking, "Will that bother you?"

"Will what bother me?"

"Going to a cemetery?"

"Why would that bother me?"

"You know…Because of Lucia."

Ah. My heart splintered, and guilt and anguish filled in the cracks. I rubbed my chest, trying to ease the ache, and swallowed hard. "It's fine."

"Ryan, I'm sorry. If you don't want to go—"

"I said it's fine."

My sister sighed heavily. "Ryan, have you been talking to anybody? You know, about what happened?"

"Et tu, Brute?"

"Huh?"

I was suddenly very tired. My bitter words had seemingly freed the stopper on my emotions, and everything rushed out in one great big torrent, leaving me empty and drained. "You're the second person to ask me about that in the past few days. And I'll tell you what I told her. I don't want to talk about it."

"Isn't that an agency requirement?"

"Not exactly." I'd be required to have one appointment with our psychological consultant in DC before I was released for full duty, but that wasn't quite the same thing. He'd just question me about my fitness for duty. I could downplay the emotional roller coaster I was currently riding enough to get the all-clear to go back to work. And that appointment was still a long way off. I needed to completely recover physically before I could even begin to think about jumping through the necessary hoops to be restored to regular duty status.

"Well, whether it is or whether it isn't, I still think you need to consider seeing a professional. I have several colleagues I can recommend."

"Yeah. Okay. Sure." I only agreed to get her to drop the subject. Unfortunately, we both knew it.

"Ryan." Rory's voice was laden with feeling, and she hesitated as if afraid to reveal her next thought. "I think you might have PTSD. And possibly survivor's guilt."

"Are you kidding me?"

"Think about it. You're not sleeping much. When you do, you have these intense, recurring nightmares you refuse to talk about. You're irritable. Where in the past you let things go or cracked a joke about them, now you get inexplicably angry or, worse, you completely shut down. You're having trouble concentrating. You won't even say Lucia's name, for crying out loud—"

"Rory, I have a master's degree in psychology. I'm familiar with the symptoms of PTSD, thank you very much. And seeing as how you're a doctor and did a rotation in psych, I'm sure I don't have to tell you that not enough time has elapsed for you to make that determination."

"Don't play the semantics game with me. Something is seriously wrong. I'm only trying to help you. Please let me."

"I just need to sleep, Rory. That's all. I haven't had a full night's rest since…" I attempted to remember back that far. "A few nights before the POTUS visit."

"What?"

I suddenly recognized exactly how much time had passed since I'd actually gotten anything close to the recommended allotment of sleep. Sure, I was used to getting much less rest than the average person, but even I had to admit this was excessive.

"Wow," I whispered to myself in disbelief.

"Please tell me you're kidding me."

"No, I'm not." Stunned, I took a second to rethink the entire course of events. "I had advance work, which is always crazy. The breakup, which was understandably stressful. Then I had to prep for Iran and write the Dougherty report. And once the Iran visit started, I had night after night of late dinners and meetings coupled with early wake-ups. After that…well, you know."

"That was over two weeks ago," Rory exclaimed, sounding exasperated.

"Wow," I said again. No wonder I was such a mess. I doubted anyone would be able to hold it together after having not slept well in that long. The idea made me feel infinitesimally better about my current inability to control my emotions and my apparent need to wallow in a whole host of negative feelings at the most inopportune times.

"Ryan, you can't go on like this."

"I know I can't. Which is why I'm going to take that Excedrin and call it a night."

"*Ay-vo.*" Rory sounded simultaneously disappointed and upset.

"*Asha*, I promise, I'll be fine. I just need a little more time. Okay?"

"Okay." Rory sounded a trifle unsure, but thankfully she didn't press the issue. "I'll see you tomorrow?"

"Yeah. Can't wait. Love you." I didn't wait for her reply before I disconnected the call.

I closed my eyes and rubbed the bridge of my nose with my forefinger and thumb. I really wanted to massage my temples to try to banish the headache gathering behind my eyes, but the stitches near the left one made that impossible. The physical pain did give me something to concentrate on besides all my emotional woes, so at least that was something.

My phone rang again, and I didn't even bother to open my eyes as I answered. "Rory, seriously, I'm fine. Please, just let me try to sleep. I'll see you tomorrow."

"You're still not sleeping?" a soft voice that definitely didn't belong to my sister asked. "How many nights has it been?"

I froze, but my intestines started doing flips, and my heart stuttered, the beats tripping and stumbling gracelessly into one another like unevenly placed dominos. Slowly, I lowered my hand and opened my eyes. "Allison?"

"Hey." Her words were barely audible, and her tone sounded tentative.

"Hey."

I closed my eyes again and smiled, filled with delight. She called. I hadn't been sure she would.

"How are you feeling?"

"I'm okay." I hesitated a beat, undecided whether to voice the clichéd thought running loud, joyful circles around the inside of my head: that I was much better now that I was talking to her. Considering the chasm that'd suddenly and unexpectedly yawned between us the previous day, it was probably better to keep that notion to myself. "How are you?"

"I'm all right."

"Are you at work?"

"Yeah." She sounded irritated. "But I just went on break, and I wanted to catch you before you went to sleep. Or tried to, anyway."

"That means a lot to me," I told her softly.

I heard Allison let slip a small sigh. "I'm really sorry I had to leave. I didn't want to."

"I know you didn't. It's okay."

"It is absolutely not okay," Allison spat bitterly.

I frowned. That sort of outburst was uncharacteristic. "What's wrong?"

"Nothing I can't handle."

"I have no doubt you can handle it. But you don't have to handle it alone. Let me help."

"I'll show you mine if you show me yours," Allison teased.

I couldn't help chuckling. My initial instinct was to shoot back with something flirty, but I didn't want to get completely off topic. Something was obviously wrong, and I really wanted to know what it was. So, I opted for the still playful yet relatively innocent "Touché."

"Come on, Ryan," Allison insisted, all business now. "One for one."

I tugged on my earlobe, trying to decide how to phrase my revelation so she felt like I was giving her something while not actually imparting too much. "You were right. I'm still not sleeping very well." When she didn't reply, I said, "I went to work today because I'm hoping that with something else to focus on, my mind will slowly let go of the nightmares I'm having."

"Oh, Ryan." Allison's voice was soft, her tenor equal parts sympathy and exasperation.

"Your turn."

"You still won't talk to me about them? The dreams you're having? Or…anything else?"

"I'd much rather talk about something that has an actual solution. Unfortunately, this just requires time."

Allison sighed heavily, but she didn't push. "Not sure my problem has an actual solution, either."

"Well, why don't you tell me about it anyway?"

"Okay. My boss is being a complete ass. He's been giving me a hard time since Hong Kong." Her voice sounded slightly shaky, a physical manifestation of the truth of the statement. "It's starting to get to me."

"What happened in Hong Kong?"

"Nothing. That's just when it all started." The words came a little too quickly, were a little too sharp. I wasn't sure I believed her, but I knew she wouldn't be pressed into revealing the truth until she was ready, so I didn't call her on it.

"I'm sorry," I told her sincerely. I had no pull on PPD, and even if I did, she wouldn't have wanted me fighting her battles for her, so I knew I couldn't do anything. But sometimes it was just nice to have somebody willing to listen.

"Ah, what can you do, right?" Suddenly she sounded very tired.

"Soldier on, I guess. Or win the lottery, quit, and move to your own private island. That's my backup plan, at any rate."

That got a sort of halfhearted chuckle. "Why am I not surprised? So, what do you have planned for tomorrow?"

"Going to the office for a bit. And then Rory and I plan to visit the cemetery."

The long, drawn-out pause on the other end of the line stretched on for so long I started to wonder whether we'd been disconnected. I pulled my phone away from my ear to check the status of the call. Everything appeared fine.

"Allison?"

"Yeah?" Her voice broke a little. She cleared her throat. "Yeah?"

"Everything okay?"

"Hmm? Oh, yeah. Fine. I was just thinking. It's nice you asked Rory to go to the cemetery with you."

"I didn't ask her. She asked me."

"Wait. What? Why would she do that?"

I chuckled at her obvious surprise. "I know, right? She never wants to know if we can go there. I always have to cajole her. Even on Reagan and Dad's birthdays she actively looks for reasons to get out of it. I don't know why it bothers her so much."

Allison hesitated a beat before replying. "Oh. I thought you meant…Never mind. Death affects everybody differently, I suppose."

"I guess that's true. But we were two when they died. It's not like we remember them very much."

"Still, I think it's nice you're going."

"Yeah."

An easy quiet settled between us, and we spent long moments listening to one another breathe. There were so many things I wanted to say to her, but I couldn't seem to make myself utter the words. I doubted they'd carry effectively across the metaphorical divide that separated us anyway.

"Listen, Ryan. I—"

A voice in the background interrupted her, and inwardly I fumed at whoever'd had the gall to intrude. Her tone had been solemn as she'd started that sentence, which indicated to me that whatever she'd been about to say had been important. I lamented that I likely wasn't going to hear the rest of it.

Allison must've pressed her phone against her shoulder the second the interloper had spoken because all I could make out were muffled tidbits. Whoever had just crashed our party must've asked her to do something because I clearly heard her ask, "Now?" in a thoroughly exasperated tone. That was followed a few beats later by her demanding to know why whatever it was couldn't wait ten minutes, until she was off the phone. That didn't sound good. Who could she possibly have been talking to, especially in such a fashion? I kept coming up blank.

"Ryan?" Allison said finally, sounding infuriated.

"Yeah?"

"I'm sorry. I have to go wash the cars." Her voice dripped with derision as she said that, and I was willing to bet she was glaring at whoever had just made the ill-timed request.

I was thoroughly disappointed for oh-so-many reasons, but I tried bravely not to let my hurt seep through to taint my words. I neither wanted to anger her further nor make her feel guilty about something obviously out of her control.

"It's okay. I understand."

"I'm glad you do, because I'm having a very difficult time figuring out exactly why I'm being forced to do something that is not my job." Allison sounded positively livid, and I was fairly certain the comment was pointedly directed.

"Um." I didn't know what to say to that.

"I'll call you soon," Allison promised, but the edge in her voice sapped the vow of all comfort.

"Okay. Good night, Allison."

The lack of reply let me know she'd already hung up.

CHAPTER FIVE

It took me a long time to drift off to sleep that night, and my mind fought it with all the ferocity of a swarm of driver ants avenging one of their own. As tired as I was, and as much as I craved a good night's rest, I knew that wasn't what awaited me. But between the exhaustion, my body's need to heal, and the cocktail of sleep aids I'd fixed myself before crawling into bed, I could only battle for so long before I lost.

The dream always started out the same. Without question. Without fail. The beginning never deviated from an apparently carefully regimented script. The theme of the ending didn't either, come to think of it. And all of it had been slowly becoming more and more vivid with each nightly rendition. Which is why it came as no surprise that my dream that evening began with me all geared up for work and standing on an eerily deserted Lexington Avenue outside the InterCon Hotel.

As I did every time, I started looking around, trying to figure out why the street was empty and where everybody was, but I didn't get very far in my analysis before gunshots rang out, and I immediately rushed inside the hotel and tried to find someone, anyone, who could give me some sort of clue what the hell was going on.

I failed, of course, as I always did, and ended up escaping the endless hallway by forcing my way onto an elevator—by way of a conveniently placed halogen tool—that managed to take me maybe five floors before suddenly careening in a wild free fall the rest of the way down to the ground. The car landed with a spectacular crash that jarred the doors open to let me out in a dusty, dark basement of sorts.

Strategically placed bare lightbulbs provided the only

illumination, and they were far enough apart from one another that everything in between the weakly cast pools of light was shrouded in shadow and difficult to see. The bulbs seemed to stretch on and on, and I was overcome with a momentary pang of dread at not being able to determine which way was out. Swallowing hard, I took my flashlight from its usual place on my belt and swept the beam over the closest area of darkness, squinting in an attempt to see through both the gloom and the considerable amount of dust the elevator's crash had stirred up.

The floor in front of me was littered with an astounding assortment of boxes, papers, and bric-a-brac, piled and strewn haphazardly with no seeming intent toward order whatsoever. Gingerly, I began picking my way through the rubble, trying desperately to avoid brushing against anything as much to attempt to keep my suit clean as to avoid toppling one of the teetering piles.

If this'd been real life, I'd have wondered at the seemingly random and oddly disassociated collection of objects hoarded in the dank basement of a hotel, none of which were situationally appropriate to the location, but dream-me didn't seem to pick up on the peculiarity of the situation. No, dream-me merely took the lone boxing glove hanging off the handlebars of a toddler's Big Wheel, which was perched precariously atop a barrel sitting next to a mannequin dressed like Doctor Frank-N-Furter from *The Rocky Horror Picture Show*, an empty fish tank full of various kinds of fruit, and a box marked STAR CHARTS in stride.

A crash sounded off to my left, and I spun, training the beam of my flashlight in the direction of the noise. The ray wasn't powerful enough to cut through the shadows to the origin of the din, so I clicked it off and reholstered it. Then I eased my right hand quietly underneath my suit jacket so I could unsnap the retention strap that held my gun in place. I wasn't ready to draw it just yet because I couldn't be sure the source of the noise was a threat, but I wanted to be able to get it out that much quicker if need be.

I slowly, silently crouched behind a weight bench almost completely shrouded with bathing suits so as to be virtually unrecognizable and gave my eyes a few moments to adjust to darkness again. I listened intently for any clue as to who or what could've knocked over all that stuff but came up empty. As far as I could tell,

I was here alone. Perhaps the pile had simply toppled on its own. Unlikely, but that was the best theory I could manage.

"What are we looking for?" a low voice whispered right next to my ear.

"Jesus Christ!" I yelped as I leapt up and spun around, drawing my weapon and aiming it in the direction of the speaker. I scrambled backward a few steps to create distance between me and the newcomer and succeeded only in crashing into the weight bench. Sharp stabs of pain shot up from the back of my right hip where I'd banged into the racked bar, and I bit back a curse.

Lucia was smirking at me in the near darkness, appearing far too amused with the situation for my liking. She was dressed for work in a tailored charcoal suit that flattered her frame and somehow, against all odds, managed to make her look feminine.

"What the fuck, Luce?" I demanded, not even bothering to try to hide my annoyance. I slid my pistol back into its holster and put my hands on my hips.

"What?" she asked innocently.

"What the hell are you doing sneaking around in the basement of the InterCon?"

"I could ask you the same question."

"I'm not sneaking. I'm looking for the way out."

"Oh, I don't think you should do that."

"Why not?"

"Well, because it isn't a good idea."

"Huh?"

Lucia regarded me sadly. "I'm sorry. I'll rephrase. I can't allow that."

I did a double take. "What? What do you mean you can't allow that?"

"I mean, you're not leaving. Not yet."

"Why the hell not?"

"You and I have some unfinished business."

A spark of anger flared inside me. "Are you kidding me?"

"No. I'm not."

I shook my head and clenched my fists. I didn't have time for this nonsense. I needed to find the rest of the detail and make sure everyone was okay. Determined to outsmart her once and for all, I turned on my heel, swept past the nuisance of a weight bench, and headed in the completely opposite direction.

Lucia stepped out from behind a child's pop tent directly into my path. "I'm afraid it's not going to be quite so easy."

Never one to be deterred—or to pick up on a hint the first time—I simply changed direction once more and tried again. This time she let me get a few steps farther before simultaneously scaring the hell out of me and foiling my escape by emerging from an old wood-burning stove.

"Damn it, Luce!" I fixed her with a menacing glare. "I have to go."

"Not yet, you don't. Sit. Relax. Let's chat." She gestured to a life-sized carousel horse as though she actually expected me to hop up onto it so we could discuss shoes and ships and sealing wax. Clearly, she was out of her damn mind.

I folded my arms across my chest and glowered at her. "Luce, we don't have time to chat. Someone's in trouble. Didn't you hear the gunshots earlier?"

Lucia's lips quirked in some semblance of a wry smile, and she mimicked my pose. "I heard them."

"Then you see why I have to get the hell out of here." My words were colored with a hint of pleading and desperation.

"There's nothing you can do about that now. What's done is done."

My heart sank. "Does that mean somebody got hurt? Was it the detail? Is the protectee okay? I have to get to them!"

"Sorry," she said with a shrug, not sounding the least bit apologetic.

"For what? Did somebody get hurt?"

"I don't know. Probably." She didn't sound like she cared. "My point is, you can't change the past. So why dwell on it?"

"What the hell has gotten into you today?"

"Ah. Now you care about my feelings."

I narrowed my eyes at her. "What's that supposed to mean?"

"Forget what it's supposed to mean. Focus on what it does mean."

"Okay, stop with the passive-aggressive bullshit. If you have something to say to me, just say it."

Lucia favored me with a thoroughly disappointed look. "I think it's more important for you to listen than it is for me to speak. You need to see, Ryan. That's the problem. You're still not completely seeing."

Okay, she'd officially lost me. And I was no longer inclined to listen or speak or see or anything else having to do with this exchange. We were getting nowhere fast, and I really needed to find the detail and see what I could do to help.

"I have no idea what you're talking about."

"Yes, you do." She sounded frustrated now. "You just don't know that you do. You need to focus."

"Focus on what?"

"Why."

I frowned. "Why do I want to know what I'm supposed to focus on?"

"No. Why is what you need to focus on."

"You're not making any sense."

"That's because you're still not listening to me."

"What do you want from me?" I asked her point-blank.

"What does anyone want from anyone?"

I scowled at her. "Is this some kind of a joke?"

"I'm not laughing. Neither are you, come to think of it. So, it must not be a very good joke."

I let out a long, slow breath and dug my fingernails into the meat of my palms. "I can't do this with you right now. I don't want to play these ridiculous games. Either help me get out of here or get the hell out of my way."

I blinked. And in the space of that fraction of a moment when my eyes were closed, everything shifted. And when I opened them again, I was staring down the barrel of a gun.

Instinct took over faster than I ever would've thought possible, and in another tenth of a heartbeat, I had my own weapon drawn and pointed right back at her. No sound shattered the stillness that stretched taut between us, as fragile as newly forming ice on the top of a lake, as we stared at one another.

"What are you doing?" I finally asked her.

Lucia's facial expression was strangely wooden, which, frankly, gave me the creeps. She watched me for another long moment before formulating a reply. "What does it look like I'm doing?"

"Luce, this is crazy. Come on. Stop it."

"I can't let you leave, Ryan. I told you that. Not until we talk. Not until you *see*."

"See what?" I demanded angrily.

"Everything."

"Why don't you save us both some time and aggravation and just tell me what everything is?"

"Where's the fun in that?"

I rolled my eyes and made a rude noise in the back of my throat.

"Besides," she went on, "I think it'll be more meaningful if you figure it out for yourself."

"Whatever."

We went back to staring at one another in silence. It was strange. Obviously, had this been reality, you'd expect I'd be nervous or anxious or terrified having this conversation at gunpoint, but all I felt in the dream was slightly irritated.

"Look," I said as I shifted so the muzzle of my weapon pointed straight up in the air. I lifted my other hand in supplication. "You holster yours, and I'll holster mine, okay?"

Lucia's grin was nothing short of maniacal. She pursed her lips and pretended to think about it, but the malicious gleam in her eye told me no way was she going to comply with my request. "Hmmm. No."

The click of her pulling back the hammer to cock the weapon was ridiculously loud and obviously done for dramatic effect, since she didn't need to do that in order to fire. She adjusted her grip and her stance slightly as she continued to stare at me mockingly over the sights of her gun.

I swung my own muzzle back down so it was pointed at her and tried not to let my discomfort with the situation show. I didn't want to shoot her, but I also didn't want her to know I didn't want to shoot her. Perhaps if she thought I was indifferent about the task, she'd be less inclined to force me to do it.

"Luce, don't do this."

"Why?" The muscles in her hand and forearm tensed as she began an agonizingly slow trigger squeeze.

"Luce, please," I whispered. My hands were trembling, now, too, but for a completely different reason. They wanted to pull the trigger, wanted to give in to the desire to preserve my own life. And I was trying so hard to best that impulse.

"What's it gonna be, Ryan? Your life? Or mine?" The expression on her face indicated she was getting some kind of perverted kick out of this little game. "That's what it all comes down to in the end, isn't it?"

"Fuck, Luce! Knock it off!"

"Tick tock, Ryan. The hammer's almost back. What're you gonna do?"

"I will shoot you."

"No, you won't."

"Don't do this." I tried one more time, attempting to rein in the fury that'd suddenly flared to life inside me.

"This isn't my doing, it's yours. That's what I've been trying to tell you. It was always yours."

"Goddammit!"

The sounds of multiple gunshots shattered the quiet and filled the air with wisps of acrid smoke. It was strange how the report echoed throughout the cluttered basement and seemed to fill the entire room. The reverberations even seemed to resound inside me.

I stood completely still for several heartbeats as the smoke wafted around me. My eyes drifted to the gun in my grip as my mouth dropped opened. Holy shit. I'd done it. I couldn't believe I'd actually done it.

I glanced back to Luce and groaned at the sight of a perfectly placed cluster of bullet holes marring the center of her dress shirt. The wounds had started to slowly ooze, staining the pristine cloth a bright, reproachful crimson. The expression on her face was one of horror-tinged surprise.

"I can't believe you did that," she said with a gasp.

My stomach lurched, and I cast my eyes downward. I needed to not look at her, and in my efforts to avoid her accusing glare, I was sickened to note the front of my own shirt was also marred with telling blotches of red. Moaning, I let my weapon slip from my grasp to land with a loud clatter on the cement floor.

I shot straight up in bed with a strangled wail struggling to escape my clenched teeth. My breathing was labored, and my heart was galloping. My entire body was chilled and clammy, covered in sweat. I gasped shakily and sat there for a long moment, my mind spinning like an Olympic figure skater going for the gold, as I attempted to figure out where the hell I was and what the fuck had just happened.

One second.

Two.

I was in my bedroom at home. The room was pitch-black, and I was alone. I sighed in relief.

Three seconds.

Four.

It was a dream. Just a dream. I hadn't shot Lucia in the basement of the InterCon. I hadn't looked into her eyes as I'd almost triumphantly pulled the trigger and ended her life.

Five seconds.

But I was responsible for her death.

The pain and guilt that rushed in after my earlier relief had all the power and destruction of a flash flood. They washed away all traces of any positive emotions I'd been clinging to so desperately.

Letting out a shaky breath, I slowly lay back down. You'd think I'd be used to the ever-present ache in my chest, but I curled into a ball on my left side as though I were bodily cradling my cracked and damaged heart.

My eyes remained open as I lay there trying to calm my nerves and slow my breathing, but I wasn't really seeing anything around me. Tears welled, but I didn't have the energy to push them back. I didn't react when they started making slow, languid tracks across my cheeks toward my pillow.

A powerful urge to call Allison struck me just then. I mulled that possibility over for a second, considering the pros and cons. On the upside, I was certain just hearing her voice would be like applying a healing balm directly to me. On the downside, calling her at this hour would definitely raise suspicions as to my motive. Not to mention that in my current state of mind, I seriously doubted my ability to play the dream off like it hadn't bothered me. And who wanted a girlfriend who called her every time she had a nightmare? Hmm. What to do?

I snagged my phone from underneath the pillow next to me and hit the button to turn on the screen, flinching when the sudden brightness hit my sensitive eyeballs like ice picks. I scrolled to my recent-calls list and allowed my thumb to hover over Allison's number as I debated whether to give in to my urges. She'd been working late yesterday afternoon, and since it was now just shy of the ass-crack of dawn, she was probably still sleeping. I shook my head and put the phone down.

No way in hell was I going to wake her up. Not for something like this. Not when—

"Hello?" a faint, tinny voice said.

I jumped and tried to sit up, letting out a strangled cry at the pain the sudden motion produced.

"Hello?" the faraway voice said again. "Ryan?"

"Shit!" I fumbled for the phone I hadn't realized I'd dialed and scrambled to press it to my ear as my heart hammered. "Allison?"

"Yeah. You okay?" Her voice was low and rough, and I knew my call had just dragged her forcibly from sleep.

"Oh, my God. I'm so sorry. I didn't mean to call you."

"S'okay," she mumbled through a yawn. "What's up?" I heard rustling and imagined she was sitting up in bed.

"Nothing important. Go back to sleep."

"Mmm. No. I've got to get up for work soon anyway."

"Didn't you work the afternoon shift yesterday?"

Another yawn. "Yeah. I short changed."

I winced. That meant she'd had exactly eight hours between the end of her last shift and the start of her next one. Short changes were a bitch, and every second of sleep counted. "Fuck. I'm sorry."

"Not your fault. You didn't make the schedule." There was more rustling on her end, a pause, and then the sound of running water that faded into nothing not long after. "So is it safe to assume you're still having nightmares?"

"Maybe I just wanted to talk to you." Even I didn't think I sounded convincing.

"At oh-dark-thirty?"

"Sure."

"Okay, so what'd you want to talk to me about?"

"Um…How much I miss you?"

"Sounds like a load of crap to me," she muttered. I wasn't sure whether she meant for me to hear that or not.

"But you obviously find my crap endearing because you continue to stick around."

Allison sighed loudly. "So that's it? You miss me?" The keen edge to her words sent a sliver of dread into my chest.

"Of course." Though I'd made it sound like a question last time, that didn't make it any less true.

"Fine."

I shivered at the iciness in her tone and paused so I could swallow and clear my throat. "So…I guess I should let you get ready for work."

"Yeah." The running water got louder again, and I heard the distinct sound of more rustling, which I assumed meant she'd taken her pajamas off and was getting ready to get into the shower.

"Well…I'll talk to you later. Have a good day."

"Thanks." She hung up abruptly, leaving me alone with my heavy heart and my unpleasant thoughts.

It was my turn to sigh loudly as I dropped the phone back onto the bed at my side and stared up at the ceiling. My chest felt like it was being squeezed tighter than when I wore my ballistic vest, and my insides were liquid and molten as though they'd melted from the blaze of Allison's ire.

I should just tell her what was bothering me, right? I mean, she obviously wanted to know. And I was only making things worse between us by refusing to clue her in. Sure, I had my reasons, but I was starting to wonder whether they were unfounded at best and selfish at worst. Lord knew what she imagined I was keeping from her. And it wasn't fair of me to keep her in the dark like this.

It was settled. Next time we spoke, I'd tell her everything.

After that decision, I relaxed slightly and closed my eyes in an attempt to doze. It was way too freaking early for me to be awake, and I definitely wasn't going to repeat yesterday's mistake of going to the office smack in the middle of regular working hours. Nope. I planned to stall and head in much later in the day, when people were more apt to be out in the field or completely finished with their workday and on the way home. Less chance of being bombarded with questions and pitying looks that way.

I fidgeted for an eternity but couldn't get comfortable enough to drift off. The sky became lighter by degrees, and I became more and more frustrated with my sleeplessness. I tried everything I could think of: counting my blessings, counting sheep, imagining I was listening to Pachelbel's *Canon in D*, which I normally found extremely soothing. But nothing worked. It wasn't until I pretended Allison was lying beside me, gently tracing light patterns on the bare skin of my back and occasionally running her hands through my hair that I finally felt comforted enough to slowly fall back to sleep.

And found myself standing on an empty street in the middle of Midtown New York. Again.

Crap.

CHAPTER SIX

W hat the fuck are you doing here?" a loud voice boomed approximately two seconds after I'd set foot into NYFO the next day.

I was still teetering on the edge of panic from the trip in and the fear that whoever'd tried to kill me was poised to try again at any moment, so I jumped and had to forcibly strangle a shriek. I turned, careful not to move too fast lest I wince and betray the pain I was feeling. Inwardly, I grimaced. Seeing who'd spoken was enough to set my nerves ablaze all by itself. The volume at which I'd been summoned didn't help.

"I work here, Bill," I replied, not bothering to keep the fatigue or displeasure from my tone.

Bill Steelman and I had never really gotten along. Our dislike for one another had been immediate. I found him smug, pompous, condescending, and a general pain in the ass. I never cared to ask exactly what his problem was with me, but if I had to guess, I'd say it stemmed from my making no secret of the fact that I thought all of the aforementioned things about him. All I knew for sure was he appeared to enjoy pressing my buttons every chance he got.

Bill strode over to me and stopped a lot closer than I'd have liked, his feet spread wide in a confident stance, his arms folded across his chest. He took his time running an appraising gaze down my body and slowly back up again. The attention was like a thousand spiders skittering across my skin, and I fought my urge to allow my lip to curl into a sneer.

The other agents in our general proximity must've heard Bill's unnecessarily loud inquiry because heads began poking out of offices and folks started making their way over. I wasn't prepared or inclined to field the questions I was sure to be asked, but, on the bright side, the presence of other people would shorten the time I had to spend engaging Bill. I always was a glass-half-full sort of girl.

Bill lifted his chin in a half nod and gave a soft grunt. "I would've thought you'd take more time off."

"Yeah, well, you know. Work to do." I tried to shuffle past him, but he didn't move. I sighed and ran the palm of my hand across the back of my neck, squeezing lightly. I really didn't have the energy to engage with him today, which should've been apparent by my complete lack of witty repartee. But if he noticed, he wasn't taking the hint.

Instead, Bill continued to stare at me, his expression unreadable, for an uncomfortably long period of time. Finally, he stuffed his hands into his pockets and ducked his head a bit so he was looking at me from underneath his eyebrows. "Glad you're okay." Then he turned and left.

Stunned, I gaped at him as he strutted away. His statement had thrown me more than his unceremonious departure, and I lapsed into musings of whether it'd been sincere or what kind of angle he could've been working. I'd been caught off guard just long enough so I couldn't escape the rest of my coworkers, who'd managed to pen me in during my brief period of inattention to my surroundings.

The next half hour was mentally and emotionally painful, to put it mildly. I'd had to spend it enduring graceless questions and inelegant statements on all manner of subjects—from how bad had it hurt to be shot, to did I have scars, to "that NYPD chick who died"—all of which made me grind my teeth and dig my fingernails into the sides of my thighs from inside my pants pockets. I tried to tell myself these nice people were concerned about me, but a part of me wished they weren't.

When I was finally able to extricate myself from the throng and seclude myself in the relative safety of my office, I heaved a huge sigh of relief and sank gratefully into the chair behind my desk. I hated being the center of attention. I hated it when people I barely knew asked me overly personal questions. And I really hated it when I couldn't think of a smart-assed quip to deflect those overly personal questions. Handling all three of those scenarios at once had taken a lot out of me.

Pushing my uneasiness to the side, I frowned at my half of the work space I shared with Meaghan. Where her side was absolutely pristine, mine was definitely not. Files were piled haphazardly on top of my desk and in little stacks on the floor surrounding it. Pens, paperclips, and Post-it notepads littered the spaces between the piles, and handwritten notes and charts were taking up what few gaps in the disarray remained. In short, my side of the room was a disaster. That was a feat, considering I no longer carried any Secret Service cases. Even I wasn't sure what half the stuff on my desk was.

Grateful for something to occupy myself, even if it was such a mundane task as cleaning, I set to work and became lost in the soothing rhythm of creating order out of chaos. It was slow going with the use of only one arm, but I didn't mind.

I was just standing back to admire my handiwork and revel in the feeling of accomplishment that the sight of my now-orderly desk created, when a shadow darkened my opened doorway. I froze, not so much afraid as wary. Most of the people I was on good terms with didn't have a habit of lurking in my doorway.

Mark Jennings, Assistant to the Special Agent in Charge of the Protective Intelligence squad and my immediate supervisor, appeared surprised to see me at first, but he recovered quickly and schooled his face into a perfectly impassive mask. He cast his eyes around, taking in my newly organized workspace.

"AT Jennings." I addressed him in an attempt to fill the uncomfortable silence that inevitably settled around us whenever we interacted with one another.

"You've been busy, I see."

In the few short weeks I'd been out of the office—first on a protection assignment and then in the hospital—I'd somehow forgotten how much his mustache lent emphasis to every single word he uttered. I couldn't stop staring at it. He probably thought I had a crush on him because of the way my eyes were always drawn to it, like they would be to a horrific car crash on the side of the highway. But it was just so… bushy. He kind of reminded me of the walrus in the cartoon version of *Alice in Wonderland.*

"Yeah, well, I don't have much else to occupy my time. I figured why not try out this whole neatness thing everybody is raving about. I'm still not convinced it isn't overrated."

"Mmm." He stared at me, and I looked expectantly back.

"Did you need something?" I asked finally. Normally, I enjoyed letting the quiet stretch taut between us until he finally felt compelled to break it. My own little power trip, I supposed. But today, I simply wasn't up to it. I wanted to finish this strained interaction as quickly as possible so I could figure out what to do with the rest of my afternoon.

Mark blinked as though he'd just been jolted out of a daydream, even though he'd been looking right at me when I'd spoken and shouldn't have been surprised. I could almost see the thoughts squirming around inside his head as he considered how best to respond.

"I didn't expect you to be back so soon."

"Yeah, well, I missed you."

He frowned, visibly stymied, but didn't comment.

Unable to stand the silence, I strove to fill it, "Besides, I couldn't let you run around here unattended, could I? Who knows what sort of trouble you'd cause? I've gotta protect the brand and prevent an international incident."

Mark's eyes grew wide, and his face paled visibly for an instant before flushing. I sighed at his complete lack of a sense of humor. Granted, that hadn't been one of my better jokes, but I'd hoped he'd cut me some slack and let my wan attempt at levity slide. Apparently not.

"I was kidding. Obviously. Or maybe it wasn't. Anyway, I came back because I was bored sitting at home."

"You don't have any PI cases to work on," he said, as though he really didn't think I was perfectly aware of my own caseload.

"I know I don't." I ground my reply out through clenched teeth.

"So, what are you going to do?"

My jaw tightened even further, and a jolt of pain on the right side forced me to make myself relax. I had no idea why he cared what I was doing here or how I planned to spend the rest of my day, but I refused to let him bully me into justifying myself.

"I don't know. Maybe catch up on my timekeeping paperwork or knock out a couple of the online learning modules I have due. Don't worry. I won't be here too long."

Mark fidgeted in my doorway, looking as though he was debating making another comment, but after a bit he simply turned and left without uttering good-bye.

I let out a huff. While his behavior was exasperating, it wasn't all that surprising. Mark liked me about as much as I liked him, which was to say about as much as I liked tomatoes or pouring lemon juice directly over a paper cut. Or Peeps. But I didn't think that necessarily took the notion of common courtesy completely off the table.

That he hadn't even thought to inquire after my well-being or remark on my recovery didn't shock me. I knew he didn't care. That he'd bothered to stop by at all had been mildly astounding, though. And I figured he'd agree with me that we were now pretty well full up on our interaction quotient for at least the next week. Hopefully, that'd keep his presence in my office to a minimum, and I'd be able to get some work done.

Now that my desk actually resembled something you might expect to find in the office of a federal agent and not a replica of what you might see in the dorm room of a college boy, I needed another menial task to occupy my time. Going to the gym was out. I was in way too much pain. Meaghan had obviously gotten called out on something because she wasn't here, so I couldn't look for any entertainment ideas there. I didn't want to leave my office to go on a quest for another errand for fear of having to make awkward conversation with my peers. That left few options. I sat down in my chair and drummed my fingertips lightly on my blotter.

An idea occurred to me, but I wasn't certain I'd be able to pull it off. Feeling a bit naughty, I glanced around, as though searching for someone who might intervene in what I was about to do. Biting my lower lip, I slowly eased my right arm out of its sling.

The process was time-consuming and borderline agonizing, but I was tired of having my arm strapped to my body, and frankly, I'd be much more likely to get things done if I could use my dominant hand.

The still-healing wound above my right shoulder protested the movement loudly and with extreme prejudice, and I had to clench my teeth to stifle a groan. Maybe because my arm hadn't really moved from that position in days. Hopefully, the ache would ebb, if only slightly, the longer my arm was free. It was a working theory, at any rate.

I let out a relieved breath as I tested the range of motion available to me, pushing against the boundaries of discomfort just hard enough to be certain where they lay. I discovered, much to my pleasure, that I was able to rest my forearm against my desk and manipulate my computer mouse without any problem. That was huge, considering it took me almost forever to get anything accomplished using only my left hand.

I opened up the website for the online learning modules we were required to complete intermittently, loaded up the one about OPSEC, and leaned back in my chair. My eyes glazed over as the presentation played. I wished this were a module I could just test out of, but unfortunately, I had to sit through the entire thing. Then I had four others to complete. Damn, this was going to be a long day.

My work cell phone rang, cutting through the low drone of the presenter's voice, and I blinked. Grateful for the interruption, I paused the video and glanced at the caller ID. It was a number out of DC but not one I recognized. That was never good.

"Ryan O'Connor," I answered warily.

Jamie Dorchester's irritated voice floated over the line. "What the hell did you do?"

I was relieved it was one of my friends and not some suit from headquarters, though her obvious irritation was much less reassuring. I played with my staple remover as I considered the question. I wanted to determine exactly what transgression she could possibly have known about before I admitted to offenses that were still a mystery. Perhaps it'd be better if I postponed answering until I had a better idea why she was annoyed.

"Hey, Jamie. What's up?"

"Don't you give me that innocent act. I'm not playing with you."

"Nice to talk to you, too. How's Jo?" Perhaps asking about her girlfriend would buy me some much-needed time.

Jamie would not be deterred. "What. Did. You. Do?"

"Um...I can honestly say I have no earthly idea what you're talking about."

"How about this: do you want to tell me why your girlfriend is in such a shitty fucking mood today? Does that ring any bells for you?"

"My what?"

Jamie snorted derisively. "Stop playing dumb when I know you aren't. You know damn well there are no secrets in the Secret Service."

I cringed. She had a point. And even though I'd basically had the same conversation with Meaghan less than twenty-four hours ago, I was still caught off guard. I hadn't really thought about it specifically, but now that I was, I guess I would've said I hadn't expected the rumors to have spread quite that quickly. Silly me.

"Oh." That was all I could think of to say.

"Yeah. 'Oh.' And don't think I don't have a whole host of follow-up questions about *that*, by the way. Starting with 'Was this going on during the last POTUS visit to New York?' But now isn't the time."

"So, uh, how'd you find out?" I didn't really care about the answer. I was just trying to stall her wrath for as long as I could.

"Well, let's see," she drawled, her tone pure sarcasm. "I was the one who had to replace Allison on the Hong Kong trip. How long do you think it took for somebody to tell me exactly why that was necessary?"

"Less than four seconds."

"You're close. Less than three."

"Do I still win the prize?"

"You're going to win my foot up your ass if you don't answer my question. The day-shift whip is in a horrendous mood today, and dealing with her when she's like this is next to impossible. So what'd you do to piss her off?"

I grinned despite Jamie's ire. "Allison was whipping the shift today?" That meant she was sort of in charge, and it was a big deal. She hadn't mentioned that to me. I was unbelievably proud of her.

"So not the point. And stop being dirty."

"I wasn't!"

"Sure you weren't. And I'm the pope. Listen, the woman has been back here for less than two days, and she's miserable. I don't know what you did, but you fix it, and you fix it now. Flowers. Candy. Jewelry. Phone sex. I don't care, and I don't want to know. Just be quick about it. Because she's almost done arguing with the boss, and my shift whip ordered me to get the briefing from her before she goes home. I'd rather eat broken glass than be anywhere near her with the mood she's in."

"That bad, huh?"

"Worse."

"What makes you think Allison's bad mood is my fault?"

"Gee, I don't know," Jamie said dryly. "Maybe the fact that she's been nothing short of even-keeled the entire time I've worked with her and has never once spoken a sharp word to anyone, and all of a sudden she's behaving like a perfect—"

"Watch it." I could appreciate that Allison's current disposition upset her, but I wasn't about to stand idly by while anyone called her names.

"Anyway. My point is, you're the difference. You're what's new in Allison's life. It makes sense that she's angry because of you."

I mulled over what Jamie had just told me. True, our conversation this morning hadn't gone as well as I'd have hoped, but I didn't think it'd gone horribly enough to have made her as angry as she sounded. Certainly not angry enough to get into an argument with her boss. Which meant the situation with him was likely more serious than she'd let on the night before. Allison hadn't wanted to give up any information on the subject, but maybe I could get something out of Jamie. The trick would be doing it without her realizing I was fishing. Not an easy task.

"So, you think she's arguing with the boss because of me?"

"No," Jamie said, sounding a little contrite. "Probably not completely because of you. They've been arguing for a while now. But it started when she left Hong Kong to come home to be with you."

"Wait. The boss she's fighting with now was in Hong Kong?"

"Yeah. He was the second supe on the trip."

"Oh."

"Yeah. So you see why I need you to fix this."

I wasn't sure how to do that or even what the problem was exactly, but I didn't tell her that. "Which boss?"

"Huh?"

"Which boss is she arguing with?"

"Oh. Beau Byers."

"Hmmm. The name sounds familiar, but I can't picture him."

"He's pretty new, considering. Been here about a year, I guess. Came from LA. He's okay."

"Squared away?"

"Yeah. He knows his stuff."

"But...?" I knew her well enough to realize there was something she wasn't saying.

She didn't answer me right away. A low hum escaped her as she considered my question. "I don't know, but something about him rubs me the wrong way."

Interesting. I wondered whether Allison would be able to articulate exactly what it was about Byers that bothered her better than Jamie had.

I didn't have much of a chance to pursue the topic any further, however. Just as I'd opened my mouth to follow up, Jamie said, "Hang on."

I heard some sort of scraping, which led me to believe she'd pressed the receiver against her shoulder or her chest. I couldn't hear what the other person was saying, but I did hear her slightly muffled response of, "No problem. I'll be right there." Then her voice grew louder. "Sweetheart. I'm sorry. I have to go. The whip's ready to give me my briefing now."

Her address tickled me. She'd never called me that before, and I didn't expect her to have very many reasons to have a change of heart now. Only one I could think of. "Sweetheart, huh? Allison's standing right there, isn't she?"

"You got it."

"Nice! Is she whipping you?"

"Absolutely. I have to go. Do you remember what you promised?"

I laughed. It had to be driving her crazy that she couldn't retort or scold me. "I'm on it," I told her. "But if she's leaving anyway, does it really matter?"

"Good. I love you, Jo."

"Is she actually buying that?"

But I never got an answer because Jamie hung up on me. I really had to get the women in my life to quit doing that.

CHAPTER SEVEN

As soon as I stopped grinning about Jamie's predicament, I eased myself into the backrest so the chair was leaning a bit and tipped my head up to stare at the ceiling. I rested my elbows on the armrests and tapped the edge of my shoe against the underside of my desk as I mulled over everything I'd just learned.

While I was pretty sure Allison wasn't happy with me at the moment, judging by our phone call earlier, I didn't think her bad mood was entirely my fault. I also didn't hold any illusions that I'd be able to completely negate whatever was going on with her boss. No matter what I did, her day wouldn't suddenly become all unicorns and rainbows. But I was reasonably certain I could do some minimal damage control. I just needed to figure out the best way without accidentally jumping up and down on her obviously already raw nerves.

Jamie was clearly being facetious when she'd brought it up, but I still considered, then discarded the ideas of flowers, chocolates, and jewelry. They'd take too long, and I was more of an instant-gratification kind of girl. I also dismissed phone sex, but that was mostly because I was sitting in my office. Also because I doubted she'd go for it in her current state. But I filed it in the back of my mind for another time.

I retrieved my personal phone from the holster on my left hip and regarded the dark screen for a long moment. Text or call, text or call? Hmmm. I did want to hear her voice, but if she was still on the White House grounds, she might prefer to keep our conversation a little more private.

Are you still mad at me?

I texted her after a long moment of deliberation and an even longer moment of intentional stalling to give her time to finish briefing Jamie.

What do you think I'm mad at you for?

For stealing your heart.

I smiled at my own joke and laid the phone down on my desk next to my mouse as I waited for her reply. Seconds dragged on into minutes, and I tried to ignore the heaviness in my chest as I restarted the OPSEC module as a sort of distraction. I was only half paying attention to it, and my eyes flickered over to my phone more often than I would've liked as my nerves sizzled waiting for Allison's reply.

I'd just about dozed off because that stupid module was so unbelievably dull when the buzzing of my phone against the wood of my desk dragged me back to awareness. I fumbled for it and cursed as pain speared several key body parts. Hastily, I opened Allison's message. It was a picture of a bottle. I frowned at it for a few seconds before firing off a reply.

What's that?

Some wine to go with all the cheese.

I burst out laughing and shook my head.

But did it make you smile?

I can neither confirm nor deny.

I'll take that as a yes.

I didn't say that.

Doesn't matter. It's what I choose to believe.

After a long pause, I received a cryptic answer.

No.

No, what? That's not what I choose to believe? Or no, you didn't smile?

No. I'm not mad at you for stealing my heart.

Oh. Well, that's good.

I mean, I made out pretty good in that deal. I ended up with yours.

Speaking of hearts, mine did its best pinball impersonation between my ribs as I read that, and I didn't even try to stop the grin from breaking out across my lips. A flirty, smart-ass retort came immediately to mind, but my thumbs hovered over the keyboard as I recalled my conversation with Meaghan about how I was never serious about anything. Maybe it was time for me to give that a try.

So if you're not mad at me for that, what are you mad at me for?

The pause that followed felt longer than an Easter Sunday church service. I twirled my hair around my finger and succeeded in creating several knots as I waited.

Mad isn't the word I'd use.

What word would you use?

This really isn't a text type of conversation.

My chest felt suddenly hollow, and her words reverberated dully against the insides of the newly created chasm.

Ah. So, can I be all adult about this and call you?

I'm still at the House. I'll touch base with you later.

I let out a shaky breath as I glanced at the clock and noted it was quickly approaching the time I needed to leave so I wouldn't be late meeting Rory.

Okay. I'm headed out to meet Rory at the cemetery. I'll be out of pocket for a little while.

Have a good visit.

Thanks. Safe trip home.

I tried not to fret over what Allison was upset about as I hastily packed up my desk and hightailed it out of the office. And thoughts of her receded altogether as soon as I hit the street, only to be replaced by the gut-twisting anxiety that was my new constant companion any time I was out in public. Apparently, it was impossible for me to fear her wrath and fear for my life at the same time.

The razor wire of unease that'd wound its way around my insides pulled tight with a sharp snap, and I suddenly had a hard time forcing the breath in and out of my lungs. It kept catching on something, and the short, shallow pants I was forced to take were making me dizzy. Despite the cooler temperatures, sweat broke out on my upper lip and my brow, and a droplet lazily made its way down the nape of my neck and under the collar of my shirt to trail down my back. My eyes darted restlessly, trying to land everywhere and size up everyone in a single glance.

My muscles were as hard and rigid as if they'd been carved of marble the entire trip. I was only able to relax once I reached the cemetery, and even then only slightly. I was finally able to take a slightly deeper breath as I started winding my way through the grave markers, and that was simply because there were fewer places for someone to hide out there, less chances for someone to catch me off guard. I forced my hands out of the fists I finally realized they'd been locked in and inspected the deep, crescent-shaped indents in my palms. They weren't bleeding, but they ached something fierce. I shook my hands a little and rubbed them together to try to alleviate the sting as I shifted my attention to the reason for my visit.

My oldest sister Reagan had been four when Rory and I had been born, and she'd been not quite seven when she'd died. It'd been one of those freak accidents that happens so often in life and can be attributed neither to rhyme nor to reason. She and my dad had been driving to the store to pick up some groceries when they'd hit a patch of black ice. My father had lost control of the vehicle, and they'd slammed into a telephone pole, which'd then collapsed on top of the car, effectively crushing both of them and killing them instantly.

The simultaneous loss of her husband and her firstborn child had devastated my mother. Rory and I had been about two and a half when Reagan and my father had passed and left my mother with the burden of rambunctious twins to take care of. When she'd talked about it in subsequent years, I'd seen a fleeting hollowness in her eyes that always made me wonder if she'd have at least contemplated completely giving up on life after that if not for the responsibility Rory and I had presented.

Of course, my stepfather, Ben, was no stranger to tragedy. About a year or so before Rory and I were born, he'd lost his first wife to cancer. He'd not-so-offhandedly mentioned numerous times in the years that followed that if it hadn't been for his two best friends literally making him move in with them and more or less forcing him to be a part of their family, he didn't know what he would've done. So, the loss of my dad and Reagan—Ben's oldest friend and his goddaughter—had hit Ben pretty hard as well.

I don't remember my dad at all. The only things I know about him are what Ben and my mom have told me. But judging by the way they talk about him—by the matching twinkles in their eyes and the genuine smiles on their faces—they both loved him very much. I've also gathered he was something of a smart-ass, and I'm never sure how to feel when they point out with wistful expressions that I am, indeed, my father's daughter.

I don't remember my sister, Reagan, either, but I do have several pictures of her. My favorite one—which is actually hanging in a position of honor in my bedroom—is a candid, black-and-white shot that shows Reagan, Rory, and me diligently constructing sandcastles at the beach. Or, more accurately, it shows Reagan showing Rory how to build sandcastles and me preparing to knock them down. At least that's what I've been led to believe. To this day, I think I was framed.

The chilly air surrounded me like a blanket as I picked my way through the forest of headstones toward the grave where my father and my sister had been laid to rest. The sounds of the traffic on the surrounding streets faded into the background the deeper I went into the cemetery until I had to concentrate to hear them at all.

It didn't take long to reach the plot, and as I always did whenever I visited, I knelt in front of the headstone and gently traced the letters etched into the block with the tips of my fingers. Silently, I reached into my coat pocket and brought out the gleaming silver flask I'd hidden there. Before I unscrewed the cap, my eyes rested briefly on the flask's inscription—TEMPORARY PERIODS OF JOY—an homage to what I'd been told was one of my dad's favorite William Butler Yeats sayings. I lifted the flask in salute to my father.

"*O m'anam*," I toasted, taking a long draught from the flask. The Jameson burned a little as it slipped past my lips and slid down my throat, but it provided a welcome heat. I blew out a shaky breath as I proceeded to pour the rest of it into the grass in front of me. It would've been rude of me not to share.

"Did you save any for me?" my sister asked from behind me.

I turned my head so I could glance at her over my shoulder. "Nope. You know what happens when you miss the toast."

"You suck."

"Tell me about it." I put the now-empty flask back into my pocket and watched as Rory laid the flowers she'd brought next to the whisky-soaked patch of grass.

The silence hung between us as I took my time settling myself so my back was leaning against the grave marker and my knees were bent in front of me to serve as a platform for my forearms. I paused to gauge the discomfort level of my injured shoulder and briefly debated putting the sling on again. But I didn't want to wrangle with it. Instead, I leaned my head back, relishing the feel of the cool marble against my hair, and closed my eyes. I felt Rory settle herself next to me and rest her head on my good shoulder.

I drew in a deep breath, pausing to regard the misty white puffs that escaped my mouth upon my exhale. It'd be winter soon. The thought alone chilled me, and I balled up my hands and pulled them into the sleeves of my coat as a light shiver wracked me.

"We should've brought a blanket," Rory said.

"Next time. I assume we'll be back in a couple of months. You know, on the day they…"

"Died."

"Yeah."

There was a long pause. "So, shit's pretty fucked up," she said softly.

"Yeah."

"Did you go talk to someone?"

I canted my face in her direction, but she didn't lift her head off my shoulder to meet my eyes. She just wrapped both of her arms around my biceps and trembled. "You mean did I manage to squeeze that in during the handful of hours since you nagged me about it? No."

"Didn't think so. Are you ready to talk to me?"

"No."

"Do it anyway."

I scowled and tried to put a lid on the annoyance that was suddenly boiling over inside me, leaving scalding splatters in its wake. "Rory."

She did look up at me then, her expression pleading. "Humor me. Please."

"I thought we were here for them," I said, banging my head lightly against the grave marker.

"And I think they'd want you to get this off your chest."

I shook my head at her insistence and sighed. "I don't even know where to begin," I confessed softly. "Maybe that's part of the problem. Maybe I'm too overwhelmed. I definitely know I'm too tired to think straight, which isn't helping anything."

Rory snuggled closer and rested her head on my shoulder again, saying nothing, apparently content to let me continue in my own time now that she knew she'd won. I propped one elbow on the fleshy part of one thigh so I could rest my chin in my hand and let the other dangle uselessly over my other calf. I raked my eyes over every part of the cemetery I could see from my position as I searched for a threat. It'd just occurred to me that Rory might be in danger simply because she looked like me. Worms of anxiety began gnawing away at the tender tissue of my belly, and I checked and rechecked the distant trees before I made myself focus on the conversation again.

"Luce is dead." I stumbled a little as I said her name out loud for maybe the third time since she'd been killed. It felt weird to me, like I didn't have the right to even say it.

"Yeah," Rory breathed softly.

I went back to studying the foggy breaths wafting in the air in front of me. "Do you think she's with Dad and Reagan?"

"I don't know. I guess anything's possible."

I wasn't sure whether the notion made me happy or not, so I didn't comment on it.

"I'm sure she's at peace, Ryan."

I frowned and gathered the strength I'd need to get through this next part. "It's my fault she died, you know."

Rory shook her head. "No. It's not."

"Kind of. I mean, I didn't actually pull the trigger, but I'm responsible."

I swallowed hard against the lump forming in my throat and willed myself not to cry. Fleeting images of Lucia's face in those final horrific moments of her life flashed in my mind's eye. My heart clenched, and my stomach churned and writhed as though it were alive.

"She was there because of me, Rory," I said, my voice wavering and weak. "She'd read a text message from Allison on my phone, and she—" I broke off to clear my throat, unable to finish the thought. Lucia had been there, and now Rory was here because of me, and if whoever was trying to kill me was following me... I inhaled sharply and compressed my impending panic into a tight, more manageable ball just below my throat. It was tough to breathe around, and my right hand twitched with the desire to reach for the weapon I no longer wore.

"Anyway, it's my fault she was there. If I hadn't hurt her, she wouldn't have come to confront me. She would've stayed at the front of the motorcade with the intel car, and she'd still be alive."

"Ryan, you don't know that. She might've come to talk to you anyway."

"Or she might not have."

Rory let out a heavy breath. "You have to let it go. As tragic as it is, she was just at the wrong place at the wrong time."

I closed my eyes and scrubbed at them with my fingertips. I didn't want to argue with her about this, but nothing she could say would make even the slightest dent in how I felt. "Maybe."

"Definitely."

"I'm a little bit pissed at her," I said after a while, figuring if I'd already gone this far, I might as well tell her the rest.

"Who?"

"Luce. For dying. As horrible as I feel about getting her killed—and I don't think I've ever felt so bad about anything in my entire life—a small part of me is almost irritated with her for starting that argument. Can you believe that? I'm actually mad at her for being in the wrong place at the wrong time. Because if she'd just listened to me and gone back to her car when I told her to, I'd be the one dead, and I wouldn't have to deal with all these stupid feelings."

Rory sat up slowly and shifted so she was more or less facing me. Her brows were pulled down, and her eyes were cold. Her mouth was set in a grim line. "Don't even joke about that."

"I'm not." When she opened her mouth to retort, I rushed on, cutting her off. "Hadn't you heard? She basically saved me by punching me when she did. Her knocking me off balance is why the bullet went through my shoulder instead of my brain stem. So not only did I get her killed, but she's actually the reason I'm here. Yet I'm still angry at her for dying and angry at her for making me feel guilty to begin with. The angrier I get, the guiltier I feel and—"

I broke off my anguished ramblings to catch my breath. The pressure collecting inside me was unbearable, like someone blowing up a balloon just under the surface of my skin. I could feel it, straining against me, pushing its way out. I was afraid of what would happen when it finally popped. I was also afraid of what would happen if it didn't.

I swallowed hard against the lump growing in the back of my throat and sniffled. "So...yeah. Shit's fucked up."

"Everything you're feeling is perfectly understandable. I'd say it's even normal."

A sound escaped my lips that was probably the worst impersonation of a laugh ever attempted. It was more like the noise you'd expect to hear if a goose honked inside of a tin can. It was sweet of Rory to pretend my thoughts were okay instead of all kinds of messed up, but she was my sister. She had to say stuff like that. It didn't make it true. "Great."

Rory was silent for a long time. "What does Allison say about all this?"

"Nothing."

"You haven't talked to her about it?"

"No."

"Why not?"

I shrugged and hissed at the pain, cursing myself for forgetting not to do that yet again. I'd never realized how often I did it until now. I rubbed at the wound until Rory yanked my hand away. "I just haven't. There hasn't really been time. She got called back to DC right after I was discharged."

"And the three days when I couldn't get her to leave your hospital room long enough to eat something that wasn't an energy bar? You couldn't have talked about it then?"

"I was pretty doped up half the time."

"And the other half?"

I hesitated and tapped the palm of my hand against the grass, using the prickling of the blades against my skin as a grounding technique. "I'm not really good at talking about stuff." I paused a moment to chew on the inside of my upper lip. "Especially not with her."

"Shouldn't she be the one person you can talk to about anything?"

"Probably."

"But…"

I wasn't sure exactly how to explain in a way that she'd really get it. Would it make sense to her if I told her that Secret Service agents are supposed to be strong? That there's this mystique about us that gives people the impression we're always even-keeled and in control? Maybe it was the focus we exhibited when we were in public. Maybe it was the sunglasses. I wasn't positive. What I did know was assumptions were made about us that we then felt obligated to live up to. We don't show weakness, we don't show emotion. We deal with situations as they are, reacting on less than a moment's notice without so much as breaking stride, and then we continue as if nothing had happened.

What if I told her that Allison was the quintessential Secret Service agent in that regard, that she was the paragon to which we all aspired? Calm, cool, and collected, Allison rarely got fired up or flustered no matter what was going on around her. She played the part so much better than I could've ever hoped to on my best day, and it was one of the many things I admired about her. Would Rory understand my reluctance to talk about my feelings if I explained all of that?

Allison really was a lot to live up to. And not just professionally, either, but on a personal level, as well. I'd always looked up to her as an agent and had wanted so badly to be someone she could be proud of, someone who was maybe a little bit worthy of her attention. I guess I'd allowed my tendency to avoid showing any type of vulnerability, my attempt to live up to some ideal she'd never even said she'd wanted, to spill over into our relationship. Maybe I hadn't trusted her to stick around if she realized I wasn't even half the superhero she was. Whatever the reason, it wasn't fair to either of us.

"Do you ever listen to any of Dad's stories?" I asked finally.

"Huh?"

"When Dad talks about big cases in the office, do you ever listen to him?"

Rory rolled her eyes. "Of course not. That stuff never interests me."

I nodded, even though I'd known that'd be her answer. "I do."

"I know you do. You always have. Even when we were kids, you always hung on every word he said."

"Right."

"I don't understand. What does that have to do with you not talking to Allison?"

I ducked my head and picked at the grass. "I knew who she was. Before I ever met her, I knew."

"What?"

"You said it yourself. When Dad talks, I listen."

"He told you about her?"

I nodded again. "When I was going through the application process, she took down one of the biggest identity-theft rings in Secret Service history. It was all he could talk about for weeks."

"I didn't think he mentioned the agents by name. Some kind of privacy thing."

"He doesn't. But he did reference her gender. That's what caught my attention. Most of the agents are men. I'd actually assumed the case agent on that investigation was a man until he said something about *her* being available to accept the Agent of the Year award."

"I still don't see what this has to do with anything."

"I spent a considerable amount of time admiring Allison as an agent before I ever met her. I was so taken by the idea of a woman doing all these amazing things and earning Dad's respect so effortlessly. I'd never heard him talk about a female agent before. There just weren't that many women around, or maybe they simply didn't work as hard as Allison did. I don't know. But hearing his stories about this superstar agent who also happened to be a woman fascinated me. I asked him about her a couple times, and he told me a little bit. The rest I found out by listening to other agents in the office before I left for training."

"Awww, you had a crush on her. That's adorable. Does she know?"

I kicked at her ineffectually and went on. "No. And you're not going to tell her. The point is, once I did finally get to meet her, once I got to know her and saw firsthand how smart and capable and driven she is...I just don't want her to think I can't handle it, you know? Because I can. I'm not going to fall apart over this."

Rory's expression softened and she let out a low exhale. "Oh, Ryan. Talking to her about how you feel isn't going to make her think any less of you."

"Maybe. Maybe not." I thought about how our past few conversations had gone and shook my head. "That's not the entire reason, though."

"Then what is?"

I paused to take a deep breath and attempt to gain control over my rampant thoughts and emotions, which was a lot like trying to stop a tornado with your bare hands. My mind was stuck in the by-now-familiar rut of reliving the moments just prior to and just after the shooting in super slow motion.

"Well, for one thing, it seems gauche to lament to the woman you're currently sleeping with about how you got the last woman you were sleeping with killed."

Rory elbowed me lightly in the side. "Stop saying that before I hit you someplace it'll really hurt. That's not what happened. And it's also not the real reason. So what is?"

"I don't want Allison to think it's her fault," I said softly after a long moment.

Rory looked confused. "What? Lucia's death?"

I nodded.

"Why would she think that?"

"Because of the text message."

"She doesn't already know about that?"

"I told you, we haven't talked about it. I haven't told anyone besides you. And I don't want to bring it up because I know her. She'll feel responsible. No matter what I say, she'll be convinced she's to blame, that Luce never would've been where she was if not for that text, and she'll be devastated."

"So, she'll board the same crazy train you're riding right now?" Rory asked with the barest hint of a smirk. "You really are perfect for one another."

I glared at her. "It's not crazy."

"It kind of is, though. Are the two of you seriously so arrogant you really believe all the events of the world revolve around your thoughts and actions? Is that an agent thing? Are you all like that? Or is it just you two?"

I huffed and looked away. When she put it that way, it did sound pretty stupid and more than a little egotistical. Not that I was going to admit it.

My frustration with Rory's refusal to empathize with my feelings was building and making it difficult for me to sit still. I slowly disentangled myself from her and struggled to regain my feet. I paced back and forth in front of the headstone, careful not to trample on the flowers as I strode. I shoved my hands deep into my pockets to keep them warm and counted my steps. One, two, three, turn. One, two, three, turn.

If I'd held any illusions that engaging in such a mundane, repetitive feat as pacing would be enough to distract me, however momentarily, from my gnawing feelings of helplessness and dissatisfaction, well, I was disappointed. If anything, it sparked a greater longing inside me. As much as I abhorred running, in that moment, I wanted nothing more than to bolt for the distant hill and never look back, to just keep going until I dropped. Logically, I knew I couldn't outrun any of this, but that didn't mean the thought of trying wasn't suddenly appealing.

The burning, roiling emotions were all twisting together and gathering strength to become the perfect storm of chaos raging in the confines of my chest. I was a woman of action. I needed to have a plan of attack to deal with and assuage my anguish head-on. And not being able to come up with one was driving me nuts.

For days now, people had been telling me I needed to talk to a professional, and while I recognized the theoretical benefits of that suggestion, I was having some serious doubts I'd be able to reap any of those merely by unburdening my soul. This sort of pain went well beyond simple verbal confessions, and if detailing all my woes to Rory hadn't taken the edge off my emotional agony, I had less than no faith that speaking to someone who didn't even know me would help.

I let out a long, loud huff. Clearly, none of my problems were going to get solved tonight. I'd just have to resign myself to enduring for another day. Maybe tomorrow I'd be able to figure something out.

Rory leapt to her feet and stepped in front of me, stopping my momentum. She placed her hands on my elbows and dipped her head when I ducked mine to force me to look into her eyes. "Ryan."

"Yeah?"

She opened her mouth but then closed it again almost immediately as she shook her head. She hesitated a moment before trying again. "I'm a little cold. Wanna go grab dinner?"

I was about as eager to prolong this experience as I was to retake the SATs. Or go back to FLETC. Or have a sit-down with my boss. All my remaining energy spilled out of me, leaving me feeling as empty and fragile as one of those blown-out eggshells they'd made us carry around in high school to simulate child care. I could probably only handle about five more minutes of this in-depth examination of my emotions before I shattered.

It was my turn to shake my head. I stepped back so Rory's hands fell from my arms and tried to smile at her. It felt wobbly and insincere, but it was the best I could do. "No, thanks. I'm not really very hungry."

Rory frowned and took half a step forward but didn't try to touch me, for which I was grateful. "Then do you want me to come over so I can take out your stitches?"

As tempting as that was, at this point, I'd rather have removed them myself. Besides, now that the tidal wave of my emotions had ebbed somewhat, I was once again reminded that she was in danger just by being near me. She needed to get as far away from me as possible and stay there, at least until I figured out exactly where the threat was coming from. "Can we do it another time? I'm kinda tired. I think maybe I'll just try to get some sleep."

"But it's barely dinnertime."

"Yeah, well, I have some serious catching up to do."

Rory's brow wrinkled, and she tilted her head as she studied me. I chewed on the corner of my lower lip as I held my breath and waited for her inspection to end. Finally, she nodded and dropped a gentle kiss on my cheek. "Of course. I'll see you soon. Sweet dreams."

"Thanks, Rory. And thanks for, you know, listening."

"Any time. You know that."

I bobbed my head, turned, and left the cemetery without looking back.

CHAPTER EIGHT

If I believed in hell, which I was pretty sure I didn't, I might've been worried that lying to my sister so blatantly would've earned me an express ticket. Even as the words were coming out of my mouth, I'd had no intention of going home. Not yet. She'd been right. It was too early for me to go to sleep. For one thing, I'd probably just toss and turn for hours, driving myself crazy by thinking. For another, it'd up the chances of me having more than one nightmare, and you couldn't pay me enough to sign up for that.

Having completely dismissed the idea of returning to my apartment, I decided to head back to my office. I still had online learning modules to complete. True, I was technically on medical leave and could put them off, but in addition to stalling my going home, doing them lulled me into such a stupor, I was pretty sure I'd be able to fall asleep with no problem when I finally did go to bed. Besides, I felt a whole lot safer in the office than I did in my apartment. A sniper would have no line of sight to my part of the building, and it'd be next to impossible for anyone to get inside and catch me off guard. Sure, it meant one more trip outside to get back home, but I'd deal with that when the time came.

I set up the module about fire extinguishers and propped the hollow of my cheek on the heel of my hand. My eyes glazed over almost immediately as it started to play, and I sighed heavily. This might not have been nearly as bad as the DVDs they used to make us watch before these mandatory modules became digitized—the one for fire extinguishers, for example, looked as though it hadn't been updated since the 70s—but it was still as boring as all hell, and I wanted to gouge my own eyes out.

After a while, I started doing the long, slow blink that meant I was starting to drift off to sleep, and my thoughts became foggy and jumbled. The corner of 49 and Lex beckoned insistently, and while I wanted to resist, I didn't have the energy to put up a convincing fight.

"I recognize that look," a familiar voice said from my doorway, wrenching me back from teetering precariously on the edge of sleep and causing me to sit up quickly and then hiss at the white-hot slash of pain the movement caused. A nod toward my computer monitor. "Bird flu?"

If I were a cartoon character, my eyes would've bugged out of my head at the unexpected sight of Allison leaning against my door frame with a tiny smile on her lips. I shook my head, feeling a little dazed. She really was there, right? I hadn't just fallen asleep and conjured her up in my dreams? "No. Fire extinguishers."

Allison's smile widened just a tad, and she stepped fully into my office and closed the door. "I miss the DVDs," she said as she took a seat in the chair opposite my desk.

"I was just thinking the same thing." My mind was still churning sluggishly as I attempted to shake off the last hints of slumber.

"They were stupid, but they were at least entertaining."

"What are you doing here?" I blurted without thinking.

Allison rolled her eyes. "Aren't you happy to see me?"

"Of course I am. It's just…don't you have to work tomorrow?"

Allison nodded and crossed her left knee over her right, then drummed her fingertips on the arms of the chair. "Yeah. I have an SA-1 day, and I'm going to try to go to the POR."

Ah, paperwork and range. "Nice. What time do you need to report?"

"Oh-nine-hundred. But I plan on being a little late."

"Won't that piss off your boss?"

Something dark flickered behind her eyes before her expression became neutral again. "I sure hope so."

I frowned. "Is that the best idea? Deliberately trying to make him mad? I mean, aren't you guys already fighting enough as it is?"

Allison's eyes narrowed. "Who told you we were fighting?"

Oops. I shouldn't have said that. "Uh...no one. I just assumed. You told me he was giving you a hard time."

"How does that translate into us fighting?"

"It doesn't. Like I said, I assumed. You know me. I like to make an ass out of myself."

The look on her face told me she didn't believe me. "It was Jamie, wasn't it?"

"Who?" Somehow I thought playing dumb was the way to go. Not one of my better plans.

She averted her eyes, shook her head, and muttered under her breath, "I should've known."

"Known what?"

I could see a proverbial lightbulb illuminate inside her as her gaze snapped back to me. "She was on the phone with *you* earlier today, wasn't she?"

I cleared my throat to buy myself a couple extra seconds to try to think of a way to pull Jamie out from under the metaphorical bus I'd just driven over her at top speed. Unfortunately, it didn't help. "What?"

Allison took a long, deep breath. "She and I will be having a talk about that when I see her again."

I stood up and walked around to Allison's side of the desk and perched on the edge in front of her. As a shift whip, Allison was sort of a peer supervisor and therefore fell into Jamie's chain of command. This could get very bad for Jamie very quickly if Allison decided she wanted to be petty. "Allison, let it go."

"No. She needs to learn to keep her nose out of other people's business."

"She was just worried about you."

"So she called you?"

"Well, we're friends."

Allison mumbled something to herself that I didn't catch and glared at nothing in the corner of the room.

"What?"

"This is why I don't like to date people I work with. Everybody gets involved."

The room suddenly became a vacuum, and breathing like a normal person was no longer an option. I forced myself to think past the ringing in my ears, to pay no attention to the flush burning beneath my skin. Dozens of comebacks started clamoring for attention, begging for permission to trip off the tip of my tongue. But I held off for a moment. I wasn't about to ruin this with my typical mouth-off-first, cringe-later behavior.

"Why did you really come here tonight, Allison?" I asked after a long moment, taking great care to make my voice as soft and gentle as I could under the circumstances.

Allison's head shot up, and for a millisecond, I'd have sworn she'd forgotten I was there at all. Her brow had crinkled adorably, and her eyes were brimming with confusion. But the moment was short lived, and she was back to herself in the time it took me to cock my head. "I thought you wanted to talk. Be all adult and whatnot. Isn't that what you said?"

"Oh." I hadn't been expecting that. "I do. I just thought we'd do it over the phone. I didn't expect you to hop a train immediately after your shift to race up here. Especially not when you have to work tomorrow."

"I needed to get away from DC anyway."

"Because of your boss?"

She regarded me for a long moment before she nodded slowly. "Yes. I know in my head he can just call me or email me, and he probably will, but something about the physical distance is comforting."

"I can understand that. I wish he hadn't forced you to go back so soon. Not because of me, although I do like spending time with you, but cutting your annual leave short was a shitty thing to do."

"Yeah, well, as it turns out, he's a pretty shitty guy."

"I'm sorry. It sucks having a tool for a boss. Believe me, I know."

"You haven't hit the lottery yet, have you?"

"What?"

"Your plan to win the jackpot, buy a private island, quit, and spend your days lounging naked on your own private beach sipping mai tais."

"I don't recall saying anything about being naked or sipping mai tais."

"Maybe that was just in my fantasy then."

Her words alone made me dizzy. The mental pictures that accompanied them completely stole my breath and robbed me of the ability to think clearly. When I was finally able to form words again, I licked my lips and said, "Uh, no. Sorry to say I haven't won the lottery yet. But you'll be the first to know if I do."

"I'd better be."

"So, are you ready to talk about why you're not-mad at me?"

Allison's expression was suddenly dark, her mouth set in a grim line. "Oh. That."

"Well, you did come up here to talk. We may as well get right down to it, don't cha think?"

"Yes, I suppose we should."

"Unless you're partly upset because I haven't figured out for myself why you're upset."

"That doesn't help."

"Well, I could start guessing if you'd like," I said as I stood and then strode back around my desk to resume my seat, "but somehow I suspect you'd tire of that game quickly."

"You're right."

"Let me take one stab at it."

Allison nodded once, an almost imperceptible lowering of her head that I wouldn't have caught if I hadn't been watching for it. She laced her fingers together and rested her clasped hands on her stomach.

"You're upset that I won't talk to you about what happened."

Allison's smirk was bitter, and her eyes remained flat and hard. "You got it. And who says all blondes are dumb?"

I wrinkled my nose. "Cute."

"I try."

I hesitated, not certain I wanted to get into all this now, not feeling as prepared as I'd have liked, but knowing I needed to wade through it sooner rather than later. "I get why you're upset. And for what it's worth, I'm sorry."

Allison's eyes narrowed for an instant, and then she shook her head. "I'm more frustrated and hurt than I am angry."

"I get that, too."

She appeared to be considering her words before uttering them. "I just wish you'd talk to me."

"Okay," I said quietly, not positive I'd spoken loud enough for her to have heard me. I took a long moment choosing random items from the top of my desk to pick up and fiddle with one at a time before discarding them for something else that'd caught my eye. How to even begin? And where? I sucked on my bottom lip and twirled a few stray locks of hair around my finger as I deliberated, keeping my eyes carefully averted from Allison until I was ready to start sharing.

"Okay," I said again, taking one last deep breath and laying both palms flat on the desk on either side of my keyboard. "So you know how I haven't really been—"

A new email notification popped up on my computer screen just as my BlackBerry buzzed to announce the same thing. Initially, I glanced at it absently because it was kind of in the way of the fire-extinguisher video that was still running silently, and I fully intended to click it away, but when my eyes snagged on the sender, my heart leapt. I stared at it for a long moment, trying to convince myself it really was the phone company with my subpoena results. Wow, a turnaround time this short was unheard of. Greg must really have some pull over there.

Allison prompted me. "How you haven't really been...?"

I kept my eyes glued to the screen as I reviewed the decryption instructions embedded in the body of the email. "Um...How I haven't really been..." Would I be able to open these from this computer with the firewalls we had set up? Would I have to wait until normal business hours to set up my decryption password, or could I do it now? I frowned as I reread the directions, absently rubbing my forehead as I tried to figure it out.

"You're checking email in the middle of our talk?" Allison asked, sounding torn between incredulity and exasperation.

"I'm sorry. What?" I snapped my head up to look at her, and her obvious aggravation made something inside me shrivel.

Allison uncrossed her legs and leaned forward in her chair. "It'd better be important."

"Oh. Just some subpoena results for a case that I wasn't expecting yet. That's all."

Her brows pulled down as she looked at me for a long moment. "Do you really need to deal with this now?"

"Um...no?" I reined in my disappointed sigh and sat back in my chair, forcing myself to close the email window before taking my hand completely off the mouse and putting it in my lap so as not to be tempted.

Allison ran one hand through her hair and stared at the ceiling for a bit before shifting her attention back to me. "Ten minutes."

"Huh?"

"You have ten minutes to deal with whatever that is. Then I'm turning your computer off, and we're getting the hell out of here."

"No, Allison. You're right. I'm sorry. This can wait. Nothing is more important to me than you." And while that wasn't necessarily a lie—while she was more important to me than anything and anyone and whatever these results showed *could* wait until tomorrow because I probably couldn't do anything with them tonight anyway—waiting to take a look at them would slowly gnaw away at my insides.

The corners of her lips turned up in a small smile, and she shook her head. "As sweet as that is, we both know only half your focus will be on our talk. And I want your attention undivided when we do this."

"Are you sure?"

Allison retrieved her personal phone from the holster on her belt and made a series of swipes and presses on the screen. When she was done, she held it up so I could see that she'd set a timer that was now counting down the interval she'd allotted. She wiggled it for emphasis. "When this goes off, you're mine."

"Yes, ma'am."

CHAPTER NINE

My mind was running like a squirrel on crack as I flew through the email decryption procedures, eager to see what the subpoena results had to say. I prayed they'd give me something other than a prepaid cell phone that was no longer active. With my newly acquired suspicions regarding the assassination plot, I doubted I'd be able to handle the disappointment and frustration that'd accompany that sort of blow.

The ringing of the main squad phone line broke though the haze of self-absorption, and I glanced at my watch. Who'd be calling the squad at this time of night? The phone rang again, and my eyebrows went up as my attention drifted around, searching for other signs of life. Pangs of sympathy echoed loudly within me. A call to the main line at this hour was never a good thing. It normally meant someone's shift was about to get extended whether they liked it or not.

The phone rang a fourth time, and since it appeared the response guys were either unable or unwilling to answer it, I mouthed "I'm so sorry" to Allison as I grabbed the receiver on my desk. Allison rolled her eyes and huffed, obviously annoyed, but she didn't try to stop me from answering or storm out, which I took as a win.

"Secret Service." My eye wandered to the caller ID display as I spoke. The words weren't even completely out of my mouth, yet when the realization of exactly who was on the other end of the phone hit me, I cringed.

"Fuck," I muttered under my breath. It was the Protective Intelligence Division in DC. *Shit, shit, shit.* Allison looked up from the report she'd been reading and raised her eyebrows at me. "It's PID,"

I mouthed. She winced and shifted in her chair, her irritation replaced by sympathy.

"Uh…Hello?" the voice on the other end said, sounding uncertain.

I closed my eyes and massaged my forehead, where I could feel one hell of a killer headache gathering. "Secret Service," I said again. My eyes popped open, and I glared around, trying to catch sight of the guys who were supposed to answer the phones. They were grinning like idiots at me from my doorway. I scowled at them and flipped them off as they laughed and ran away.

"Hi, this is Agent Phelps from PID. Who's this?"

"Hey, Scotty. It's Ryan."

"Hey, Ryan." His tone was bright and a little too enthusiastic for my taste. "Even when injured, you just can't stay away from work, can you?"

I clenched my jaw against a rising tide of annoyance. "Something like that."

"You okay?"

"Peachy." But that wasn't even remotely true. I was completely immersed in my own problems, and I didn't welcome the interruption. Couple that with the aches and pains I was trying to manage without the assistance of painkillers, and you ended up with one very unhappy federal agent.

"You sound a little off to me," Scott informed me, either not picking up on my mood or, more likely, not caring that he was poking the proverbial hornet's nest with a stick. "Shouldn't you be cursing me by now?"

I took a deep, deliberately controlled breath and let it out slowly. I wasn't sure who I was pissed at, exactly. Maybe myself for not being able to shake the feeling that I should've suspected sooner that I was actually the target of the assassination attempt. Maybe the universe in general for repeatedly sabotaging my attempts to have a real conversation with Allison. I slapped the palm of my good hand down on the desk and began rooting around in my top drawer for a pen.

"How can I help you, Scott?" I asked tightly, shooting another dark look in the direction of the guys who were on duty and actually supposed to be fielding this call.

"Wow. This is serious. Not a single swear word to be heard. I'm going to start thinking you don't love me anymore."

"It's the new and improved me," I told him sarcastically. "Professionalism is my middle name."

"I thought Ryan was your middle name."

It wasn't. But now didn't seem like the time to get into all that. "I was thinking of having it changed."

Scott hummed. "No. It doesn't have the same ring to it. I'd keep it the way it is."

"Thanks for the tip."

"That's what I'm here for."

I said nothing, but I tapped the end of the pen against the mouthpiece of the phone impatiently.

"Aw, come on, Ryan. Why do you never sound happy to hear from me?"

"Because you never tell me anything I want to hear. In fact, I think I'm going to hang up on you now." Allison appeared amused by my threat, and I grinned at her.

"Ah, ah," he chided in a singsong voice, sounding almost smug. "You know that's against the rules."

"Yeah, well, who's gonna know?" I shot back. "I'll just deny I ever picked up the phone. I'm not even supposed to be here."

Scott laughed lightly. "These lines are recorded. You know that."

"Is that even legal?"

"DC is a one-party-consent state. So is New York, actually."

"How do you even know that?"

"Do you really want to know?"

I laughed in spite of myself. "You're a shit."

Scott laughed, too. "There's the trucker I know and love."

"Okay, you got me to laugh. Good for you. I'll send you a fucking medal. Just tell me what you want so I can pass it to the response guys and go the hell home."

"Actually, Ryan, it's kind of a good thing you picked up the phone." I sensed a slight hesitation behind his words.

"Oh, what the hell? Why?" This seriously wasn't my day. I saw Allison sit up straighter and lean forward, the report in her hands apparently forgotten.

"You remember Adam Royce Walker?"

My mind raced furiously to decipher exactly what he was asking me because he sure wasn't being literal with his question. "Of course. What about him?"

Scott sighed. "He's out."

I was stunned. I opened my mouth but then shut it again and frowned. That wasn't good.

"Ryan? You there?"

"What do you mean, he's out?"

Allison's face registered her concern, and she mouthed, "Who?" I shook my head a little and held up one finger, silently asking her to wait.

"Just what I said. He's out."

"How the hell did he get out?" Whoever'd been literally gunning for me couldn't have arranged this, could they? No. That was impossible. I was just being paranoid. Shit. I really needed to not start looking for conspiracies everywhere.

"Saint E's let him go. A few weeks ago, actually." Saint E's— short for Saint Elizabeth's—was a mental-health facility located in DC.

"Why?"

"Apparently it was time."

"And why weren't we notified?"

"I don't know, Ryan. I honestly don't. But that isn't what you need to be concerned about right now. We have a much more pressing problem."

"Okay," I said slowly. I failed to see how DC's pressing problem became my immediate concern. I mean, sure, I thought I knew where he was going with this conversation, but I was going to exist in a state of blissful denial on the subject for as long as I could and make him spell it out for me.

"He just called to say he's on his way to New York."

There it was. That's what I'd been waiting for. A humorless little laugh bubbled up in the back of my throat, bitter and rancid. "Of course he did. Why wouldn't he be?"

Scott sounded sympathetic. "He's taking the train to Penn Station right now. Or so he says. He should hit town in about two and half hours, give or take. Want to guess where his first stop is likely to be when he gets there?"

I groaned and put my head in my hand. My shoulders sagged,

increasing the ever-present ache, and I hissed. "No. I think I can figure it out on my own."

"I haven't notified the detail yet. You were my first call. Frankly, if you hadn't picked up the phone, my next call was going to be to your cell."

"Lucky me."

"Well, you were his case agent when he was in New York. I figure you know him better than anyone else."

"Yeah. That makes sense. Thanks, Scotty. I mean it. I'll take care of notifying the detail. I'll tell them to call you, so you know the message was passed. And then I'll take care of him."

"You sure?"

I bit my bottom lip thoughtfully, pondering the situation and all the ways it could play out. "Yeah," I said after a long moment when I realized he was waiting for a reply. "I'm sure. Listen. Can you fax me everything you have for him? I kind of fell out of touch with his situation when he relocated to DC. Oh, and the train number, if you have it."

"Thanks, Ryan." I thought Scott sounded a touch relieved. And why shouldn't he? He was handing the metaphorical ball off to someone else. This wasn't his responsibility anymore. He, at least, would get to go home at the end of his tour.

I hung up and immediately met Allison's worried gaze. "That didn't sound good," she said after a beat.

I raised my hands in a helpless gesture and then raked my fingernails lightly down my cheeks. "It really isn't. I'm so sorry about this."

Allison's expression grew dark. "They're not seriously making you go to work right now."

"I have to."

"You just got out of the hospital."

"Tell that to the threat subject on his way to New York," I said with a twisted attempt at a smile.

"This fucking agency," she muttered under her breath, throwing the report in her hand onto my desk top with a forceful breath. "Who is it?"

I hesitated. "Adam Royce Walker."

Her eyes widened. "What?"

"Yup."

"He's out?"

"Apparently."

"When did that happen? Did they notify the detail?"

"Yours or Hurricane's?" I asked playfully.

"Either."

"I don't know about yours. I get to go tell Hurricane's."

Allison scowled and flounced back into her chair, folding her arms across her chest. "Can't you just call them?"

"I can. But if he shows up, someone's going to have to handle him. Seeing as how he was my case when he was still here, it really should be me."

"You can barely walk without limping, you're not supposed to move your right arm at all, and you're going to go have it out with a crazy man more than twice your size. Great."

"Hey." When she didn't look at me, I eased myself out of my chair and moved to her side, trying unsuccessfully to minimize the limp she'd just mentioned as I went. I placed a hand on her shoulder and waited for her to meet my eyes. "You know I don't want to do this, right? That I'd rather be going home with you?"

She stared at me for a long moment before finally taking my hand. The knot inside me loosened at the gesture and unraveled completely when her expression softened. "I know you don't. I'm sorry. I'm not mad at you."

"Not about this," I was unable to stop myself from saying.

A wry smirk tugged at the corners of her mouth. "No. Not about this. But it looks like we don't have time to get into that right now."

"Talk about saved by the bell, huh?"

"Do you really want to be flip with me right now?"

"No. I don't. I'm sorry. And I feel awful that you came all the way up here for nothing."

Allison stood up and contorted her body back and forth to stretch out her back. "Who says it was for nothing?"

I furrowed my brow, unable to mask my confusion. "Uh…It's just that there's no way to know how long this is gonna take. I doubt you want to sit around and wait for me to get done."

"You're right. I'm not going to just sit around. I'm going with you."

"What?"

"You heard me."

"I did. I just can't imagine you're serious."

"Trust me, I'm serious."

"But…why?"

The look she gave me then, all soft and affectionate and indulgent, instantly burrowed beneath my skin and lit fires inside me in all the best places. "I've heard you're pretty good at this."

"What? Dealing with threat subjects?"

"Mmm-hmm. Word on the street is they wanted to send you down to Beltsville to teach the Protective Intelligence block, but you're technically too junior, so they're waiting."

I narrowed my eyes at her, trying to determine if she was messing with me. It was tough to tell. She'd been on the job longer and had contacts I didn't, so it was possible she was telling the truth. But I wasn't necessarily ready to believe her. "Really?"

"Yup. And I'd never forgive myself for passing up the chance to see you in action."

A small smile tugged at the corners of my lips, and I rolled my eyes at her. "Sure. Well, let's go then." I started to walk toward the door, but she stopped me with a hand on my arm.

"Why don't you go round up the two-to-ten guys. I'll meet you back here in a few minutes. I want to hit the restroom before we leave."

"Okay."

I trailed along behind her, and we got as far as my doorway before she abruptly spun around. I froze and held my breath as we stared at one another. My nerves danced and my heart thundered the longer the silence stretched between us. I licked my lips and balled my hands into light fists to disguise their trembling.

The air between us was thick and heavy and crackled with promise as we stared at one another. I tried to inhale when she reached out to trace the stitches near my eyebrow with a gentle fingertip, but the breath got stuck in my throat. She smiled softly at me then and leaned down to capture my lips in a languid kiss.

When she eventually pulled back, it took me a second to make my eyes work, and even then, they fluttered a bit before I convinced them to stay open. "What was that for?" I asked, my lips still almost brushing hers, my voice barely louder than a murmur.

She smiled at me before giving me another gentle peck and saying, "Just because."

Chapter Ten

After Allison left to go to the bathroom, I stood in the doorway to my office for a long moment trying to compose myself. My cheeks felt flushed, and my lips were still tingling from her kiss. I had to shake my head and slap myself lightly on the face to push away thoughts of what Allison and I could be doing with our evening and back to what we were going to be doing.

Following a brief trip to the water fountain to get a long, cold drink, I set about trying to find the on-call guys. It didn't take long to locate them. They were tossing a small Nerf football back and forth across the long hallway around the corner from the squad, killing the last few minutes until the end of their shift. The irony of the situation as I recalled my last thought about Scott and his metaphorical handoff wasn't lost on me.

"Time to go to work, fellas," I told them, effortlessly snatching their ball out of the air with my left hand and tucking it under my arm as I strode away.

"Hey!" Austin Ford cried indignantly after me as I headed in the direction of my office. "That's our ball."

"Yeah, Ryan," PJ Clark chimed in, from right behind me. "If you wanted to play, all you had to do was ask."

I tossed the ball carelessly over my shoulder without looking and heard PJ let out a muffled curse. I smiled. "Sorry, guys. Game's over."

"Ryan," Austin said, sounding a trifle annoyed. "It's almost the end of our shift. The midnight guys should be relieving us any minute now. Whatever it is, let them take care of it."

I sighed and stopped walking so I could turn to face them.

"Actually, I need them, too. No one's getting off light with this one. I'm sorry." And I was. No one likes to be told at the very end of the night that the shift has been extended indefinitely. But that's what we got paid for. Hell, it wasn't like it happened very often. At least they could be gracious about it on the rare occasion it did.

"Aw, Ryan, come on!" PJ grumbled. If the white knuckles on his hands were any indication, he was squeezing that football pretty hard in his frustration.

My patience snapped. "Look. I don't like this any better than you do. I'm not even supposed to be here, for crying out loud. But something came up, and now we all have to work together to deal with it. Okay?"

That seemed to mollify them, if only a little, and their expressions were somewhat contrite. Austin sighed and ran his hand over the layer of fuzz covering his head. "What's going on?"

"You remember Adam Royce Walker?"

Austin shrugged lightly. "Sure. What about him? He's in DC, right?"

"Not anymore."

Austin's eyes popped open wide. "What?"

"He's out, and he's decided to come pay us a visit."

"Adam Royce Walker?" PJ drew out the words, and his brow furrowed in concentration. "Why do I know that name?"

I shifted my attention to him. His words had reminded me he was pretty new to the squad and had probably not been around when Walker had still been here. "He's one of our more…interesting PI subjects. They actually talk about him in training now when they're covering the Intelligence block. I had to make a PowerPoint presentation for them," I told Austin with a little smile.

Austin laughed. "You're kidding."

"Nope."

"Please tell me there are pictures! I love the one I took of you guys in Central Park with that silver street-performer guy. It was priceless."

I made a face at him and returned my attention to PJ. "Adam Royce Walker is a paranoid schizophrenic with delusions of grandeur who's off his medication as often as he's on it. He has a fairly predictable cycle. He goes off his meds, gets a touch vocal about his ideas, threatens to kill himself and/or someone else, depending on his mood, and ends up being committed because he's a danger to himself and/or others.

"While he's in lockup, they get him back on his meds, he comes down, appears rational and reasonable, and they have no cause to hold him anymore, so they cut him loose. At which point, he decides he's fine and goes back off his meds. And round and round it goes." I sighed at the inherently frustrating nature of the mental-health system. It was a vicious circle, and as far as I could tell there was no way out of it.

"All the earmarks that the instructors in training tell you to look for in a PI subject to assess each one's relative threat level? He hits them. With gusto," Austin informed PJ. "He kept us on our toes when he was here in New York, that's for damn sure."

"And it looks like the DC guys weren't enough of a challenge for him. He called the office down there to inform them that he was on the train headed back to New York. Three guesses where his first stop is probably going to be."

"Shit," Austin whispered softly.

"That about sums it up," I said.

"Well, at least he called instead of just showing up," Austin pointed out.

"True. We have him pretty well trained that way. But then his innate craving for attention would never have allowed him to get away with not telling us."

"Where's he headed?" PJ wanted to know.

"His direction of interest is Hurricane." I felt an acute stab of sympathy underlying the general feeling of helplessness that washed over me. That poor girl just couldn't catch a break. Sure, all of our protectees had people who took an unusual interest in them, both positive and negative, but I'd never seen any collection of individuals as motivated to overt action as the ones who were obsessed with Zoey Carmichael. The worst part about it all, as far as I was concerned, was that Zoey hadn't done anything to deserve any of this unwanted attention. She hadn't asked for this. She was targeted solely because of whose daughter she was.

I shook my head a little to dispel the cobwebs and got back to business. "I'm going to call the midnight response guys and tell them to get over to the Sin Bin ASAP and just hang out on the street with their eyes open."

"I'm sorry, the what?" PJ asked.

It took me a second to realized what I'd said, and I struggled not to outwardly evince my mortification at the slip. "The CP."

"That's not what you said."

I sighed. "No, it isn't. But it's what I meant. Now—"

"I thought the code name for the CP was Platform."

"It is." I glanced to Austin for help, but he was busy smirking at me.

"What did you just call it?"

When it became clear Austin wasn't going to interject, I huffed. "The Sin Bin. So, if we could just—"

"Why did you call it that?"

"It's what the detail calls it, okay? I need you to—"

"Why?" PJ pressed.

"PJ! Focus! Forget about the CP. I need you two to go to the train station and try to catch up with him when he arrives. I'll email you the exact train number as soon as I get it from DC. I'm waiting for a secure fax now. Call me the second you have eyes on him, but don't try to forcibly detain him. Especially not there. He'll make a scene, and Penn Station definitely isn't a place we want him doing that. See if you can catch him outside and try to take him to dinner or something. So far, he hasn't technically done anything wrong so we can't pick him up, but I do think we need to have a chat with him."

Walker making it a point to travel back up here had set off all sorts of alarm bells in the back of my head, and I wasn't eager to see how this would all play out. Not when I had to be so closely involved.

"How?" PJ frowned slightly. "I mean, if he's this fired up to get to Hurricane, what can we possibly say that'll slow him down?"

"I don't know," I snapped. "Think of something. Tell him I'm on my way and want to talk to him. I don't care. Just stall him. I need time to get there to intercept."

"Will that help?" PJ asked, apparently not even remotely fazed by my ire. "Telling him you want to see him, I mean."

"Maybe. Could push him over the edge the other way and make him more determined. It's hard for me to tell, not having spoken to him. I'm not sure where in his cycle he is at the moment or how long he's been off his meds. Hell, I'm not even positive exactly how long he's been out. I'll call DC back and see whether they can get me a good number for him. A cell or something. If I can talk to him, I'll have a better idea what we're up against."

"What are you going to do?" Austin wanted to know. "While we're waiting for him at the train station?"

I took a deep breath. "I'm going to personally inform the detail that this is headed their way. And then I'm going to figure out how to take care of Walker."

"Any ideas?" PJ asked, clearly dubious.

"Not yet. Walker and I go back a long time. He was one of my first cases when I transferred to the squad. I dealt with him for the better part of a year. I know him pretty well. I ought to. I lost track of how many phone calls I got because of him. I spent easily half my time working on his case. Maybe I can talk him down or something. I'll put Bellevue on notice that we'll most likely be bringing him in."

"Do you think we'll need the mobile crisis unit?" Austin asked.

"God, I hope not," I muttered. "But I'll see who's running tonight and maybe let them know to keep an ear open in case we need help."

Austin clapped PJ on the shoulder and made a jerking motion with his head, clearly urging the kid to get a move on. "We'll call you when we hit the train station."

"You remember what he looks like?"

Austin nodded. "Sure do. I interviewed him with you enough times. I'm not likely to forget."

"Okay, well, an updated pic in the file should be on its way from DC. I'll send it over to you as soon as I get it. Okay?"

"Sure thing, Ryan," Austin said, heading toward his desk with PJ trailing close behind asking him to explain the CP's nickname to him.

I took a long moment to try to control my reeling thoughts, attempting to force my mind to just stop for a second so I could get my bearings. Of all the things I didn't need right now, Walker's reappearance had been so outside the realm of possibility it would never have occurred to me to even put it on the list.

Shaking my head, I headed toward my own office to grab my keys, stopping by the secure fax as I did so to retrieve the file DC sent up. I was so completely wrapped up in scanning its contents I didn't notice I wasn't alone until I'd turned the corner and stumbled upon someone at my desk.

Gasping in surprise, I jerked, startled. Mark Jennings was standing behind my desk frozen in place, his face a mask of astonishment that was probably an exact mirror of my own. My eyes flicked down to see he had one hand in my bottom desk drawer where I kept all my old case files and timekeeping paperwork. I frowned, and when I glanced back up to meet his eyes, I thought he looked more than a little guilty.

"Hey, Mark." I managed to keep my tone even as I cocked my head to one side and deliberately dropped my stare back to his hand. I felt more than heard Allison move up behind me but didn't turn to acknowledge her.

Mark hastily withdrew the offending appendage and stood up to his full height, straightening the lapels of his suit jacket, though whether it was out of necessity, habit, or nervousness, I couldn't have said for certain.

"Ryan," Mark said quickly. "Hey, I was just looking for you."

"In my desk?" I transferred the sheaf of papers I was holding to one hand and walked around to retrieve my bag. The move trapped him behind the desk, and his gaze flickered toward the door, though I couldn't tell whether he was looking at Allison or merely glancing to his only escape route.

"Of course not. I meant I came to your office looking for you, and when you weren't here I decided to leave you a note. I was looking for paper."

I doubted that was even remotely true. I suspected he was actually searching for ammunition with which to get me fired. Like I didn't have enough headaches at the moment. Without taking my eyes from his, I took a couple steps forward and picked up a Post-it notepad from the top of my now-pristine desk. The silence between us was heavy as I held it out to him.

"And a pen," Mark said.

At that, I extended my arm and plucked out the pen I could see peeking over the top edge of his breast pocket. I held it up so he could see it. The uncomfortable moment seemed to stretch on into eternity as we stared at one another. I knew he wasn't looking for writing implements. He knew that I knew. And obviously neither of us was going to talk about it.

"What did you want to tell me, Mark?"

There was a long pause, and his eyes flickered to Allison's direction again. "You have a secure fax coming in from DC."

"I know." I held up the papers as evidence before carefully placing them in my shoulder bag. I grabbed my car keys out of the little wooden bowl they rested in when I was in the office and moved to the door, pointedly pausing when I reached it so I could turn to look at him. My hand was poised over the light switch. I liked to think my meaning was clear. "Thank you for telling me."

Mark seemed to deflate slightly, and something strange flickered behind his eyes as they raked over my desk one last time as he departed, making me wonder idly what it was he'd been searching for so diligently. Exchanging a puzzled glance with Allison, I turned off the lights and made sure the door was locked behind us as we left.

CHAPTER ELEVEN

A quick check of Hurricane's schedule before I left the office revealed she was hosting a private party at her residence. I sighed in relief when I read that. It'd be much easier for her detail to contain any possible situations that might arise if they were on their home turf, so to speak. I'd have been much happier if the entire detail had been out of district, but you took what hands you were dealt, I supposed.

I called Rico while I was on my way over to share the joy of our new assignment with him. Naturally, he made a smart-assed remark about how I really needed to come up with better excuses to see him. I told him I expected him and his annoying partner on site within the hour before I hung up on him in protest.

I then received a call from Austin and PJ. They estimated they'd arrive at Penn Station in another few minutes or so and planned to contact the on-duty Port Authority sergeant and then start looking for Walker immediately. After extracting several unneeded promises from them to call me the second they spotted him, I took a deep breath and got out of the car.

As soon as my feet hit the pavement, the hair on the back of my neck snapped to attention, and a shiver flowed down my spine and chilled my extremities. I clenched one hand on the edge of the car where the door met the roof and warily looked up. I scoured every window I could see as quickly as I could, but it was dark, and would I really be able to tell if a sniper was lurking in any of them, waiting to end me? I doubted it. And that knowledge made my blood run as cold and fast as the Colorado River in January.

I let out a shaky breath and pushed off the car, all the while chanting over and over to myself that it was going to be fine, that neither Allison nor I was about to die, that no one was waiting to shoot me on this street corner because no one had any way of knowing I was here. Except no one should've known the president of Iran was at that meeting, which meant no one should've known to take the shot then, but they had. I still hadn't figured out how that'd worked.

Forcibly ignoring the roaring pressure swirling around inside my chest, I made myself walk—not run—toward Hurricane's building. A big, black Suburban sat idling at the curb with the silhouettes of two people visible inside. Recognizing the larger of the two, I grinned at Allison, held one finger to my lips to tell her to keep quiet, and crept stealthily over to the driver's side door. I was pleased to note the window was down a bit despite the chill in the night air.

"Yo. I need to get uptown in a hurry." I made it a point to hit the stereotypical New York accent hard and barely managed to restrain my laugh as I spoke. "There's a twenty in it for you if you step on it."

The man in the driver's seat whirled around at the sound of my voice, his face a comical mask of mixed surprise and irritation. "I'm not a cab driver—" His eyes widened. "Ryan?"

My laugh bubbled over and broke free. "Hey, Tuck. What's shakin'?"

Tucker Doyle, a longtime member of Hurricane's protective detail and a former New Yorker, rolled the window down all the way and grinned back at me. "What the hell are you doing here?"

"Testing your perimeter defenses. Bad news. You failed." Allison scoffed at that and shook her head.

Tuck snorted. "Failed, my ass."

"You're getting soft in your old age. I was going to ask why you're down here on motorcade duty instead of one of the junior guys, but now I know. You need the practice."

Tuck cast a sharp glare at his companion when she snickered and then returned his attention to me. He looked me up and down appraisingly. If it'd been anyone else, I probably would've bristled, but I'd known Tuck for years. I wasn't positive what he was looking for, but I did know there wasn't anything sexual or suggestive in the inspection.

"How are you?" Tuck's voice was soft, his tone concerned.

I glanced at Allison out of the corner of my eye and then began the pretense of picking nonexistent lint off the front of my suit jacket. I probably should've expected the question and the not-so-hidden nuances his tone implied, but I hadn't. I'd been too focused on my reason for being there to have even considered it.

"I'm good. How are you? It's been a long time."

The look in Tuck's eyes told me he didn't believe me. "Yeah. You've been busy."

"No busier than anyone else." I extended my arm in through the window across Tuck's body and held my hand out to his partner, barely containing the wince at the tug in the muscles of my injured right shoulder. "I'm Ryan, by the way." I shot Tuck a disapproving look for not introducing me. "And this is Allison Reynolds. You probably know her. She's on Harbinger's detail."

Allison nodded at them in silent greeting as the woman in the car took my hand firmly. "Marissa St. John."

"Oh, yeah. You're from Nashville, right? I think we worked together during UNGA once."

Marissa nodded. "That's right. Three years ago. Lesotho. Good memory."

"Nice to see you again. Welcome to New York. Sorry you have to put up with this guy. I'll submit your name for a cash award for your trouble."

Marissa's eyes slid over to Tuck's face, and I saw the briefest hint of tenderness there before she shut it down and a wry expression overcame her features. "He can be trying."

Tuck raised one eyebrow at me but chose to let it go. "What brings you over here to our neck of the woods?"

"I have some info I need to pass. Who's the on-duty supe?"

Tuck rubbed his chin with the heel of his hand. "Doctore's upstairs."

I blinked at him. "Uh...Doctore?" I had no idea who that was or what the hell he was talking about. I'd never heard of an agent by that name, and that was definitely something that would've caught my attention. It was probably some sort of nickname or inside joke. This detail always had struck me as a sort of insular, march-to-the-beat-of-their-own-drummer kind of group. I glanced to Allison for a hint, but she just shrugged, so I waited for Tuck to elaborate.

"Yeah. Doctore. Valenti."

"*Hannah* Valenti?"

The corner of Tuck's mouth twitched. "Who else?"

"Why do you call her Doctore?"

"Because she whips us. Regularly and with great enthusiasm. Just like the guy in charge of the gladiator school in *Spartacus*."

I ignored the labored comparison. "Hannah's the shift whip? Seriously?"

Tuck grinned. "Yup. And she won't let any of us forget it, either."

Hannah Valenti and I had gone through the academy together and had actually gotten along extremely well despite the fact that we were almost complete polar opposites. Our easy camaraderie had been a relief, as she'd been the only other female in the half of the class whose last names began with the letters M through Z, and we'd spent a great deal of time partnered up for various training scenarios and control-tactics drills by default.

Hannah had been a very solemn, extremely determined, almost freakily intense recruit—I fondly recalled I'd spent easily half my time trying to get her to crack a smile or lighten up—and somehow I wasn't surprised to learn she was whipping the shift tonight. She'd definitely take her duties very seriously. I grinned at the prospect of seeing her in action.

"Well, this'll be more fun than I thought. I'll catch you later, Tuck." I turned to head inside, but the telltale movement of Tuck lifting his wrist mike to his mouth caused me to stop. I put a restraining hand on his arm. "No. Don't."

"Still testing our security?" Tuck's eyes twinkled with obvious amusement.

That was a silly question, considering the cameras in the CP were most likely trained on the Suburban even now as Tuck and I talked. His allowing us to pass would be clue enough to the guys upstairs we were good to go. And if that didn't do it for them, my lapel pin should be identification enough. That's assuming the guys we ran into didn't know us by sight, which the majority of them should. Many of the guys on the detail were former New Yorkers we both knew personally. The ones who weren't had probably seen us around; me when I'd supported the detail in a PI capacity when Hurricane had attended public events and Allison when Hurricane attended joint events with her father. No, in reality, I'd stopped Tuck from calling out over the air because I hadn't wanted him to let Hannah know I was coming. I wanted to surprise her.

"You know me. I'm nothing if not thorough."

Tuck chuckled. "Go easy on them. Okay, O'Connor?"

"No promises." I turned to head toward the entrance to Hurricane's building.

"Wait. Wasn't she just shot?" I heard Marissa ask as I walked away.

"Shhh!" Tuck hissed.

I cringed but resolutely kept going, taking minimal comfort from the slight pressure of Allison's hand on the small of my back. Marissa was very nice, but I wasn't in the mood for Twenty Questions or gaping stares at the moment. Or ever, if I was going to be completely honest.

I waved over my shoulder as I ambled toward the door of the building. Would Tuck actually let us go in unannounced, or would he warn his team we were coming? Of course, he could always tell them to give us a hard time. That notion made me grin, and I listened intently but didn't hear anything go out over the radio through the earpiece nestled snugly in my left ear.

The agent standing post in the lobby raised an eyebrow at us as we approached. His handsome face was completely impassive, which made it impossible for me to determine whether he'd recognized us as fellow agents.

"Agent O'Connor." He nodded slightly in greeting and then nodded at Allison. "Agent Reynolds."

Guess that answered that question. I held out my right hand. "Ryan. Please. Nice to meet you."

He took my hand in his, and as he did, his eyes flitted to my right shoulder as though he could see my newly acquired bullet hole through my suit jacket. I reassessed his reaction to my arrival and wasn't surprised when my face blazed and my chest suddenly felt tight. I told myself my annoyance was unjustified. I mean, it wasn't every day an agent got shot multiple times in the line of duty. It was only natural people would become curious. Perhaps. But that rationale did nothing to ease my tension.

"Isaac Artaega." His handshake was just shy of vigorous, and it caused a faint throb in the area of my injured shoulder that I tried bravely to conceal. "And if I may say, it's an honor."

I froze, utterly flabbergasted and not a little panicked. An honor? To meet me? Hardly. I opened my mouth to make some sort of trademark smart-assed remark but stopped. I really was no good in these situations. What the hell did one say to something like that?

"Uh...Thanks. Is Hannah Valenti around?" My skin crawled and itched under the intensity of his attention, and I just wanted to get upstairs, pass my info, and get back out on the street before Walker arrived. I really didn't have a lot of time to be engaging in these sorts of conversations.

"Doctore's upstairs." He handed me a key card and nodded in the direction of the elevator. "Top floor. Just swipe that against the pad before you press the floor to gain access."

"Great. Thanks."

"You're a celebrity," Allison said wryly when the elevator doors slid shut.

"Great. Because you know how I love being the center of attention."

She shifted closer to me and deliberately brushed her pinkie against mine. "It'll die down soon enough, I'm sure."

"You feel like messing up in some spectacular way to take some of the heat off me? I'd owe you one."

Allison chuckled. "As tempting as that sounds, I think I'll pass."

"Damn it."

The elevator doors opened into a nearly empty hallway. The telltale sounds of a party drifted through one of the only two doors on the entire floor, but if they registered with the agent standing post in the hallway, she gave no indication.

Ivy Peltier looked a bit taken aback by our arrival, but her features quickly split into a huge grin. She wasted no time in folding me in an enthusiastic hug. I returned the greeting with equal zeal.

"What the hell are you doing here?"

"Hey, Ivy. Nice to see you, too. Do you know Allison Reynolds?"

"Of course," Ivy said, shaking Allison's hand. "I've seen you around."

"Tuck just said the same exact thing to me downstairs," I said.

"Is that the standard greeting you all are instructed to use on us NYFO guys? Or is it specific to me?"

Ivy laughed. "Just you, baby."

"Fantastic. You know how I love to be singled out."

Ivy's eyes twinkled, but they flickered briefly to the papers in my hand, and the good humor slowly seeped out of her expression. "I take it this isn't a social call."

I smirked wryly. "Sweetie, I know I've been out of touch lately, but I promise you when I finally get my shit together, I'll do better than to bug you while you're working."

"Hey. I didn't mean it as a criticism."

"Good. Because I didn't take it as one."

"Hell, we all know that you've been..." Ivy frowned slightly and appeared unsure how to complete that sentence. She cleared her throat and glanced uneasily at Allison. "Well, anyway, I'll never give you a hard time about being out of touch after what you went through."

The uncomfortable feeling that'd started when I'd overheard Marissa asking Tuck about the shooting and had gained strength during my brief encounter with Isaac in the lobby was now raging. I raked one hand through my hair and willed myself to relax. It wouldn't do anybody any good for me to lose focus now.

"So, is Hannah inside? I need to speak with her for a minute."

"Yeah, she's in there. Probably standing motionless and unobtrusive in a corner somewhere. Possibly behind a large potted plant, if there is one." Ivy's affection for the woman who was essentially her boss was obvious. "Want me to get her?"

I grinned. "Nah. I'll do it. You guys are on Tango, right?"

Ivy nodded.

I adjusted the earpiece in my ear and lifted my wrist mike to my lips. "Valenti, Valenti, location?"

Ivy covered her mouth with her hand and chortled quietly. Her eyes shone with barely restrained glee.

There was a long pause, and I could imagine the expression on Hannah's face as she tried to determine who was hitting her up over the air. She'd have immediately realized it wasn't one of her regular guys. How long would it take for her to figure out who it was? Would she even be able to?

A click sounded in my left ear, followed by Hannah's voice,

deliberately low and almost completely masked by the sounds of the party. "Go for Valenti."

My grin widened, and Ivy and I exchanged an amused glance. "Valenti, location for a meet?"

Another long pause. Then, "Peltier, Peltier from Valenti. Can you step in here, please?"

Ivy laughed. "You're so bad. You know it's driving her crazy that she can't figure out who you are, right?"

"Oh, I know. That's why I did it."

Ivy shook her head, a small smile still pulling at her lips. "God, if that's what you do to people you like, remind me not to get on your shit list."

"Not to worry. You're safe."

"Why doesn't that make me feel any better? I'll give you a call. We'll hang out soon, okay?" She gave my arm a squeeze and headed toward the door to the suite.

"Sure thing. Stay safe."

"You, too." And with that, Ivy disappeared into Hurricane's apartment, leaving me to attempt to figure out how to break the news to Hannah that things were about to get a helluva lot more exciting over here.

CHAPTER TWELVE

The door to the loft was only opened for a few seconds, but it was long enough for the sights and sounds of the party to waft around me, breaking my concentration. Then the door was shut once more, the noise reduced to a muted tumult. And I was left in the hall about to ramp up Hannah Valenti's already unusually high pucker factor another ten notches. She looked exactly as I remembered her, which helped relax me somewhat. I couldn't help smiling.

"Ryan?" Hannah's hazel eyes were serious and tinged with the barest hint of confusion. She glanced from me to Allison and back again.

I motioned to Allison, wishing I had a name tag or something for her so I didn't have to keep introducing her to people. "You know Allison Reynolds?"

"I think so," Hannah said, shaking Allison's hand.

"Also, I'm not calling you 'Doctore,' so don't ask."

Hannah rolled her eyes. "Good. I hate it when they call me that. What are you doing here?"

"Why does everyone insist on asking me that? I can't just stop over to say hi?"

Her expression was thoughtful as she looked at me. "Of course you can. I just assumed—"

"Well, I didn't," I said with a grin. As always, her innate seriousness seemed to bring out my teasing side. I was never able to be in her presence for very long without getting on her case about something. The activity likely amused me so much because most of the time she didn't seem to realize I was just messing with her.

"Oh. I'm sorry. Of course not. What did you need?"

I rolled my eyes and shook my head, fondly exasperated with her. "Hannah, you're killing me. Get over here, would you?"

And before she could even think to protest, I folded her in a gigantic hug. She stiffened immediately, most likely because she had some sort of problem with hugging while she was on duty as the acting supervisor. But, never the kind of girl to let that sort of thing stop me, I merely squeezed her tighter and then took it a step further and swayed her almost violently from side to side. I capped the display off with a big kiss on her cheek—complete with loud, over-exaggerated smacking sounds—before I finally released her and took a step back.

Hannah's face was at least eighteen shades of red, and she ducked her head, clearly mortified. "You just got lipstick on my cheek, didn't you?" Her brows pulled down in a scowl, and she scrubbed at the spot with the heel of her hand.

I beamed and gave a curt nod, pleased with myself. "Yes, I did."

Hannah's eyes tightened and her brows pulled down, and she opened her mouth, presumably to scold me for what she probably considered unprofessional behavior, but the dinging of the elevator signaling a new arrival saved me from a tongue-lashing.

SAIC Claudia Quinn, Zoey Carmichael's detail leader, stepped off the elevator and into the hall, her black business suit impeccably pressed, her dark hair perfectly braided with not a hair out of place, her green eyes intense and missing nothing. I felt that gaze lock onto me, and instinctively I stood up a little straighter.

We'd never officially met, but the woman was an absolute legend. A highly decorated former NYPD detective and one of the youngest SAICs the Secret Service had ever promoted, SAIC Quinn had a rocket strapped to her back. Rumor had it she was about to be named the head of the Office of Protective Operations. Then every detail in the agency would report to her, not just this one. Of course, that was assuming she didn't leave the agency altogether to jump over to the Department of Homeland Security, which I'd heard had also been courting her for some time. I mentally smacked myself upside the head for not once considering I might run into her here. In addition to her mere presence making me nervous, I had the uneasy feeling it might complicate matters greatly.

"Agent Valenti," SAIC Quinn murmured in a low voice. "Agent

Reynolds." Her words were obviously directed elsewhere, but her attention was still fixed on me.

"Ma'am," Hannah and Allison both replied in unison.

I had to fight not to give voice to the quip bubbling behind my lips that Hannah never called me ma'am even though I was technically senior to her because I'd been hired two days earlier than she had. Somehow I doubted this woman would appreciate my particular brand of humor. And while she wasn't my boss, she was most definitely someone I didn't want to piss off. I held no illusions I'd be able to make a good impression on her, but I was pretty sure I could avoid making a bad one. Well, probably.

The SAIC's eyes took in my earpiece and lapel pin, and she held out one hand to me. "Claudia Quinn."

I met her handshake with a firm one of my own, gritting my teeth in an effort to disguise my discomfort. "Ryan O'Connor. I'm from NYFO. It's very nice to meet you, ma'am."

The SAIC's expression turned speculative as she continued to assess me. "Yes. Of course. How's the shoulder?"

Allison stiffened beside me, obviously uncomfortable with the question, but I was mostly surprised. That SAIC Quinn knew who I was had taken me aback, although it probably shouldn't have. That she thought to inquire about my injuries, well, that provoked another feeling entirely. It wasn't necessarily one I'd categorize as pleasant. More like falling through ice into a freezing cold lake. "Fine, ma'am. Thank you for asking."

Something flashed behind her eyes, but it was impossible to determine exactly what it meant, if anything at all. One dark eyebrow lifted slightly. "And your other injuries? Forgive me. I can't recall where they were or how many you sustained."

Allison's body was now completely rigid with tension, and I bit down on the inside of my lip and took a deep breath, willing the discomfort to fade. My hands curled into tight fists, and my muscles also went rigid with tension. I'd been a curiosity for much longer than I'd ever wanted to be, which was never. The press, other agents, occasionally even strangers on the street seemed to either want to avoid discussion of the topic of my injuries in favor of staring at me with pitying glances or to ask me overly personal questions as though they were entitled to the answers. Both reactions were becoming rather stale.

But then, to be fair, I imagined SAIC Quinn most likely knew all about that. As far as I'd heard she never talked about it, but everyone knew she'd been shot in the line of duty while responding to a domestic-violence call when she'd still been a beat cop. Several times, if memory served. She probably knew exactly how I felt on almost every level, except she hadn't lost anyone close to her. Not in the way I had. And not when the whole thing was entirely her own fault.

I glanced at her but saw neither pity nor morbid curiosity. And for the first time since I'd been shot, I realized I might actually be able to talk about it without wanting to throw up. The deep breath I'd inhaled came out slowly, and with it went the majority of the tension I'd been carrying around since my arrival at the residence. I met the SAIC's stare.

"Five bullets hit me. One tore through the muscle just above my right shoulder. My vest caught two that would've ripped straight through my back, one at the height of my right lung, the other in the area of my right kidney. I sustained minor damage to the back of my right hip, where my handcuffs more or less deflected the fourth bullet. And the last caused a minor flesh wound to the outside of my right thigh that'll leave a scar, but no major lasting injury."

SAIC Quinn regarded me for a long moment. "Well, I'm glad you're okay. It isn't often we get called on to take a bullet for our protectees, obviously. And I'm happy the outcome wasn't more grave."

I winced as my mind immediately flew to Lucia and how the outcome couldn't have been worse for her, but I forced myself to skip over that thought. I may've been a hot mess of conflicting and wildly vacillating emotions when I was alone, but I'd be damned if I'd let anybody else see that. I refused to appear as anything less than strong and put together to anybody I worked with. Especially not SAIC Claudia Quinn.

"Did you have something you needed to report, Agent O'Connor?" SAIC Quinn derailed my runaway-thought train and dragged me back on topic.

My heart leapt into my throat as her eyes fell to the papers in my hands. My previously assuaged tension immediately snapped back into place with all the subtlety of a taxed rubber band. Would her presence be a problem for me? It appeared I was about to find out the hard way.

While SAIC Quinn was definitely in charge of this detail and should absolutely be privy to all of the information I had to impart regarding Walker, I hesitated to include her in this discussion. For one thing, I didn't have either the energy or the inclination to go another round with Mark about following protocol and respecting the chain of command. And me briefing a SAIC without going through my superiors would definitely fall outside the chain of command. For another, she was bound to have a million questions, and I didn't have time to indulge her curiosity. I'd already spent longer than I'd planned on this notification. I needed to finish this and get back down on the street, pronto.

Hannah, ever the astute little agent, interjected before either the SAIC or I could utter a word. "Ma'am, Hurricane asked me to send you in as soon as you arrived. She needs to discuss something with you regarding the preparations for the charity auction next week. There's been a change."

I was fairly certain the SAIC knew she was being dismissed—as I've previously stated, the woman missed nothing—but she didn't address the issue.

"Thank you, Agent Valenti." The SAIC tipped her head in my direction. "Agent Reynolds, I'm sure I'll see you soon. Agent O'Connor. Perhaps we'll have a chance to speak again."

"I'd like that." I held my breath until she'd entered Hurricane's apartment and closed the door firmly behind her. Once Hannah, Allison, and I were alone again, I fixed Hannah with a grateful look. "Thanks."

"For what?"

"You saved my ass just now, and don't try to pretend you don't know what I'm talking about."

Hannah shrugged. "I knew you wouldn't want to relay whatever information you have in front of her. I can always fill her in later at my discretion. Besides, I still owed you."

"Owed me? For what?"

"The bar?"

Oh, fuck. Not this. Not now. Allison was studying me a little too closely with a curious glint in her eyes. Maybe if I just glossed over it... "You didn't owe me anything. So, about this notification—"

"It was a huge deal, Ryan. And I don't know if I ever told you how grateful I was."

I focused intently on Hannah because I really didn't want to make eye contact with Allison at the moment. And I could feel her staring at me like her eyes were lasers and were searing my flesh. "Really. It was nothing. Literally. And I told you when it happened not to mention it. You suck at following instructions, by the way."

Hannah's expression was serious. "It was everything. And you know it."

I huffed and wrinkled my nose as I looked away, scratching the side of my neck self-consciously.

"The SAIC doesn't know." Hannah's voice was quiet. "At least, I don't think she does."

Oh, God. What did I have to do to get her to let this go? "That's cuz there's nothing to know."

Hannah was dredging up some memories that were best forgotten. It was years ago, before Claudia Quinn had transferred to Zoey Carmichael's detail. Even if the SAIC had been briefed, it probably wouldn't have mattered much.

In recent years, it's seemed to be a growing trend that the president's children act out. I don't know if they're just rebelling against the unfairness of being under constant guard during their formative years or if each new generation is trying to outdo the one before it with increasingly brazen acts of audacity. I'd often speculated that they all spoke to one another and egged each other on, but I had no concrete proof. Yet.

Zoey Carmichael and her two older brothers had been under one type of protection or another longer than anyone in recent memory. Her father had served as the governor of Idaho—which, incidentally, has no term limits—for sixteen years before being elected president. She'd been in protective custody since she was four years old.

While she may've grown up somewhat in the past few years and now seemed to take our presence in stride, that hadn't been the case when we'd first started protecting her. In the beginning, Zoey Carmichael had been...Well, a little wild, to put it mildly, and she'd been proud of it. So proud, in fact, she'd requested her code name be changed from Halo to Hurricane. She was rumored to have stated she thought it suited her better.

And she'd definitely been a force of nature. Her brothers were both older, and they'd either sown their wild oats and gotten the rebellion out of their systems before their father had become the leader of the free world, or they were leagues better at hiding their activities. Hurricane, on the other hand, simply hadn't cared. Rumor had it she'd regularly slipped away from the watchful eyes of her agents and roamed around for hours with no one having any idea where she was or who she was with. The American public had no clue, of course, because we don't tell tales out of school—although keeping that quiet in this day and age had been a feat—but among the agents, the secret wasn't that well-guarded. However, knowing a thing to be true and encountering it up close and personal were two different matters entirely.

I'd stopped into a bar in the Village one night after a late shift so I could have a quick drink and had been floored to see Hurricane there. She'd been just barely underage at the time, so she shouldn't have been able to get past the bouncer at the door. But what'd surprised me even more had been that she'd been completely without protection. I probably should've figured straight away that'd be the case, as I'd heard the rumors like everyone else. But like I said, knowing facts and seeing them firsthand are two different kettles of fish sometimes.

Anyway, long story short, I'd sent Hannah a text message on her personal phone telling her where Hurricane was and that I'd keep an eye on her until the cavalry arrived. Then, I'd surreptitiously put myself into a position where I'd be close enough to keep an eye on her so she wouldn't be able to slip away without me noticing, yet far enough away that hopefully she wouldn't realize I was watching her.

What I hadn't counted on, unfortunately, were the overtly amorous attentions of a man in the bar who apparently couldn't take no for an answer. He'd become decidedly aggressive with his overtures, despite Hurricane's repeated insistence that she wasn't interested. Hurricane had been a lot more polite to the guy than I would've been in her position, but the situation had started to draw the notice of several of the bar's other patrons and had the potential to escalate into quite the scene.

Not sure what else to do and wanting to avoid a spectacle more than anything else—I'd been fairly certain the more attention the debacle attracted, the more likely it'd be someone would recognize Hurricane, which had the potential to unleash a whole host of problems I'd just as soon avoid—I'd confidently strolled up to the pair and addressed Hurricane as though we were intimately acquainted. I apologized for my lateness, promising to make it up to her, with just the right amount of flirtation coloring my tone, and spirited her away to the other side of the room, shooting the guy my very best death glare to discourage any further attempts to win Hurricane's affections.

Hurricane must've decided I was her best chance of getting out of the fiasco unscathed, because not only had she gone along with my ploy, but she'd further surprised me by upping the ante.

And that's how Hannah had walked in on me kissing one of our protectees. Or, more accurately, Hannah had arrived just in time to see Hurricane kissing me and me not knowing what else to do except go with it and kiss her back. For the record, Zoey Carmichael is an excellent kisser. I'm just saying.

"I'd like to tell her," Hannah broke into my reverie.

Holy shit! "What? Why?"

"She might be comforted to learn you looked out for Hurricane when none of us was around to do the job," Hannah said. "I mean, if it weren't for you, who knows what could've happened? It had the potential to be disastrous."

Oh. Right. That. Whew. Because my mind had just been swimming in memories of the kiss, I'd automatically assumed she'd been talking about that. That wouldn't have been good. Claudia Quinn didn't need to know I'd made out with a protectee. Ever. As far as I was concerned, no one needed to know that. Especially not Allison.

"Well, it all worked out okay," I told Hannah, hoping no one noticed the flush I could feel burning in my cheeks.

"Still, I wish you'd let me say something to her."

"Oh, Hannah, come on. That's not necessary. There's really no point."

"She's a good person to have in your corner. She's very well connected, not just in the Service but everywhere."

"Why would you think I'd need her in my corner? Or anyone, for that matter?" I waved an impatient hand to cut her off. "You know what? It doesn't matter. Let's forget it. Here." I handed her the papers I'd been holding and gave her a moment to peruse them.

The expression on Hannah's face was grim as she flipped through the file. She glanced at me without lifting her head. "Is there a particular reason you're bringing me this?"

I nodded. "There is. Saint E's let him out. He's on his way here."

Now Hannah's head did snap up, a dangerous glint in her eyes. "He's headed here? As in the Platform, here?"

"Well, to New York, at the very least. We don't have any concrete indication he'll head here, necessarily. But it's only a matter of time. If he doesn't come straight from the train station—which, frankly, would be a surprise—he'll make an appearance here at some point in the not-too-distant future."

Hannah's expression darkened, and her eyes took on a faraway cast, as though she were mulling over the situation. "How concerned do I need to be?"

"As concerned as you'd be for any other threat subject with an interest toward your protectee, I suppose."

Hannah reflected on that scenario for a long moment. "Do you have a plan of action in place?"

"Come on, Hannah. Really? I'm offended."

Hannah cracked a tiny smile. "What've you got?"

"The on-duty response team is waiting for him at Penn Station. They can't detain him because he hasn't technically done anything wrong yet, but they'll be following him once he leaves the station. Which"—I consulted my watch—"has probably actually already happened. I'll call them when we're done here to verify. The midnight shift is on the street outside keeping an eye out for him, and I plan to be his personal welcoming committee when he arrives."

Hannah frowned again. "I don't like this. Knowing a threat is on its way here and just sitting here waiting, doing nothing. It feels... wrong."

I couldn't help smiling. She was so type-A and proactive. Not moving to either address the threat or flee from it had to be killing her. "You may not be doing anything, but we are. This is a team effort, remember? I know you're used to calling the plays, but just let us have the ball. It won't kill you to sit this one out." Clichéd sports metaphors again. I couldn't get away from them.

"I know," she said. But she clearly wasn't convinced.

I put a hand on her arm. "Hey, relax. This is what we do, okay? All day, every day. Don't worry. He won't even make it into the lobby. I promise. Just keep Hurricane in the apartment, and everything will be fine. I'll call you later with an update."

Hannah took a slow breath and rolled the papers into a tube. "Do you want any of our guys to back you up?"

I tried not to let my smile morph into a full-fledged, shit-eating grin. Apparently, my clichéd sports metaphor had gone completely over her head.

"You don't need to. Between the five of us," I glanced at Allison, "well, technically six, I think we've got it covered. And we're the ones that're going to have to report this to DC and handle the follow-up paperwork. But it's your sandbox. I'm not going to tell you that you can't play in it."

"Okay." She tapped the tube of papers against the palm of her free hand. "Just brief Tuck and Marissa downstairs so they can watch your backs. And call me when everything's settled."

"Will do."

The door to Hurricane's apartment opened abruptly, and my body went cold. Then my stomach folded in on itself when I realized Hurricane herself was at the door. Normally, being around our protectees didn't faze me—I was generally too focused on my job to leave room for emotions of any kind—but encountering her so soon after recalling our kiss from a few years ago admittedly threw me. And having Allison standing right next to me and looking back and forth between us with a shrewd gaze only made things exponentially worse.

"Hey, Hannah, did you—" She broke off when she saw me and studied me a little too closely for my liking. "I'm sorry. I didn't realize we had company."

The previously dampened fire in my cheeks roared back to life, and I hastily pressed the button to call the elevator. "I'll give the key card back to the guy in the lobby," I muttered to Hannah out of the side of my mouth, turning so my attention was completely focused on my escape route.

"Ooh, more Secret Service."

I may not've been looking at Hurricane, but I didn't need to see her expression to know something about this situation amused her. The intonation of her words was evident.

I looked to Allison for help, but she just raised her eyebrows. I sighed softly. "Yes, ma'am."

"I can always tell. There's just something about you guys that gives it away. Even when you're in down clothes."

I found her statement intriguing. It either meant she'd known I was an agent when she'd kissed me all those years ago and had done it anyway, or she wasn't quite as adept at picking us out as she liked to think she was. Which was it?

"Are you joining my detail?" Hurricane asked.

"No, ma'am. I'm not."

"Hmm. Pity."

I didn't have any idea what she meant by that, but Hannah must have because she chastised her with a soft, "Miss Carmichael."

"What? Noah likes to look. And he'd definitely love looking at her. Do you want to transfer to my detail? I can make a call."

Oh, dear God. I had to fight not to give in to the urge to put my head into my hands. And if body language was anything to go on, Allison wasn't thrilled with the comment either. I didn't know why the president's daughter was actively recruiting agents to her detail as eye candy for her fiancé, and I wasn't about to ask any follow-up questions. I did cast my eyes heavenward and silently lament that this was obviously the slowest elevator in all of human history.

"Miss Carmichael!" Hannah's tone now was aghast.

"Come on. I was kidding. Mostly. What did we say about that stick, Hannah?" Hurricane was teasing her.

I snorted, unable to rein in my laughter at the good-natured barb. It appeared Hurricane and I had something in common. I silently wished her luck on getting Hannah to lighten up and wondered if she had any clue what a massive undertaking that was. I'd known Hannah for years and was still struggling with it. I hoped Hurricane enjoyed the challenge as much as I did.

"Do I know you?" Hurricane asked me as she moved closer. Her hands were on her hips, and out of the corner of my eye, I could see her intensely searching expression. "You seem very familiar."

I looked to Allison again, silently pleading with her to jump in. She shook her head almost imperceptibly and shoved her hands into her pockets. I took a deep breath and reluctantly faced Hurricane's curiosity. I didn't really want to converse with her, but it probably would've been rude of me to ignore her outright or to answer her while staring a hole in the elevator doors.

"This is Agent Reynolds," I said finally, elbowing Allison hard in the side. "She's on your dad's detail."

Hurricane spared her a cursory glance. "Hmm. That makes sense. But I was actually talking about you. Where have I seen you before?"

"Probably just at one of your events, ma'am. I'm from NYFO."

Hurricane's brow furrowed. "What's nigh foe?" she wanted to know, stumbling over the pronunciation as though if she only said it slowly enough, she'd be able to decipher what I was telling her.

My face flushed even hotter. "My apologies, ma'am. It stands for the New York Field Office. N-Y-F-O. We just say it like it's a word."

A sort of mischievous little smile pulled at the corners of Hurricane's lips. "Huh. You agents and your acronyms and code words. It's like your own little language."

"Yes, ma'am. It is."

Hurricane's smile faded, and that pensive look trickled back into her eyes. I could practically see her mind working as she tried to figure out how she knew me. Feeling unbelievably self-conscious, I pressed the button for the elevator again because it's common knowledge that pressing the elevator call button repeatedly makes it come faster.

"It isn't that," Hurricane murmured, almost to herself. Her expression now was deeply thoughtful. "It's from someplace else."

Thankfully, the elevator chimed its arrival, and the relief that rushed through me actually made me a little tingly. "If you'll excuse me, I have some business to attend to." I shot Hannah a warning glare. "I'll call you later."

The elevator doors closed on Hurricane looking frustrated and Hannah looking horrified. I breathed in relief, but my respite was short lived because I could feel Allison's gaze burrowing into me. I slowly turned my head to meet her eyes, a little afraid of what I'd see.

"Something you want to tell me?" she asked as she leaned against the opposite wall and folded her arms across her chest.

"Such as?"

"Such as what the hell that was back there with Hurricane?"

Okay, this was definitely not a conversation I wanted to have. And while I was completely on board with implementing a policy of complete honesty between us, now really wasn't the time to get into this. I still had a paranoid schizophrenic to deal with. "Can we maybe add this to the list of things we need to talk about later?"

Allison's eyes got wide and her jaw dropped as she gaped at me. "Oh, my God. You slept with her, didn't you?"

"Seriously?" I demanded.

"I've gotten pretty good at reading you, Ryan. You were definitely uncomfortable up there. Plus, I don't think I've ever seen you blush that hard."

"Believe me, if I'd slept with her, she'd remember it." I paused. "Or is this your way of telling me I'm not that great in bed?"

Allison seemed chagrined. "Definitely not. You know I think you're amazing. And you're right. She'd remember that."

"Thank you." My BlackBerry went off just then, and I shifted my focus back to more pressing matters. "He's almost here," I told Allison after reading the email.

"Don't think I'm going to forget about this."

The elevator door opened on the lobby, and I started making my way over to Isaac so I could return the key card to him before I forgot. "I wouldn't expect you to, although I'm concerned we're going to lose track of all the things we need to discuss. Maybe we should be writing them down."

"Don't worry. I'm keeping a mental note."

I smiled. "Why am I not surprised? You ready?"

Allison smiled back, and my chest constricted in the most wonderful way. "Let's go get him. The sooner we take care of this, the sooner we can attend to our own business."

I took a second to shake off my regular demeanor in favor of the game face I wore when I was working. I stood up a little straighter and squared my shoulders as I headed for the door. "Okay. Let's go."

CHAPTER THIRTEEN

Though I'd been all fired up and eager to get the party started a second ago, I couldn't help hesitating just inside the outer door. Panic slammed into me, leaving me slightly breathless. My pulse jumped, and my grip on the door handle became viselike. Not only was I worried about someone trying to splatter my brains all over the front of Hurricane's building, but now I was also terrified that whoever was gunning for me would miss and hit Allison. Fuck. I needed to get her away from me ASAP.

Gathering the courage necessary to walk back outside—and into the open where any would-be assassin would have a relatively clear shot at me—was a lot like trying to pick up several pounds of cooked spaghetti with my bare hands. I'd probably have stood there longer trying to manage it if I hadn't felt Allison's presence behind me. Not wanting to either let her see my fear or risk having to engage in a conversation about why I'd stopped, I hastily flung open the door.

"Elvis has left the building," Rico's best—and far-too-often practiced—announcer voice informed me via the earpiece nestled in my left ear as I stepped back out onto the street.

Despite my clattering nerves, I rolled my eyes, shooting a dark glare down the street in the direction of his car, where he and Eric had positioned themselves at the end of the block I couldn't see very well from my vantage point. Leave it to him to distract me from my fears of impending death with utter ridiculousness.

I ambled several paces from the front entrance of Hurricane's building toward the corner Austin had told me Walker would likely be approaching from, given his direction of travel, and leaned against a wrought-iron fence. I rested a casual elbow against the top of it to help disguise the motion of lifting my microphone to my lips. "Really, Rico? Elvis? Do I look like the kind of girl to wear a rhinestone jumpsuit?"

"I really wish I had a radio," Allison muttered out of the side of her mouth.

"Sorry," I whispered back.

"Ha. Right. Elvira, then? I know you've got some dresses that would put that outfit of hers to shame." I could hear his grin, and I shook my head.

"Two words for you, buddy: leather pants."

"That was a low blow."

"Agreed. But you're too far away for me to smack you, so I went with what I had. Remind me to retaliate physically later."

"Roger that. Oh, and the eagle has landed."

"What?" I was back to scrutinizing every square inch of the street for threats. Even though I was positive I'd never see the bullet with my name on it coming, I still couldn't help but look.

"The fox is in the henhouse." When I didn't respond, he tried again. "The cheese stands alone."

"Oh, good grief. You couldn't just be a normal person and say you've spotted him on the northwest corner of Sixth or something?"

"Nah. That's no fun."

"You're an ass." But we didn't have much time to get involved in a really good bickering match because, as I said that, my target lumbered into view.

Adam Royce Walker was a very big man. I'd known that, of course, but time had muted my memory, and I'd apparently forgotten exactly how big he was. Even if I'd been wearing heels, I'd have barely cleared his shoulders, and I doubted I'd have been able to touch my fingers together should I ever be seized by the urge to wrap my arms around him. However, that wasn't a theory I planned to test any time soon.

He was dressed in baggy jeans and an oversized zippered hooded sweatshirt over what appeared to be a grungy tee. His white sneakers made a faint scrape-slap noise as he wandered down the street, and his head was canted slightly toward the ground, as though he were looking at the pavement in front of him as he walked. From what I could see of his expression through the darkness, broken only by the occasional streetlamp, he appeared to be very deep in thought. He didn't seem to notice anyone was even sharing the street with him at all, let alone that it was me.

"Ryan, we're at your six," PJ informed me. "Right in front of the door."

"We've got eyes on, too, Ryan," Tuck told me as he opened the door to the Suburban. I heard the movement both over the radio via the earpiece nestled in my left ear and through the still night air.

I clicked my microphone twice with my thumb to indicate I'd heard them and turned to Allison. "Do me a favor and go set up with PJ and Austin in front of the door?"

Allison tilted her head and gave me a scathing look. "Really?"

"Do you want to have to explain to your bosses or mine what you were doing interviewing a PI subject out of your district when you're not even in a field office? Because if you stay here for this, you're going to have to go into the report."

Allison scowled and shook her head. "No."

"Besides, if he does get past me, you three are going to need to keep him out of the building. I promised Hannah he'd never even make it into the lobby. Do you want to make a liar out of me?"

"No."

"Okay, then."

"I don't like leaving you here to talk to him alone. It's not safe. You're not even armed."

"It'll be fine. You guys are all nearby. And this'll go better if it's just me and him. Trust me."

Allison took a long, slow breath. "I do," she said quietly.

"Thanks."

"Be careful."

"Always."

As soon as Allison turned to leave, I shifted so I was once again facing Walker. I split my attention between watching his approach and scanning the entire street for threats. My skin was crawling with equal parts anticipation and anxiety, and I rubbed my palms against my pant legs to rid them of the sweat I could feel gathering there.

When Walker was still a good ten feet from me—which put him approximately thirty-five feet from the door to Hurricane's building—I finally pushed off the fence I'd been leaning against and stepped into the middle of the sidewalk to engage him.

"Hey, Adam," I said, my voice just loud enough for him to hear me. "Bit late for a stroll, isn't it?"

Walker's steps faltered, and his head shot up, giving me the first clear glimpse of his face. His eyes were wide and positively wild. My heart immediately sank. I'd have bet this month's salary he was completely off his meds again and had been for some time. This was not going to end well. I reached across my chest and brushed the fingers of my right hand against my lapel pin, which rested on the left side of my suit jacket, an indication to Rico that I wanted him to move a little closer. I was willing to bet next month's salary this was going to escalate quickly, and I wanted my backup to be able to jump into the fray before it went too far south.

"Agent O'Connor," Walker said after a beat, his voice a raspy growl as he ground out the words.

Out of the corner of my eye, over Walker's left shoulder and out of his line of sight, I saw Rico and Eric slowly creeping toward us. I fluttered the fingers of my right hand where they now rested near the outside of my thigh. Rico caught the motion and put his hand out to stop Eric's forward progress. Thank God, Rico and I had worked together as often as we had because these signals we'd utilized countless times before were really coming in handy.

"What's going on, Adam?" I asked, trying to keep my tone as light and conversational as possible.

"What're you doing here?" he demanded. His voice wavered, and his eyes had grown wide again. My mind immediately likened him to all the frightened animals I'd ever seen on those television nature shows about creatures going wild and attacking innocent bystanders. Walker was unpredictable when he was like this, and that made him dangerous.

"I came to see you," I told him simply.

"How'd you know I would be here?"

I gave a half shrug with my good shoulder and casually put my left hand behind my back, indicating to Austin and PJ with one finger that I wanted them to hold where they were. I chanced a quick glance to my right, where I could see a glimpse of their reflection in a darkened store window. Austin nodded and murmured to Tuck and Marissa over the radio to stay put.

"You told the guys in the Washington office you were coming to New York."

Walker's countenance darkened faster than I'd have thought possible, and he took half a step toward me. His fists were clenching and unclenching at his sides, and all of his fear seemed to have completely evaporated at my statement. His body was rigid, and tension rolled off him in heady waves. Peripherally, I could see Eric starting to move, but thankfully Rico held him back.

"That's not true, Agent O'Connor. Don't lie to me!" His voice rose into an enraged screech, and I had to fight not to wince.

"I never lie to you, Adam," I informed him smoothly. I tried to let my tenor evince a level of calm I didn't remotely feel.

He jutted his chin out and pointed at me menacingly. "You just did."

"How did I lie to you?"

His brows pulled together in a furious scowl. "You just said Washington told you I was coming to see Zoey. I never told them that! You lied to me!"

I shook my head. "I never said they told me you were coming to see Miss Carmichael."

Walker hesitated, and I could almost see him replaying my words in his head. "Yes, you did. Stop trying to confuse me."

"No, Adam. I said they told me you were coming to New York. That's all I said."

"No, it isn't." But his anger faltered, and the timbre of his words gave away his uncertainty.

"Yes, it is, Adam."

"Well, then how did you know I was coming here? I didn't tell them. And I didn't call you."

I agreed. "No, you didn't call me."

"Are you reading my mind again?"

"No, Adam. I'm not reading your mind. I can't do that, remember? I've told you that before."

"What color am I thinking of right now?"

"Red, Adam." I was deliberately overusing his first name in the hopes that if I kept personalizing the conversation, he'd be less likely to fly off the handle. It didn't always work, but that didn't mean I wasn't going to try.

"See?" he shouted. He flailed his arms wildly, his movements quick and jerky. "See? You're reading my mind. I knew it. I knew you could do that."

I fought not to smile. "Adam. You always pick red when we play this game."

Walker became still and eyed me suspiciously. "Yeah?"

"And you get mad at me when I guess another color. Do you remember?"

"Yeah. Because I know you do it on purpose to make me think you can't read my mind. You try to trick me. But I'm onto you. Because I'm smarter than you are."

"That's right. And that's why I always answer you correctly. Because I know better than to try to trick you. What number am I thinking about right now?"

"Eight."

"That's right. So, maybe you can read my mind."

Walker laughed and relaxed a little. "No, Agent O'Connor. I can't read your mind."

"Are you sure? Maybe you're trying to trick me."

"I don't want to trick you, Agent O'Connor."

"Then why don't you tell me what you do want, Adam?"

Walker's frustration roared back to life, painted with broad swaths of sadness and desperation. He slammed the side of one fist against his thigh. "I want you to let me see my wife. Why won't you ever let me see my wife?"

I sighed heavily. I'd had hopes he hadn't progressed this far into his delusion just yet because there was no reasoning with him at this point in his fantasy, but clearly that'd been too much to ask.

"Adam, you're not married."

"You always say that. You always say it, and it's not true. I am married. And you're standing in the way of my happiness. Zoey and I belong together! She needs me. And I need her." His fingers were clenching and fluttering, and he kept shaking out his hands, which was an outward sign of his increased agitation. I had to force myself not to react, not to take a step back, even though my body was screaming at me in bold, underlined, italicized all caps to increase the distance between us.

"Adam, you and Miss Carmichael aren't married. I told you that the last time I saw you."

"You always say that. Every time you see me, you say that."

"And it's always true."

"It isn't true," he insisted. I couldn't tell whether he was trying to convince me or himself.

"Why would I lie to you, Adam?"

"You just want me all to yourself! That's why you lie to me. That's why you won't just let us be together. But I don't want you. I only want her. Why can't you just get the fuck out of here and leave us alone?" He pressed his hands to the sides of his head so hard I could see the strain in his arms.

I couldn't help it. I laughed out loud. He'd never said anything like that before, and the completely out-of-left-field idea had taken me by surprise.

Naturally, that was the absolute worst way for me to respond. Something not unlike comic surprise stole over Walker's features at the sound of my chuckles. His arms dropped heavily to his sides. Then his eyes narrowed, and his nostrils flared as he glared at me. "You're laughing."

Uh-oh. "I'm sorry, Adam. I didn't mean to."

"Why are you laughing at me?"

I briefly deliberated pointing out it was the very idea of me wanting him I'd found so gut-bustingly hilarious but decided against that much honesty. I'd probably do well to settle for only a small portion of the truth.

"I wasn't laughing at you, Adam. It's just that I don't date men."

He appeared to be considering that scenario. "You're a dyke," he said slowly.

I managed to restrain my chortle but only just. Something about his ultra-serious and yet at the same time wildly inappropriate characterization of me tickled me to no end. I nodded. "Yup. I'm a dyke."

Walker's eyes went wide as though something had just occurred to him. "You want her," he whispered, his voice a harsh, grating rasp.

Oh, no. Not good. I really hoped he wasn't implying what I thought he was implying, because if he thought I had any romantic designs on the supposed love of his life, he was likely to become really violent really quickly. I was definitely not in the mood for another hospital stay. I decided to confirm my suspicions before digging myself into an even deeper hole.

"Who do you think I want?"

"Zoey. Oh, my God! That's it! I can't believe I didn't see it before." He flailed his arms again and sort of paced back and forth in a small, two-step path. His fingers tore at his hair and scratched at his cheeks hard enough to leave red trails, though not quite hard enough to actually draw blood. Yet. "I can't believe I let you trick me. All this time." His voice trailed off into incoherent mutterings, and his eyes glazed over as he marched and ranted to himself.

I needed to regain his attention before he got himself even more worked up than he already was. Sometimes I could distract him and lead him in a different, less rage-filled direction. Another technique that didn't always work, but it was worth a shot.

"Adam, what animal am I thinking about right now?"

But he didn't appear to have heard me. At least, he didn't answer me directly. "That explains everything. Stupid, stupid, stupid." He punctuated each utterance of that word with a forceful smack to his own forehead.

"Adam, calm down. Tell me about the Giants' chances this season." At this point, I was just trying anything I could think of to get him to shift topics.

Walker continued to mutter to himself as though I hadn't even spoken. "That's why she was so insistent on keeping us apart. I never understood why…I didn't get it. But I get it now." He turned to face me, looking me directly in the eye. The cold fury I saw there sent an icy tendril of fear slithering down my spine and spiderwebbing abruptly outward once it reached my hips. "I get it now."

I pursed my lips as I watched him. This was unquestionably a new take on the situation, and I wasn't at all certain how to handle it. Up to a point, he and I'd been more or less wandering down a familiar path, our dialogue so established it could almost have been a script. I'd thought I'd known our destination as well as the roads we'd travel to get there. But then he'd taken this sudden sharp turn and jumped the proverbial shark, leaving me navigating unfamiliar waters and totally out of my element.

Distraction hadn't worked at all thus far, so maybe it was time to just engage him about his latest theory. "What do you get now, Adam?"

He favored me with a look of disbelief tainted with suspicion. "Why you would never let Zoey and me be together."

"Miss Carmichael can't be with you, Adam. She's with somebody else."

"Liar! Zoey would never cheat on me! Ever!" He went back to his enraged pacing.

I huffed and rolled my eyes. His refusal to remain grounded in reality as well as my own inability to get him to see reason was irksome. I could only put up with either for so long before I became frustrated.

"Adam. Miss Carmichael just got engaged. To somebody else. You know that."

Walker froze in his pacing and slowly turned his head to look at me. The gesture was so wooden I imagined I could hear the creaking of the tendons in his neck that accompanied the motion.

"What?" He spat the word at me as though he couldn't stand the taste of it, and he glanced at the ring finger of my left hand, presumably to confirm I wasn't wearing an engagement ring. Inwardly, I breathed a sigh of relief that I wore my rings on my middle fingers. I just hoped he'd take specific notice of the placement and not just see the adornment and jump to conclusions.

"It was all over the news and in the papers. Everyone was talking about it. You had to have seen it."

Walker shook his head, snorting in derision. "No. That was a hoax. A fake. To make them think she was one of them. She's infiltrating. It's all part of the plan."

Oh, boy. This was going to be good. "One of who?"

Walker's expression became full of uncertainty. He was obviously deliberating whether to tell me something. I waited as patiently as I was able, not wanting to push him too fast. Years of experience in dealing with him had taught me that forcing him to do or say something before he was ready never had the end result I wanted it to. And since he wasn't making any moves to enter Hurricane's apartment building, and there was no way Hannah was going to let Hurricane venture out here, the situation wasn't exactly dire. I didn't have a problem engaging Walker or moving at his pace for a little while longer. Besides, I was much better equipped to handle his conspiracy theories than his beliefs that I was cock-blocking him. Those, at least, I'd dealt with before.

Walker worried at his lower lip with his fingers as he evaluated me, and his eyes darted around as though searching for something. Or, more likely, someone. He was probably looking for evidence of "them," whoever they were. I held my breath, waiting to see what his reaction would be to the other agents on the street who were watching this drama unfold. If he noticed them at all, he must've deemed them unimportant because he didn't even blink.

"I can't tell you," he said finally, sounding truly sorry.

"Well, that's okay, Adam. I wouldn't want you to get into trouble for telling me something you shouldn't."

Walker beamed at me like a proud father. "You passed the test!"

Okay. I had no idea what the hell he was talking about. We were definitely off book now, and it didn't appear likely that we'd be returning to our regularly scheduled programming anytime soon. Damn. And I'd had such hopes, too. Oh, well. Time to improvise. Should I pretend I knew about the test or act surprised? Hmmm.

I decided to favor him with a secretive smile and incline my head slightly while lifting my hands in a careless gesture. He could interpret that pretty much any way he wanted.

"I knew you would, but I had to be sure." His tone was apologetic.

"Hey, don't worry about it. If anyone understands, it's me."

He nodded thoughtfully at my logic. With one last careful look to the left and right, he took a few steps toward me and entered my personal space, beckoning me to lean in so I'd be able to hear what he was about to tell me.

I never got the chance to hear what he had to say. Walker had just opened his mouth when he was unceremoniously tackled by a flying blur that moved too fast for me to see. I blinked, and when my eyes finally managed to shape the sight before me into a comprehensible image, I was utterly stunned and horrified to see Walker and Eric rolling around on the ground. Eric was yelling the usual commands we were taught in the academy—"Police," "Don't move," "Stop resisting"—as he struggled to get a now-writhing Walker under control.

Walker was bucking and thrashing violently, trying with everything he had to break free. The sounds coming out of his mouth were more like the incoherent roars of a wounded lion. Or at least what I imagined a wounded lion would sound like. Admittedly, I didn't have much of a real-world reference to back up that analogy.

Once I understood what I was seeing, I rolled my eyes and huffed as I threw my hands up in the air. I scowled and shot Rico a dark glare before I reached down to pull Eric and Walker apart. I had no earthly idea what'd made Eric suddenly decide he needed to let out his inner football player, and while I'd definitely be having a serious discussion with him about that later, now I needed to break this up before somebody got seriously hurt.

"Eric, stop it!" I managed to get one arm around his neck and slide the other underneath his arm to wrap around his chest, ignoring the tiny explosions of pain the move set off inside me. "What the hell?"

To my surprise, Eric didn't fight me. I'd sort of expected he would, or at the very least he'd ignore me in favor of continuing his current activity. Instead, he allowed me to yank him off Walker easily and favored me with a look of confusion once I'd gotten him back on his feet.

I shoved Eric back a step and angled myself so I'd be able to stop him if he went after Walker again. I might not've been prepared for it the first time, but I wasn't about to be caught off guard again.

I frowned at Eric and shook my head once, keeping one hand on his chest, trying to convey without words my sheer disappointment in his off-the-wall behavior. I didn't want to get into a discussion of tactics with him in front of the guy he'd more or less just assaulted, but I hoped he realized we'd be addressing the issue later and at great length.

As I had most of my attention focused on Eric, I didn't realize Walker had moved until it was too late. He'd popped back to a standing position almost immediately after Eric had, apparently. And in the blink of an eye, he'd moved to retaliate. He was startlingly adroit and agile for his size. I'd never have imagined a guy that big could move that fast. But move he did. Like a flash.

I, unfortunately, did not. Move like a flash, that is. At least not until it was too late to completely evade what was coming my way. Oh, sure, I tried. Sort of. My reflexes would never have allowed me to do otherwise. I might've even managed to come out of the encounter completely unscathed, too, if Eric hadn't been standing so near to me as to nullify my preferred avenue of escape. But close only counts in horseshoes and hand grenades. It definitely doesn't count when you're trying to avoid getting knocked upside the head.

Out of my peripheral vision, I caught the motion of Walker's punch at the last nanosecond. Long enough to think, *Oh, shit*, and not much else. I think he was probably aiming for Eric, but at that point, I doubt it really mattered much to him that I was standing more or less in between them.

Walker was right-handed, which meant that, naturally, the big, winding roundhouse he threw in our direction came from his right hand. Unfortunately for me, that's the side I was standing on. And since I'd just had to make myself a physical buffer between Walker and Eric, that meant the blow would hit me long before it got to what I presumed was the intended target. Because that's just the kind of luck I had.

Realizing that scrambling out of his reach wouldn't work out well for me—not when I'd only be crashing into Eric, effectively trapping me literally between the oft-talked-about rock and a hard place—and that ducking would result in having my almost-completely-healed left eyebrow split wide open instead of my jaw, I opted for the only course of alternative course of action I could come up with: I stepped into the punch.

As I took a step forward, my left arm came up in an attempt to deflect some of the brunt of the strike. It worked somewhat. I mean, he caught me with a glancing blow of his gargantuan, meaty fist on the back of the head, behind my left ear, but it could've been worse. The stars I saw directly after the contact were only white. They weren't glittery or anything. If I'd taken the full brunt of his punch, I imagined they'd be bigger and sparklier and probably singing and entertaining me with a well-choreographed dance number. At least until I lost consciousness.

Walker's mouth formed a comical-looking "O" of surprise that I saw for the briefest of instants as I took him to the ground, having hooked my right foot behind his and kicked back against his Achilles tendon with the heel of my shoe. Hard. Between the leg sweep knocking his foot out from under him and the driving momentum of both my hands against his shoulder, he had no choice but to fall.

He landed on his back with a resounding thud that practically shook the leaves off the nearby trees, and I wasted no time clambering up his body so I could kneel on his shoulder with my left knee, effectively pinning him to the ground. This didn't sit well with Walker at all, and he took up his incoherent roaring again as he thrashed and kicked, attempting to break free.

"Adam, stop resisting, stop resisting," I told him as I wrestled his arm between my thighs and torqued it back against the right one in such a way that I was exerting pressure against his elbow, pushing it in the direction elbows weren't meant to bend. Not hard enough to do any lasting damage, but enough to send the clear message that I could if I wanted to. And I would if he didn't stop fighting me.

It took a lot longer to describe that than it actually did to do it. I'd wager the whole thing probably took about four seconds. I'd barely had time to get Walker relatively under control before Rico, Austin, and PJ jumped in. As Rico was closer than the other two, he'd immediately taken up a mirroring position with Walker's left arm, and, if the angry look on his face and Walker's subsequent howl were any indication, he'd been a lot less gentle in wrangling it into position than I'd been.

Despite the fact that Rico and I were basically poised to dislocate both of his elbows, Walker still continued to struggle. His face was an alarming shade of red and contorted into such a snarling expression of rage that I felt slimy vines of fear wind their way into my very soul. He continued to undulate, bucking his hips and lashing out at everything and anything with his legs.

For all the times Walker had flipped out on me over the years—and those times were too numerous to count—I'd never once seen him look even half as crazed as he did right now. He was gnashing his teeth and had turned his head so he could try to bite me, all the while calling me every filthy name I'd ever heard and a few I hadn't. I'll admit, I was mildly impressed with his vocabulary. If the insults hadn't been backed by as much pure anger as they were, I undoubtedly would've found them hilarious. Now, however, I was filled with a growing sense of unease.

The five of us—Allison, Tuck, and Marissa had wisely taken up strategic positions on either end of our brawl to watch our surroundings for us so we wouldn't be blindsided by something or someone unexpected rolling up on us while we were preoccupied—rolled Walker over onto his stomach, handcuffed him, and then shoved him into the back of Rico's car quicker than you can say seventy-two-hour hold.

Once inside, he'd immediately flopped onto his back on the backseat and attempted to kick the rear passenger window out of the car with both his feet, which I think would've worked a lot better if the door had actually been completely shut. As it was, all he did was manage to kick to door back open to PJ, who caught it and cursed. The move earned him a swift jab to the outside of his thigh with the butt of a baton and a set of industrial-strength zip ties binding his feet together. Then Rico and Austin had to fight with him to get him seat-belted into place so he wouldn't be able to try that again.

When they finally shut the door on him and his mad rantings about how I'd set him up and he was going to get me for this if it was the last thing he ever did, I let out a shaky breath and sagged bodily against the trunk of the car. Now that the situation was relatively under control, the adrenaline had worn off, and with it went my imperviousness to pain. My head was throbbing like a demolition derby was taking place inside my skull, and all of my not-quite-healed wounds were screaming at me in languages I'd never even heard of. I tried to ignore them.

"You okay?" Allison asked lightly, concern etched onto her face in broad, Technicolor strokes. She rested a gentle hand on my upper arm as she studied me.

"Yeah, I'm fine," I said through gritted teeth as I tried to keep my breathing even.

"Let me see."

"Allison, really, I'm fine." I tried to jerk away from the hands she'd extended my way, but the move reignited the stars that'd just stopped dancing in my periphery.

"I'm sure you are," she replied smoothly, unfazed by my attitude. "Just let me look."

"Yeah, O'Connor," Rico chimed in. "You got pounded pretty hard back there."

"Really?" I said to him. "You, too?"

"Let her look," Rico said. "You know Paige is going to kick my ass if I just take your word for it that you're okay."

I rolled my eyes and followed Allison's finger as she waved it back and forth in front of my eyes. I tried not to blink too much when she shone a tiny penlight into each eye. And I dutifully if a little balefully held still so she could examine the knot growing behind my ear. I tried not to wince, but I'm afraid I failed. Even though I was looking at Allison, I was directing my words at Rico. "Did you ever think of just not telling your wife about every little thing that happens?"

"I have, actually," Rico replied, sounding amused. "But the woman's kind of hard to resist."

"She also has your balls in her purse."

"That, too."

"So, what do you think, Doc?" I asked Allison softly, staring into her eyes. "Am I gonna live?"

"You'd better," she murmured back, brushing my hair back off my face.

"Let me see," Rico interrupted, pushing Allison out of the way to prod at me himself.

"Ow!" I slapped at his arm. "What the hell? That hurts!"

Rico stopped his probing and grinned, hooking his thumbs into the front pockets of his jeans. He shrugged. "I just wanted to be able to accurately describe the size of that knot when I'm retelling the story. The devil's in the details, baby. You taught me that."

I shook my head at him before the searing stabs of pain forced me to stop. And then I turned to Eric, who was standing a few feet away from us, quieter than I'd ever seen him. Normally, he wore an air of cockiness that wafted off him like too much bathroom-vending-machine cologne, but at the moment he just looked defeated.

"What happened?" I asked him.

Out of the corner of my eye, I saw Rico open his mouth to chime in, but I put a restraining hand on his arm. The way I figured it, Rico could tear him a new one later if he wanted to, when they were alone somewhere. Rico, as the backup of the Counterfeit Squad, was nestled in the middle of Eric's chain of command, so he'd be well within his rights to do so. Now, on the street and in front of four other coworkers, wasn't the time.

Eric ducked his head and scuffed the toe of his boot on the ground like a scolded child. "I thought he was taking a run at you," he mumbled.

"What?"

Eric took a deep breath and tipped his head up slightly, favoring me with fleeting traces of eye contact. "When he stepped toward you that last time, I thought he was getting ready to assault you. He looked like he was reaching for your head."

I nodded. I'd suspected as much, but I'd still wanted him to confirm it. And what could I really say to that? More than half of police work involved split-second judgment calls. If I'd been in his shoes and that'd been my interpretation of the situation, I might've jumped in to save another agent a certain ass-whooping, too. Okay, I probably wouldn't have literally jumped in until after the brawling had started just so I could be positive I wasn't making a mistake like the one Eric had just made, but different strokes, I supposed.

I shared a meaningful look with Rico, punctuated by the wild screams of the man under discussion. The whole car rocked with his frantic attempts to get free from his seat belt. With as big as he was and his hands cuffed behind him the way they were, he couldn't twist around far enough to reach the mechanism to unfasten it, and he was showing his displeasure loudly and with extreme prejudice.

"I've never seen him this wound up," Austin confessed, reholstering his phone. I assumed he'd just briefed Mark and the two-to-ten supervisor on what'd happened out here, but I didn't care enough to ask.

"Me, either," I said, massaging my right temple absently in an attempt to assuage the massive headache collecting behind my eyes. "On the bright side, I can't imagine Bellevue's going to have any problem taking him."

"Is that where we're headed?" PJ wanted to know.

"That's where *we're* headed," I said, indicating Rico and Eric with a wave of my hand. "You two are headed home to get some sleep."

"Are you sure you guys have got this?" Austin asked. He looked and sounded exhausted, but I knew he wouldn't leave until he was practically ordered to go.

"We're good. I'll see you guys tomorrow."

As they ambled off, I turned to Rico and Eric. "You two want to transport him? I doubt he'd be particularly receptive to my presence at the moment."

"No problem," Rico replied.

"Good. I'll follow you guys over and call the ER so they know we're on our way in." I refocused my attention on Tuck and Marissa, who were waiting patiently next to their Suburban.

"Christ, Ryan," Tuck murmured, shaking his head.

I wasn't in the mood. My head felt like it was literally being cleaved in two. My shoulder was on fire. And the way my shirt was sticking to me made me suspect I'd popped a couple of the stitches on my back. Either that, or I was sweating a lot more than I'd realized. I was strangely both wired and utterly spent. And my night was probably only about half over. I still had to take Walker to the hospital and get him committed and then make about a million notification phone calls to everybody in the free world and their grandmother. I doubted I'd get to bed much before two, and I was pretty damn surly about it. Especially since it meant I wouldn't get to spend any quality time with Allison. Although, on the bright side, that did mean a delay of my inevitable descent into a nightmare. And who knew? Maybe I'd be too tired after all this excitement to dream at all. A girl could hope, right?

"Can you do me a favor and call Hannah for me?" I asked Tuck. "Tell her we've got him, and we're taking him to Bellevue. She can hit me up tomorrow for the specifics if she wants."

"Sure thing. You're going to take him to the hospital now? Why not let those other two guys handle it?"

I sighed as I walked past him toward my car. "Because apparently there's no rest for the wicked."

CHAPTER FOURTEEN

I'd been so off in my estimation about my bedtime it was tragic. By the time I'd finished up with Walker at the hospital—as well as with my own checkup because somebody who shall remain nameless but looked fantastic in a business suit and a concerned scowl couldn't wait to tell the doctor I'd been clocked and should be checked over—and called the whole thing in to DC so they'd be in the loop, it was just shy of three a.m.

If Allison hadn't been in town, I'd have gone straight home and crawled exhaustedly into bed. Actually, I'd suggested that she come home and crawl into bed with me, but she'd declined. Apparently, she seemed to think trying to get any sleep was foolish since she had to be at the train station in about two hours, and I wasn't about to let her sit up somewhere by herself. Which is how I found myself across from her at a diner in Midtown killing time before she was scheduled to depart.

"You sure you won't get into trouble?" I asked for probably the third time, trying unsuccessfully to stifle a yawn. I stirred my coffee, unsure whether I'd already added sugar or whether that'd been what I'd been about to do. I frowned at my cup as I tried to make a determination.

"You sure you want to drink that?" Allison asked before taking a sip from her own mug.

"Huh?" I blinked at her wearily.

She motioned with one hand, keeping the other wrapped completely around her drink. "You didn't order decaf."

I made a face. "Of course not. I hate decaf."

"One might think you're trying to ensure that you don't sleep."

"I'm more worried about you not sleeping. *You* actually have to go to work today."

"Oh, who are you kidding? You'll go in anyway. Apparently medical leave isn't a thing to you."

"Probably. But I can go in whenever I want. If I want. Or I can stay home. You're scheduled to report in."

Allison pursed her lips and narrowed her eyes for a moment. "It's cute how you think you can get away with changing the subject."

"What subject? I didn't realize we had landed on anything yet."

She smirked at me and shook her head. "Okay. You want me to be direct? How's this? Are you finally ready to talk to me about your nightmares?"

I sighed and rubbed my eyes with the pads of my fingers. We'd been over this several times when I'd awoken in various states of distress in the hospital, and I didn't want to get into it with her any more now than I had then. But I'd promised myself I'd tell her everything. I just wished it didn't have to be right this instant.

"I'm sure you can imagine what they're about," I said finally, my voice low. My stomach writhed like something alive inside me, and my mouth was suddenly dry. I tried to swallow reflexively, but the action was uncomfortable.

"Lucia dying."

"Yeah. They don't start that way, but they all end up there. No matter what I do."

"Why didn't you tell me she was dead?" Allison asked after a long moment. Her voice held the tenor of so many different emotions, I was almost distracted from her words by her tone. But after a beat, they sank in.

My head shot up, and I noticed that she had carefully arranged her face into the neutral mask she always donned when she didn't want to appear upset. The one she always adopted when I hurt her. "What?"

"Lucia. You never told me she was there. You never told me she died."

I furrowed my brow. "I…I thought you knew. I thought everybody knew. It was all over the news. And the gossip in the agency is rampant. I just assumed…" Had she really not known? Was that why she'd been so distant? Because she'd thought I was keeping that from her?

"And I was on a plane home from Hong Kong, and then I was

in your hospital room. I never even turned on the TV. So, no. I didn't know."

"I'm sorry. I wasn't trying to keep it a secret. I just…didn't really want to talk about it."

"Because she was your ex?"

I shook my head and took a deep breath. This was it. Fuck. I wasn't ready for this. I didn't think I'd ever be ready for this, but somehow I'd thought the revelation would come under different circumstances. I should've known better.

"Because I feel like it's my fault she's dead. And it's only because of her that I'm even alive."

The words fell from my lips almost absently, and dimly I noted how hollow my voice sounded as I said that. It'd just occurred to me that I'd only ever admitted that out loud to Rory before, which almost didn't count because we were sisters, and that'd made the admission safe. It unsettled me how easy it'd been to disclose that fact to Allison. For all the agony the concept had caused, I felt it should've been more difficult for me to say.

"What are you talking about?"

I glanced around the nearly empty diner. Nobody appeared to be paying any attention to us, and I was grateful for that. I figured this part really would be easier to show than it would be to tell. I shimmied my way slowly out of my side of the booth, gritting my teeth and holding my breath in an attempt to keep the pain from showing on my face. When I finally made it into the aisle, I held out a hand to her.

Allison eyed my hand warily for a second before glancing back up at me. "What's this for?"

"Stand up for a minute?"

"You're not asking me to dance, are you? Because that'd be a weird way to try to change the subject. Even for you."

I couldn't help smiling, despite the seriousness of the conversation. "No. I'm not asking you to dance." When she still didn't move, I rolled my eyes. "Please? It'll only take a second."

With a tiny huff, Allison took my hand and extracted herself from behind the table. "Okay, now what?"

I positioned myself so we were standing face-to-face roughly the same distance Lucia and I had been before everything had gone to hell. My hands were trembling slightly as I rested them on her shoulders.

Allowing my fingers to caress them lightly for a moment, I pushed down on her. Not hard. Just enough to convey my wishes. And when she didn't react right away, I was forced to explain.

"You're taller than Luce is." I cringed as I realized what I'd just said. "Was." I corrected myself thickly. "You're taller than Luce was."

Allison's eyes flooded with understanding, and she bent her knees until I'd stopped exerting pressure on her. I swallowed hard and took a deep breath.

My emotions lately had been as rough and changeable as the ocean during a hurricane, with ebbs and flows that seemingly had no pattern and left me vaguely breathless. I'd been paying close attention to the cycle over the past few days, and while I might not have been able to predict exactly when the shifts were going to happen, I'd certainly been able to recognize when one was looming. I could feel that by-now-familiar building of sentiment gathering inside me like an oncoming storm. I was afraid of where this particular wave might carry me.

"If we were alone, I'd have taken my shirt off for this," I told her, trying to lighten the mood. The joke landed flat and leaden between us, and I took a deep, shaky breath, swallowing the rancid taste that coated the back of my tongue.

I took her left hand in mine and balled it up into a fist. Then I maneuvered it so her knuckles were resting along the right side of my jaw. Her eyes were once again boring into mine, and the eddying emotions I saw there led me to believe she'd already deduced exactly where this little demonstration was going.

Holding her fist to my jaw, I leaned to my left, mimicking the chain of events that'd followed Lucia's punch in super slow motion. When I'd reached what I figured was roughly the right position, I stopped.

The atmosphere between us was heavy, and I was having trouble breathing. The surge of emotions churning inside me was quickly becoming overwhelming. Still holding her fist against my chin with my right hand, I started tracing gentle circles on the skin of her neck with my left. I didn't tell her I was marking the place where the bullet had torn Lucia's life away from her. I didn't have to. The expression on Allison's face said it all. She knew.

Unable to stand the intensity of the moment for even another instant, I abruptly pulled back and scrambled to retake my seat, hissing at the little bursts of agony my haste ignited. I went back to absently stirring my coffee, blinking against the scratchiness in the backs of my eyes, as I waited for her to say something.

After a long moment, she finally sat back down across from me. I held my breath and stared into my cup until she folded her hands over mine. I swallowed hard and looked up at her from underneath my lashes without lifting my head.

Allison's face was brimming with sympathy and something else I couldn't quite grasp but which made my intestines squirmy and knotted. I couldn't clench my hands because she was holding them, so I started wiggling my toes instead. Anything to burn off some of this tension.

"That was an unfortunate coincidence, Ryan," Allison murmured softly.

I lifted my left shoulder in a half shrug. "Whatever you call it, it still makes me feel like shit."

"I suppose throwing out the term 'survivor's guilt' won't do much for you?"

I smiled a little at that. "No. But it was a nice try."

Allison sighed and started tracing light patterns on the backs of my hands and forearms with her fingertips, making me shiver. "We're only responsible for our own actions."

I tilted my head and gave her what I hoped was a quizzical look.

"You didn't pull that trigger. You can blame Lucia's death only on the person who did."

I sagged a little in my seat. "In my head, I get that…"

"But it doesn't make you feel any better."

I shook my head. "Not even a little bit."

She studied me for another long moment. "There's something else, isn't there? Something else you're not telling me about what happened?"

I scowled at her. "Okay, you seriously need to tell me how you keep doing that. Are you psychic or something? A cyborg? Do you have access to some sort of machine that's watching me every hour of every day?"

Allison raised an eyebrow at me, and one corner of her mouth lifted in a small smirk. "Like I said before, cute. But it's still not going to work."

I gently took back my hands and started scraping my nails one at a time against the creases in my fingers. My pulse was hammering, and my nerves rattled and shook, which made my hands tremble. This was the part I'd been afraid to tell her, the part I had no idea how to even begin to convey. I chewed at my lips as I considered. "Luce was working at the time of the…incident." I smirked bitterly to myself at the moniker, unsure whether I'd just used it ironically or whether I'd simply been unable to call it what it really was. "She'd replaced another Intel detective who'd had to leave."

Allison nodded slowly. "I'd already sort of figured that."

"She'd left the Intel car to come return my phone."

I left the words to hang in the air for a long moment, hoping Allison would grasp the implication and not actually make me utter the words. I wasn't disappointed. After frowning for a second, her eyes grew wide, and she gasped softly. She sat back in her seat with a stunned expression.

"She's the one who had your phone?"

I nodded. "Mmm-hmm."

Allison closed her eyes, lifted one hand to her temple, and started rubbing small circles. My heart cracked at the sight. "She read the text message, didn't she? The one I'd sent you after we…?"

"Yeah," I said softly.

"That's why she came back to talk to you," Allison said, sounding more like she was talking to herself than to me. "That's how your phone got broken. That's why she punched you. She was pissed we'd slept together."

"Yeah," I said again, trying to ignore the violent swirling that'd started low in my gut. I was on the verge of moving around to Allison's side of the booth to put my arm around her when she opened her eyes, pinning me in place.

"That's what you didn't want me to know."

I nodded silently.

"Because you blame me for what happened?"

I was stunned. "No! Of course not. Because I didn't want you to blame yourself. I was…I was trying to protect you," I said lamely.

Allison's face was a mask again, and when she spoke, her voice had been carefully stripped of all emotion. "I don't know if you've noticed, but I'm a big girl. I can take care of myself."

"I know you can. But I can take care of you, too."

She lapsed back into brooding silence, only moving occasionally to sip her tea. Since I'd just dropped a huge bomb on her, I was reluctant to intrude on whatever her thoughts might have been. I merely drank my coffee and watched her warily, trying to turn her own mind-reading trick around on her to figure out what she was going to say or do next.

"Is that it?" she asked finally, startling me out of my own reverie.

"Huh?"

"Is that everything you've been keeping from me?"

Inwardly, I bristled at her chosen phrasing, but I didn't have the energy to argue with her about semantics. "That's everything."

"Okay."

"Is that why you've been not-mad at me?" I was unable to resist asking. "Because you felt like I was keeping things from you?"

"You mean because you *were* keeping things from me? Yes. And I told you before, I was more hurt than mad."

"I'm sorry. You're right. I should've told you sooner."

She took my free hand in both of hers, a faint smile ghosting across her lips. "I get why you didn't. I do. But that doesn't mean I have to like it."

"No. I wouldn't expect you to. I don't like it when you keep stuff from me, either." My words were deliberately light, but inside I was praying she'd realize I was referring to her situation with her boss and take the opportunity to open up to me.

No such luck. She tilted her head and eyed me playfully. "Well, then, we have to stop keeping stuff from one another."

I had a heavy, sinking feeling and wanted to roll my eyes at her, though I wasn't sure if was deflecting or whether she really hadn't picked up on my hint. So much for the subtle approach. Guess I was going to have to take a page out of her book and go the direct route, after softening her up a bit. No need to kill her good mood right this second. "We do."

"All kidding aside, we need to talk more, Ryan. In general. If this thing between us is going to work, we need to start being honest with one another. About everything."

"Everything, huh?"

"Mmm-hmm. Everything."

"You're sure about that."

"Absolutely."

"So, you want to hear that I'd rather shove hot marshmallow

skewers directly into my eyeballs than watch *The Notebook* with you even one more time?" I'd gotten a huge kick out of discovering that she was a hard-core, closet romantic. It'd seemed so at odds with her public persona, and I'd found it unbelievably endearing, even if it did mean I had to suffer through movies I normally wouldn't have been caught dead watching.

Allison chuckled. "Well…"

"And you seriously want to endure the look on my face when you finally 'fess up to the fact that you actually hate cherry topping on your cheesecake, and you only ever order it to share with me because you know I like it?"

Allison drew back to fix me with an astonished look. "You knew about that?"

"I've told you before. I'm a trained criminal investigator."

"Point taken," she said with a small, affectionate smile. "Maybe there are some things we can lie about."

"Good. Because I really didn't want to get into the whole issue I have with your cat." I shot her a grin.

Allison's eyes narrowed, and she pinned me with a dark glare. "What's wrong with my cat?"

"See? Some secrets are good." I hesitated, a little nervous about seguing into the next topic. But since she clearly wasn't about to confess on her own, it was up to me to prompt her. "But in the interest of talking more and being honest with one another, do you want to tell me what's really going on with your boss?"

Allison tensed beside me and suddenly became inordinately interested in studying her silverware where it rested on the table beside her saucer. My heart seized as I wondered whether I'd crossed a line. I didn't know what was going on down there on PPD, but her body language told me it definitely wasn't anything good. In fact, I suspected it might even be worse than I'd originally feared. I ached to help her but was afraid there was nothing I could do. And I definitely wouldn't be able to offer any assistance if I didn't even understand the problem. I waited somewhat patiently for her reply.

"We had a difference of opinion," she said finally, still refusing to meet my eyes.

"About what?"

A brief pause, as though she were choosing her words carefully. "About me coming home to New York after you were shot."

I sat back in the booth as far as I could, completely stunned by her answer. "You mean because you were in the middle of an advance?"

She nodded, gaze still locked anywhere but on me.

I frowned. "But...I mean, apparently everybody knew, so..." I didn't even know how to finish that thought.

Allison shrugged. "Yeah, well, I guess that didn't really matter."

My frown deepened, and I shook my head. "There has to be more to it than that."

Allison glanced at her watch, and her expression was apologetic when she finally looked at me. "There is. Unfortunately, we don't have time to get into it. Not tonight. I have a train to catch."

I wanted to argue with her, wanted to point out that she was the one who'd been touting the need for complete disclosure in our relationship, but that would've been futile. If she had to go, she had to go. I glanced at my own watch and sighed.

"Okay," I replied finally. "But the next time I see you, I'm going to get you a cheesecake with blueberry topping, and you're going to tell me everything."

Allison's smile was back. "Deal." She stood and threw a handful of crumpled bills on the table before extending a hand in my direction. "Walk me to my train?"

I took her hand and allowed her to help me to my feet, smiling back at her. "I can't think of anything I'd like more."

CHAPTER FIFTEEN

After seeing Allison to her train, I was finally able to answer the sweet siren call of sleep. Unfortunately, I was wrong in my obviously misplaced hope that I'd be able to have just one night dream free. That definitely did not happen.

No sooner had my head hit the pillow than I was back on that cursed street corner in the city, staring at a bunch of empty motorcade cars. At least this time I knew I was dreaming. That was something. But that didn't appear to influence the conversational flow of the dream, which, I assumed later, is why I spent the majority of it standing on said street corner engaging in an inscrutable discussion about the interconnectedness of life's events and how they all came back to trust in the end. And it also didn't stop me from awakening with a cry, tears of frustration rolling down my cheeks at my inability to save Lucia. Again.

Naturally, by the time I dragged myself out of bed the next day, I was a total wreck. Exhausted, I looked like I'd fit in perfectly with the extras of any zombie movie currently in production without a trip to makeup. If Jamie could've seen me, she no doubt would've made a sarcastic comment, but I was so tired I couldn't have formulated a witty reply. And you know things are serious when I don't have the energy to be sardonic.

Cursing myself for not talking to Rory during our lengthy early dinner about getting my hands on something to force me into unconsciousness—a sledgehammer came immediately to mind—I booted up my computer and set my brain to going over the recent subpoena responses. The ones I hadn't been able to even glance at because Walker had decided to come back to town.

First were the records for Akbari's new cell phone, the one he'd given Meaghan and me the number to the Thursday night we'd first interviewed him. Beginning there would make it easier for me to keep track of the trail that way.

Even before I'd asked Greg to subpoena those phone records, I knew it'd been a burner phone. Now I was hoping that all the numbers these records provided me weren't to burner phones as well. That'd make my job ten times more difficult, and I simply didn't have the energy for that.

I was extremely interested in learning who—if anyone—Akbari had called immediately following our departure. If the theory that Rico and I'd hammered out held any water, it was likely Akbari had told someone I'd been to speak to him. And as I'd left him my business card, it wouldn't have been difficult for him to pass my name and description along to whoever he was working for.

Aha. According to the time stamp on the call logs, Akbari had called someone from his burner phone barely two minutes after we'd left. And surprise of surprises, the number he'd called was the one I'd gotten from the JTTF database for Fallahi. I hadn't expected that. Interesting.

I pushed the paperwork pertaining to Akbari's records to one side and shuffled through the reports I'd gotten back on Fallahi, looking for the date of the interview. It didn't take long to locate the call from Akbari. I wanted to see who Fallahi had called immediately after.

His first call had been to Golzar. I'd known they were associated with one another, as well. I just wasn't sure how I felt about the fact that it was now starting to look like they all knew about me. Obviously, if recent events were any indication, being on the radar of suspected terrorists didn't generally work out well. And if I had in fact been the intended target of that assassination attempt—and it was looking more and more like I had—somebody would want to finish the job. And soon.

Pushing that notion—and the bile that rose along with it—aside, I shifted my attention to Golzar's phone records. I quickly located the call from Fallahi and jotted down the number of the phone he'd called immediately after. It didn't match up to Golzar's most frequently called numbers, so it wasn't someone he spoke to often enough to have garnered my attention before. But whoever it was had it now.

Just out of curiosity, I took all three sets of records and flipped forward a few days to the day I'd been shot. Akbari's and Fallahi's phones each had a couple of calls, but not to any numbers I recognized and not during any time periods that had any specific resonance for me. Golzar's records, on the other hand, were a completely different story.

I knew from the call logs of my own agency-issued cell phone roughly what time the first shots had rung out, as the last call I'd gotten prior to the shooting had been from Allison. That time was now seared into my brain, which made it easy for me to scour the page for the exact moments I wanted. There, practically jumping off the paper, were two telephone calls placed back to back. Each one had lasted less than thirty seconds, and they'd both been made approximately ten minutes before the first shot had been fired. The first number was an incoming call from the number Golzar had called the night of the Akbari interview. The second was an outgoing call to a number I didn't recognize. I didn't yet know who either number belonged to, but I was willing to bet one of them was the shooter.

I conducted as many database searches on those two phone numbers as I could but determined only that the numbers were registered to burner phones, and none of the systems I had access to at the Secret Service office had any record of either. I intended to scour the JTTF databases for both numbers just to exhaust all possible leads, but I also didn't expect to find any answers there. That prompted me to speed up the process.

I shot Greg a quick email explaining what I'd found and asking him to issue follow-up subpoenas for the two unknown phone numbers Golzar had called the day I'd been shot. On a whim, I also asked him to request cell-tower information for both. Maybe learning where the callers had been when Golzar had spoken to them would give me a better idea of their identities. I fully expected to get bullshit names and addresses when the records came back, so what towers the phones had pinged off would likely be my only viable clue. It wouldn't be much, but it would be better than nothing.

Greg emailed me back immediately to let me know he was on it and would get it rushed through. I thanked him profusely, though waiting frustrated me.

I sighed as I clicked the button on my mouse to close the message and leaned back in my chair. My eyes roved over the contents of my office as my mind raced. I needed to find something else to do to keep me from going crazy. Sitting here with nothing to do but think was only going to—

My thoughts seized, then shuddered and lurched in a new direction as my eyes fell on the two cell phones perched innocently on the edge of my desk. The corners of my mouth curled up in the beginnings of a grin.

A phone call. Of course. I don't know why I hadn't thought of that before. It was the oldest trick in the book and one I'd used on several occasions. It didn't always work, of course. Nothing in life ever did. But if I called either of the two numbers I might get whoever answered the phone to slip and give me a name or something to go on. If it didn't work, well, I was no worse off than before.

I licked my lips in anticipation and picked up my work cell phone, the number of which was always blocked from anyone's caller ID. My insides fluttered as I dialed the first unknown number, the one Golzar had called the night I'd spoken to Akbari. I'd decided I'd use my well-tested GEICO representative ruse in my fishing expedition, which had been successful in the past.

As the first traces of ringing from the other end of the line floated through the speaker to my ear, I got up and strode over to my door, intent upon closing it. It was late, and the office was practically deserted, but I still felt like I wanted as much privacy as I could get for this.

I reached the doorway to my office by the end of the third ring and had started easing it shut as the fourth started up. Out of my other ear—the one not pressed against my cell phone—I could hear the shrill ring tones of someone else's cell phone wafting out of an office down the hall. That made me glad I'd decided to close my door. Apparently, the privacy would be more necessary than I'd originally thought.

"Hello?" a gruff male voice finally answered.

I blinked at the unexpected phenomenon of hearing a voice say the same thing down the hall. I pulled the phone a few inches from my ear and strained to listen.

"Hello?" the voice said again, sounding more irritated this time.

Again, I heard the voice come through the speaker a fraction of a second after I heard someone say the same thing down the hall. Feeling vaguely uneasy and unbelievably confused, I hung up.

Frowning, I held up my cell phone in front of me and stared at it, as if waiting for it to explain to me what'd just happened. Light wisps of dread had started winding around my internal organs, sparking a chill deep inside the marrow of my bones.

My heart pounded as I crept down the hall toward where I'd thought I'd heard the voice. My mind was screaming something at me, loudly and using many expletives, but I was ignoring whatever it was trying to say as I concentrated on making my way as silently as possible.

When I was close enough, I leaned back against the wall and slowly pressed the redial button with a trembling thumb. My heart was thudding violently, and my breathing was ragged. I opened my mouth and took slow, deep, and hopefully silent breaths.

The ringing started again, both in the office and through the speaker of my cell phone. Once. Twice. A thir—

"Hello?"

My heart stopped and plummeted, landing with an impressive splat in my gut. The rest of my body began trembling right along with my thumb, and bile rose in the back of my throat. I attempted to both insist upon and deny what I now knew to be true.

"Hello?" the voice barked again, causing me to cringe.

Hastily, I pressed the "call end" button with my thumb and stood frozen as the owner of the cell phone muttered angrily about butt dialing and telemarketers.

I continued to stand there, rooted in place, for what felt like an eternity as I tried to force my mind to accept what'd just happened. I knew who that voice and that phone belonged to. And no amount of mental gymnastics or logical argument could change it or make me unknow it. My world slowly started to crumble.

I knew whose pocket that burner cell phone was sitting in even as I lurked outside his office door.

I now knew who Golzar had called that night.

I now knew who tried to have me killed.

My boss. Assistant to the Special Agent in Charge Mark Jennings.

Holy. Fucking. Shit.

CHAPTER SIXTEEN

As quickly and as quietly as I possibly could, I fled back to my office, terrified and desperate. My feelings decreased only marginally when I reached my office and silently shut the door.

Okay, don't panic. Don't panic. Don't panic. I leaned against the door and took a deep, shaky breath as I tried to will my traitorous heart to slow down from its gallop. Trembling badly, I wasn't surprised when my legs gave out, and I slumped down to the floor.

Reaching up behind my head, I thumbed the deadbolt. I'd have felt a million times better if I'd had my gun, but I still wasn't back to full duty, so I wasn't allowed to carry it. Did my dad have it at his house, or had he moved it to the safe in his office? Not that it mattered much. No way was I going to chance the journey up to Mahogany Row, where all the big bosses sat, in order to retrieve it. Not when I couldn't be 100 percent positive that Mark wasn't lying in wait for me somewhere out there.

Merely thinking of him made the adrenaline spike painfully in my system again, and I shook even worse. I pulled my knees up to my chest and wrapped my arms around them, ducking my head. I closed my eyes.

Ten seconds, I told myself firmly. *You can have ten seconds to freak the fuck out. And then you really need to get your ass in gear and take some sort of action.*

I inhaled deeply, slowly counting out five languid beats. Then I paused for an instant and exhaled as completely as possible, counting the remaining five seconds of allotted break-down time. When that was over, I repeated the process, rationalizing that twenty seconds wasn't too much to ask.

Mental disintegration put on hold for the time being, I crawled over to my desk and hid on the floor behind it. Part of me felt like an idiot, cowering the way I was, but the majority of me agreed that if a man—a federal agent, no less—could order a hit on one of his own employees, then logic was clearly out the window, and the notion of an office murder was possible.

Frowning, I reflected on Mark's behavior the past few weeks and saw each interaction in a new light. His demand to know why I'd been on Utica Avenue the night I'd interviewed Akbari. His fishing for further information regarding the subsequent investigation. His insistence that I keep him in the loop on the case's progression. His sudden appearances at my office during the oddest times, only to look surprised to find it occupied. His rooting through my desk the other night in search of some mysterious object. When I'd thought about it— which, truthfully, hadn't been either deeply or often—I'd dismissed his actions as part of his latest campaign to get me fired or have me transferred out of his squad. Now, however, when played against the backdrop of what I knew, all those scenes took on a much more sinister connotation.

Now that I knew more or less the who behind the assassination attempt, I needed to figure out the why. I chewed on my lower lip and rested my chin in the palm of my hand as my mind worked furiously to try to come up with a possible motive. I mean, I knew Mark hated me, but to actually want me dead? That seemed like overkill. Pun intended.

I pulled the phone records from Golzar's phone from my desk down into my lap and began to sift through them, looking at the other days I'd previously ignored. I wasn't particularly surprised to see the number I now knew to be Mark's frequently peppered into Golzar's call logs. Clearly, the two had a relationship of some kind. And, according to the records I'd subpoenaed, it'd been going on for quite a while. Before the Akbari interview even. What the hell?

I tried to come up with something, anything, that could possibly tie them to one another, because based on what I was reading in these records, their relationship definitely hadn't started because of me. I kept chewing on my lower lip as I thought, considering and then discarding one inane theory after another.

The counterfeit connection seemed to be the most plausible link. Golzar had long been suspected of financing a good deal of his activities through the sale of counterfeit currency. We'd never been able to make that charge stick before because the AUSAs in New York seemed to require a confession inked in someone's own blood that that's what he was doing. And that all of Golzar's supposed minions were caught with different types of counterfeit bills had confused us no end. Normally, perps tended to pick one type of bill to print and stuck with it. The entire situation had frustrated the bejeezus out of us, but we hadn't yet been able to acquire enough concrete proof that he was the mastermind behind the entire ring.

So, throwing solid, tangible evidence out the window and applying the standard of reasonable doubt, perhaps Golzar was in fact using counterfeit currency to fund his activities. That I could fathom, but I couldn't wrap my head around Mark's role in this twisted play.

Mark had been the AT of the Counterfeit Squad right before I'd transferred in a few years ago. He'd actually been leaving just as I'd been reassigned, so our paths hadn't crossed. I tried to recall who'd been in the squad with him when he'd been the boss. Rico had already been there when I'd transferred in, so he must've worked for Mark for at least a couple of months before the switch. I'd have to ask him.

So, I had Golzar's connection to counterfeit and Mark's connection to counterfeit. But what was their connection to each other? How had they met? And when? What'd been the progression of their relationship to have left us here? And did the fact that they both had knowledge of counterfeit currency—albeit it from completely opposite perspectives—have any bearing on the situation?

Cocking my head to one side, I listened intently, trying to determine where Mark was at the moment. His office was too far away from mine for me to tell whether he was still there, but I didn't hear any footsteps approaching my workspace. That was a good sign.

Feeling a little bit less terrified with a puzzle to distract me, I slowly eased myself up so I could reach my laptop. With a few well-placed keystrokes, I was into the main file server that our office shared and had instigated a search for any files containing the keywords "Jennings" and "Iran." I drummed my fingertips on the top of my desk in what must've been quadruple time as I watched the system execute its search.

The ringing of my cell phone sliced into the near silence with a suddenness that made me shriek. I clapped my hands over my mouth and prayed to any deity who'd listen that Mark hadn't heard me. I doubted my ability to act normally around him at the moment, and I really didn't need him to suspect I was onto him. I didn't put it past him to lead me out of the office at gun point and kill me, leaving my dead body in the marshes of Long Island where all those hookers had been found several years ago. And if there was one place I definitely didn't want my body discovered, it was Long Island. Dead was the only way to get me there willingly.

I clawed at the phone where it rested on the edge of my desk, determined to silence it. Naturally, I simply managed to smack it, and once I did, it fell off the desk and skittered across the floor out of my reach. I felt like a cartoon as I leapt across the room to throw myself bodily on top of it in an attempt to at least muffle the ring. *Holy hell, that hurt.* I groaned and tried not to move as my body adjusted to the pain.

When the ache had been downgraded from agonizing to almost bearable, I resumed my quest to quiet my phone. Wincing against the clatter my chair made as I kicked it and it rolled across the floor, I wrapped my butterfingers around the slippery little device just as the ringing ceased. With a gargantuan sigh of relief, I lay panting on the floor, as much from physical pain as emotional turmoil.

A knock against my closed office door stopped my heart for what felt like an eternity, and when it finally resumed pumping again, it was racing so fast I couldn't distinguish the individual beats from one another. It just felt like one painful, continuous roar. A cold sweat broke out across my brow, and I struggled to make as little noise as I could while attempting to regain a standing position. I refused to be on my knees when I faced the man who tried to have me killed. I also wasn't going to make this easy on him in the slightest. If he wanted me dead, he'd have to do it here and now. No way was I leaving the office with him. Fuck that!

"Ryan?" The voice was muffled by the metal between us, but I'd have recognized it anywhere. I was just having trouble figuring out why I was hearing it at all.

Stymied, I opened the door, chancing a quick glance around what I could see of the rest of the hallway to make absolutely certain Mark wasn't lurking anywhere. "Allison? What are you doing here?"

I grabbed her hand and pulled her into my office before poking my head out to take one last look. Then I silently shut the door again and turned to face her.

Allison's normally sparkling black eyes were dull and lifeless, highlighted by dark circles underneath. The familiar air of confidence-bordering-on-cockiness that she normally wore—the one I was as attracted to as I was irritated by—was absent. Her shoulders were slumped, her clothes slightly rumpled. She looked beaten.

"Are you okay?" she asked me, looking me up and down.

"Are you?"

"I asked you first."

"Sure. I'm fine. Why?"

"You look a little...I don't know...shell-shocked." She glanced around my office as though she were looking for someone.

"What are you doing here?" I asked again.

She made a face. "Nice to see you, too."

"I didn't mean it like that. It's just...I wasn't expecting you." As soon as the words were out of my mouth, all the air whooshed out of my lungs like I'd been sucker punched. Had Mark seen her? Oh, shit! She'd been with me the night before when Mark had been rummaging through my desk. If he paid any attention to the office gossip, he already knew she and I were together, which meant she was probably in more danger than I originally feared. Fuck! We had to—

"Clearly. I went by your apartment first, but you obviously weren't there. I figured this was the next logical place to find you."

My pulse pounded just beneath the surface of my skin, and I was suddenly light-headed. "Did anybody see you?" My voice sounded small and far away, like someone else had spoken.

Allison frowned. "No. I don't think so."

My dizziness lessened, and the world seemed more in focus, though I wasn't completely relieved. "Good."

"Is this about people knowing we're together?" She sounded hurt. "Because I told you I don't care."

"What? No, no. It's not about that. I wasn't even..." I buried my face in my hands and clawed at my forehead with my nails. "Jesus Christ."

Soft hands closed gently around my wrists and pulled my hands down. Could Allison tell they were trembling? She had to be able to. I took a deep, shuddering breath before I met her eyes, praying I didn't look even a fraction as panicked as I felt.

"Ryan, what's going on?"

I tried to swallow, but my mouth was dry, and my throat felt like it'd swollen shut. The muffled sounds of voices approaching and then passing my office made me freeze, and though I was thrilled that neither was Mark, I realized that I had no idea where he was at the moment. My breath was coming in short gasps, and mental images of Allison bleeding to death on the ground assaulted me. I drove them away with a violent shake of my head and forced myself to concentrate on her.

"Are you armed?" I blurted out.

"What?"

"Are you armed right now?"

"Of course."

"With just your service weapon? Or do you have your backup piece on you, too?"

"Just my service weapon. Seriously, Ryan. You're starting to scare me."

I paused, deliberating whether it was safe to talk about this in my office. I had no idea whether Mark had planted any sort of listening device in there to keep tabs on me, and while I was likely just being paranoid, I figured there was a reason for the adage "discretion is the better part of valor." I flipped on the radio that sat atop a corner filing cabinet and drew Allison to the other side of the room. "Humor me for just a second first, okay?"

"Okay." She dragged out the word, obviously wary.

"Pop the retention strap for me?"

"What?"

"The retention strap on your weapon. Pop it for me." She rolled her eyes but did as I asked. "Okay. Now just keep your hand there."

"On the butt of my weapon?"

"If you don't mind." I wanted at least one of us to be prepared in case Mark stormed in. I'd rather it be me, but I doubted she'd give up her gun even if I asked nicely.

"Fine. Now will you tell me what the hell this is all about?"

"So, funny story…Uh…You know the assassination attempt on the president of Iran?"

Allison's face darkened, and the muscles in her jaw jumped. "Yes." The word was clipped, the tone bitter.

"Right." I palmed the back of my neck with my right hand, wincing at the ache the motion produced in my shoulder. "Well, here's the thing. It wasn't an assassination attempt on the president of Iran as much as it was an assassination attempt on me." I glanced at the door and strained to hear any movement from the hall, but all I could pick up were the strains of the music wafting throughout the room and the roar of my heart thundering in my ears.

Allison stared at me for a long time, not saying anything. I tried to read her expression, but her face was completely neutral and gave me no clue. "Who would want to kill you? And why?"

"You believe me?" Somehow I'd expected a little more resistance to the idea.

She cocked her head and raised her eyebrows at me, as if silently inquiring whether I'd really just asked her that. "Of course. Although I do have some additional follow-up questions. Starting with the ones I just asked."

The band of pressure around my chest loosened, and I was thrilled at how much easier it was to breathe. "Remember the paperwork for that counterfeit case you found mixed up with my advance paperwork?"

"Yeah."

"I think it's connected to that."

"How?"

My insides crawled as though I were stuffed with an army of ants, and I placed one hand across my midsection to dispel the unpleasant sensation. "The guy has ties to several men who are suspected of funding terrorism with the sale of counterfeit currency."

Allison's eyes widened, and the ants marched up and swarmed my heart as I was suddenly awash with the renewed realization that my situation was perilous enough without Mark's involvement.

"And?"

"What?" I scrambled to recall where we were in the conversation, but I was hitting a wall.

"I assume there's something else. What is it?"

I hesitated and looked toward my door again. The words I wanted to speak crowded into my mouth, all sharp points and angles, but as much as they pained me, I was reluctant to spit them out. *Please, dear God, don't let him have planted a bug in here.* Just to be safe, I pressed my lips right against her ear and murmured, "I think Mark's somehow involved."

"Mark who?" she asked, loud enough to make me cringe and glance at the door.

"Shhh. Jennings." When she merely blinked at me, I clarified softly. "My boss."

Allison's face crumpled, and it was her turn to stare at my door. She looked torn between believing me and denying that anyone we worked with could be party to something so dark. I knew the feeling.

"Can you tell me why you think that?" she asked finally.

I explained the situation in detail, using a dry-erase marker on one of the frosted-glass windows, the one that backed up to the office behind mine, which should be locked at this time of night.

"And you know for sure this is"—she glanced at the door again— "his phone?"

I nodded and tried to ignore the nausea pressing against the walls of my stomach. My tongue was too big and unwieldy in my mouth. "Yeah. I just called it. And he answered."

Allison sucked in a sharp breath, and her eyes darted back over to my closed office door. The muscles in her hand tensed as she tightened her grip on the butt of her gun. "He's here in NYFO, isn't he?"

"Yeah."

She refocused on me, and the terror bleeding into her eyes only made me more aware of my own. "Does he know you're here?"

"I don't think so."

"Does he know you're onto him?"

I shook my head and gritted my teeth against the pounding behind my temples. "I doubt it. If he did, I don't think you and I would be talking right now."

Allison looked horrified. "Don't even joke about that."

"Unfortunately, it's not a joke."

"You think he'd kill you."

"It looks like he's already tried once, and that was before I suspected him of anything. Do you really think he'd let me live now that I actually do?"

"Shit."

"Yeah."

"This is bad."

"Tell me about it."

"What are we going to do?"

I let out a shaky breath, capped and discarded my marker, and lifted my hands. "I honestly don't know."

"He needs to be off the street and out of contact with these guys. Like now. As long as he's free, you're in danger."

I stopped right at the edge of pointing out I was likely in danger anyway. We both were. Had it gotten hot in here? I'd just noticed I was sweating again and was suddenly aware of the way my shirt was sticking to my skin. "I know. But I can't think of anyone with the pull to get a warrant drawn up this fast."

"What about the SAIC?"

"You mean *my* SAIC?"

Allison shrugged. "Why not? You don't think he knows about this, do you?"

I wanted to laugh, but I didn't want to have to explain why the idea was so funny. Instead, I shook my head. "No. But I don't know that dragging him into this would be the best idea."

"Why not?"

"Well, for one thing, if anyone else besides the SAIC gets wind of this, I can't be sure Mark won't find out somehow." For another, I couldn't be sure my dad wouldn't just kill him, which was the main reason I was reluctant to involve him at this stage.

"The gossip in this agency really is out of control."

"Tell me about it."

"Okay, so anyone from NYFO is out. You're on the JTTF. Don't you have any connections in another office or another agency you can tap?"

Her words were like a flare being ignited in a darkened room, making my next course of action suddenly, blindingly clear. And now that my path was illuminated, I wanted nothing more than to follow it. Immediately. No, scratch that. Yesterday. I still wasn't sure exactly why Allison was here, but whatever it was, it could wait. But I couldn't guarantee the outcome for either of us if someone didn't deal with Mark soon.

"There is one person who might be able to help us. We'll go see in a minute."

I checked on my computer search. Being a government agency, we saved everything. On a normal day, I lamented that fact, as I'd found the practice more than tedious. Today, however, I was unbelievably grateful.

I took a moment to skim the files my search results had set aside for me, simultaneously elated and sickened that I'd unearthed more or less what I'd thought I would. According to these records, Mark had been assigned as the detail leader for almost every single visit the president of Iran had made to the United States in the past five years. There were a handful of exceptions, of course, notably the most recent visit. Mark had not been the DL on the day of "the incident." But, according to what I was seeing, he was supposed to have been and had been switched out at the last minute. I'd have said it was a coincidence if I'd believed in those, but I didn't. I hit the Print key and moved on to my next search.

"What are you doing?" Allison came to stand beside me and peered over my shoulder at the monitor. Her proximity allowed me to feel the heat of her skin, and I trembled, fumbling the mouse.

"Just tying up a few loose ends," I replied, cringing at the waver in my voice. "Give me another second. I'm just about finished. Then we can go."

A few more taps of my keyboard, and I was looking at the entrance logs for the building. Every employee had an access code necessary to gain entrance to the office, one of the many ways we kept our facility secure. The code needed to be typed into an electronic keypad that controlled the locks to every exterior office door. And each entry was logged into a system of records that kept track of everyone's coming and goings. Again, I hadn't seen the need for such a procedure before, but now I was thanking my lucky stars the federal government was so anal-retentive.

I didn't have time to go through every single day for the past few years, and I wasn't well versed enough in this particular system to do an advanced search for one particular access code, even if I'd known which one I was looking for. I also didn't know how to conduct a search so the system displayed only a specific name. But as the names were the only identifiers displayed when each employee logged in, it was simple to scroll through a few random dates, manually scouring for Mark's.

When I wasn't so pressed for time, I'd have to review all the records and see if I could pull the logs specific to him and consolidate them on one page. But for now, just seeing that Mark had a fairly consistent pattern of showing up at the office around four a.m. approximately two to three times a week as far back as three years ago was enough for me.

I hit the Print key again. The picture was starting to come into sharper focus now. But I didn't need complete clarity. The way I saw it, I had just enough rope to make Mark believe I knew everything and leave it to him to hang himself. Now all I needed was an executioner.

I turned to face Allison, startled that she was still so close. Her breath ghosted across my lips and made my head foggy. My throat was tight, and I cleared it before I spoke. "You ready to go?" My voice was barely a whisper.

Allison pulled the corner of her lower lip in between her teeth and nodded slowly. A lock of hair tumbled down her forehead and into her eyes as her gaze flickered to where the tip of my tongue had darted out to moisten my lips.

Against my better judgment, I reached out to tuck that stray tress behind her ear and then caressed her cheek, all but falling into her eyes for the moment she held my gaze before she closed them and nuzzled into my touch. I used my other hand to cup her face tenderly and ran one thumb over her bottom lip. Christ. Even though facing imminent death, the woman was like my own personal black hole. I couldn't get within five feet of her without her pull ensnaring me.

Allison and I stood there together like that for a while, seemingly content to coexist in the silence of my office. I took advantage of the opportunity to study her while her eyes were closed, and I couldn't help the smile that blossomed across my own lips as it occurred to me, not for the first time, how heartbreakingly beautiful she was.

She let slip a soft sigh, and her hands came up to rest lightly on my hips, causing my own breathing to hitch and my mind to wrench violently off its current innocent track, only to crash-land on another that was most definitely not. The desire to kiss her breathless suddenly consumed me, followed closely by the yearning to strip her completely naked, place her on top of my desk, and take my time slowly exploring every inch of her hot skin with my tongue until she came undone and screamed my name.

Good Lord. I swallowed hard as the mental images of that scenario played out inside my head. The woman didn't even have to try to turn me on. My fingers tingled and burned with the need to touch her, which was startling in its intensity.

Focus, O'Connor, the voice in my head snapped. You're dealing with a life-and-death situation here. Keep your eye on the damn ball.

I indulged myself one more moment and set my thumbs to roam over the silken skin of her cheeks before I gently let her go. I cleared my throat again. "So…you ready to get out of here?"

Allison's eyes fluttered open slowly, and she appeared dazed for a second before her expression cleared. The speed with which she snapped back to being all business was as impressive as it was hot. She took a step back, and her hand drifted to the butt of her gun again.

"You think he's still here?"

"I don't know. Maybe."

"Any way to find out?"

"Aside from walking down the hall to his office or calling his extension? No. Not one that wouldn't require involving other agents."

"Which we don't want."

"No."

"You armed?" she asked.

I shook my head. "Nope."

"Shit. Where's your gun?"

"They took it from me when I was shot. I can't get it back until I'm cleared for full duty."

"Do you know where it is? Is it here in the office? Can we get it?"

"I don't know. My—the SAIC said he had it locked up, but I don't know if it was here or at home. His home. Not mine. Obviously."

She narrowed her eyes at me, and my cheeks blazed under the intensity of her stare. I held my breath as I waited to see whether she'd press me on why I'd just stuttered like a fool. She didn't. Instead, she asked, "Where's your vest?"

My breath rushed out of me, and I didn't know whether to be

grateful she was taking this seriously or horrified that she also considered Mark might actually shoot me in the office. "My raid vest is in the trunk of my car. And the vest I bought to wear on protection is probably with my gun. Or maybe the FBI has it as evidence. I don't know. I haven't seen it since I was shot."

She huffed and shook her head as she shrugged out of her suit jacket. Her hands went to the buttons of her dress shirt and started unfastening them.

"What're you doing?"

"What's it look like I'm doing?"

"Now seems like a bad time to get naked. Not that I don't always want you naked, but I shouldn't always get what I want."

"You're an idiot, you know that? I'm giving you my vest."

I placed my hands over hers. "I'm not taking it."

"Well, I'm not letting you out this door unprotected."

I tried to smile at her. "I'm not unprotected. I have you."

Allison rolled her eyes. "You know what I mean."

I did know. And while I could appreciate the sentiment—while it warmed me in a way I couldn't have imagined—the idea of holding her while she bled out because she'd given me her vest and forgone protection was far scarier than my own death. "Yeah. I do. But it's not going to happen." When she opened her mouth to interrupt, I pressed on. "We don't have time to argue about this. Let's just get the hell out of here."

She stared at me for a long moment, and I could see the temptation to keep pushing sparking behind her eyes. But in the end she merely nodded once, shrugged back into her suit jacket, and turned toward the door. I took a deep breath and reached out to open it, but she stopped me with a quiet, "Wait."

I glanced at her, surprised. "What's up?"

She eased her weapon out of her holster and adjusted her grip so both hands were wrapped tightly around the butt, muzzle pointed at the floor, finger high along the slide and out of the trigger guard. "Which way is Mark's office?"

"To the left."

She nodded. "Okay. Then we go out the door and head right. We'll make our way to the elevators the long way. I'd rather take them because we know they have video surveillance. I doubt he'd try to take you out knowing he's on camera. Since I've got the gun, I'll cover your six until we're away from his office. Then I'll take point. Standard evacuation protocols and signals. Make sure you take quick peeks around the corners before you advance."

I was so keyed up about the next few minutes, it barely even occurred to me to point out that I was an agent, too, and I knew damn well how to evacuate from a building. Only the lump in my throat and the pressure building in my chest kept me from replying. My insides clenched as I tried not to imagine all the ways this could go horribly wrong.

I wiped my sweaty palms on my pants and took another deep breath before slowly easing the door open a crack. I took a moment to listen for footsteps, movement, anything that would indicate someone's approach, but I heard nothing. I caught Allison's eye, and we both nodded. Then I flung the door back and took off down the hall with her right behind me.

CHAPTER SEVENTEEN

By the time we reached the parking garage, I was wound up tighter than the inside of a baseball. I tried to slow my ragged breathing as I slammed my car door and hastily scrambled to insert the key into the ignition. It took me a couple of tries, and every cell in my body was on high alert as I fumbled, but eventually I made it work. I let out a long, shaky breath as the engine caught and had to force myself not to speed out of there like I was trying to win the Indy 500.

"So that was…something," Allison said as I eased the car onto the street. Her work phone buzzed, and her expression was annoyed as she pulled it out to check it.

"Mmm."

"You okay?"

"Yeah. Sure. You?"

I heard her huff, and when I glanced at her, I saw that she'd tilted her head back and was glaring at the ceiling. "You don't really expect me to believe that, do you?"

I shrugged. "What do you want me to say?"

Allison didn't reply, but she did go back to glaring at her phone, her fingers hovering over the keyboard as though she was itching to type something but was either trying to think of an appropriate reply or to talk herself out of replying altogether.

I sighed heavily and rolled my good shoulder in an attempt to ease some of the tension in the muscles of my back. We had at least ten minutes until we reached our destination. Not at all an ideal amount of time, but with the way our lives had been going, it looked like we'd need to squeeze in the important talks when and where we could. Now seemed like a good time.

"What's wrong?" I asked quietly. My fingers trembled on the steering wheel, and I held my breath as I awaited her answer.

She was silent for a very long time. So long, in fact, that I'd started running through a list of other possible questions I could ask her that would get her to talk to me. I'd just decided on one and was trying to locate the courage to actually voice it when she spoke. "Nothing."

"I don't believe that any more than you believed me when I said I was fine." I made sure to keep my tone light, not wanting her to think I was being snarky right now.

She rubbed the palm of one hand across her forehead. "Fair enough."

The blanket of quiet that settled on us then was a little too heavy. I swallowed against the buzzing in the back of my throat. "That your boss?"

"How'd you guess?" I didn't think her cutting tone was necessarily meant to wound me.

"You don't usually glare at your phone like you're trying to set it on fire. Not unless it's a telemarketer."

My attempt at humor fell flat, and Allison went back to alternating between staring at her phone and gazing out the window.

We rode along in silence again for a bit before I couldn't stand it any longer. "So are you going to tell me what's bothering you?"

Allison shook her head, eyes still focused on the outside world. "Not right now."

"Oh. Okay. And why's that?"

"It's just not the time to get into this. My stupid boss can wait. We need to focus on Mark now."

"But you will tell me? Later?"

Allison finally turned to look at me, and the glimpse I caught of the sad smile she favored me with made me ache. "Yes. Of course. I'll tell you later."

"Okay."

We rode the rest of the way in silence. She was right. We did need to put our personal issues aside so we could concentrate on this situation. But that didn't stop me from obsessing about them in between wondering whether this hail-Mary play I was about to attempt was even going to work and fearing for our lives.

We pulled up in front of Hurricane's building and hopped out of the car. Again, I scanned every inch of the street I could see, searching for any type of threat, but I didn't detect anything. Nevertheless, my heart thundered the entire time we were making our way from the curb to the door, and the skin between my shoulder blades prickled and burned as though I were being watched.

"What are we doing here again?" Allison asked me as we entered the lobby.

"I don't think I told you what we were doing here in the first place," I murmured absently, focused on calling the command post upstairs. Since Hurricane didn't have an event, there was no agent in the lobby, so I needed them to key the elevator to let us up. I'd emailed Hannah before we'd left NYFO to make sure she wasn't busy, so she was expecting us.

"That's right. You didn't." Allison's tone was sarcastic. "Surprise, surprise."

I grinned at her, edging in the direction of so exhausted and burnt out that everything was hilarious. "You said it yourself. We need help."

"Oh, of course. Well, that certainly clarifies everything."

The elevator ride up to the floor where Platform was located was silent. Allison had once again lapsed into silent brooding, while I was diligently going over what I was planning to say in my mind. I'd only get one shot at this, and I didn't want to mess it up.

Hannah greeted us on the landing, looking as serious as ever, but I caught a faint undertone of concern in her eyes that sparked a measure of guilt in me. I hadn't meant to worry her. I just hadn't been sure who else to turn to.

"Hannah. You remember Allison, right?"

Hannah inclined her head toward Allison in greeting, a gesture that Allison returned. "Is everything okay? Your email was a little cryptic."

"It's complicated. And I'm sorry about that. I…uh…I need to get in touch with SAIC Quinn. I don't suppose she's still here, is she?"

It'd occurred to me briefly before leaving NYFO that I might've asked that question before coming all the way over here, but in the end I'd decided it didn't matter if she was here or not. In the event she wasn't, I figured I could either wait for her or, if she was out of town altogether, get Hannah to assist me with a conference call.

Hannah looked completely stunned. Her brow furrowed in confusion, and she put her hands on her hips. "Yeah, she's upstairs. Hurricane literally just walked back in the door, and they're going over her schedule for tomorrow. Why?"

I fiddled with my necklace, nervously using the vaguely pleasant scraping of the chain at the nape of my neck to keep me present in the moment. "Would you mind asking her if she has a minute? I need to speak to her about something."

Hannah stared at me for a long moment before pushing the call button for the elevator. "Let's go upstairs and see if she's free yet."

When the elevator arrived, we all piled on wordlessly. I didn't have a clue what the other two were thinking. My own thoughts were a wild tangle I was desperately trying to unravel. Butterflies took wing in the pit of my stomach, and I rested my hands across my abdomen in a vain attempt to quiet them. Despite the fact that she was clearly in a terrible mood for reasons I could only imagine, Allison placed a reassuring hand on the small of my back. I shot her a grateful look.

The SAIC was just coming out of Hurricane's apartment as we stepped off the elevator, and my nerves sizzled. She was dressed impeccably in a black pin-striped suit with a white button-down shirt. Her hair was loose and a little tousled, as though she'd been running her hands through it and had then attempted to finger-comb it back off her face. She also looked exhausted, which took me by surprise and highlighted for me even further how inconsiderate I felt for just dropping by like this.

A flush rose in my cheeks. I barely knew the woman, and here I was interrupting her evening without knowing whether she was even the right person to turn to. I just had to cross my fingers she was—or that she could point me in the right direction if she wasn't—because I was out of ideas.

SAIC Quinn fixed me with a curious look when she noticed me, and I took that as my cue to start speaking.

"SAIC Quinn. I know it's late. My apologies for breaking in on your night. I'm not certain if you remember me. I'm Ryan O'Connor. We met the other day." Had it only been yesterday? I wasn't sure.

The days had become a blur to me. "And you already know Allison Reynolds."

"Of course I remember you. And it's nice to see you again, Agent Reynolds. Please, call me Claudia. What can I do for you?"

"Again, I'm terribly sorry for intruding on your evening. May I have a moment of your time? I need to discuss a sensitive matter with you. And Hannah." Technically, Hannah shouldn't have been involved in this any more than the SAIC should've been, but I was craving the moral support her presence provided.

SAIC Quinn's face now was businesslike and deathly serious. She glanced at the agent standing post in the hall before she motioned for us to follow her. There was only one other apartment on the floor, and as far as I knew, no one lived there, so I wasn't sure where she was leading us. I glanced to Hannah, but her expression gave away nothing.

SAIC Quinn dug around in her suit pants pocket for a moment before producing a key. She opened the door and took a few steps inside. I hesitated, and SAIC Quinn turned around to face me.

"Come on in."

"Oh, no, ma'am. We couldn't impose like that. We can discuss this here, if that's all right." I didn't really want to get into all of this in front of the agent standing post in the hallway, who I didn't think I'd ever seen before, but I also didn't want to encroach upon her evening any more than I already was.

"Nonsense. There's no reason to stand in the hall. We might as well get comfortable. I was planning to make some coffee anyway. Join me." And with that, she turned away, leaving us to follow her.

I shared an uncomfortable look with Allison before trailing Hannah inside. I had no idea why she'd have keys to an apartment on the same floor as Hurricane's and was unwilling to entertain any of the scenarios my mind was throwing out. It seemed strange to me that she'd want to reside this close to her protectee. Neither Allison nor I had that type of experience with anyone we'd been responsible for safeguarding, so we were both obviously uneasy with the situation.

When I finally made it into the kitchen, SAIC Quinn was already getting out mugs for everyone.

"So…uh…I didn't know you lived here," I said in a feeble attempt to make small talk while SAIC Quinn made sure everyone was set up with something to drink before we all got settled in the living room.

Allison shot me a dirty look, and I lifted my hands in reply. She had to know I was going to ask.

"Oh, I don't," the SAIC said as she retrieved some creamer from the fridge. "No one does, actually. Building management lets us use it on the sly since they don't have a tenant. I'm short-changing tomorrow, and I occasionally crash here so I don't have to lose sleep on a long commute."

I winced at the news and surreptitiously checked my watch. I was seriously cutting into her sleep time, and the knowledge hit me hard and sparked a little fire of guilt inside my chest.

"So, what can I do for you?" the SAIC asked as soon as we all had our respective drinks and had taken seats in the living room.

I swallowed hard, playing with my coffee cup as I attempted to decide where to begin. Trying to mentally calm my jangling nerves, I took a deep breath. "What I'm about to tell you is extremely unbelievable. It isn't going to make a whole lot of sense to you—hell, it doesn't make a whole lot of sense to me—and I know I'm breaking a whole slew of rules and jumping about eighteen chains of command by coming to you with this."

"Why did you come to me with this?" SAIC Quinn asked. Her voice held just the right amount of gentleness and curiosity to put me at ease. Well, as at ease as I could be, considering the circumstances.

"Hannah trusts you," I said immediately, sharing a meaningful glance with the woman in question. "She told me once you'd be a good person to have in my corner. I need you in my corner now."

SAIC Quinn appeared to consider that statement for a moment. She sat back in her chair and crossed her right ankle over her left knee and took another sip of her coffee. "Go on."

I exchanged a look with Allison, who was sitting next to me on the couch. Without a word, she slipped her hand in mine. I smiled at her a little nervously, hoping my gratitude for the gesture showed in my eyes.

"I need to talk to you about the assassination attempt on the president of Iran," I said, mulling over the words as they left my mouth. I was still a trifle uneasy about discussing this whole thing outside of the JTTF. I wasn't technically supposed to talk about a terrorism-related matter with anyone but another task force member; and while I'd kept the discussion with Allison vague enough that the rules were bent instead of broken, I wouldn't have that luxury now. In order for

SAIC Quinn to be able to help me, I'd need to get into the weeds with her. I didn't like it, but the way I saw it, I needed someone with her pull and connections in DHS to help me sort this out as quickly as possible. I figured that necessity overrode rules. Probably. And if it didn't, well, I really hoped I could rock orange as well as the women from that prison show.

Both SAIC Quinn and Hannah appeared shocked. Allison seemed more anxious than anything else, but that was to be expected, seeing as how she knew exactly what I was about to say. I felt her hand clamp tighter on mine, and she fidgeted in the seat next to me.

"Only it wasn't an assassination attempt on the president of Iran," I went on. I cleared my throat. This next part was only one of the ones I was worried about. If they didn't take my word for this, it was unlikely they would believe me about who was responsible. "It was an assassination attempt on me."

SAIC Quinn's eyes drifted away from mine to focus on something I couldn't see in the corner of the room. Her gaze became distant, glassy. I kept all my attention on her, afraid to see Hannah's reactions to that revelation.

"That makes sense," SAIC Quinn said slowly.

"It does?" I didn't even try to hide my shock at her words.

She nodded thoughtfully, still staring blankly into that corner. "It does. You were the Intelligence Advance for the visit, correct?"

"Yes."

"And where were you standing when the shots were fired?"

"Next to the trunk of the limo. I'd just been pushed off the door by one of the shift guys and was headed back to my own car."

"So you were, what? About four feet from the president?"

"Maybe five. I'm not good with distances."

SAIC Quinn finally shifted her eyes back to me. "You were too far away from the president for him to have been the target. And all of the shots hit you. None of them got anywhere close to him. Or anyone else, for that matter, with one obvious exception. If someone goes to the trouble to hire a hit man, he doesn't hire one that sloppy. You generally don't get a second chance at an assassination attempt. So when you have your opportunity, you make it count."

I let out a shaky breath and collapsed back into the couch, completely drained. "You believe me."

Her lips quirked in some semblance of a wry smile. "Would you be surprised to learn I've actually been thinking about that day a lot and that several things about it never quite added up?"

My relief was palpable. It hadn't dawned on me until that moment how much I'd needed to hear that I hadn't been imagining things, that I wasn't crazy. Even though I possessed hard evidence to support my theory, a teeny part of me had doubted anyone would accept it.

"But I suspect that's not exactly the entire reason you came to see me tonight," SAIC Quinn said.

I sighed, knowing the most unbelievable part was yet to come. "No, ma'am. It isn't. I'm here because I know who tried to have me killed."

SAIC Quinn regarded me intently for a long moment, and I held her eyes, still deliberately ignoring Hannah and Allison. But I didn't need to look at Allison to know her entire body had tensed and she was seething. I was touched to learn she could be spurred to violence on my behalf. It was very sweet, in a twisted sort of way.

"Shouldn't you have gone to your boss with this information?" SAIC Quinn wanted to know.

I snorted, unwilling and unable to hide my derision. "I can't exactly do that. Seeing as how my boss is the one who tried to off me."

"What?!" Hannah almost shouted.

"That's a pretty serious allegation," SAIC Quinn said after a moment.

"I know. Believe me, I wish it weren't true." My tone was caustic as I spoke, and I scowled.

"Can you tell me what makes you think that?" The SAIC's tenor was even, impassive.

And with a deep breath, I launched into the story. I told her how I'd first started looking at Akbari and about Mark's odd behavior when he'd found out. I laid out the trails I'd followed between telephone numbers: from the number Akbari had dialed immediately after Meaghan and I'd left the night we'd interviewed him to Fallahi, from Fallahi to Golzar, from Golzar to the unidentified burner phone. I spelled out how that same burner phone had also made several calls to Golzar in the days leading up to "the incident," including one about ten minutes before I'd been shot, and how after that call, Golzar had then immediately called another burner phone that I suspected belonged to the actual shooter. The hardest part to tell, as it turned out, had been how I'd just discovered that the first burner phone, the one that'd been called the night this ball had started rolling, had belonged to Mark.

"Holy shit," Hannah whispered softly.

"Yeah." I smiled at her a little ruefully.

We were all quiet for a long time.

"You have documentation to back this up, I assume?" the SAIC asked finally.

I nodded, unable to speak. A lump had formed in my throat that was making it hard for me to swallow, let alone form words. Much like with Lucia's death, reality washed over me at the oddest times, crashing into me hard and then ebbing away, only to sneak up on me later and pound me all over again like a vengeful sea. This was one of those latter times. *My boss tried to have me killed.* Life was so surreal sometimes.

"I don't know why he still has the phone," I murmured almost to myself. "If he'd just gotten rid of it, I never would've known it was him."

"Well, lucky for us, he does have it," SAIC Quinn announced. "It'll be easy for us to track him with it. And tough for him to deny involvement after he's arrested holding it in his hand. But it does make time an issue. We need to move on this before he dumps it."

"It doesn't make sense." I was still trying to accept the situation for what it was and failing miserably. "Why wouldn't he have tossed it? He's a federal agent, for crying out loud. He knows better. He can't be that stupid."

"Who cares why he still has it?" Hannah asked. "All that matters is we can link him to the sniper."

Against my better judgment, I glanced at Allison. Her face was a mask of righteous fury, her dark eyes glinting with barely contained rage. When she noticed me watching her, however, she took a deep breath and adopted an air of forced calm. My heart fractured at the gesture. It shattered completely when she slipped her arm around me and pulled me closer. I sighed and rested one hand on the top of her thigh.

"There's just one thing I don't understand," SAIC Quinn said.

"What's that?"

"Why didn't you go to your SAIC with this?"

The tension that shot through my body at the question was acutely painful, and I sat ramrod straight, aggravating my still-healing injuries something fierce. I'd known it was coming, of course. There was no way SAIC Quinn wouldn't have demanded a thorough explanation as to why I was going completely outside of my chain of command to bring this to her. That line I'd fed Allison about office gossip possibly tipping Mark off wouldn't fly with SAIC Quinn. I'd known I'd have to come clean about my true motives. But that didn't mean the question didn't put me on edge.

"I can't tell my SAIC about this," I admitted quietly, dreading Allison's reaction to the bombshell I was being forced to drop. "It's a conflict of interest."

"You can't think he's somehow involved," SAIC Quinn stated, her voice mostly flat save for the bright notes of disbelief. "I've known Ben Flannigan for years. He's a good man and as honest as the day is long. There's no way he had anything to do with this."

I couldn't help the smile that stole over my lips at her opinion of my boss. He'd undoubtedly have been pleased to hear it. I'd have to remember to tell him later.

"No. I don't think he was involved. But I do think he's too close to the situation to be even remotely objective. A fact that, come trial time, a defense attorney will have a field day with." I hesitated a beat. Two. Three. The expectant silence that shrouded us was heavy and thick. I turned to face Allison. I wanted to look her in the eye when I finally confessed this to her. "He's my father."

Allison hissed and drew back, putting space between our bodies quicker than I ever would've imagined possible. I immediately missed her warmth but didn't have the nerve to rectify that situation. Each and every emotion that flowed over her face as my words sank in— confusion, hurt, betrayal, anger—was like a knife straight through my heart. The way she was looking at me now, it was doubtful she'd ever forgive me. My stomach clenched painfully.

If either the SAIC or Hannah noticed the rift the revelation had sparked between Allison and me, they were polite enough not to mention it. In fact, Hannah didn't seem particularly surprised.

"Well, that explains why you were some sort of freaky super recruit in the academy," she said dryly. "You had an inside edge. You knew exactly what to expect."

I nodded miserably. I clasped my hands together in my lap and wrung my fingers. As I was intently studying Allison's features, I saw with aching clarity the exact moment the puzzle pieces clicked into place for her as she recalled the day we'd met—the conversations we'd had about my upcoming training, my correct use of agency vernacular, our trip to the range, my proficiency with our firearms—and certain things finally added up for her. God, I wished I hadn't had to hit her with this in front of an audience. My dad's favorite adage about wishing in one hand and spitting in the other flitted uselessly through my thoughts.

For her part, SAIC Quinn appeared completely oblivious to the personal drama unfolding around her. Her expression was serious and thoughtful as she obviously considered what to do with the information I'd just presented her. Her fingertips tapped out an idle, staccato rhythm on the tops of her thighs as she deliberated.

"I'm going to have to tell Ben," SAIC Quinn announced just when I'd been about to break the silence myself. "I can't just have one of his agents arrested without warning him first."

"I know. But, if it's not too much to ask, do you think you could tell him right before you're about to do the takedown? I think it'll be easier for him if he doesn't have a lot of time to dwell on the situation. It'll take away the burden of having to decide whether to give in to his personal feelings and act on the information or remain professional and let the scenario play out without him."

"I agree with you. That'd probably be best."

"Also, would it be all right if I went with you when you do tell him?"

For some reason I didn't even have the energy to attempt to fathom, the SAIC seemed pleasantly surprised. "Of course."

"Thank you."

"I'm going to make a few phone calls. I want you to go home and try to get some sleep. We can meet up early tomorrow morning to review your evidence before we present it to the assistant United States attorney. I want to swear out a warrant for this guy and execute it as quickly as possible. The sooner we do this, the better chance we have of catching him before he dumps that phone. You're free tomorrow, I assume?"

I nodded, thankful she wanted to inform an AUSA that quickly. I was fairly positive I wouldn't be able to breathe easy until Mark was behind bars. "Yes, ma'am. I'm still on light duty, so I can't be assigned. I have nothing planned."

"Good. Expect to hear from me bright and early tomorrow morning, then. I'll let you know where to meet when I call you. Obviously, we don't want to do this at your office. And the fewer people who know about this, the better." She paused, obviously considering something. "Perhaps it's just easier for you to bring everything here."

"Whatever you think is best, ma'am. I defer to your experience and expertise on this one."

SAIC Quinn appeared mildly amused by my reply but opted not to comment directly. Instead, she said, "Perfect. We'll use the morning to get all our affairs in order, and we'll have the chief of the Counterterrorism Division of the Southern District meet us here for the case presentation after lunch."

I felt as though a huge burden had been taken off my shoulders. I guess that's what happened when you found someone to share the load. With the weight distributed among several people, it suddenly didn't seem quite so heavy. The irony that I'd spent so much time trying to shield Allison from the weight of any and all of my burdens wasn't lost on me. I simply chose not to dwell on it for the time being.

We all stood and made our way to the front door. Allison exited the apartment without a word or a backward glance, and I tried not to wince at her attitude. It wasn't easy. I turned back to SAIC Quinn and held out my hand. "I can't thank you enough, ma'am, for everything you're doing for me. I really appreciate it. I didn't know who else to go to with this."

The SAIC took my hand in hers and shook it solemnly. "Don't mention it. I'm greatly looking forward to nailing this bastard to the wall."

I couldn't help but smile. "And I'm looking forward to handing you the hammer."

CHAPTER EIGHTEEN

The elevator ride back down to the street was even more awkward for me than the ride up had been. Allison refused to look at me, and I was too mentally drained to think about trying to come up with something to say to her. I just wanted to crawl into bed and sleep for a year. Of course, my hopes for that scenario playing out in my favor were slim, since I hadn't had a decent night's sleep in forever. I didn't even attempt to rein in my exhausted sigh.

No one was more surprised than I when Allison wordlessly climbed into the car with me. And I sure as hell hadn't expected her to remain silent when I asked her where she wanted to go. I'd assumed she would head to a hotel or go straight back to DC or something. I would've liked to say I was pleasantly astonished by this turn of events, but given Allison's current mood, I wasn't convinced this was a good development.

The entire ride, Allison sat pressed against the passenger door, as far away from me as she could possibly get without actually being in a different car. She had her arms folded tightly across her chest and her jaw clenched so forcefully I could hear her teeth grinding together over the din of the city traffic. Her eyes remained fixed out the window as we rode, but she didn't appear to be seeing anything that we passed. The only words that came to mind to describe her expression were "darkly furious."

We made it into my apartment without a word between us. I felt like a live wire had been applied to the surface of my skin. My nerves were frayed to the point of disintegration. Trying to stall the inevitable,

I took a long time hanging up my suit jacket and placing my house keys on the hook next to the door, trying not to notice that my hands were shaking.

I inhaled a deep, steeling breath and paused to wipe my palms on my pants before shoving my hands into my pockets. Allison's face, the absolute, pure rage swirling in her eyes as she glared out the window at the Brooklyn skyline, told me this was going to be bad. Exactly how bad remained to be seen.

I endured the charged silence as long as I could before I finally grew weary of waiting and decided to force this conversation. "Allison, I—"

She whipped around to face me, causing the words I'd been about to utter to shrivel and die on my lips. My breath whooshed out of me in a painful rush as her gaze locked onto mine and she stared all the way into my soul. I squirmed under the attention.

"Don't," Allison growled. She pointed one finger in my direction. "Don't speak. Not. One. Word."

"Okay," I whispered.

Allison shot me a look meant to wither and clasped both hands on the back of her neck. She stalked back and forth across my living room restlessly, her eyes darting around seemingly at random. She was obviously considering what to say. I simultaneously prayed she'd hurry up and dreaded her ever speaking.

I remained as still as possible while she roved. Only my eyes followed her progress. I definitely didn't want to incur her wrath before it was absolutely necessary, no matter how much I might've felt I deserved it.

She strode purposefully in my direction and stopped directly in front of me. Mere inches separated her body from mine. She was so close to me, I could feel the heat rolling off her in waves.

"A year, Ryan. We were sleeping together for an entire year, and you never once thought to tell me you were the SAIC's daughter?!" Her eyes appeared a shade of black that seemed to leech light from the room, and her body vibrated as she seethed. Her fists clenched and unclenched at her sides, and I suspected she was struggling to best the impulse to slug me.

"I know, Allison. I'm sorry." What the hell else could I say? She was right. I should've told her sooner. But was now the right time to reiterate the complexity of the relationship to her? Somehow, I doubted it'd help matters.

"I can't believe I didn't see it before," she muttered, more to herself than to me, I suspected.

I answered her anyway. "How could you have? We have different last names. And we don't interact much when we're in the office—we don't have to—so it's doubtful you'd ever seen us together except at the hospital a few days ago."

Allison ignored me to resume pacing and muttering to herself. "I should've known. The day we met, there were so many clues, so many things you said and did that should've tipped me off that you had family in the agency. You asked if I'd done my detail time yet. You handled an MP-5 like you were born with one in your hand. You put up a shot grouping with my pistol that I've never seen even from agents who've been on the job for decades. How could I not have realized it?"

"Because you were so blinded by how adorable I am?"

She rounded on me, her glare withering.

I held up both hands in supplication and took a step back. "Sorry. Not the time."

"Who else knows?" she demanded.

"Who else knows what? That he's my dad?"

Allison bobbed her head once in an angry imitation of what the agents in the field had not-so-kindly dubbed "the PPD nod." I had to fight not to roll my eyes or allow myself to give in to the distraction the gesture presented and pursue it with a sarcastic comment. Later, I'd have to remember to be proud of myself for that restraint.

"No one," I told her honestly.

Allison glared at me with evident suspicion and disbelief. "No one. Not even Meaghan or what's-his-name? Your work husband?"

I blinked at her, startled she even knew about Rico. He and I hadn't become close until after she'd left, and I knew for a fact I'd never mentioned him to her. No way, after seeing us dance together at that wheels-up party, could she have reached that conclusion. Not unless—

Allison broke into my mental conjecturing. "I heard somebody say it." She didn't look happy, although it was tough for me to tell whether that humorous descriptor of my relationship with Rico had anything to do with her displeasure.

"No," I told her firmly, keeping the conversation on topic. "Neither of them knows."

"You really expect me to believe you never told them?"

"I can't believe you seriously think I'd tell either of them something I hadn't even told you." Her lack of faith in me was acutely painful. Yes. I realized that reaction probably leaned strongly toward hypocritical, considering all the things I'd kept from her, but that insight did nothing to negate the feelings.

"Did he know?"

"I just told you Rico didn't know."

"I wasn't talking about Rico."

"Oh. Who were you talking about, then? And what do you want to know if he knew?"

"The SAIC. Your *father*. Did he know about us?"

Oh. We were changing direction again. Okay. I took a moment to consider her question, attempting to figure out where the hell her little deviation was taking us. As was usually the case with her conversational twists and turns, I was completely clueless.

"No. He didn't." I reflected on that statement for a second and then amended it. "At least I never told him. But I don't know what he heard through the grapevine. I can promise you he never mentioned it to me, though. And I honestly think he would've said something. To Rory, if not directly to me. And she definitely would've mentioned it." Pumped me for information was more like it, but I didn't think now was the time to be picky about semantics.

"You never mentioned it to him. Never let it slip. Not even once." She appeared skeptical.

"Well, you were pretty insistent that we keep it a secret," I fired back. "I assumed that meant from him, too."

Allison continued to glare at me, her eyes searching mine intently. For what, I couldn't have said. "Does he know now?"

"Does he know what now? About us?"

Allison's glare darkened, which I would previously have thought impossible, and a shiver went up my spine. She leaned in even closer. If she hadn't looked so livid, I'd have sworn she was about to kiss me.

I tensed as a trickle of fear wound around my insides, slithering around my organs and making me faintly queasy.

"Yes." Allison's jaw was clenched again, and she ground the word out through gritted teeth.

"Are you asking me if he's aware or are you asking specifically if I told him? And are you asking if he knew about us then or if he knows about us now? Because the answers to those questions are different."

"Then answer all of them."

"I honestly don't know if he knew then or if he knows now. I have no clue what he hears through office gossip or if he even pays attention to it. But I haven't gotten around to telling him yet. We've had a lot of other stuff to talk about lately. You know, what with the assassination attempts and all."

And just like that, her anger evaporated. Like a bouncy castle whose air pump has been turned off, she deflated and collapsed into a heap onto the couch, staring at one of the legs of my coffee table. It was perhaps the most anticlimactic ending to an argument I'd ever experienced, and I wasn't sure what to make of it. I didn't trust it. Not completely. Definitely not enough to drop my guard.

"I can't believe you lied to me," Allison whispered so softly she might've been talking to herself. Her eyes were downcast. She couldn't even look at me.

I opened my mouth to point out that technically I hadn't lied to her—I'd never said Ben wasn't my father—but somehow I doubted she'd appreciate the distinction. I snapped my mouth closed and sighed.

I sidled closer to her, lacking the courage to actually attempt to sit beside her or touch her. But I couldn't suppress my desire to be nearer. I shoved my hands back into the pockets of my dress pants and clenched them into fists, yearning for contact.

It took a few minutes, but eventually, Allison remembered I was there. She tipped her head up so she could study me, and the pain laid bare on her face made me ache.

"I know this doesn't change anything, but for what it's worth, I really am sorry."

"Why didn't you tell me?" she murmured, her voice so shaky and fragile I wanted to cry.

"I'm sorry," I repeated softly. "I wanted my career to be my own. I didn't want to just be Ben Flannigan's daughter. Surely you can understand that. I know it doesn't excuse me hiding it from you for so long but…" I was unable to even conjure up a justification for my actions.

"And yesterday? When I asked if you were keeping anything else from me?"

I frowned. "I…I thought you meant about the whole thing with Lucia. I—I didn't…I mean, this never even occurred to me."

"Would you have told me then if it had?"

"Well, we didn't have a lot more time to talk, if I recall correctly."

"So that's a no, then."

"Allison, of all the things I've got on my mind at the moment, this was among the furthest. So, no. Probably not. But not because I was still actively keeping it from you."

She appeared slightly mollified. "You're right. I'm sorry. I just… The news caught me off guard, and I'm not handling it very well, I'm afraid."

"I know it's a lot to take in. But I swear I never meant to keep it from you for this long."

"So why did you?"

"I don't know. I guess when we first got together, I was afraid you wouldn't want anything to do with me if you found out who I was. But I also thought we were just fooling around, so I didn't think you really needed to know. Then when things started to get serious between us, I could never seem to find the right time. And the longer I waited, the harder it became. Then we broke up and you went to DC, so I didn't think it mattered anymore. Now, I've just been preoccupied. But I was going to tell you."

"Before or after you took me home for Christmas?" she asked bitterly.

It was tough not to laugh. I always did feel the urge to giggle at the most inappropriate times. "Definitely before. I'd want to adequately prepare you for the way that man can inhale a turkey. No one should have to see their boss like that without warning."

Allison sighed and flounced farther into the couch, propping her feet up on my coffee table. I leaned back to sit alongside her, our shoulders almost but not quite touching. "I want to believe you."

I rolled my head so I could watch her out of one eye. Her words steamrolled my heart flat. "But…"

"But it's going to take a little while for you to regain my trust."

I mulled that comment over for a long moment. "Are you going to give me the chance to?"

Allison rolled her head so she was staring back at me, her expression the one of fond exasperation I was pretty used to seeing when she looked at me. "Of course."

I beamed at her as my heart suddenly reinflated and then became almost too big. "Good."

"But I meant what I said yesterday. Complete honesty between us. Cheesecake, cats, strange obsession with weird space TV shows. I want us to share all of it."

"Okay."

Her expression softened, and she cupped the side of my face. "Because I love you, and there's nothing I don't want to know about you." She paused and grinned at me. "No matter how nerdy."

I laughed and smacked her lightly on the stomach. "Deal."

We sat there smiling at one another like idiots for who knows how long before I decided I had to kill the mood with a yawn.

Allison immediately stood and held out her hand to help me up off the couch. I appreciated her assistance since it hurt a lot less with her pulling me up than me trying to propel myself.

"What do you say we continue this in bed?" she said softly, once we were again face-to-face.

"Okay, seriously. How do you really do that? You're a mind reader, aren't you? It's okay. You can tell me. I won't say a word."

Allison chuckled. "Very funny, smart-ass." She punctuated her statement with a light slap on my butt. "Get going. You're going to get some sleep tonight if I have to exhaust you myself."

My entire body short-circuited, and my gut clenched as I started thinking of all the ways she could possibly achieve that goal. I closed my eyes and took a moment to savor the lightning strikes of desire crashing into all the most wonderful places before I whispered, "That could take all night."

"Then let's not waste any more time."

CHAPTER NINETEEN

The atmosphere that hung between Allison and me as we locked the apartment and turned off the lights so we could get ready for bed was thick and pungent with promise and tentative anticipation. I went through all my usual nighttime apartment prep in sort of a daze. My heart thudded loudly, and the palms of my hands tingled with the need to touch her. But underneath that was a discordant jangling of nerves I couldn't seem to banish. I knew it was stupid. Allison loved me, and we'd slept together countless times. But somehow knowing that this would be the first time since I'd been shot had me all keyed up, and not necessarily in a good way.

"Do you have an extra toothbrush?" Allison asked softly, scattering my worried thoughts as we lingered together in the doorway to the bathroom, stealing shy, sidelong glances at one another.

"Sure," I told her, my voice catching slightly. I went to retrieve one from the hall closet where all my spare toiletries lived. "Do you need something to sleep in?"

"If you don't mind. I didn't exactly come prepared."

Only when she said that did it register that I hadn't seen a bag. Not even a purse. She had nothing except whatever was in the pockets of her suit. I turned to face her, intent on reading her expression. "You came up here without anything?"

Allison shrugged and looked away. She bit her bottom lip, and the barest traces of a flush tinted her olive-toned cheeks. "It was sort of a spur-of-the-moment trip."

I smiled slightly, taking care not to let her see lest she be embarrassed, and handed her the toothbrush so she could begin her nightly ritual. I couldn't help the immature rush of pleasure that the notion of her sleeping in my clothes ignited, and I didn't bother to try. On the contrary, I purposely chose one of my old JJRTC shirts for her to wear simply because it had O'CONNOR emblazoned on the back in big, bold, black letters.

After changing into my own pajamas, I knocked lightly on the mostly closed bathroom door, holding the T-shirt and boxer shorts I'd retrieved for Allison in my other clenched fist. I had to wait a few moments before she opened it with an expectant look on her face, the skin of which was now slightly damp and beautifully makeup free. I held up the clothes so I could hand them to her as she stepped to one side, allowing me into the bathroom.

I turned the taps in the sink, testing the temperature several times. Then I grabbed a cotton ball and the bottle of eye makeup remover and started taking off my eyeliner and mascara, basking in the pleasure this scene of domesticity invoked.

Allison made no move to leave. Rather than retreating to my bedroom to get dressed, she propped one shoulder against the doorjamb to the bathroom and stared at me.

"What?" I asked, giving her a quick, puzzled look.

"I like the shirt you chose for me," she teased.

My face flushed, and I was grateful I could avoid looking at her in favor of washing it. I took my time wetting, lathering, and rinsing my skin. Then, for good measure, I repeated the process.

Still silent, I snagged the hand towel from the rack next to the sink and patted my face dry. I then began to brush my teeth. All the while, Allison rested smugly against the door frame, watching me with a vaguely cocky smile.

"It's too bad I didn't think to bring one of my shirts up for you," she mused, as she cast her eyes back to the name stenciled in black Magic Marker on the back of the tee she'd stretched out between her hands.

"You want me to have one of your shirts?" I mumbled around a mouthful of toothpaste and bristles. I spat once and resumed brushing, watching her carefully. Exchanging training shirts would've been rather akin to teenagers exchanging watches or letterman jackets. Did she find the notion cute or hopelessly juvenile?

Allison glanced up at me, her eyes wide. Judging by the glimmer of fear that flashed beneath her eyes, I deduced she hadn't meant to speak aloud. She hesitated for what felt like an eon, an unsettling mix of emotions dominating her features.

"It wouldn't be the worst thing," Allison said finally. Her expression now showed an interesting mix of embarrassment, hope, and determination.

"Kinda like staking your claim on me, huh?" I joked, mumbling through minty foam.

"It's better than branding you, don't you think? Or would you prefer I tattooed my name on your forehead?" She tried to make it a joke, but I was onto her. I don't know what'd made her think that would work. I'd invented that technique.

I scoffed. "No tattoos," I said, not bothering to remove the brush from my mouth. "But shirts are okay." I reverted my attention to the sink. Somehow I thought she'd be more comfortable and inclined to continue this discussion if I didn't make it a big deal.

"You're all right with that?" Her tone was mild, and in the mirror I could see her inspect her fingernails in a blatant attempt to avoid eye contact.

"With what?" I was torturing her a little bit now, but I couldn't help myself. I wanted to hear her admit it rather than just agree with something I'd said.

"Wearing my shirt. Me staking my claim on you, as you put it."

I spat once again, more a feeble stalling technique than anything else. I needed a moment to decide how to respond. Then I went back to brushing, at a much slower pace. I nodded in answer, having teased her enough for one evening. "Mmm-hmm."

"Really?"

"Mmm-hmm."

"Even if I give you the one where my name is stenciled on crooked?"

I laughed. "Even that one."

Allison grinned. "Good. Although, honestly, the idea of you sleeping in it when I can't be here captivates me. Kind of like I'm holding you even when we're apart." Her voice had dropped almost to a whisper, and I had to wonder whether that sentiment had slipped out as well.

I spat the remainder of the toothpaste into the sink and rinsed my mouth. Then I put the toothbrush back into its holder and stepped in front of her, taking her hands in mine, clothes and all.

"I kind of like the idea of that, too," I told her sincerely.

Allison's face lit up, and she beamed at me, though I caught the faintest undercurrent of relief. "I'll have to remember to give you one, then."

"I'll hold you to that." I felt a tug around my heart as I realized that when I demonstrated the depth of my attachment to her, she acted self-satisfied, but when she came close to providing evidence of her fondness for me, she became self-conscious and unsure, almost as though she fully expected to have her feelings mocked or rebuffed.

But I merely returned her smile and led her down the hall to the bedroom. It was a minor miracle that she allowed me to.

Silence reigned. I took as much time as possible preparing the bed for sleeping so I didn't have to watch her change into her borrowed pajamas. I didn't want to make her feel uncomfortable or self-conscious by leering at her, and I didn't want to become all hot and bothered and anxious.

The click of the lamp turning off was unexpectedly loud, but I was grateful for the sudden darkness. It didn't shatter the intimacy that'd crept up between us, but it'd softened it, made it more bearable. As much as I loved Allison, I was still sometimes caught off guard by certain facets of our relationship and welcomed anything that made them easier for me to endure. Like now.

I climbed into bed and turned so I was lying on my left side with my left hand curled beneath my cheek. Allison had adopted a mirroring pose just a few inches away. It took a moment for my eyes to adjust to the darkness, but once they did, I couldn't look away from her. And, as it always did, her beauty took my breath away.

"What are you thinking about?" Allison whispered softly.

"You."

Allison's lips curved into a small smile. "What about me?" She caressed my cheek lightly with her fingertips.

I wrapped my fingers gently around her wrist, needing to feel her, and matched her smile with one of my own. "How beautiful you are and how happy I am that you showed up at my office tonight."

"You are?"

"Of course."

"I'm glad." Allison hesitated, and even in the dark I could see her uncertain expression. "I wasn't sure how you would react."

"I'm always happy to see you. But I was surprised, especially since you were just up here yesterday. And you never did tell me what prompted the visit."

"Do I need a specific reason to spend time with you?"

Hmm. Her tone had been light, teasing, but I caught the hint of strain underneath. She was trying to avoid this topic for some reason. If I decided to push the issue, if I opted to ignore her earlier plea to table any serious discussions for the remainder of the night and try to cajole her to answer my questions, I'd need to tread extremely carefully from this point on.

"Not at all. But knowing you, I suspect there is one. I could hazard a guess."

"You could, huh? Enlighten me."

I slowly slid my hand up Allison's arm and tried not to wince at the ache in my shoulder as I wrapped it around her waist and tugged, urging her closer. She slid over, pressing the entire length of her body against mine. Her calf found its way atop both of my own, and I smiled at the sensation, then took a deep breath, inhaling the last traces of perfume that lingered on her skin.

"You missed me terribly. That's a given," I said.

"Mmmm. Could be. Though I'd never admit it. Your ego is big enough as it is. Go on."

"You couldn't manage even one more moment of not being able to gaze longingly into my eyes."

Even through the darkness, I could see that Allison rolled hers. "Oh, boy. It's getting deep in here."

"You knew you wouldn't be able to fall asleep without a good-night kiss."

Allison chuckled softly and captured my lips with her own. As always, their softness and their heat struck me dumb, as did their ability to effortlessly reignite the flames of desire that were pretty much always smoldering for her.

"I guess I can go now," Allison murmured thickly when the kiss finally ended, her lips still brushing against my own as she spoke. "You know, now that I've gotten what I came here for."

It took a few seconds for my brain to register her words and then to assign meaning to them.

"Probably a good idea," I said softly back, working my hand underneath the hem of the T-shirt she was wearing to rest against the small of her back. I started making slow circles on her skin with my fingertips. The more I touched her, the more I ached to touch her. The raw need building inside me was making it difficult for me to concentrate. "However, it is a long train ride back home. I could almost certainly be talked into giving you one more. You know, for the road. If you asked nicely."

"Oh, really?" Allison shifted her position so her thigh now rested on top of mine, just above the still-healing scar I now sported. She rocked her hips slightly and continued caressing my cheek. "How unbelievably generous."

"What can I say? I'm a giver." I allowed my hand to drift up her side so my palm just glanced along the outer curve of her breast and smiled when she was unable to rein in a tiny whimper.

"Lucky me."

"I'm glad you recognize that," I teased as I bridged the millimeter gap between us and took my sweet time memorizing the feel of her lips and tongue.

One of Allison's hands fisted in my hair, pulling me even closer, as her other one rested outside of my shirt on the swell of my breast, right over the top of my heart. Her fingertips were caressing my chest gently, which was a pleasurable contrast to the ones clutched fiercely in my now-tangled locks. It was my turn to let out a whimper.

"What was it? Really?" I whispered when our lips finally parted an eternity later.

Allison ignored me in favor of trailing feather-light kisses across my jaw and down my neck. Shivering, with goose bumps breaking out across my body, I slipped my free hand into the soft hair at the base of her neck and cradled her against me, encouraging her to go on.

For the longest time, I was positive she wouldn't answer me, and I allowed myself to drift, carried away by the waves of erotic sensation her clever lips and teeth and tongue were igniting. I'd actually almost forgotten I'd ever asked her a question when she suddenly murmured against the skin at the juncture where my neck met my shoulder.

"What was that?" I hadn't caught the words she'd uttered.

"I said, 'All of the above.'"

"And?" The word trailed off into a moan.

Heaving a gigantic sigh, Allison lifted her head so she could look at me. "And we had a conversation to finish."

"We did, huh?" I skimmed my thumb gently across her cheek and slid my other hand—the one that'd been thoroughly enjoying teasing the silken flesh of her torso—around her back and low enough so my fingers could slip just beneath the waistband of the borrowed boxer shorts she was wearing.

Allison's eyes fluttered for a second as a look of pained desire crossed her face. She pressed her lower lip between her teeth for an instant as the hand resting over my heart clenched the material of my shirt. "Mmm-hmm."

"You know, just because we decided to air all our dirty laundry to one another doesn't mean we have to do it all in two days."

Allison hesitated, obviously choosing her next words carefully. "Things have been strained between us since the day you left the hospital. Ever since the day we met, we've always connected effortlessly. Even after years of not speaking to one another, we fell right back into our old routine the instant we were in the same room together. Then all of a sudden, this weird distance sprang up between us."

Allison ducked her head and refocused all her attention on tracing the ridged collar of my shirt with her fingertips. I could tell this was difficult for her to say for some reason, so I concentrated on sketching soothing patterns on her body while attempting to exercise my almost-nonexistent patience.

"We bridged most of it last night, and I know there's no rush, but I didn't want to wait any longer than I had to before completely settling things."

"And do you feel like things have been settled now?"

"We still need to talk about a few things, but yeah. I think we're good."

Despite her words, her expression was somehow achingly sad as she made it a point not to look at me. My heart crumbled. Even through the dark I could see each thought and emotion etched deeply into her eyes.

"Do you want to talk about them now?" I asked, trying not to yawn again.

Allison shook her head, clearing her melancholy away. "Not tonight. And before you say anything, no. I'm not stalling. I just…have other plans for you. The things we have left to hash out can wait another day or two."

"So, really you just came up here to get laid," I said with a grin.

Allison gave me an exaggerated eye roll. "Of course you'd focus on that."

"Yet I notice you're not denying it."

"How is it I'm so much more mature than you are?"

"Probably because you're older. Much older."

Allison gaped at me, her expression now part disbelief and part exasperation with a hint of outrage. "Are you calling me old?"

"Do you need a hearing aid? Have things already progressed that far? Wow."

"I can't believe you just said that." Allison's eyes narrowed.

"If the orthopedic shoe fits…"

"Oh, that's it," Allison growled playfully in the back of her throat, rolling us so she was straddling me, careful to keep as much of her weight off me as she could. She took my wrists in her hands and pressed them into the mattress on either side of my head, being cautious not to press too hard on my right one. "You're in serious trouble now."

Whatever lingering anxiety I'd still been harboring over our first sexual encounter since the incident had completely evaporated. Now I was a little afraid she'd decide I was still too injured for this and want to stop. I gritted my teeth against the burning in my shoulder and took a deep breath, trying to steady my voice before I spoke. "Oh, I am, am I?"

"Believe it."

"What're you going to do?" I taunted her, struggling a bit against her hold with my left hand for show. We both knew I didn't really mean it, didn't really want her to let me up. "Bore me to death by summarizing the entire history of the world since your birth eight hundred and ninety years ago?"

"Just because you look twenty-one doesn't mean you have to act like it," she shot back.

"Clearly, I need a thorough lesson in respecting my elders," I replied, struggling not to laugh.

Allison leaned down so our noses were almost touching and looked directly into my eyes. The passion I saw eddying beneath her own took my breath away. "Impertinent, as always."

"I try. And you love it."

"Shut up." She pressed her lips to mine in a possessive, bruising kiss. As if I weren't turned on enough already, she had to throw gasoline on the fire by kissing me like that. It was official. The woman was trying to kill me.

I pushed my hand against her hold as I kissed her back, desperate to wrap my arms around her and pull her tight against me. Allison endured it for a while, but eventually her patience wore thin.

"Stop fighting me," she warned, her lips still brushing mine as she spoke, her voice a low rumble that made me whimper.

"Or what?" I retorted, unable to rein in my pride long enough to ask her for what I really needed, which was to hold her.

"Or I'll get out the handcuffs," Allison whispered back, a devilish gleam in her eyes.

Oh, dear God. A tidal wave of arousal threatened to drown me, and I closed my eyes and inhaled sharply. I thrust my hips up against her in a pathetic attempt to hurry this little game of hers along, ignoring the tiny flares of pain that exploded along my back. I didn't think I could take much more of her teasing.

Unfortunately, Allison refused to be rushed. Instead, she shifted so she could murmur against my ear, rubbing her center purposefully against my lower abdomen as she did so. I could feel the passion radiating off her body, and that only stoked my own fire.

"You'd like that, wouldn't you?"

"Mmm?" I was only half paying attention. Between the timbre of her voice, the feeling of her holding me down, and that thing she was doing with her hips, it was a wonder I could focus that much.

"I think you would," Allison went on, caressing the outer shell of my ear with her lips. "Being handcuffed to the headboard so you're completely at my mercy and helpless against anything I might do to you."

"Fuck you." I was trying for impudent, but my voice was much too breathy and desire-laden.

"I think you'd like that, too," Allison mused as she shifted her attentions to the sensitive skin of my neck.

"Oh, Christ," I moaned, arching into that touch, sparks blazing blistering trails across my skin wherever she was pressed against me.

Allison hummed and pulled back, taking a long moment to regard me as she obviously considered something. Lust and mischief sparkled in her eyes as she watched me, and I gulped. Her lips curved into an absolutely wicked smile, and I knew I was in serious trouble.

She leaned back over so her lips were once again within kissing distance, but when I tried to take advantage of the position, she moved away, not granting me what I so badly wanted. I growled in frustration and glared at her.

"Ah, ah, ah," she admonished me in a singsong voice that was far too amused for my liking. "Behave yourself."

"Allison," I whined, attempting to kiss her again.

She allowed it, but if I'd held any illusions that she was conceding control of this situation to me, well, I was mistaken. I tried to deepen the kiss only to have her pull back again.

"Here's what's going to happen," Allison said softly, punctuating the statement with a teasing brush of her lips against mine. "You"— kiss—"are going to lie here"—kiss—"and not move a muscle"— kiss—"and just watch the show." Another, much longer kiss.

"What show?" I asked, dazed, when we finally parted for some much-needed oxygen.

Allison released her hold on my wrists and sat up, holding my gaze as she pulled her T-shirt over her head and tossed it lazily to the floor. I drank in the sight of her naked flesh, and my breath escaped my lungs in a soft whoosh.

"Oh." That was all I could think of to say. Granted, it wasn't one of my better comebacks, but it was a miracle I could form words at all.

Allison grinned at me but said nothing. Instead, she ripped off her boxer shorts and went right back to straddling me, her thighs pressing gently against the outside of my hips. Having her heat so close to my own center made my eyes flutter closed, and I let out a shaky breath.

"Open your eyes," Allison commanded in a husky voice.

My chin trembled as I obeyed, although I wasn't sure how long I'd be able to refrain from touching her, and I definitely didn't want to find out what the punishment would be for giving in to that impulse.

Allison rewarded me with a sultry smile that made my pulse jump, and my fingers twitched involuntarily. I ached to feel her hot skin against my hands, my cheeks, my lips. The longing caused my insides to writhe and roil, and I was having a hard time staying still.

If Allison was aware of my inner turmoil, she gave no indication. She merely murmured, "Good girl," as she closed her own eyes and allowed her head to loll back.

I was about to protest the unfairness of the situation when her hands started to move, trailing up the tops of her thighs from her knees toward her hips. The words of objection evaporated in my mouth, which was suddenly unbelievably dry. I attempted to lick my lips, but that action was the exact opposite of helpful.

I stared in wonder as Allison stroked feather-light patterns on the soft skin of her own thighs, straying dangerously close to her center only to slide away at the last possible moment. A throaty groan broke the silence. It might have been mine. I hardly cared.

Allison's hands blazed an excruciatingly slow path over her flat abdomen and up to her perfect breasts. Her nipples were already hard, and the desire building inside me to claim them as my own was overwhelming.

"Allison," I whispered, softly, my tone just this side of pleading.

"Shhh." Her palms skimmed lightly across her nipples and continued up her chest, past her shoulders and over her neck to bury in her long dark hair. As she did that, her head tipped back even farther, her lips parted as she let out a low moan of her own. Her hips rocked against me, her arousal soaking the shorts I was still wearing.

My brain was absolutely fried. My breathing was shallow. My heart was a dull roar in my ears. My own sex was swollen and throbbing, and I was positive if I wasn't allowed to touch her soon, I would go irrevocably insane. Her touching herself as she sat astride me had to have been one of the most erotic sights I'd ever beheld.

"Let me touch you," I implored her.

Allison's hands resumed their leisurely exploration. My eyes were riveted to the sight of her expert fingers rolling her hardened nipples around. She played with those stiffened peaks for a few moments before allowing her right hand to slip down between her thighs.

"Oh, Christ," she hissed, then groaned loudly as her fingers brushed through her obviously soaked folds. "Oh, Ryan, this feels incredible."

"Fuck." I was teetering on the edge of a decision. Did I lie still and watch her get herself off on top of me? Or did I flip her over and just take her? I couldn't make up my mind.

Allison moaned again loudly when she slid her fingers slowly inside herself, and as she rocked her hips in time with her own motions, I suddenly forgot what I'd been struggling to make up my mind about. My attention remained fixated on the sight of her hand buried deep within her heated sex as though I were staring into the face of God Himself.

Allison stilled above me and withdrew her fingers, causing a small noise of extreme disappointment to escape the back of my throat. I glanced up at her. She was smirking at me, triumphantly. I almost spontaneously combusted. She was so unbelievably hot when she was smug, although I'd never admit that to her lest she use the information against me.

"Since you're being so good," she said. And then she traced the contours of my lips with the hand that'd just been inside of her, painting them liberally with her wetness.

I took her fingers into my mouth, sucking on them lightly and swirling around the digits with my tongue. She made a tsk sound and shook her head as she removed them, but her indulgent smile and the twinkle in her eyes told me she wasn't nearly as exasperated with my rebellion as she was pretending to be.

I sighed and refocused my attention on the task of removing all traces of her arousal from my lips, relishing the unique taste of her and feeling humbled and awed that it was all for me. My heart swelled inside my chest, and I stared up at her, completely overwhelmed.

"I love you," I whispered quietly.

Allison's eyes softened at my words. "I love you, too."

"I can tell," I teased her, allowing my gaze to drop down to where her hand was once again toying gently with her silken folds.

"Shut up. You're breaking my concentration."

I laughed. "And they say romance is dead."

Allison shot me a mock glare but didn't retort. Instead, she said, "Give me your hand."

I hastened to comply, thrilled that I was being allowed out of the penalty box and would actually get to play.

Allison caught my fingers with her free hand just before I could touch her.

I growled at her, thoroughly frustrated. "You said to give you my hand," I complained. The woman was going to drive me crazy.

"Not that hand. Your other hand."

I stared at her blankly for a long moment, curious as to why it mattered.

Allison raised my right hand slowly to her lips and dropped a tender kiss on my knuckles before placing it on the outside of her hip. She covered it with her left hand to keep it in place and reached for my left hand with her right.

"I don't want to hurt you," she said softly, stroking the wound on my shoulder carefully. "And I can tell that moving this arm at all bothers you. So we're going to give it a rest until you're healed a little bit more, okay?"

"Okay." A small part of me was touched by her thoughtfulness. But the majority of me just longed to be inside her already and was beyond caring how that happened as long as it happened soon.

"Don't move."

"Okay."

"I mean it. At all. Stay completely still or I stop."

"I said okay."

Allison flashed me a quick smile. She appeared to understand my predicament because she wasted no more time on teasing or explanations. She merely guided my left hand to the apex between her thighs and impaled herself roughly on my fingers.

She was hot and wet, and I groaned at the sensation of sliding effortlessly into that slippery heat. She began riding my hand, rolling her hips in the most sensually erotic way. Between the feel of her writhing against my own overheated skin and the sight of her wantonly taking her pleasure from me, I was in complete sensory overload. It was an epic struggle not to move, but there'd be hell to pay if I did, so I held my breath, listening to her small gasps and moans mingling with the pounding of my heart as she drove herself to climax.

She stared down at me with the most amazing expression of

lust-tinged adoration as her inner walls clenched around my fingers. My right hand tightened on her hip hard enough to leave a bruise as I watched her ride out her orgasm.

After a long moment, her body stopped spasming, and she collapsed forward onto her hands so that she was hovering over me once again. I got lost looking into her eyes before she kissed me softly.

"Incredible," she whispered almost inaudibly against my lips.

"Yes, you were."

Allison pulled back with an affectionate smile. "Flatterer."

"It happens to be true."

She rewarded my words with another lingering kiss before sliding slowly down my body. I lamented the loss of my advantageous hand positions as she slipped out of my reach, but she quickly soothed that ache by drawing my shirt up over my chest and showering my breasts with languid kisses.

My breath caught in my throat at the sensation of her lips ghosting across sensitive nipples—just hard enough to torment me, but not nearly enough to sate my desire—and continuing their leisurely exploration of my entire chest. I tangled my fingers in her hair and desperately pressed her closer, rocking my hips against her stomach in a silent plea.

"Oh, Allison." I sighed softly as she finally wrapped her lips around one aching nipple and sucked, flicking the tip of it with her tongue.

My entire body was humming. Even without her earlier show to drive me to a desperate state of yearning, I was on fire. It'd been far too long since she'd touched me. The last time had been—No! I forcibly dragged my thoughts away from that topic as well as the memories of the consequences they stirred. I wanted, I needed Allison so badly I was almost in pain, and I was determined not to ruin this by straying out of the here and now.

"Please don't tease me," I begged softly. "Not now. Not tonight." I didn't think I'd ever needed to come so badly, and if she dragged this out any longer, she was sure to kill me.

"Okay," Allison murmured softly, nuzzling the swell of my breasts with her cheek as she spoke. "Okay."

Her hot fingers curled inside the waistband of my shorts and tugged a little. At her silent request, I lifted my hips so she could remove them and relished the feeling of cool air against my burning flesh.

I half expected her to take her time and draw out her exploration despite her assurances she wouldn't torture me anymore, but she surprised me. She paused only long enough to place gentle kisses on the stitches on the outside of my thigh before she shot me the fleeting traces of a dazzling smile and immediately adjusted her position so she was settled comfortably between my legs.

At the first feeling of her tongue against my folds, I almost burst into tears. A hoarse, ragged cry, somewhere between a laugh and a sob, escaped my throat. I spread my legs wider and tangled my fingers back into her hair roughly.

"Oh, fuck," I mumbled, squeezing my eyes shut and rolling my head back and forth against the indescribable ecstasy she was wringing from me.

My body was completely beyond my control, the entire experience a blur of sensations. I was panting heavily, little mewling cries of pleasure falling from my lips. Her nimble lips and tongue explored me surely, knowing exactly where and how to stroke to drive me closer to the edge.

I held my breath in anticipation of the inevitable, torn between wishing for the orgasm and never wanting to leave the place I was blissfully floating in. In the end, Allison decided for me. She thrust two fingers into me roughly, curling the tips to ensure she hit just the right place inside, wrapped her lips around me, and sucked.

"Oh, God, Allison," I cried as I came, clenching and unclenching my fists in her hair in time with the quaking of the rest of my body.

Allison continued, albeit much more gently, drawing out the exquisite sensations for what felt like an eternity. Eventually, it was too much for me, and I tugged gently on her hair in an attempt to get her to stop.

"No more," I gasped, as a shiver racked my body. "Please."

Allison beamed up at me and placed one last light kiss on my sex before readjusting her position so she lay stretched out next to me on the bed. I wasted no time cuddling up to her, resting my head on her chest and wrapping my arm around her waist.

"Thank you," I whispered softly, turning my head slightly to place a grateful kiss against the curve of her breast.

"The pleasure was all mine. Believe me."

"Remind me to properly express my gratitude later," I mumbled through a yawn.

Allison nuzzled the top of my head. "Don't worry. I will. Now, go to sleep."

"Mission accomplished," I murmured.

"What?"

"You wanted to tire me out," I said. Or tried to.

"Shhh."

"Mmm. Okay." I sighed heavily and snuggled deeper into her embrace, relishing the sound of her heartbeat beneath my ear. It was a soothing, comforting sound, and it helped lull me into a state of even further relaxation.

It wasn't long before I drifted off, too beat to entertain much more than a fleeting concern about waking her with one of my bad dreams. But it turned out I didn't need to be worried because for the first time since "the incident" I slept—actually slept—secure in the knowledge that I was safe and loved and free from all nightmares.

CHAPTER TWENTY

The next morning, I snuck into the JTTF office ridiculously early. Allison had had to catch an early train back to DC in order to be on time for her afternoon shift, so I hadn't exactly been forced to drag myself away from her. However, she did almost miss the departure because we took way too long fooling around in the shower. I'd have been more than happy to endure that consequence, but she doubted it would've amused the guys working the day shift.

While I'd been sad to see her go, a small part of me was relieved she wouldn't be around for what lay ahead. I was having enough trouble coming to grips with the reality of the situation. The last thing I needed was the distraction of her presence. I really needed to be on my A game for this.

I quickly printed out copies of all the emails I'd exchanged with Greg on the subject of the phone calls, as well as all the emails and documents I'd received from Sarah relating to Akbari. I already had hard copies of the subpoena results, as well as the printouts of the building entry logs and the list of who'd been assigned to work the Iran delegation for all their visits during the past few years. Pausing only long enough to throw everything into a folder and snag a blank legal pad, I fled back to the relative safety of my apartment.

To say I was a little on edge would've been the understatement of the century. From the time I'd set foot outside to the time I was safely back home, I'd been keyed up and jumpy. Every unexpected noise had made me start. Every eye that lingered on me too long on the street had made me tense. I'd have given anything to have the peace of mind that carrying my weapon had provided me. I hadn't realized how much I'd relied on that sense of security until now.

Once I was safe in my apartment with a doorman and a locked door between me and potential death, I started making a chart and organizing all my documents in a way to make it easy for the AUSA to follow. I didn't want to leave any room for doubt. I wanted to be able to answer any question he put to me quickly and convincingly. I could only pray it'd be enough for him to issue a warrant for Mark's arrest. SAIC Quinn's certainty that it would helped to ease my mind. Well, somewhat.

A knock on my door interrupted my arts-and-crafts session, and I froze, my lukewarm cup of coffee halfway to my lips. Well, my body froze. My heart, on the other hand, began a wild gallop that would've put Seattle Slew to shame. Gingerly, I set the coffee mug down and reached for my gun, wincing both at the tug the motion produced in my shoulder and at the realization I wasn't wearing it. You'd have thought I'd have been used to its absence by now, but clearly years of wearing it every day overrode common sense.

I cast around my living room for some sort of weapon just as the knocking sounded again. Whoever was at my door had made it past the doorman downstairs. Normally, the front desk called up to verify that all visitors and deliveries were expected and welcomed. That I hadn't received a call led me to believe that whoever my uninvited guest was, they'd badged their way past the front desk. Considering that the man who wanted me dead possessed a badge, the notion didn't fill me with a warm, fuzzy feeling.

Snagging the largest butcher knife I owned out of the block on my kitchen counter on the way by, I crept to the door. My palms had started to sweat, necessitating a quick swipe against the leg of my pants to dry them and a readjustment of my grip on my makeshift weapon. Licking my lips, I chanced a quick glance through the peephole to see who was in the hall.

At first I didn't recognize the slight figure standing with its back to me clad in a dark raincoat with the hood pulled up. I blinked and took another look through the peephole as the figure turned. The relief that flooded me when I finally realized it was SAIC Quinn threatened to knock me off my feet. I fumbled with the locks a bit before throwing the door open wide to grant her entrance.

"SAIC Quinn," I said, flushing at my surely disheveled state.

SAIC Quinn favored me with a puzzled look as she stepped inside and pushed the hood back off her head. "Claudia, please. I thought I told you that last night. Are you okay?" Her eyes flicked uncertainly to the knife in my hand and then back up to me.

I blushed harder and hastened to deposit the knife on my kitchen counter. "Sorry about that. It's just I wasn't expecting anyone, and you know…"

SAIC Quinn—Claudia—shut and locked the door behind her. Her expression now was knowing and sympathetic. "You're right. I should've called first. I'm sorry."

"Please, don't apologize. It's my fault. I hope I didn't scare you."

She grinned at me. "Are you kidding me? I used to live in Crown Heights back in the day. An upset woman with a butcher knife is the least of my concerns."

I laughed at her dark joke. "Can I offer you anything to drink or eat?"

"Coffee would be great, if you have any."

I went about fixing her a cup, recalling how she'd prepared it for herself the night before. "So, not that I'm not happy to see you, but what are you doing here? I thought you were going to call me with a place to meet you in a couple hours."

Claudia accepted the offered mug and followed me to the living room, where she took a seat on the couch beside me. She took off her raincoat and adjusted the rubber band that held her hair. "I was. But then it occurred to me that having you leave your apartment might not be the best idea."

The blood in my veins turned to ice. "You think I'm being followed." It wasn't a new idea—hell, I'd been keyed up by the notion all morning—but for some reason hearing her say it out loud still gave me chills.

"I can't say for certain you are," Claudia said. "But I thought it best not to tempt fate."

I nodded slowly, and then a sharp sliver of terror pierced my heart. "Allison," I gasped softly.

Claudia regarded me with a quizzical look.

"She came looking for me at the office last night. She spent the night here. She left early this morning to go back to DC. What if she—"

I clamped my lips together and swallowed hard, unable to even finish the thought.

Claudia put her coffee cup down and rested a reassuring hand on my arm. "Ryan, relax. I'm sure she's fine."

"You can't know that. I have to call her." I reached for my cell phone.

"By all means, if it makes you feel better. But let me remind you that Allison spending the night here isn't necessarily going to raise any red flags with anyone. I mean, it's not exactly a secret that you're together. Mark won't think her being here has anything to do with him."

"I know that," I told her as I waited for my cell-phone provider to connect the call to Allison's cell. "But he tried to have me killed, which means he's desperate. And we both know the lengths desperate people will go to."

"True. But he also doesn't know you're onto him, so we've got that point in our favor."

I didn't answer. My entire being was focused on my phone, and I lamented that it took damn near forever for a call to connect sometimes. Allison's phone went straight to voice mail. Okay. That wasn't necessarily a reason to panic. Maybe the train was in one of the underground stations along the way. My mind whirled as I attempted to recall what time her train was supposed to leave and calculate roughly where she should be at the moment, if the train was running on schedule. It was too much to contemplate, so I gave up and shifted my energy to trying not to freak out. "Trying" being the operative word. I left what I hoped was a regular-sounding message asking her to call me when she could and put the phone back on the table. I slumped into the cushions of the couch and let out a long, slow breath.

Claudia shot me another sympathetic look and shifted her attention to the piles of papers on my coffee table. She inclined her head in their direction. "Is this everything?"

I forcibly tamped down on my near terror that something had happened to Allison and attempted to banish that feeling. I definitely wasn't completely caught up on sleep yet, but what rest I'd managed to get the previous evening seemed to have restored some of my normal self-control. I was still scared for her, but I was able to push past that fear enough so I could concentrate on the task at hand.

"It's everything I have." I was thankful I'd almost finished compiling all the documents into order just before she'd knocked. "I hope it's enough."

"Let's see what you've got."

We spent a considerable amount of time going over everything from beginning to end. As I presented each new piece of evidence to her, I studied her face for any telltale expression—good or bad. Unfortunately, she'd been an agent way too long, and her countenance gave away absolutely nothing of her thoughts. Shame. I'd have liked to have some indication.

"Well?" I asked finally. I'd shown her everything, and she'd sat quietly for quite some time after I finished. I hated to rush her, but this was sort of a life-and-death matter. "What do you think?"

"Are we waiting on anything else?"

"Yes. Subpoena information on the two telephone numbers Golzar had contact with just prior to the shooting, including cell-tower information. I asked for those just before I came to see you last night. Given the circumstances, the AUSA said he would put a rush on it for me."

The ghost of a smile dusted Claudia's lips. "Good thinking."

I lifted my good shoulder in a half shrug. "I figured if one of them belonged to the shooter, the cell-site information would confirm it. I didn't know the other phone was Mark's when I asked, but cell-site info will help us confirm it's his, too. I just don't know how long it'll take to get those results."

Claudia's smile widened, a sly, almost predatory gleam in her eyes. "We'll have them before the warrant is cut, I promise you."

"Really?"

"Do you honestly think that between me and the chief of the Counterterrorism Division of the Assistant United States Attorney's Office, there's anything we can't get when we want it?"

Now I was grinning. "No. I guess not."

"So, what's this, then?" Claudia asked, sliding the photos Meaghan had taken the night of the Akbari interview out of the envelope they'd been residing in for the past couple of weeks. She spread them out on the table in front of her and studied them.

"Oh. One of my colleagues, Meaghan Bates, took those on the

streets around Akbari's apartment the night we went to talk to him. She's big into photography and had some fancy night-vision stuff she wanted to test."

"Hmmm." Claudia's eyes were roving over the pictures, and she sounded distracted.

"We actually had to wait a while until after we'd left for it to get completely dark before she could take them," I told her, more to fill the silence than to actually impart any useful information. "I hadn't wanted to, honestly, but Meaghan had done a favor for me by even coming out there so—"

"Did you look at these?"

"Briefly, the day after she took them. Why?"

"Do me a favor and examine them again? Maybe, in light of everything you know now that you didn't know then, something'll jump out at you."

"Okay." I took the offered photos and started perusing them. Claudia contented herself with sipping her coffee and checking her emails on her BlackBerry while I looked. At first glance, nothing struck any particular chord with me, but I figured since I had time to kill, I might as well take one more, closer look.

I got up to grab something out of my bag and was met with a curious glance from Claudia as I sat back down. I flashed her a smile and held up the object in my hand. It was the loupe I used to use to examine counterfeit currency. "It couldn't hurt, right?"

Claudia's countenance was one of mild surprise. "No. I suppose it couldn't."

"How much time do I have until we have to meet the AUSA?"

She consulted her watch. "He'll be here in about an hour."

Now it was my turn to be surprised. "He's coming here?"

"It seemed like the best course of action."

I nodded thoughtfully and went back to examining Meaghan's pictures. It was slow going, as I wasn't sure precisely what I was supposed to be looking for. After the second one, I felt like my eyes were starting to cross.

On picture number six, something gave me pause. I snagged my flashlight from my bag and shone the light directly on the photo in the hopes it would help me determine whether it was anything to get excited about.

"Did you find something?"

"Maybe," I murmured. I leaned even closer, as though having my eyes mere inches from the loupe would help somehow. I slid the picture closer to Claudia and gestured. "Tell me what you see."

"A car. Late-model sedan. Dark. Maybe a Toyota? I'm not sure. Jersey plates. And there's a sticker in the back window." Claudia frowned in concentration and leaned nearer, just as I had. "Some kind of pirate flag or something. Skull and crossbones. Might be writing underneath the image, but I can't make it out." She looked up at me but didn't lift her head. "Does that mean something to you?"

I took a deep breath as I considered the question. "It's probably nothing, but Mark has a thing for pirates."

"Does he own a personal car?"

"He lives in Jersey, so it's likely. I doubt this is his—I mean, that'd be way too easy—but I'd like to run the plate anyway, just to rule it out. What time does Hannah come in today?"

Claudia nodded. "She said she planned to head in early so she'd be in a position to help us if we needed it. And Hurricane had no scheduled movements, so unless she had a sudden urge to go out and do something, Hannah should be in the CP."

"Great." I sent Hannah a quick email asking her to run a DMV check on the plate number from the photo. "I'd rather have Hannah run it than ask someone in NYFO. You know, just in case it does come back to Mark. I'd hate to inadvertently tip our hand."

"Good thinking."

I fiddled with my BlackBerry anxiously as I waited for Hannah to answer. "So, do you think this'll be enough for the AUSA?"

"Absolutely. You've got a great foundation with this alone. If the cell-site info tells us what you think it will, it's a slam dunk."

"I hope so. The sooner we grab this guy, the happier I'll be."

"You and me both. I'm absolutely furious that one of our own resorted to such tactics. It's terrible for a civilian. For one of us, it's unconscionable."

"He's clearly not worthy of trust and confidence," I said, referring to our agency motto.

Claudia laughed. "You're taking this pretty well."

"Ha. You should've seen me last night when I called that phone and Mark answered. Believe me, I was the exact opposite of well."

"You bounce back quickly, then."

"Yeah. I'm a regular real-life Weeble," I drawled sarcastically, thinking about the past few days and how well I had not handled anything.

"Is your dad free early this afternoon? I'd like to have a quick chat with him before I go grab Mark."

"I checked both his and Mark's schedules this morning," I said, wiggling my BlackBerry at her. "They're both supposed to be in the office all day."

"Perfect. Should be easy, then. One-stop shopping. I can brief your dad and then go pick up Mark."

"Here's hoping," I told her as my BlackBerry chimed to indicate an incoming email message.

"What is it?" Claudia asked.

"It's Hannah." A slow smile stole over my features.

"It's his car, isn't it?"

"Got it in one."

"This should be enough for the AUSA. I can't imagine he'd need much else."

"Even if it's not, you can still interview Mark and just lay it all out for him. I know him. He's a bully, but it's all an act. He's a coward to the core. If he thinks you can hit harder than he can—which we both know you can—he'll tell you everything you want to know. All you need to do is get him to confess, and the warrant will write itself."

Claudia glanced at her watch again. "We should know soon enough. It's almost time for our meeting. You ready?"

I grinned again. "You have no idea."

CHAPTER TWENTY-ONE

The meeting with the chief of the Counterterrorism Division of the United States Attorney's Office for the Southern District of New York went a lot quicker and a lot smoother than I'd ever have thought possible.

Claudia also hadn't been kidding when she'd told me that, between the two of them, they could get me that subpoena information for those phone numbers faster than Joey Chestnut could eat a hot dog. In the space of two well-placed phone calls, I was the proud owner of cell-site information for the suspect numbers in question. And, surprise, surprise, the results showed exactly what I'd expected. The one number hit off towers in the vicinity of Mark's home and our field office. The other number hit off towers in the area near the InterCon on the day I was shot. If I were a different kind of girl, I might've done a victory dance at receiving that information. But as I'm a consummate professional, I danced only on the inside.

Between those subpoena results and all the other facts I'd gathered, the AUSA had no problem drafting a warrant for Mark's immediate arrest. He hadn't been in my apartment for more than forty minutes before he'd excused himself so he could go back to his office to write it up. He promised he'd get it before a judge, and we'd have it in a matter of hours.

That actually worked out perfectly because it gave us plenty of time to go over to NYFO so we could brief my dad. I was admittedly a little nervous to see how he would react to this news, both as an agent and as a father. I was also curious to see which part of his personality would win out. For his sake, I hoped it'd be the agent side, but I simply couldn't be sure.

I knocked tentatively on the edge of his door frame, reluctant to interrupt whatever he had going on but knowing this needed to be done ASAP. He looked up from the document he'd been perusing and blinked at me, obviously surprised.

"Ryan, what are you doing here?"

"Sir? Do you have a minute."

He frowned slightly at the request—or perhaps at the formality of it, I couldn't be sure—but didn't comment. "Of course. Please, come in."

Claudia and I entered, and I shut the door gently behind me. With a fortifying breath, I turned to face him. "Dad, I'm sure you remember SAIC Claudia Quinn from Hurricane's detail."

My father blinked at me, presumably startled by me addressing our relationship in front of someone else, but then stood and came out from behind his desk to shake her offered hand. "Of course. Good afternoon, SAIC Quinn. It's nice to see you again."

"Come on, Ben. We've known each other too long to stand on that kind of ceremony. Call me Claudia, please."

Dad grinned at her, making me wonder exactly how well they knew one another and whether I'd be able to get either of them to dish whatever dirt they may've had on each other.

"Please, have a seat." Dad gestured to the couch and chairs on the other side of his office away from his desk. He allowed us all a few moments to get settled before speaking again. "So, you ready to make the transition to OPO, Claudia?"

"Absolutely. The official mail notification should go out in the next few days or so. I've already pushed my date up, so the move will be quick."

I was surprised they'd talk about something that was so closely guarded right in front of me, but if the notification was impending, I supposed it didn't really matter in the long run. Besides, while Claudia might not have known me that well, my dad knew I wouldn't tell anyone.

"They couldn't have picked a better agent for the job," Dad told her sincerely. "But I doubt you need me to stroke your ego. I imagine you're here for a reason. What can I do for you?"

Claudia shot me a glance out of the corner of her eye. On the ride over, we'd discussed our strategy for breaking this news to him and had decided he might take it a little better if he heard it from me. It was just a theory we were working on, but it'd sounded as good as any other when we'd talked about it.

"Dad, I have something to tell you, but you have to promise to just listen to me and not freak out. Okay?"

My dad narrowed his eyes at me. "That's normally not a good start to a conversation."

"And it isn't this time, either, I'm afraid," Claudia interjected smoothly. "But before Ryan fills you in, I want you to know we have the situation under control. There's absolutely nothing you need to do and nothing for you to worry about. This is just a courtesy notification. That's all."

"Also not a phrase that generally bodes well," Dad remarked dryly.

I rubbed the back of my neck with the palm of my hand. "Ah. Yeah. Well, here's the thing. Remember the other day when I told you I wanted to find out who killed Luce?"

"Of course. Although I'm surprised you do. You were pretty drugged. So, did you?"

"Not exactly. I mean, I think I found the burner phone the trigger man was using when he got the call to take the shot. But I couldn't get much further with him."

"I spoke with my contact in the FBI a few minutes ago," Claudia informed him. "Their sources indicate the shooter was likely brought in for this one specific job. He used a fake ID and credit card to rent the room at the W that he fired the shots from, and the room was wiped completely clean. The crime-scene unit who worked it couldn't find a single usable print. Not for prior guests, housekeeping staff, nothing.

"The surveillance footage from the cameras in the common areas at the hotel allowed us to get a pretty good look at his face and to determine that he slipped out a side door less than a minute after the shots were fired and got into a yellow cab. The driver has already been interviewed, and he stated he'd been paid to wait at the curb, which he did for about fifteen or twenty minutes before the guy came down. Then he dropped the guy off at JFK, where the guy paid his fare in cash.

"They considered dusting the back of the taxi but figured it'd be a moot point. There'd be hundreds of prints in there, if not thousands.

Even if they could identify which ones belonged to the shooter, it's doubtful they'd get a positive ID on him. The chances he's of record with anyone are slim. And he's almost certainly long gone by this time. It's very likely he'll never be positively identified through conventional investigative means. However, the Bureau is following up with the security cameras at the airport to see if they can pin him down to a specific airline, and they're considering releasing the photos to the media to see whether anyone recognizes him."

Dad's expression was thoughtful. "I see. So, if you didn't identify the shooter, who did you identify?"

"We know who orchestrated the hit."

"Wonderful. Is he in custody?"

Claudia and I exchanged a glance. "Not yet, Dad. That's actually why we're here." I paused to give myself enough time to gather the courage sufficient to utter the words that were almost certain to throw my father into a tailspin. "It's protocol to inform the SAIC of a field office when one of his agents is about to be arrested for something of this magnitude."

Dad stared at me blankly for a very long time. Then he shifted his attention to Claudia and back to me again. I could see the realization trickling slowly, almost reluctantly, into his eyes. "You're saying one of my guys is responsible for this."

Claudia took her BlackBerry out of its holster and began punching in the password required to unlock it. I appreciated her attempt to give us some illusion of privacy for this moment.

"Yes," I replied simply.

My father had dedicated his entire life to the Secret Service. He loved this agency with every fiber of his being and was unbelievably proud of his tenure here. To hear that a fellow agent was responsible for something like this had to be breaking his heart, the fact that one of the casualties in the hit was his daughter notwithstanding.

Dad had clenched the arms of the chair he was sitting in so hard his knuckles were white. I could see the muscles in his throat work as he swallowed. "Do you know who?" His voice was calm, but I could tell that was forced. His lip twitched.

"Yes, Dad. It was Mark."

"Mark who?" Dad's tone had adopted a cutting edge, and his eyes were dark with rage.

"Mark Jennings, Dad. My AT."

"Ben," Claudia said softly. "I just got an email from the AUSA's office. We have the warrant. I reached out to my contacts at the JTTF, and they sent someone over to Southern District to swear it out. Three other guys from the JTTF are waiting in the lobby to make this arrest. They're in suits, so they won't attract any unnecessary attention when I take them to Mark's office. I just need for you to sit here for a few minutes until we have him in custody."

Dad shot to his feet, and the anger radiating off him was enough to sour the air in the entire room. "I'm going with you."

"We can't, Dad," I told him gently. "We have to stay here and trust Claudia to do her job."

"I have a right to be there when one of my agents is arrested. Especially when the charges are of this nature."

"You don't, Dad. And neither do I. This hits much too close to home for either of us to be remotely objective. And as much as we both want to be there, you know any defense attorney worth his salt will find a way to use it to his advantage if either of us is present for this."

"Fine. Then I want to be there when you interview him."

I let out a huff of annoyance. Clearly, the personal was winning out over the professional here. Good to know. You know, for the next time one of my coworkers tried to off me. "No, Dad. We can't sit in on the interview either. We don't want him to walk on a technicality. Any technicality. We have to stay here until Claudia says it's done."

"This is ridiculous," my father muttered darkly under his breath and began pacing the room. "Someone from the Service should be conducting this interview."

"I'll be there," Claudia told him. "I've discussed it with the JTTF reps, and they're fine with me taking the lead in the questioning."

"I'd like to be there, too." Dad seemed adamant about that.

"Look, Ben." Claudia placed a gentle hand on his arm, which stopped his back-and-forth. "I'll tell you what. Let's compromise. If you can promise me you'll stay out of the room—and I mean a solid promise—I'll interview him in one of your rooms downstairs, and you guys can watch." Claudia pointed a warning finger at him and pinned him with a threatening look. "If the door handle to that interview room so much as jiggles while we're in there, there's going to be hell to pay."

I smirked at the sight of my father being told what to do but managed to school my face back to a neutral expression just in time for him to look back at me. I blinked at him innocently and waited.

"Is that okay with you?" he asked.

"It's fine. Whatever gets his ass in jail faster, I'm all for it."

"I figured you'd want to talk to him. Find out why he did it."

I shrugged slightly and lifted my hands in a careless gesture. "I gave Claudia my list of questions. She knows what I want to ask him. Besides, this isn't her first rodeo. She can handle a custodial interview."

"Ben, we have to go. We need to do this now. Can I trust you to stay here until I come get you?" Claudia's eyes were serious as she assessed him.

Dad's whole frame sagged as he sat down hard on the chair he'd been occupying previously. He waved one hand toward the door absently. "Yeah. Go do what you have to do."

"Thanks," Claudia said. She fixed me with a long look and squeezed my bicep once reassuringly. "I'll be back for you in a few minutes," she said softly.

I caught her hand as she turned to leave. "Mark almost never wears his gun when he's here in the office. I don't know where he keeps it, so I don't have any idea how accessible it is to him, but I can count on one hand the number of times I've seen him with it on. For safety's sake, since I can't tell you where the weapon is, you might want to either get him outside of his office altogether or, if you want to avoid a scene, at least get him out from behind his desk and into the center of the room to give you more time to react if he lunges toward something."

Claudia smiled at me—probably because she'd been doing this for a lot longer than I had, and yet I'd still obviously felt compelled to give her a safety speech—and nodded once in acknowledgment. "Don't worry about us. We'll be fine."

I nodded back and released her hand. "Go get him, then."

After Claudia had departed, I sat back down on the couch and started studying the carpet. I could see the tracks left by the vacuum and let my eyes wander up the line of one pass and down the next. Silence reigned between us for a very long time.

"Now what?" Dad said finally, his voice low.

"Now we wait."

CHAPTER TWENTY-TWO

We didn't have to wait long. Maybe ten minutes. And while it was probably the longest ten minutes in my life to date, it wasn't awful. I mean, it was nothing compared to the time one of my friends dragged me to a Cher concert. That had been torture. And I reminded myself of the differences in the experiences repeatedly as the seconds ticked slowly by. I also hummed "Gypsies, Tramps, and Thieves" under my breath.

Finally, Claudia came back to the office to retrieve us. She informed us that Mark hadn't fought them, and that outside of a few tense moments during which it had appeared that he might've been considering it, the entire experience had been pretty anticlimactic.

She then escorted us to a viewing room downstairs. I suspected she did that because she wanted to make sure neither of us went rogue on her and tried to burst in and beat the hell out of Mark, but I didn't say that out loud. I merely chuckled silently to myself and trailed obediently behind her.

I left the lights in the viewing room off and stepped right up next to the one-way glass. I was trembling a little, but it was tough to tell whether that was due to fear, anger, or relief. Probably a mixture of all three. I didn't have it in me to analyze it closely.

Mark was sitting in the room next door, one hand attached to a bar bolted to the wall by a set of handcuffs, looking dejected and beaten. I didn't think I'd ever seen him look so small.

"He does, doesn't he?" My dad's whisper came from over my shoulder.

Curious, I glanced over at him. "What?"

Dad's eyes never left Mark. "Look small."

Oh. I hadn't realized I'd voiced that thought aloud. I didn't reply. There wasn't much else to say.

I adjusted the sound on the speaker embedded in the wall next to the glass as Claudia and one of the JTTF guys entered the room. I didn't recognize him, but the JTTF was pretty big, so that wasn't necessarily unusual. I wished I knew what squad he was in.

My eyes were glued to the scene in front of me. Claudia's face was completely impassive, which I deemed to be a pretty impressive feat, considering I knew she wanted to throttle the man sitting across from her. I placed my palm against the glass, allowing the cool smoothness to anchor me and keep me focused on something besides my spasming intestines.

"So, Mr. Jennings," Claudia said, and I couldn't help but grin at her deliberate failure to use his title. "I assume you know why you're here."

Mark was staring at the table in front of him with an intensity he normally reserved for scrutinizing my paperwork for mistakes. He didn't answer for a very long time. I was actually starting to doubt he was going to—which frustrated and angered me to no end—when he cleared his throat. His eyes slowly tracked across the tabletop to Claudia's hands, then trailed up her arms to finally land on her face. He nodded once.

"Good. Then I have some questions for you."

"Aren't you going to read me my rights?" Mark asked, a glimmer of his old swagger starting to appear.

"No," Claudia replied. "I don't have to. When the government has reasonable belief that lives are at stake, we're allowed to demand answers to certain questions without providing you the benefit of a Miranda Warning." A beat. "But you already know that."

"Yes." Mark had gone back to staring at the table again, his voice a hoarse whisper.

"So, Mr. Jennings. Let's get right down to it. Who, besides the president of Iran, is being targeted by your little sleeper cell?"

I shot a wary glance at my father, who was glaring holes at Mark through the one-way glass. Claudia and I had deliberately avoided telling him I was the target of the assassination attempt and not the president of Iran. We'd discussed the issue and decided we wanted to see whether she could get Mark to admit it. We'd also thought that if my dad had been privy to that information before Mark was taken into custody, no power in heaven or on earth would've kept him from killing Mark. I knew we only had so much time before that little nugget of joy came out during the questioning, and I wasn't sure having my dad here to witness the confession was the best idea. But I also didn't know how to get him to leave.

Mark had lapsed back into silence, during which Claudia and her partner—whose name, I was ashamed to admit, I hadn't caught when we'd been introduced earlier—merely continued to watch him. They were both the picture of patience. It was a damn good thing they were in there instead of me. I wasn't very good at waiting when I wanted something. I probably would've resorted to tactics in direct violation of the Geneva Convention. And I wouldn't have felt bad about that ever.

"Let me put this another way, Mr. Jennings. While we can tie several of your coconspirators to the plot to assassinate the president of Iran and have teams en route to pick them up, who do you think the Southern District of New York is going to be inclined to throw the book at? To make an example of? A bunch of Iranians? Or a special agent who swore an oath to protect and defend this country against all enemies both forcign and domestic?"

Mark still didn't reply, but he squirmed in his seat a bit. My jaw was clenched tight, and every muscle in my body was rigid as I watched this scenario unfold. The fury churning within me was making it difficult to keep still. Only the knowledge that my interference might blow the entire case kept me in that room, but only just.

"Another thing for you to consider," Claudia went on, as cool and casual as you please. "Do you really think for one second that your Iranian friends will protect you? Do you really think they won't try to offer you up as part of a plea deal to save themselves some jail time? Because if you honestly believe that, well, you're even dumber than I realized."

Mark's eyes shot up to meet hers, and he glared at her for a long, tense moment before the whole of what she'd said sank in. The ire in his gaze withered and died, and a flicker of something akin to fear took its place.

"We don't need you to tell us who else might be a target, Mr. Jennings. I was merely trying to offer you the professional courtesy of giving you the opportunity to talk first. But if you're refusing to speak to us, well, we can just get right to booking you." Claudia paused and glanced at her watch. "It's late in the day, which means you'll need to be housed at MCC for the night. There's no way you'll be able to see a judge today. Hopefully they can get you on the docket early tomorrow morning. Although, if I were you, I wouldn't count on making bail. I don't like to brag, but I made a couple of calls, and I can say with a fair amount of certainty you'll be remanded until trial."

A grin stole across my lips at her words, and I bit back a sharp laugh. Damn, she was good. As much as I itched to be driving the interrogation myself, I was really getting a kick out of watching her run the show. Not to mention the fact that she apparently had weapons in her arsenal I could only dream of.

"She can't be serious," Dad muttered under his breath. "She didn't get a damn thing out of him! She can't just process him and dump him without getting something."

"Just watch," I told him.

Dad turned to me with an incredulous expression. "How the hell can you be so calm?"

"I'm not. Believe me, I'm absolutely seething. But I trust her. She'll get what she's after."

Dad just nodded in irritation and returned his attention to the silent showdown in the next room.

Claudia appeared mildly bored now and pushed a piece of paper across the table at Mark, along with a pen. "Here's the Miranda Warning you wanted. I don't know about you, but I actually have things to do tonight, so the sooner we can get you processed and dropped off, the sooner I can get on with my life. Just sign this paper, invoke your right to counsel, and let's be done with this."

Mark's expression now was borderline panicked. I didn't know which part of Claudia's little speech had struck a chord with him, but it looked to me like he was on the verge of some sort of breakdown.

"Wait," Mark said quickly. "You can't really send me to MCC for the night."

Claudia shrugged lightly and shot her colleague a meaningful glance. "What else are we supposed to do with you? I'm sure as hell not sitting here and babysitting you. Do you really want one of the NYFO agents to come do it? How do you think they'll take it when they realize you're responsible for all this?"

Mark dropped his head heavily into the hand that wasn't cuffed to the wall and started scratching his scalp. His ministrations made his hair stick up, which somehow added to the air of pathetic wafting off him. Couple that with the now-wild eyes, and he was quite the sight.

"I can give you the names of the other guys involved," Mark said. He was obviously quickly approaching desperate.

Claudia was busy making notes on a notepad and didn't even look up when he spoke. "You're welcome to confirm them for me, if you like. But I already told you, we know who they are."

"Then what do you want from me?" Mark's voice broke as he asked that, and it looked to me like he might be trying hard not to cry.

Good, I thought, experiencing a surge of childish triumph at his distress. I was glad he was fighting tears. Scared was the very least of what I wanted him to feel.

"I don't want anything from you," Claudia told him absently, still focused on her notepad. "Not anymore. I was merely giving you a chance to clear the air and come clean about the other targets for the sake of your conscience because I thought you might have a shred of humanity left in you and want to preserve a life or two. But if you have no interest in doing that, we can move this right along."

Mark bowed his head and clenched his fists. He started taking deep, gulping breaths of air, and he was trembling. The contrast between the blowhard of a boss who'd made my life hell and the broken man before me was startling.

Mark whispered something softly under his breath I couldn't hear. I frowned and leaned closer to the glass, as though that'd actually help. Claudia stopped writing and looked up.

"What did you just say?" she asked. Her voice was shot through with dark tendrils of warning.

Mark cleared his throat but didn't lift either his head or his eyes. He kept his focus on the Miranda Warning form in front of him. "I want to see her." After a long pause, he uttered a barely audible "Please."

"You want to see who?" Claudia demanded, her eyes narrowing.

At that, Mark did lift his head, his hollow expression mildly disconcerting. "You know who."

He turned his head and looked directly at the one-way mirror toward the exact spot where I was standing. I knew he couldn't see me, couldn't possibly know I was there, but the illusion was eerie.

Claudia followed his eyes and then shook her head. "Out of the question."

"I'll tell you everything you want to know," Mark said, his voice slightly louder, his eyes still locked with mine. "But I won't say a single word until you get her into this room."

"You know why she can't be here," Claudia said.

Mark continued to stare at the glass for an indeterminate amount of time, during which I held my breath. Not until he finally shifted his attention back to Claudia did I let it out. My lungs burned. I licked my lips and tried to swallow, but my throat was dry. Absently, I prodded the stitches still present in my left eyebrow, somewhat reveling in the ache the motion caused. It helped keep me grounded.

Almost angry now, Mark picked up the Miranda Warning form and started scribbling on the bottom of it frantically. His brow was pulled down in a scowl, and his mustache was set in the line that indicated his lips were pursed behind it. After a time, he finished whatever he was writing with a grand, theatrical flourish and threw the pen on the table. He then slid the paper across the tabletop so it stopped in front of Claudia.

Claudia raised one eyebrow at him and perused whatever he'd written there. Then she pinned him with an intense stare. "You can't be serious."

"I'm absolutely serious," Mark informed her.

Claudia inhaled long and slow as she reverted her attention to the paper so she could reread whatever he'd written. Then she inclined her head to her partner, and they both stood up.

"I'll see what I can do," Claudia told him as she exited the room.

"That's all I ask," Mark murmured softly as the door clicked shut.

CHAPTER TWENTY-THREE

The door to the viewing room was flung open seconds later, and Claudia strode in looking positively vengeful. Her free hand, the one not clenching Mark's Miranda Warning form, was balled into a fist. The muscles in her jaw jumped as she ground her teeth together hard enough to shatter her molars. Her partner opted to stay in the hallway. I couldn't blame him. I kinda wanted to join him myself.

"What did he write?" my dad demanded almost immediately.

"It doesn't matter. He isn't getting it," Claudia almost snarled.

"I'll go talk to him," I said softly. Both Claudia and Dad fixed me with matching incredulous stares. I ran one hand through my hair, feeling self-conscious.

"No."

"Absolutely not."

"It isn't that big a deal," I said. "Besides, he's handcuffed to a wall. What else can he do to me at this point?"

"It's out of the question." Dad's tone made his words less a statement and more of a command.

I didn't dignify his outburst with a response. Instead, I met Claudia's eyes. "That's what he wrote on the paper, isn't it? That he'd waive his right to counsel if I sat in on the interview."

"Yes."

"Call the AUSA," I told her. "Clear it with him, and let's go back in there and get this done."

Claudia studied me intently for a long moment, then rested a gentle hand on my good shoulder. "You don't have to do this. We don't need his confession. We've got enough without it."

"I know," I said. "But aren't you curious what he has to say that he'll only say to me?"

The corners of Claudia's lips twitched like she wanted to smile. "If you want the God's honest truth, I'm extremely curious."

"Okay. Then let's do this."

Claudia nodded. "Give me a second. I'll make the call."

She stepped out into the hall to use the phone in relative privacy, leaving my dad and me alone in the viewing room. I couldn't have said what he was thinking. I wasn't paying much attention to him. I was too busy playing over all conversational paths this discussion could possibly take and promising myself I wouldn't give Mark the satisfaction of losing my temper.

After several long minutes of silence I announced to no one in particular, "We should tape this." When Dad didn't answer, I looked up at him. "You know, just so he can't make any wild accusations about what went on in there later."

Silent, Dad continued to glare at Mark through the one-way glass. I glanced toward the door Claudia had disappeared through a few minutes ago. What was taking her so long? For lack of anything better to do, I started setting up the video equipment.

"I can't tell whether you're inventing things to worry about or whether you're worrying about things you can't change," I remarked as I crawled on the floor to plug the camera in. "But I have it on good authority neither of those activities will get you anywhere."

I stood up and brushed my hands off on my suit pants as I waited for Dad to respond. He blinked at me in mild surprise before allowing a tiny smile to play at the corners of his mouth.

"That's some pretty good advice," he said, having realized immediately that I was quoting him.

"It's all right," I shot back with a grin of my own.

"Whoever told you that must be an absolute genius."

I rolled my eyes. "Well, he certainly thinks he is."

The door to the room opened, and Claudia poked her head in. "We're all set. You ready?"

I motioned to the video camera and sound equipment I'd set up. "Is it okay if we record this?"

"Sure," Claudia replied with a slight shrug.

I took a deep breath as I turned to follow her out into the hallway.

"Ryan." My dad stopped me with a hand on my arm.

"Yeah?"

A myriad of sentiments played out across his features, none of them particularly pleasant, and each of which made me wish I was good with words so I could comfort him or put him at ease. Since I wasn't, I merely waited in silence for him to compose himself enough to speak.

"Give him hell," Dad said finally.

My earlier grin came back. "Count on it."

My nerves jangled as I followed Claudia into the interview room where Mark waited, but I tried to tell myself any number of things in an attempt to soothe them. I had a hard time convincing myself this wasn't just a new facet of my recurring nightmares. Briefly, I wondered why Mark had never appeared in any of my dreams.

So many strong emotions were battling for dominance in the forefront of my mind there wasn't enough room for me to feel any of them completely. As I settled into the chair across from Mark, I decided I was grateful for the phenomenon. I wouldn't be able to fully concentrate on interviewing him if any one of those feelings were any more vivid.

The three of us sat together in absolute silence for what felt like an eon. I could actually hear the faint ticking of Claudia's wristwatch. I raised an eyebrow at Mark as we continued to stare at one another.

The familiarity of the situation hit me, amusing me. Mark and I had been here before, countless times, which helped keep me composed. Made it easier for me to breathe, to think. I folded my arms across my chest and stopped trying so hard to keep my delight off my face.

Out of the corner of my eye, I saw Claudia take a breath and open her mouth. Without turning my head, I lifted one hand in a silent request for her to stop. She and I were on the same side here. As far as I was concerned, her actions were my actions. If she spoke first, we lost the upper hand. That's how this game between me and Mark had always been played.

Mark's stare never wavered. He and I had engaged in innumerable staring matches throughout the time he'd been my direct supervisor, and during those times, I'd seen all sorts of emotions lurking beneath his gaze. But today was the first time I'd ever seen him look even remotely unsure of himself. It gave me the creeps.

Claudia's hands dropped to the tops of her thighs under the table and started tapping out a restless rhythm against the fabric of her pants. This little power struggle was getting to her a bit, probably because she was irritated that we'd essentially capitulated to Mark's demands. I didn't like the idea of giving him anything he asked for either, but that merely strengthened my resolve not to be the first one to speak. I was unbelievably grateful Claudia was allowing this to play out without interfering and made a mental note to thank her later.

"It's not what you think," Mark murmured in a low voice. He'd spoken without warning, and his statement struck me as odd. That hadn't been what I'd thought he would open with. Not even close. Already, all of the conversations I'd played out in my head were out the window. Story of my life.

"Why don't you tell us what it is, then?" Claudia drawled smoothly.

Mark and I continued to maintain our charged eye contact. Claudia might have been the one asking the questions, might have been the one engaging him, but he was definitely talking to me.

"I know the media and the public are going to say I did this because I'm unpatriotic, anti-American," Mark said slowly. "I know you'll think I did this because I hate you."

I smirked and slightly lifted my eyebrows, simultaneously amused and intrigued that he was cutting to the chase so quickly. I'd been prepared to pull this out of him slowly and painfully, one loathsome revelation at a time. My, my, but he was full of surprises today.

Both Claudia and I continued to watch him quietly, allowing him the time to map out what he wanted to say to us without pressure or intrusion. I was interested to hear what was about to come out of his mouth. Frankly, the two theories he'd already dismissed had been the only two I could come up with. To hear there was a third, alternate reality fascinated me.

I could see the muscles in Mark's throat working as he swallowed several times in rapid succession, as well as the tears forming in his eyes. When he finally broke eye contact with me in favor of staring at his hands, I shot Claudia a puzzled look. By the matching expression of confusion on her face, neither of us expected such raw emotion from him. At least not emotion of that variety. I couldn't speak to what Claudia had been prepared for, but I had thought we'd see anger or defiance. Heartbreak and despair hadn't even occurred to me. I wasn't sure how to react.

Part of me was furious, of course, that he'd dare break down like this in my presence. I wanted to grab him by the back of his head and smash his face repeatedly against the table, wanted to revel in the murderous satisfaction as I heard the crunch of bones breaking and saw his blood smeared across the pale wood. He'd tried to have me killed. He'd succeeded in causing the death of an NYPD detective, who'd also been my lover at one time. He had no right to feel remorse, let alone parade his guilt in front of me like this.

A deep, ragged inhale from Mark interrupted my brooding. It was followed closely by the clearing of his throat and indicated he was finally about to speak. I snapped my attention back to the present and did my best to school my face into an impassive expression. I didn't want him to know I felt anything at all or that I was interested in what he had to say. I wanted to come across as coolly detached. I figured it was my best hope of making it through this interview without an outburst. When I was younger, I'd once heard someone say, "Act as if," and that'd stuck with me. I'd employed that technique numerous times throughout the years and prayed it'd come through for me now.

"I know this doesn't justify anything," Mark said. His nose was stuffed up now, and his voice was thick with unshed tears. "I know what I'm about to tell you isn't any kind of excuse for the horrible—" He cleared his throat again, sniffling pathetically as he struggled not to cry.

Claudia shot a meaningful look toward the one-way glass and inclined her head once. I assumed she was telling her still-nameless partner to bring us some tissues. Obviously, neither she nor I had any, and it appeared we needed them. Either that, or Mark would have to wipe his nose on his sleeve.

Mark sniffed again and shook his head a little roughly, as though attempting to shake some sense into himself. This waiting for him to speak punctuated by his small flare-ups of sentiment was starting to grate on my nerves. I took a deep breath of my own and clenched my teeth together hard.

"My wife," Mark tried again, his voice wavering. "Dharma. She… she has a…rather serious…" He opened his eyes wide as though he could dry the tears through sheer will alone. He also stretched his jaw and let out a heavy sigh.

What? I screamed on the inside as I tried to ignore the tendrils of pity threatening to work their way into my hardened heart. *What does your wife have?* My mind ran swiftly through all the possibilities I could come up with. Cancer? Lupus? An obsession with Hummel figurines? What could his wife possibly have that would result in all of this? I couldn't figure it out.

"Gambling problem," Mark spat finally, as though he'd been attempting to choke back the words, but they'd broken free anyway. I could see by his expression how much that'd hurt him to say. "Dharma has a very serious gambling problem. We've lost everything. We have no money. Our house is mortgaged to the hilt. Our oldest daughter started college last year, and my youngest goes next year. We struggle to pay our regular bills, to say nothing of the gambling debts she's racked up. We're beyond flat broke."

As Mark lapsed back into silence, I considered what he'd just said. And while that new revelation certainly explained the screaming phone call I'd unwittingly heard between him and his wife a few weeks ago, it still left several unanswered questions. Primarily, how could his wife's gambling problem land him in a place where he'd felt homicide was the only available option? Maybe I was a little bit biased—okay, I was definitely biased—but I was having a lot of trouble wrapping my head around whatever thought processes might've made him conclude that I needed to die.

Claudia's partner, who I decided in that moment to call Bob, quietly crept into the room and handed over a box of tissues. Claudia pulled a few out and pushed them across the table to Mark, who took them without a word. He ducked his head and scrubbed at his nose, violently. Claudia nodded her thanks to Bob, and he left as noiselessly as he'd come in. After the door had clicked shut, silence reigned again, broken only by the occasional sounds of Mark's sniffling and clearing his throat as he attempted to compose himself enough to go on.

Mark coughed once. "A few years ago, she started getting involved in sports betting. High stakes, high dollar. She got in pretty deep with some bookies and ended up taking out a loan from some loan sharks to pay off the debt. That wouldn't have been too bad if she'd just stopped betting, but…" The implications of his sudden silence were abundantly clear.

I didn't have much real-world experience with loan sharks. I'd met only two during the course of one of my investigations—my target had owed them money and had put up some of his personal effects as collateral against that debt, personal effects that I'd had a search warrant to go through—and they'd seemed like nice enough guys. They'd given me permission to search the property and had been completely cooperative with my investigation. But, to be fair, they'd had no reason to be anything except perfectly pleasant to me. I hadn't been the one who'd been unable to pay them back.

In the movies and on television, loan sharks tended to be brutal, ruthless men who would begin breaking body parts in order to remind you of your obligation and would continuing doing so until you repaid your debt. I had no idea whether that was the case in actuality, but the look on Mark's face now caused a heavy weight of dread to settle in the pit of my stomach.

"How much do you owe them, Mr. Jennings?" Claudia asked.

"Almost five hundred thousand dollars."

My eyes almost bugged out of my head. He hadn't been kidding when he'd said his wife was into high-dollar gambling. I couldn't conceive how often or how much you'd have to bet to dig yourself a hole that deep. Nor could I understand how, at a certain point, long before you were down almost half a million dollars, you didn't just cut your losses and call it a day. I guessed that was why it was considered an addiction.

"And how did you manage to keep this information from coming out during your last background update?" Claudia sounded particularly curious about that part.

Mark's face flushed, and he had the grace to look embarrassed. "The problem wasn't anywhere near this bad during my last background update. And no one noticed it then. At least, no one asked me about it. But the situation has become considerably worse in the past few years, and my next update isn't far away."

"And you were trying to control the situation before your credit report was run again for your next update so your security clearance wouldn't be revoked and you wouldn't lose your job." Claudia made a notation on her pad, and I suspected someone in Human Resources would get a very stern talking to sometime soon for having missed this the last time Mark's finances were looked at. But then she refocused on our current predicament. "So, how, exactly, does your financial situation translate into attempting to orchestrate a hit on the president of Iran?"

Mark blinked, startled. "It wasn't…Surely you've figured out that it's not—" He broke off and fixed me with an intense look. The expression in his eyes as he stared at me was almost beseeching, although what he was asking for, I couldn't have said. Perhaps he wanted forgiveness. Maybe he was hoping I'd interrupt and not make him say the words out loud. Unfortunately for him, it'd be a cold day in hell before I bailed him out of anything.

Mark seemed to realize this because he sighed heavily and scratched his cheek. He shifted his attention to Claudia as though he couldn't bear to meet my eyes when he disclosed this next part. "The president of Iran wasn't the target." A long pause. "But you already knew that, didn't you?"

"We did," Claudia said with a slight nod.

"You just wanted to hear me say it?"

"Yes. But more than that, we want to know why."

Mark's facial muscles bunched, and I imagined he was pursing his lips behind his mustache. Or maybe chewing his bottom lip. It was tough to tell. His brow furrowed, and after a long moment of obvious consideration, he met my eyes again.

"You should've just left it alone," he whispered softly, sounding truly sorry. "None of this would've happened if you'd just left it alone like I told you to."

"The Akbari case," I said, finally opting to actively participate in the conversation. The fact that he was more or less placing the blame for this entire debacle squarely on my shoulders was utterly absurd and infuriated me. But pointing that out to him would be akin to trying to reason with my conspiracy-theory-laden buddy Walker. I'd get nowhere and would only end up more frustrated for having tried. So I bit my tongue, figuratively speaking, and waited for him to go on.

"Yes. The night you went to interview him, I got a call that you'd been there. You were too close. And you're like a goddamn dog with a bone. I knew you'd just keep digging and digging and that you'd eventually unearth me. I couldn't risk it, so I tried to get you to stop, but you wouldn't listen. You just had to keep going."

"Well, killing me would have definitely made me stop," I remarked dryly, trying not to let him see exactly how deeply that notion chilled me.

"Yeah." Mark's countenance now was glum. His eyes were bloodshot and rimmed by dark circles. He appeared very tired. Idly, I wondered if he'd been having as much trouble sleeping lately as I had. The thought pleased me no end.

"Weren't you at all concerned that it'd have been tracked back to you anyway, even if I were dead?"

Mark shrugged. "I didn't see how. The Akbari case was completely unrelated to what was supposed to look like an assassination attempt on the president of Iran. Who would've ever connected them?"

"Except for me."

"Yeah, well, you weren't supposed to live, so I hadn't counted on that."

"The best-laid plans and all that," I quipped icily.

"For what it's worth, it wasn't my idea."

"I'm sorry?"

"Killing you," Mark clarified. "It wasn't my idea. They kept asking me if you were going to be a problem and if I'd managed to get my hands on whatever notes or documents you had on the case, but I couldn't find anything. I looked."

"That's why you kept coming to my office and seeming surprised to see me there," I said softly, just now putting the last few pieces together. "You were there to snoop around. You were expecting it to be empty. That's why I found you going through my drawers. I always thought you were looking for ammunition to get me fired."

Even when I'd realized his involvement, I still hadn't been able to figure out exactly why he'd been ransacking my office. It made sense now that he said it, and I could've smacked myself for not having seen it before.

"I was looking for something that would keep the Iranians off my back. I thought if I could give them whatever you'd gathered on the case they might…It sounds stupid now."

"It really does," I said coldly. "Forgive me for not sounding more sympathetic, but it doesn't sound like you tried all that hard to talk them out of killing me."

"What was I supposed to do?" Mark shot back. "They were set on it. Do you really think anything I said would've made a difference?"

"Tell me something. Did you help them in any way?"

He hesitated for a fraction of a second. "What do you mean?"

"I mean exactly what I said. Did you help them try to kill me? Did you provide them any information they'd have found useful? Such as the location of the delegation? I only ask because we were supposed to have been at the UN long before the shooting occurred but only stayed where we were because the president had an impromptu meeting. So there's no way the shooter could've known where we were if someone didn't tell them."

Mark averted his eyes and pretended to adjust his handcuff. "Maybe the shooter just camped out in that room and waited for a clear shot."

"But he didn't, did he? Because the protectee was never supposed to have been at the InterCon, which meant all of his arrivals and departures would've been from the covered garage of the Waldorf. And if someone took a shot at me when the protectee was nowhere nearby, it wouldn't have looked like an assassination attempt on him. It would've looked like exactly what it was: an assassination attempt on me. No. Someone had to advise them on when would be the absolute best time to try that, and I think that someone was you."

Mark's jaw clenched, but his eyes remained riveted to his handcuff. It didn't appear as though he would chime in with any sort of rejoinder any time soon, so I went on.

"Did you have somebody set up that meeting?"

Mark's left eye twitched, and the corner of his mustache jumped immediately after. "My contacts did, yes. Through some of their associates. I didn't get involved in the details. I didn't want to know."

I didn't comment on that last part. "Because you needed to make sure he'd be out in the open or what you had planned wouldn't work."

Mark nodded. "Yeah. But my contacts weren't positive about the date or the time. They said they couldn't risk making too many calls back and forth because the feds were already watching them. That's why I had to be involved."

"So you could give the shooter the correct location and time."

Mark nodded again, and his eyes glazed over.

"How did you know what the detail was doing?"

"Most of the time I just listened to the radio."

"And the other times?"

He hesitated. "I called Michael Prince and asked him."

I closed my eyes for a second as that news washed over me. "Michael had no clue why you were asking, did he?"

"No. I kept our conversations short and made it sound like I was checking up on him more than the detail."

God, I hoped Michael never found out about that part. He'd be devastated. "You told them where to shoot, too, didn't you?"

Mark didn't lift his head, but his gaze snapped up to meet mine. "What?"

"You told them I was wearing a vest. You told them they'd have to aim high so they could avoid my body armor."

"Maybe they just assumed you were wearing body armor and compensated accordingly."

"They could have, but I don't think they did. I think you told them. I think that, left to their own devices, they'd have gone for a center-mass shot because it's the easier target. And the vest I wear for protection is low profile. You can't tell I'm wearing it underneath a suit, so they wouldn't have known. No, I think you filled them in on that fun fact. And because you told them to aim high, Lucia is dead."

"That wasn't my fault. She wasn't supposed to be there," Mark cried, sounding indignant.

I was fuming. For the first time in my life, I understood what people meant when they said they saw red, but after a long moment of considerable internal struggle, I decided I didn't want to get into that line of discussion with him. No good could come of it. Clearly, he was hell-bent on shifting the blame for Lucia's demise off his shoulders altogether. Attempting to get him to see my point of view on the subject would get one of us beaten to within an inch of their life, and it sure as hell wouldn't have been me. In the interest of avoiding my own trip to prison, I opted to change the subject.

"Speaking of things that weren't counted on, what about your burner phone?" When Mark merely blinked at me, obviously confused, I clarified my sudden topic shift. "Why do you still have the burner phone you'd been using to communicate with the Iranians? After 'the incident,' surely you had to know it was dangerous to keep it. Why didn't you get a new one?"

Mark sighed heavily. "I was going to. But then Dharma told me she'd given that number as a contact to a new guy she owed money to, and I was afraid if I dumped the phone, he'd think she was trying to get out of paying up."

"You were afraid he'd find her and kill her."

Mark nodded. "It wouldn't have been hard for him to do it. She keeps to a pretty regular schedule, comes and goes at the same time every day. He could just grab her. Or the girls. I couldn't risk it."

Something occurred to me just then, at his mention of comings and goings. "The building entrance logs."

"What?"

"You've been coming in early a few times a week for years."

"How do you know that?"

"I looked." I frowned as I attempted to discern why he might've done that. The flashbulb that went off in my head was almost blinding. "You've been taking counterfeit bills we've received from businesses and banks that haven't been entered into evidence yet out of the vault and giving them to the Iranians. That's why we kept seeing so many different types of notes connected to them. They'd been using all different kinds of notes because that's what you'd been giving them."

The sheer volume of counterfeit bills we received that way was staggering, and although our administrative staff worked tirelessly to keep up with the flow, they were fighting a losing battle. Unless we hired another two dozen people just for the purpose of logging in those bills that slipped through the proverbial cracks and weren't identified as fake until it was too late, it'd always be like Sisyphus trying to push that gigantic boulder uphill only to have it roll back down before he could reach the top.

That shouldn't have been a problem, though, because the bills were put in safekeeping in a special place in the evidence vault where they were supposed to stay until they could be properly catalogued, logged, entered into the system, and officially stored. The only people who had access to that vault were the bosses and the evidence technicians. If I wanted to go in there, I had to find someone to let me in. Whenever the administrative personnel went in to log the bills, they had to find someone with access to open the doors for them. And then there were standards and protocols in place for signing in and out of the vault that we were all instructed to follow. When I'd borrowed the prop counterfeit bill I'd brought with me the night I'd gone to interview Akbari, I'd had to sign that out, too.

Those policies and procedures coupled with the fact that we were all supposed to be "worthy of trust and confidence" meant that, in theory, the system should've worked perfectly. "Should have" was the key phrase in that statement. Clearly, the system had broken down somewhere. I guess when the higher-ups had been designing it, they hadn't counted on someone perpetrating a breach of trust like the one Mark had just engineered. To be fair, I doubt anyone could've seen that coming.

Mark's incredulous expression told me I was right. It also told me he couldn't believe I'd managed to figure it out. That made two of us. I couldn't have said why I'd had that thought just now. And I didn't care. All that mattered was that I was correct.

"Have you been helping them perfect their own note, as well?" I wanted to know, thinking of the newest version of the Iranian note Rico and I had talked about the other day.

Mark averted his eyes and looked ashamed. "Yes." The answer was barely audible.

"How much did they pay you for your services?" Claudia inquired.

"Enough to keep the loan sharks from pressing us too hard to repay our debts. We don't always pay them as much as they'd like, but we can give them enough that they content themselves with various verbal threats and don't resort to physical violence."

It was my turn to sigh, and I slumped back in my chair. I folded my arms across my chest and scowled. This entire situation was all kinds of fucked up. I understood Mark had felt a duty to protect his family, I understood desperation, but to resort to those measures? I couldn't fathom it. Not even a little. I contemplated the nuances of the situation repeatedly and still couldn't come up with any plausible reason for why Mark had gone along with the plot to kill me. The longer I sat there mulling it over, the angrier I got. And underneath all that anger were scalding feelings of disappointment and betrayal. He may not have liked me, but damn it, he was supposed to have my back, not help someone try to put a bullet in it.

And speaking of murderous tendencies, I wanted to know one more thing. "Are they going to try again?"

Mark didn't say anything, but he also didn't look at me, which told me everything I needed to know. My heart started doing somersaults, and my hands trembled. I swallowed and clenched my fingers into my pant legs at my knees.

"How much do they know about me?" I asked. "How much did you tell them? Do they know my schedule? Where I live? Do they know about Allison?"

Again, Mark didn't reply. I closed my eyes as a wave of terror threatened to drown me. My lower lip quivered, and I placed the palms of my hands over my roiling stomach as I tried to talk myself out of throwing up.

"Well, Mr. Jennings." Claudia spoke up, breaking into my tumultuous thoughts and causing me to open my eyes. "I think we have all we need. Thank you so much for your candor. Is there anything else you'd like to add before we begin processing you?"

Mark was silent for a long time, his eyes downcast, looking like a completely broken man. I hadn't thought he was going to answer her question, so I got up to leave. I'd made it as far as the door before his voice stopped me.

"I'm sorry." It was soft. The barest trace of a whisper. But it was enough to make me pause with my hand on the doorknob.

I was unsure how to respond. His apology changed nothing. Lucia was still dead. I still carried the almost-unbearable weight of guilt for that because it was partially my fault. Allison and I—and maybe even Rory—might still be in danger. He'd taken the trust and loyalty of the men and women of this agency and trampled on it, an action that would likely have resounding repercussions. And not just for me, but for a whole host of agents—past, present, and future. Pretty words, no matter how heartfelt, couldn't undo any of that. My hand tightened on the knob, and I swallowed against the churning in my gut.

"Ryan," Mark said louder. "You have to believe me. I really am sorry."

I stood there for another long moment with my back to him, trying to sort through all the possible responses that bubbled up behind my lips like a poker player sorts through the cards in their hand, choosing which to keep and which to discard. I had a ton of retorts to pick from, and they ranged from snarky to pathetic to heartfelt to downright cruel. In the end, I settled for silence and walked out of there without a backward glance.

CHAPTER TWENTY-FOUR

Y ou knew, didn't you?" my dad said without preamble when I stepped into the hall. He'd been waiting for me and had ambushed me the second the door to the interview room swung shut behind me.

I studied him for a long moment as I debated the merits of playing dumb and asking him to clarify. Ultimately, I was simply too exhausted and too preoccupied to prolong this exchange.

Checking my phone to see whether Allison had responded to my message from that morning, I answered him. "Yes. I knew."

I turned away and started walking down the hall, as much in an effort to get on with the rest of my life as to lure him away from the interview room before Claudia emerged with Mark. I didn't need my father to assault a prisoner who'd just confessed to deliberately trying to have me killed. A jury probably wouldn't look too kindly on that. And I wasn't going to risk having Mark walk on a little technicality like being roughed up by his boss before he was even fingerprinted.

"You don't think the fact that you were the intended target of that assassination attempt was something you should've told me?" Dad demanded as he matched me stride for stride.

I looked at him and then went back to staring at my phone, my internal organs twisted into several Gordian knots. *Where the hell is she? Why hasn't she answered me?* My ears were ringing, and my nerves crackled and snapped.

I said aloud, "Why? What good would it've done?"

"How long have you known?"

"How long have I suspected? Or how long have I actually known? Because they're two different things."

"Both."

I sighed softly as I punched my access code into the keypad next to the door in order to let us out of the hallway where all our interview rooms are housed. As soon as the door snicked shut behind us, effectively putting a barrier—albeit an easily overcome one—between my father and Mark, some of my tension ebbed. I took a few steps away from the door and fiddled absently with the handcuff key I always carried in my pocket, pressing the pads of each of my fingers and thumb against the sharp corner in turn, only to start over again.

"Not as long as you're thinking," I answered finally. When he shot me a look of disbelief, I went on. "It occurred to me a couple days ago I might've been the target and not the president of Iran. But I didn't have anything concrete to base that suspicion on. And I only just found out yesterday that Mark was involved in the whole thing."

"I see."

"You're angry."

"That's putting it mildly."

"I suppose that's understandable."

"Gee. Thanks for giving me permission to be upset."

That retort took me aback. This type of reaction wasn't like him at all. He was normally very even-keeled, even in the face of crises. I frowned thoughtfully, not certain of my next course of action.

"I don't want to fight with you," I told him quietly, grateful the hallway we were lurking in was completely deserted.

Dad huffed once in obvious irritation and ran one hand though his hair. "I'm sorry. I'm not mad at you. It's just that you're here and are therefore a convenient target for my resentment."

"I know. It's okay." A beat. "But you get why I didn't tell you sooner, right?"

"I understand. I even agree with the decision on some level. I'm just frustrated, and I'm having a hard time maintaining perspective, that's all."

I managed to refrain from pointing out that was exactly why I hadn't come to him when I'd discovered Mark was involved. Somehow I doubted that what would basically amount to an "I told you so" would be helpful in any way. "If it makes you feel better, I'd probably have a hard time, too, if our positions were reversed."

Dad favored me with a small smile. "I don't know whether that makes me feel better or not, actually."

I lifted my hands in a helpless gesture. "I wouldn't know either, if I were you."

"I don't suppose you're up for coming with me to make a couple of phone calls. I have to get ahead of this thing. The news will break before long, and I want to ensure all the appropriate parties are in the loop. You know how much the headquarters suits hate to be the last to know."

"I do, yes. Do you really need me there for this?"

My father's expression became apologetic. "Unfortunately, I do. They'll almost certainly have questions I won't be able to answer. It'll be a lot easier, and the call will go a lot quicker if you're on hand to fill in some of the blanks."

I hesitated, trying to think of a valid reason to beg off. Not only was I not in the mood to answer a million questions, but I was unbelievably distracted. Even though Claudia had assured me that Mark's accomplices would be picked up at roughly the same time he was, even though getting them into custody should negate any threat to me or my loved ones, I still couldn't be 100 percent positive Allison was all right, and that was demanding all my attention. I wouldn't be able to focus on anything else until I heard her voice reassuring me she was okay.

"What's the matter?" Dad asked.

"Nothing. I'm just thinking."

"I know it's a lot to ask after everything that just happened. But, on the bright side, the sooner we do this, the sooner we can put the entire thing behind us."

"Yeah," I remarked bitterly. "Until the press gets wind of it. Then I go back to being a headline again."

"It sucks. I know that. But there's no way around it."

I sighed heavily. "I know."

"I'm sorry. I'd save you from all of it if I could."

"I know that, too."

But that was the least of my concerns. My mind drifted. I was busy deliberating whether I should try again to get ahold of Allison. If she was busy or wanted some space, I didn't want to bother her. But if something bad had happened to her, I'd rather know sooner than later so I could begin to formulate some sort of plan of attack. And until I knew for certain she was safe and sound, my mind would work overtime fabricating horrific scenarios it was unlikely anyone outside of a movie would ever find themselves in. My father wasn't the only one who invented things to worry about. I could fret with the best of them.

Perhaps Jamie would have some clue as to where she was. She already thought Allison was pissed at me. If I called Jamie to check up on Allison, she'd just think Allison and I hadn't made up yet. Or, more likely, that we'd fought again. And I seriously doubted she'd let Allison know I was asking around about her. A spark of hope ignited inside of me as I pulled my phone back out so I could call her.

My feet must've had a mind of their own because they turned and marched me down the hall toward the elevator. I barely noticed. I continued to stare at my phone as I walked, as though I'd be able to make a message from Allison appear by force of will alone. My thumb ghosted over the phone icon, itching to make that call to Jamie. Of course, if I made it now, I'd have to prolong my presence in the office because there was obviously no reception in the elevator. No, better to wait the few minutes until I was outside on the street. Surely, I could contain my overactive imagination for that long. Well, probably.

"Ryan?" Dad stopped me with a hand on my arm.

"Huh?" I blinked at him, stymied. "What?"

Dad regarded me with a completely impassive look. Whatever he was thinking as he studied me was carefully and deliberately concealed behind his painstakingly crafted game face. Years of being an agent had taught him that look. I don't know what made me think I'd be able to crack it and see behind the mask. But that didn't stop me from trying all the same.

"What?" I asked again when the awkward silence between us had grown far too uncomfortable for me to stomach even one moment longer.

"I asked you if you were okay."

"Oh. Sure. I'm fine."

"Do you want to tell me what's bothering you?"

"Nothing specific," I lied. "I've just got a lot on my mind."

"I'm sure everything's fine," Dad said softly after a beat. A small, fond smile was playing at the corners of his mouth.

"Huh?"

"She's probably just busy."

"Who?" I inquired, out of habit.

"Agent Reynolds." When I merely goggled at him, he went on. "That's who you're so tied up in knots over, isn't it?"

Huh. Guess he was more in the gossip loop than I'd originally thought. I briefly considered lying to him again but dismissed the notion. Worrying my lower lip between my teeth, I nodded mutely. The lump in my throat made a verbal reply nearly impossible. I attempted to swallow against it, but it didn't work as well as I'd hoped. Actually, it didn't work at all.

"How'd you know?"

Dad's smile never wavered. "You keep looking at your phone like you're waiting for something, and each time you do, you seem disappointed."

"But how'd you know I was worried about Allison?"

Dad huffed and shot me a disbelieving look. "I may be a little rusty, but I'm still a trained criminal investigator. And I'm sure she's fine."

Instead of elaborating on what I considered to be perfectly valid reasons for my fears, I resumed my stride down the hall toward the elevators, leaving Dad to follow, or not, as he chose. I was getting the hell out of this building, and I was doing it now. If he wanted to pursue the conversation, he'd have to keep up.

He did. But in a surprise plot twist, he didn't say anything else. He merely walked with me to the elevator and stood quietly next to me as I waited for it to arrive. Neither of us spoke. We didn't even look at one another. We simply stood. I can't say I wasn't happy about that. I hadn't really wanted to continue that discussion. A small part of me had been terrified that once I'd let my fears for Allison's safety slip past my lips, I wouldn't be able to contain the torrent of emotions flailing around inside me, straining to break free. And I didn't have time for a breakdown at the moment. My schedule was pretty tight.

The elevator eventually chimed, signaling its arrival, and that was when I finally met my father's eyes. He gave me a fond, loving smile as I stepped forward to enter the car. I stopped in the threshold and turned back to face him, holding the door open with my arm.

"Will you be able to handle talking to headquarters without me?"

"Absolutely. I'll likely email you a list of a few questions I anticipate they'll ask. If anything else outside of those comes up, they'll have to wait."

The pressure in my chest was back again as my father's willingness to let me go though he really needed me here moved me. A million little thoughts drifted across my mind, each sparking to life in a brilliant flash only to blink out of existence just as quickly. I wanted to say so many things to him, but I couldn't find the words to adequately express a one of them.

"Thanks," I told him sincerely.

The elevator began making the ear-shattering buzzing noise that indicated that the door had been held for too long. Dad gave me a reassuring smile and enfolded me in a tight hug.

"Be careful," he whispered in my ear. "And give me a call when you get there."

"Will do," I whispered back, blinking back the tears that sprang up in my eyes. He knew me so well. I should've figured he'd know exactly what I was going to do without being told.

Shooting him one last watery grin, I hopped onto the elevator with the sounds of Rico's announcer voice declaring that "Elvira has left the building" ringing in my head.

CHAPTER TWENTY-FIVE

The train ride down to DC was easily the longest trip I'd ever taken, and I'd been on a C-130 to Cape Town, South Africa, so that was saying something. I'd called Jamie as soon as I'd stepped out onto the sidewalk outside of NYFO, but she hadn't answered. I'd more or less already decided I'd be making the trip down regardless of whether I'd received confirmation that Allison was okay, but now that I was still in the dark, well, the trip seemed imperative.

In an attempt to distract myself from fretting, I'd endeavored to read, sleep, listen to music, and play numerous games on my phone. But I had roughly the attention span of a four-year-old hopped up on cotton candy at a carnival. I could concentrate on the task at hand for maybe twenty seconds before my mind drifted. It was maddening.

Unlike the imaginary, metaphorically sugar-stuffed toddler, however, I never let my thoughts stray anywhere pleasant. Despite my best efforts, I could only think about the many grisly fates that could possibly have befallen Allison if anyone connected to Mark's little band of merry men had gotten ahold of her. I took my title of Queen of Inventing Things to Worry About extremely seriously.

Each call I'd placed to Allison's cell phone since I'd left NYFO that went straight to voice mail only increased the already leaden weight residing in my gut exponentially. She would've arrived back in DC hours ago. She'd had to report to the White House for her shift at fourteen-hundred hours. It was macabre that I hadn't heard from her and her phone was still off.

Finally tired of trying and failing to reach Allison, I'd broken down and called Jamie again. I hadn't realized it was her day off, but she'd immediately assumed my attempts to locate Allison were directly related to my desire to make up with her and been more than happy to tell me what she knew. Which wasn't much.

She said Allison had switched her schedule the day before so she'd be whipping the afternoon shift today instead of the day shift—presumably so she could come to New York to spend the night with me—and that POTUS hadn't had any movements on the books for the day. That meant Allison should've been at the House all afternoon. She'd offered to call someone else on the working shift to confirm that Allison had definitely made it in, but I'd told her that wasn't necessary. By that time, the train was already in Maryland. Whether Allison was at work or not, I was going to DC and didn't need to call anyone else anymore. After having spent the day worrying myself sick, I needed to see her anyway.

So, I suffered through the remainder of the longest train ride in human history, followed by the longest cab ride in human history, which preceded the longest wait that any human has ever had to endure for any reason since the beginning of time. I paced back and forth in a small line at the top of the Ellipse, feeling each second drag excruciatingly by as they ticked slowly toward the end of Allison's day.

I alternated between wringing my hands and checking my cell phone, hoping Allison would contact me. My mind raced. Actually, it whizzed back and forth like a Ping-Pong ball during a gold-medal match at the Olympics, complete with hollow-thwack sound effects. With each shift in thought, I could almost hear a thunk.

What if she wasn't here? What if she hadn't shown up? Maybe she hadn't been feeling well and had called in sick. But wouldn't she have called to tell me? Unless she'd just wanted to sleep without being interrupted. However, that was a really long time to sleep. She might need a doctor. Maybe I could swing by her apartment to make sure she was okay. Did Jamie know where she lived, because I hadn't been to her apartment yet. But what if she hadn't made it out of New York? Would Mark have said something to me if he'd arranged for someone to grab her? Used her as leverage to broker himself a deal? Or would he have been afraid that'd get him into more trouble than he was already in? If they were going to take anyone, wouldn't it have made more sense to snag me? Where would someone take her if they'd grabbed her? Wouldn't someone have noticed an abduction on a busy Manhattan street? Weird things did happen in New York, though, so maybe no one paid any attention. Of course, maybe it was something more run-of-the-mill. A car accident or medical emergency of some kind, completely unrelated to Mark. How was I going to find her? Her cell phone was off, apparently, but did that mean it couldn't be tracked? On TV, they could still track cell phones as long as the battery was in. Did that translate to real life? Aside from subpoenas, which provided me with historical data, I had nothing to do with cell phones. I had no idea how or even if I could track her cell phone in real time and whether the phone needed to be on in order for me to do that. Who would know the answer? Givens, maybe. Or Cohn. Possibly Johnny Bravo, which wasn't his real name. We all just called him that because he looked like a real-life version of Johnny Bravo. Did he mind that we called him that?

That was as far as I progressed in my mental gymnastics because about that time people started trickling out of the southwest gate to head to their cars. With the appearance of each new person, my hopes soared, only to crash again when I realized it wasn't Allison. An unbearable tightness began to collect in my chest, and my already singed nerves started to sizzle and smoke.

The throng of bodies exiting the White House complex had swelled and then ebbed again, and now it was nearly nonexistent. I stared at the gate expectantly, willing it to open, but nothing happened. Maybe Allison had gotten caught up talking to someone, but perhaps I needed to accept the fact that she simply wasn't there.

Okay, time for Plan B, I told myself. Except I didn't really have one, which sort of threw a wrench into this whole adventure. I wandered over to a tree and leaned heavily against the trunk with little thought that I was likely getting my suit dirty. I twirled a lock of hair around my index finger as I considered my options.

I could call Jamie back to see whether she knew where Allison lived so I could check her apartment. If Jamie didn't know, I'd have to gain access to one of the secure computers, so I could scour our database for that information on my own. And if I somehow managed to accomplish all of that and still couldn't find her, well, I didn't know what I would do. Go crazy with worry, most likely. As if I wasn't two-thirds of the way there already.

I glanced at my watch and frowned. Allison hadn't been missing long enough for me to sound the alarm and call in a full-scale police investigation. Not yet, anyway. We were still several hours away from that. I wasn't sure I'd be able to handle sitting around and doing nothing for that long.

I dug my cell phone out of the holster on my belt and began searching my dialed-call log for Jamie's number. I planned to call her to ask her whether she could get in touch with one of the shift agents I'd just seen walking to their cars to determine whether Allison had even shown up for work. I also intended to ask for Allison's address. If I still came up empty after all that, well, I'd cross that bridge when I came to it.

The creak of the southwest gate opening caught my attention, and I looked up, full of both hope and trepidation. I held my breath as I waited for the figure to come into view and let it out in a long, loud rush when I recognized it.

"Allison," I whispered under my breath, tears of relief and joy springing to my eyes. She was alive. She was okay. Thank God!

I pushed off the tree I'd been leaning against and shoved my hands into my pockets, now feeling like an utter idiot for rushing down here. I wanted to call out to her, walk over to her, something, but I stood there, frozen. My heart felt like it had tripped, remained suspended in midair for an instant, and then taken a spectacular tumble down that infamous flight of stairs from *The Exorcist*. Not for the first time that evening, I was plagued with indecision.

Allison's expression—what I could see of it through the dim light being thrown off by the nearby streetlamps—was dark and brooding. Her brow was pulled down in something akin to a scowl, and her lips were set in a tight line. She was stalking toward the Ellipse—and, by default, me—with a purpose, and for one brief, terrifying instant I thought her sulky mood was because of my presence.

As she came ever closer, I finally registered a guy walking maybe a step and a half behind her, his eyes focused feverishly on the back of her head. I couldn't hear what he was saying to her, but I could see his lips moving. The man was definitely talking fast, trying to get her to come around to his way of thinking perhaps? I hardly cared.

I took another step away from the tree, a little closer to the edge of the shadow I was currently hiding in, closer to the light. I opened my mouth to call out to her, but my voice shriveled and died in my throat, blown away on my next deep sigh like so much dust on the wind.

Allison stopped walking suddenly and spun abruptly on her heels, putting her back to me. I couldn't catch exactly what she was saying to the man—who was near enough to where I was standing now that I could see he was extremely distraught—but by the cadence of her tone, it wasn't pleasant. I winced in silent sympathy. I'd been on the receiving end of Allison's temper before. It wasn't fun.

As unexpectedly as she'd turned to engage the unknown man, Allison whipped back around and resumed her deliberate trek to the car. The completely useless and highly inappropriate thought of *God, she's beautiful when she's angry* flitted through my mind before I decided to grow a pair and just approach her, temper and consequences be damned.

"Allison," I called out, my voice mingling with the unknown man's as he said the same thing at exactly the same time. I took two more steps forward so she'd be able to see me.

Allison froze, which caused the man following her to crash into her back, but her eyes had already caught mine and their gaze never wavered. I could dimly hear him muttering apologies to her for his clumsiness, but she didn't so much as cock her head in his direction. She merely stared at me.

I held my breath again as I watched a parade of emotions march plainly across her face. Doubt, confusion, and fear were immediately recognizable, and my heart sank. I was debating the merits of apologizing to her myself when a new emotion broke through to stake a claim on her features: joy.

Allison's eyes lit up, and a huge grin broke out across her face. For the second time that night, I let out a huge sigh of relief and felt my lips curve into a smile to match hers. Leaving the man to stare stupidly after her without even a good-bye, Allison rushed over to me, only stopping when perhaps six inches separated our bodies.

"Hey." I greeted her softly, widening my smile impossibly.

"What are you doing here?" Allison asked, her tone laced with a fragile sort of disbelief, as though she still wasn't positive I was really standing in front of her and was afraid to hope.

"You think you're the only one who can organize surprise visits?"

Her smile was flat and a touch insincere. "No, seriously. Is everything okay?"

"It is now. I'm sorry to just show up like this. I tried to call you first. All day, actually, but your phone—mmmpphhhh."

Allison cut off my nervous ramblings by pressing her lips gently against mine. Time seemed to grind to a halt for me, and the rest of the world faded into nothingness as we kissed. I'd sort of expected her to pull away after a second or two—neither of us was really the PDA type, and we were standing in the shadow of the White House at the moment—but she didn't. Instead, she tenderly cupped my face between her hands, allowing the tips of her fingers to play with the wisps of hair just behind my ears as she slowly moved her lips in time with my own.

The kiss was long, languid, and deep, and when she finally did pull away, I was gasping and faintly dizzy. Every nerve ending in my entire body was reverberating with the echo of it, the way the tone of a bell continues to resonate long after it's been hit with a striker. I beamed at her bemusedly as she lovingly wiped at my lips with her thumb.

"Not really your shade, sweetheart," she teased.

I halted her attempt to eradicate all traces of her lipstick as well as that mind-blowing kiss from my lips by clasping her hand and dropped a soft peck on the edge of her fingers. "If I'm going to get a welcome like that, I'm thinking I should show up unannounced more often."

"You won't hear any complaints from me."

"I'd better not. Although, I admit, I'm mildly intrigued as to what a complaint from you might look like and whether it'd involve punishment of any kind." I raised my eyebrows once in a playful gesture.

Allison smirked at me, and then her expression quickly became concerned. "What happened today? Did you arrest Mark? Did he—"

It was my turn to silence her. I kept my kiss shorter and slightly more chaste than hers had been, but its effect on me was no less visceral. Desire made my insides clench, and I couldn't help moaning softly.

After a moment, we broke apart and stood there staring at one another stupidly, smiling. A pleasant hum ran throughout my body like an electrical current, and I shivered.

"Yes, we did. Everything's fine," I told her sincerely. And it was. Because she was okay.

"Huh?" Allison blinked at me, looking puzzled.

"You asked me what happened," I reminded her, secretly pleased that I could short-circuit her as easily as she did me.

"Oh. Yeah. Right."

"Glad to find at least one way to get you off topic. I have a few other possible distraction methods I'd like to test, when we get someplace more private."

Allison rolled her eyes at me good-naturedly and busied herself adjusting the lapels of my suit jacket. "Not that I'm not thrilled to see you, but what are you doing here?"

My cheeks burned, and I ducked my head. I started to throw out a quip but discarded that notion in favor of the truth. "I was worried about you. You know, because of Mark and everything. When you didn't call me back, and you didn't answer your phones, I thought..." I couldn't even voice my fears aloud.

Something dark and dangerous swam beneath the depths of Allison's eyes, there and gone in the time it took me to blink. The muscles in her jaw tightened, and she swallowed once. Then her face became a perfect mask of impassivity.

"I'm so sorry, Ryan. My phones died sometime last night—both of them—and I left my chargers at home. I never got your message."

"Oh," I replied softly, feeling like a moron. If I'd just had Jamie call someone at the House—hell, if I'd done it myself and just asked for her—I wouldn't be standing here in front of her feeling like the biggest idiot on the planet.

"Hey," Allison said, a small smile playing across her lips. "I'm glad you're here."

"Yeah?"

"Definitely," she said with a nod as she wrapped her arms around my waist and pulled me closer.

"Well, then, I'm glad that you're glad," I said, threading my own arms around her neck.

"Good. Everybody's happy," she murmured, her eyes dropping down to my lips and making my heart stumble gracelessly.

"Uh...Is that your boss?" I asked. I didn't really want to shatter the moment, but I could feel the man's eyes on us, and it was starting to make me uncomfortable.

"Where?" Allison asked, sliding her hands under my suit jacket so she could trace delectable patterns on my dress shirt over the small of my back with her fingertips. And though she verbally inquired, she couldn't have been terribly interested in the answer as she never for even one second shifted her attention from my face to look.

Between the heat in her eyes and the maddeningly gentle touch of her fingers, I almost forgot what the hell I'd just been talking to her about. I paused, taking a moment to enjoy the little sparks of pleasure she was igniting within me before answering her question. I nodded to my right, where, out of the corner of my eye, I could see the man gaping at us.

"Over there. The guy who practically chased you out of the White House and is now staring at us like we're some sort of rare and fascinating zoo attraction."

Something dark and ominous passed across Allison's features, and she tensed in my arms. She turned her head to glare at him, and they engaged in a silent showdown that would've put my staring contests with Mark to shame. When she started to break her hold on me to move toward him, I tightened my grip and pulled her even closer.

"I'll take that as a yes, then," I said lightly, flashing her a small grin.

Allison sighed heavily and returned her attention to me. "Yeah. That's him."

"The one who's been giving you such a hard time lately?"

"Yes."

"You just made out with me in front of your boss?"

Allison laughed at that. "I guess I did."

"Hmm," I mused, running my fingers through her hair and reveling in the slide of those silken strands over my skin. "The president could've been looking out his window just now. He could've seen us, too."

Allison's eyes twinkled. "Could have."

"Why, Agent Reynolds. Who knew you were such an exhibition-ist?"

"I'm just full of surprises."

"I'll bet."

"Are you complaining?"

"Not even a little bit."

"Then shut up." She kissed me again, and, as always, the rest of the world completely ceased to exist as I got caught up in the feel of her in my arms and the sensation of her lips moving against mine.

When she finally pulled back—far too soon for my tastes—I smiled at her dreamily, feeling ridiculously happy.

"Will you go out on a date with me?" I blurted.

Her brow furrowed, and her face crumpled into an adorable frown. "What?"

"I'm asking you out on a date."

Allison's frown faded somewhat, but she didn't appear any less confused. "Um...Isn't it a little late for that sort of thing?"

I ducked my head and licked my lips, considering how to explain myself to her. I'd given the matter a lot of thought when I'd been stuck in the hospital. You'd have thought I'd have been better prepared to answer that question.

"We never really dated," I said slowly. "We sort of just fell into whatever it was we were before. It started out with sex. Mind-blowing, earth-shattering, phenomenal sex," I said with a grin. "But still, just sex. I think it was sort of an accident that we fell in love. I don't know if either of us intended that. But for all the time we spent together, I think I could count on one hand the number of times we actually went out anywhere. And even then, it was usually just to grab a quick bite before heading back to one of our apartments."

"Huh," Allison murmured as her expression became pensive. I could see she'd never really thought about it before.

I took a deep breath to prepare myself to voice this next part. I recognized that it likely sounded better in my head than it would on the air, but I was determined to say it anyway.

"I want to court you," I told her seriously.

Allison blinked at me blankly, so I went on. "You never really seemed to want that before. You know, dates and flowers and my inept, bumbling attempts at romance. You didn't seem interested in that. You might not be now, and that's okay. If you're not, you can just tell me, and we can forget it. But for what it's worth, I think you're absolutely amazing. And I also think that, in addition to being with someone who can give you the most incredible orgasms you've ever experienced, you also deserve someone who's going to spend at least some time every day showing you how extraordinary they think you are. You know, with clothes on. And I'd like to be that someone. At least I'd like to try. If that's okay with you."

My words hung heavily between us as silence descended in the aftermath of my announcement. I fidgeted in her arms, feeling silly and anxious and hopeful. The longer she merely stared at me dumbfounded, the longer she offered no response, the more nervous I felt until finally I lost my nerve and attempted to backpedal.

"Never mind," I mumbled, ducking my head to hide my blush. "It's stupid. Forget I said anything."

"No way," Allison exclaimed, using the edge of one finger to tilt my chin back up so she could meet my eyes. Her own were dancing, and her lips were curved into a smile. "Are you kidding me? You offered. There's no getting out of it now."

It took a second for her words to work their way through the tangled mess that was my mind, but once they did, I goggled at her, unable to believe my luck. "You're saying yes?"

Allison shot me an exasperated look. "Geez, Ryan. One would think you'd actually expected me to say no."

I shrugged my good shoulder and allowed my own grin to steal over my features. I slid my fingers through her hair again. "I never know what you're going to do at any given time. I didn't want to be presumptuous and assume."

"I thought you liked making an ass out of yourself."

"Damn you and your fantastic memory."

"I want you to know I expect you to go all out with this. I won't accept anything half-assed. You know the kinds of movies I watch and what kinds of books I read. The bar's pretty high."

"Hey!" I protested, mildly insulted. "First of all, I never do anything half-assed. You should know that by now. Need I remind you—"

"Yes, yes. The Peeps. All-consuming hatred. I know."

I shot her a dirty look. "Secondly, if you wanted creative control over the courting process, you should've asked me out. I guess that makes me the man." I smirked at her, pretty pleased with myself.

"Really? If you're the man, then why am I the one who wears the strap-on?"

I flushed, alternately mortified that she'd actually said that aloud in public and unbelievably turned on by the mere thought of her wielding that particular accoutrement, to say nothing of the memories the notion stirred. "I have no response."

"Didn't think so. But I do feel it's only fair to give you adequate warning that I have one dating rule that must, without question, be adhered to."

"Oh, yeah? What's that?"

"No sex until the fifth date."

"I'm sorry?"

"You heard me."

"I did hear you. I just couldn't conceive in what reality you might actually be serious."

"Well, I am serious."

"Oh." I stared at her, still not convinced she really meant it. It had to be some kind of a test.

"Yeah. Oh."

"I see."

"Is that going to be a problem?" Allison was studying me intently, waiting for my answer.

I considered her mandate for a moment. Not whether I'd be willing to comply with her request. That was a given and required no thought whatsoever. If she truly wanted to wait, we would. No, I was busy contemplating whether she'd let me get away with cramming five dates into one day, the number of cold showers I was likely going to have to endure in order to be able to survive my imposed abstinence without any permanent nerve damage, and if it was possible for one person to single-handedly cause a drought.

"Absolutely not," I said finally, brushing my lips gently across hers in a tender kiss. "The wait will definitely be worth it."

Allison kissed me back slowly. "Definitely." She released her hold on me and turned toward her car. "Come on."

"Where are we going?" I asked innocently.

"To my place. Let's go. Move with a purpose."

"I didn't realize we were on such a tight schedule," I quipped, falling into step beside her.

"I'm short-changing again," she said. "So we don't have a lot of time. I'd like to get at least a little sleep tonight. But I have some pretty specific plans for you before that happens."

"What kinds of plans?"

"Plans that involve your naked body, a bottle of chocolate sauce, and you screaming my name."

"What happened to no-sex-until-the-fifth-date? Or am I just so irresistible that you've caved already?"

"We haven't even been out on our first date," Allison reminded me as she opened the door to her car and gazed at me over the roof with hooded eyes. "Therefore, the no-sex clock hasn't started yet."

The sounds of my laughter rang out in the cool night air, and I followed her into her car, eager to see whether she'd be as selfish with the chocolate sauce as she was with the strap-on and wondering if it'd occur to me to complain if she was.

About the Author

Kara A. McLeod is a badass by day and a smart-ass by night. Or maybe it's the other way around. Or quite possibly neither. A Jersey girl at heart, "Mac" is an intrepid wanderer who goes wherever the wind takes her. A former Secret Service agent who decided she wanted more out of life than standing in a stairwell and losing an entire month every year to the United Nations General Assembly, she currently resides in Colorado and is still searching hither and yon for the meaning of life, the nearest Comic Con, and the best deal on a flight to London.

If anyone has any leads on any of the above, she can be contacted at kara.a.mcleod@gmail.com.

Books Available From Bold Strokes Books

The Sniper's Kiss by Justine Saracen. The power of a kiss: it can swell your heart with splendor, declare abject submission, and sometimes blow your brains out. (978-1-62639-839-9)

Divided Nation, United Hearts by Yolanda Wallace. In a nation torn in two by a most uncivil war, can love conquer the divide? (978-1-62639-847-4)

Fury's Bridge by Brey Willows. What if your life depended on someone who didn't believe in your existence? (978-1-62639-841-2)

Lightning Strikes by Cass Sellars. When Parker Duncan and Sydney Hyatt's one-night stand turns to more, both women must fight demons past and present to cling to the relationship neither of them thought she wanted. (978-1-62639-956-3)

Love in Disaster by Charlotte Greene. A professor and a celebrity chef are drawn together by chance, but can their attraction survive a natural disaster? (978-1-62639-885-6)

Secret Hearts by Radclyffe. Can two women from different worlds find common ground while fighting their secret desires? (978-1-62639-932-7)

Sins of Our Fathers by A. Rose Mathieu. Solving gruesome murder cases is only one of Elizabeth Campbell's challenges; another is her growing attraction to the female detective who is hell-bent on keeping her client in prison. (978-1-62639-873-3)

Troop 18 by Jessica L. Webb. Charged with uncovering the destructive secret that a troop of RCMP cadets has been hiding, Andy must put aside her worries about Kate and uncover the conspiracy before it's too late. (978-1-62639-934-1)

Worthy of Trust and Confidence by Kara A. McLeod. FBI Special Agent Ryan O'Connor is about to discover the hard way that when you can only handle one type of answer to a question, it really is better not to ask. (978-1-62639-889-4)

Amounting to Nothing by Karis Walsh. When mounted police officer Billie Mitchell steps in to save beautiful murder witness Merissa Karr, worlds collide on the rough city streets of Tacoma, Washington. (978-1-62639-728-6)

Becoming You by Michelle Grubb. Airlie Porter has a secret. A deep, dark, destructive secret that threatens to engulf her if she can't find the courage to face who she really is and who she really wants to be with. (978-1-62639-811-5)

Birthright by Missouri Vaun. When spies bring news that a swordswoman imprisoned in a neighboring kingdom bears the Royal mark, Princess Kathryn sets out to rescue Aiden, true heir to the Belstaff throne. (978-1-62639-485-8)

Crescent City Confidential by Aurora Rey. When romance and danger are in the air, writer Sam Torres learns the Big Easy is anything but. (978-1-62639-764-4)

Love Down Under by MJ Williamz. Wylie loves Amarina, but if Amarina isn't out, can their relationship last? (978-1-62639-726-2)

Privacy Glass by Missouri Vaun. Things heat up when Nash Wiley commandeers a limo and her best friend for a late drive out to the beach: Champagne on ice, seat belts optional, and privacy glass a must. (978-1-62639-705-7)

The Impasse by Franci McMahon. A horse-packing excursion into the Montana Wilderness becomes an adventure of terrifying proportions for Miles and ten women on an outfitter-led trip. (978-1-62639-781-1)

The Right Kind of Wrong by PJ Trebelhorn. Bartender Quinn Burke is happy with her life as a playgirl until she realizes she can't fight her feelings any longer for her best friend, bookstore owner Grace Everett. (978-1-62639-771-2)

Wishing on a Dream by Julie Cannon. Can two women change everything for the chance at love? (978-1-62639-762-0)

A Quiet Death by Cari Hunter. When the body of a young Pakistani girl is found out on the moors, the investigation leaves Detective Sanne Jensen facing an ordeal she may not survive. (978-1-62639-815-3)

Buried Heart by Laydin Michaels. When Drew Chambliss meets Cicely Jones, her buried past finds its way to the surface. Will they survive its discovery or will their chance at love turn to dust? (978-1-62639-801-6)

Escape: Exodus Book Three by Gun Brooke. Aboard the Exodus ship *Pathfinder*, President Thea Tylio still holds Caya Lindemay, a clairvoyant changer, in protective custody, which has devastating consequences endangering their relationship and the entire Exodus mission. (978-1-62639-635-7)

Genuine Gold by Ann Aptaker. New York, 1952. Outlaw Cantor Gold is thrown back into her honky-tonk Coney Island past, where crime and passion simmer in a neon glare. (978-1-62639-730-9)

Into Thin Air by Jeannie Levig. When her girlfriend disappears, Hannah Lewis discovers her world isn't as orderly as she thought it was. (978-1-62639-722-4)

Night Voice by CF Frizzell. When talk show host Sable finally acknowledges her risqué radio relationship with a mysterious caller, she welcomes a *real* relationship with local tradeswoman Riley Burke. (978-1-62639-813-9)

Raging at the Stars by Lesley Davis. When the unbelievable theories start revealing themselves as truths, can you trust in the ones who have conspired against you from the start? (978-1-62639-720-0)

She Wolf by Sheri Lewis Wohl. When the hunter becomes the hunted, more than love might be lost. (978-1-62639-741-5)

Smothered and Covered by Missouri Vaun. The last person Nash Wiley expects to bump into over a two a.m. breakfast at Waffle House is her college crush, decked out in a curve-hugging law enforcement uniform. (978-1-62639-704-0)

The Butterfly Whisperer by Lisa Moreau. Reunited after ten years, can Jordan and Sophie heal the past and rediscover love or will differing desires keep them apart? (978-1-62639-791-0)

The Devil's Due by Ali Vali. Cain and Emma Casey are awaiting the birth of their third child, but as always in Cain's world, there are new and old enemies to face in Katrina-ravaged New Orleans. (978-1-62639-591-6)

Widows of the Sun-Moon by Barbara Ann Wright. With immortality now out of their grasp, the gods of Calamity fight amongst themselves, egged on by the mad goddess they thought they'd left behind. (978-1-62639-777-4)

Arrested Hearts by Holly Stratimore. A reckless cop who hates her life and a health nut who is afraid to die might be a perfect combination for love. (978-1-62639-809-2)

Capturing Jessica by Jane Hardee. Hyperrealist sculptor Michael tries desperately to conceal the love she holds for best friend, Jess, unaware Jess's feelings for her are changing. (978-1-62639-836-8)

Counting to Zero by AJ Quinn. NSA agent Emma Thorpe and computer hacker Paxton James must learn to trust each other as they work to stop a threat clock that's rapidly counting down to zero. (978-1-62639-783-5)

Courageous Love by KC Richardson. Two women fight a devastating disease, and their own demons, while trying to fall in love. (978-1-62639-797-2)

One More Reason to Leave Orlando by Missouri Vaun. Nash Wiley thought a threesome sounded exotic and exciting, but as it turns out the reality of sleeping with two women at the same time is just really complicated. (978-1-62639-703-3)